Lucky 22

Lucky 22

ASHLEY ECKSTEIN

AND

SAMANTHA CHASE

BLUE BOX PRESS

Lucky 22
By Ashley Eckstein and Samantha Chase

ISBN: 978-1-968707-99-6

Published by Blue Box Press, an imprint of Evil Eye Concepts, Incorporated

Printed in China

Dedication

To the Lucky reader of this book. May you always have hope that every birthday will be the beginning of your best year yet. Make wishes, dream big, and claim what's yours.

A Note from the Author

Dear Reader,

If you've read my husband David Eckstein's memoir, *Just Enough*, then you already know that our love story began with a moment that felt—honestly—a little like movie magic. I grew up in a world where fairy tales were part of everyday life, and I never stopped believing in them.

This book is based on the true story of how we fell in love, and this is my chance to use that sense of wonder as the foundation for Ella Rose and Christian's tale. It's sweeter than the stories you may be used to. Gentler. A little more stardust than spice. But it's also deeply true to who I am, how I was raised, and the way I fell in love with the man who became my best friend, my Prince Charming, and my soulmate for life.

To me, there's nothing better than a beautiful romance—the soft, slow-burn kind that changes everything quietly. The kind built on trust, laughter, and the sort of everyday magic that lasts.

Thank you for taking this journey with me. I hope this story brings a little warmth to your heart and a bit of wonder to your day.

All my love,

Ashley

Prologue

The stadium roars with life around me—an electric, relentless hum of cheers and chants. It's almost deafening, but you can't help but get caught up in it. Bright lights bathe the diamond in a surreal glow, catching every glint of sweat, blade of grass, and nervous twitch of the players. In my head, I'm cheering just as loud as everyone else. It's like I'm trying to telepathically say, "You've got this."

But sitting in the stands, in a pocket of solitude amid the chaos, I am alone.

Literally.

My husband is mere seconds away from winning the World Series, and minutes ago, security came to get all the players' friends and family to bring them down so they could run onto the field when the big moment arrived.

But I stayed behind.

I never should have looked at my phone.

Heck, it should have been turned off. But I'm in the middle of shooting a movie here in St. Louis, and I already know I need to be on set in the morning. The producers were kind enough to work around the World Series schedule, but I need to be aware of any schedule changes.

Hence, the phone being on.

My heart races, and my hands feel clammy as I clasp my cell to my ear. I'm watching what's happening on the field, even as I listen to my agent presenting the biggest role of my career. This is what I've been working toward since I was a kid. If ever there was a dream part, this is it. Unfortunately, her timing couldn't be worse. Everyone knows I'm here to support Christian.

This is *his* moment.

I wish she had considered that and waited until tomorrow to call.

A tiny voice in my head reminds me, "*It's Christian's moment*," but this is important, too.

Not that anyone understands that.

My husband does. Truly. But the looks I got as the rest of the friends and family were ushered away—and the snarky comments from some of the players' wives—told a different story. Words like *selfish, self-involved,* and *rude* were whispered.

I'm an actress, and things like that aren't anything new. But this time, the words stung quite a bit more than they usually do.

I look down at my free hand—at my wedding ring sparkling in the stadium lighting. It represents the promise that Christian and I made to each other.

So many promises.

So many sacrifices.

I hear the exuberant announcement. "And the Archers have won the World Series!"

"Ella? Ella, are you listening to me? This is an incredible opportunity. They want an answer from you tonight."

Everyone's running onto the field, laughing, cheering, hugging their loved ones. I should be down there. But I'm not.

"I'm going to have to call you back," I say. "I need to run."

I hear a loud sigh on the other end. "Seriously? This is the chance of a lifetime. What is there to think about?"

"We'll talk tomorrow, okay?"

"Jeez, Ella." Another sigh. "Are you sure he's worth it?"

One

Three years ago…

Today was supposed to be a great day.

Personally, I think every day offers an opportunity to make it great, but today was supposed to be a little extra dazzling because I'm flying back to Los Angeles for an audition. I had a great time visiting my family in Tennessee, and knowing I was heading back home for a potential role made leaving a little easier. I've been living on my own for a couple of years now, but I truly believe this is my time.

The year of Ella.

I giggle to myself because it's kind of silly. But I have worked so hard to get where I am as an actress, and I'm ready for the next step.

"Ladies and gentlemen, we're sorry for the delay," our captain announces. "We are currently waiting on a couple of passengers on their way from their connections. They're running to the gate as we speak. Once they arrive, we'll be ready for takeoff. Thanks for your patience."

Great.

Delays are totally normal, but I was psyched when it looked like everything would be on time. I'm a nervous flyer—always have been—

and sitting here on the ground waiting just gives my anxiety more time to kick up a notch. My flight from Memphis to Dallas was completely uneventful, and I hoped my good luck would continue on through to LA.

Sighing, I give the empty seat beside me a cursory glance—another thing I was psyched about. The empty middle seat means I can stretch out a bit and relax. And believe me, if there's ever been a time for me to relax, this is it.

Because my ex is sitting in the row directly in front of me.

With his new wife.

And their baby.

Luckily, they didn't see me. I boarded first, and I've got on my favorite baseball hat pulled down low to hide my face a bit. But I saw *them.* I hear them cooing affectionately to their baby, and the whole thing makes me feel like an awkward voyeur.

So not my day…

With nothing to do and in desperate need of a distraction, I pull out my journal and decide that a bit of mindless doodling might work. I could watch a movie or play a game on my phone, but I feel like I need to be actively doing something. With my notebook open in my lap, I draw my favorite number.

Twenty-two.

That may seem juvenile to some people, but it's very calming to me. The number twenty-two makes me happy and gives me hope whenever I see it. Call it my lucky number or just a positive sign from the universe, but the number seems to randomly find me wherever I go. You see, I was born on September 22 and am turning twenty-two in a few weeks. It will be my golden birthday—when the date of your birth coincides with your age. In fourth grade, my teacher explained that concept to me—well, to the entire class—and said that something special would happen on that day. And I've basically been waiting for thirteen years to find out if that's actually true.

It is, I tell myself. *It has to be.*

Just thinking about it and all the possibilities makes me giddy.

I continue doodling my number, over and over—big and blocky, script, ornate—until someone plunks down loudly in the seat beside me. I give him a brief look, but his back is to me as he gets himself settled.

I go back to my notebook, silently praying that we take off soon. I'm in the middle of a rather adorable twenty-two when my new seatmate bumps into me, causing my pen to slide across the page, ruining all my hard work of the last few minutes.

He mumbles, “Sorry,” but goes back to getting comfortable. He’s fidgeting a bit, and I have to wonder if maybe he’s a nervous flyer like me. I’m not sure I want to open that dialogue, though. You know, sometimes, you get lucky and sit next to someone awesome, where you can chat the entire flight and feel like you have a new best friend.

Other times…

You get that person who’s totally not into making friends—or being polite—and you’re left feeling awkward for even starting a conversation.

Do I really want to take the chance? Between the flight delay and my ex in front of me, I’m not liking my odds. So, rather than risk disappointment, I opt to pull my hat down a little farther and settle against the cabin wall.

Out of the corner of my eye, I steal another glance at the guy sitting beside me. Dark hoodie. Strong jawline. He’s reading something on his phone, completely absorbed, his brow occasionally furrowing like he’s not happy about whatever’s on the screen.

I shift slightly, adjusting my legs and angling my body just enough to get a better view. I don’t know why I’m doing this. Maybe because we’ll be sitting next to each other for the next few hours. Or maybe because he barely acknowledged me when he sat down. He taps the phone with a quiet flick, and I catch a glimpse of his hand—clean, neatly trimmed nails, and a giant gold ring on his right ring finger.

My eyes dart back to my drawings before he notices me staring. Although he seems really engrossed in what he’s reading, so I doubt he even noticed me.

Within minutes, I’m listening to the flight crew preparing us for takeoff.

Finally.

“At this time, we ask that you please fasten your seat belts, stow your tray tables, and ensure that your seatbacks are in their upright positions.”

I glance around and see who’s disregarding the rules. I’m always a little surprised by how many people wait until the flight attendant tells them to do this stuff.

“We’d like to take a few moments to go over the safety features of this aircraft, even if you fly with us often. Please give us your attention.”

So, I do.

I'm a rule follower, mostly. I mean, I've been known to push a few boundaries here and there, but only if it's for a good reason. Like the time I lied about my age when I auditioned for the role of a much younger girl. The thing is, I look young for my age. Always have. So maybe that wasn't an actual lie. More like a lie of omission.

Maybe.

"Thank you for your attention. We wish you a pleasant flight." Our flight attendant finishes her speech, and we start taxiing to the runway.

I shift slightly and go back to my drawings. I could turn on a movie or something once we're in the air, but for now, I'm perfectly content doing this. Besides, it's sometimes nice to unplug and be creative.

Even if it's just doodling.

I pause and peek out the window because we seem to be barely creeping along. The runway queue is stretched farther than I can see.

Well, that's disappointing.

Returning my focus to the paper, I'm about to start another blocky twenty-two when the guy next to me gently clears his throat.

I look up and meet a pair of piercing blue eyes.

"Excuse me," he begins quietly. "I don't mean to be nosy, but…are you drawing the number twenty-two?"

I look up from under my hat and smile shyly as I nod. "I'm just trying to pass the time until we get in the air. I wasn't ready to watch a movie or anything yet. But, um…yeah."

His eyes go a little wide, but he doesn't say anything else right away. Just when he seems about to, the captain interrupts with an announcement.

"Hey, folks, this is your captain speaking. Just wanted to let you know we're all set and taxiing out now. We've got a couple of planes ahead of us, and we're currently number four for takeoff. Shouldn't be too long—maybe ten, fifteen minutes tops—and we'll be on our way. Sit back, relax, and we'll get you up in the air shortly."

"We are never going to take off," I murmur, more to myself than the guy next to me. "It's just been one delay after another."

"Yeah. Sorry about that."

Looking over at him, I frown and whisper, "Excuse me?"

"That first delay was my fault. Well, mine and another guy's. Our flight from Atlanta was delayed, so we landed late. I honestly didn't expect them to hold the plane, but I'm really glad they did. The next flight to LA doesn't leave for something like four hours, and I would have been on standby."

"That would totally give me anxiety," I tell him. "I need to know that I have a seat and will get where I'm going."

"Same." He nods at my drawings again. "That's your favorite number, huh?"

I smile. "It is!" I say, and then immediately lower my voice. "It may seem silly, but it's more than my favorite number. I guess you could say it's my lucky number." He's looking at me, his expression completely neutral, and I wonder if he thinks I'm unhinged. "What about you? Do you have a favorite number?"

He nods again but doesn't answer. Instead, he quietly asks, "Why are you whispering?"

It's a valid question. After all, plenty of people are speaking in normal tones all around us. But I'm purposely keeping my voice down so I don't draw attention to myself.

I nod to the seats in front of us and silently mouth, "*That's my ex and his wife. I don't want them to see me.*"

Now, he's frowning. "What?"

I mouth it slower this time. "*That's…my…ex…*"

He shakes his head, and I realize I'm either going to have to say it aloud or just let it go. But then inspiration hits, and I write it down on the paper in my lap instead.

That's my ex and his wife with their new baby in front of us. I really don't want them to see me, so I'm trying to stay quiet.

"Ah, got it," he murmurs, giving me a thumbs up. His smile is sweet, but I can tell he's not comfortable with this conversation. After a small nod, he shifts in his seat—like he's putting some distance between us—and just like that, we're done talking.

I'm about to ask again about his favorite number, but I see that his arms are crossed, his head is back, and his eyes are closed.

Yeah. Conversation's over.

Oh well.

I'm mildly disappointed because he seems like a nice guy. He has kind eyes and a sweet smile. I wouldn't have minded chatting with him to pass some time on the flight. But…it's obviously not meant to be.

Eventually, we take off. Once we reach our cruising altitude, I put my notebook away, pull out my phone, and take advantage of the complimentary Wi-Fi to find something to watch. I have three hours until we land at LAX, so I make myself comfortable and settle in quietly for the rest of the flight.

Back in LA, my life is as chaotic as usual. My audition was amazing, but I'm still waiting to hear if I got the part. Meanwhile, I spend my nights working at a local coffee shop. I wouldn't say I like it, but it sort of goes with the territory when you're an aspiring actor. You do auditions during the day and work—often as a waiter or waitress or barista—at night.

So, really, I'm right on track.

And honestly, I've embraced the lifestyle. And sometimes, I even feel like I'm thriving. I've gotten some wonderful roles that I'm incredibly thankful for.

Unfortunately, nothing's steady at this point. I'm paying my bills and able to travel home to see my family, but it would be nice to have a consistent acting gig. After all, that's the dream.

Growing up, my father worked at Wonder Land in Florida—one of the biggest theme parks in the world and part of Storyteller Studios. The first time I walked through those gates with my family, my fate was sealed. I knew it was where I wanted to work, too. Well, I wanted to start by dancing in a parade or something equally cool at the park and then go on to act in one of Storyteller Channel's shows.

I'm proud to say that I *did* work at the theme park, I *did* get to dance in a parade, and I *did* eventually end up with a recurring role on *That's So High School,* a hit Storyteller Channel show. But now, I'm ready for that next step, the big break, and I look at every part I get as a way to meet new people and make connections. It's very important to do that sort of thing in this business because you never know when you'll end up talking to the person who will change your life.

I've met some incredible people and already made some great connections that got me from my small town in central Florida to where I am here in LA, but nothing big has happened yet.

Soon, though. I can feel it.

Taste it.

It's so close, it's like I can reach out and touch it.

"Can I get an iced coffee and a blueberry scone?" the next person in line asks.

But for now, this is my life. I take orders, pour coffee, serve baked goods, and do it all with a smile. But when my shift is over, I gleefully sprint out the door. Especially since tomorrow is my day off.

When I get back to my tiny apartment, I'm beat. I kick off my sneakers, yank the scrunchy off my ponytail, and shake out my long hair. I smell like coffee, and I contemplate a shower, but the sound of an incoming text makes me pause.

Jim: *Hey! We still good for the game tomorrow? I can pick you up at 4.*

Oh, right. The baseball game. I groan as I flop down on my bed.

Jim and I have been dating casually for five months now. I know he's serious, and is maybe even in love with me, but I'm not there. I think he thinks I'm "the one," but sadly, he's not the one for me. I just don't feel the same way. And really, I don't know why.

On paper, he's perfect. He's nice enough and cute, but I don't feel the spark. My mom always tells me that when you meet your person, your soulmate, you'll just know. Well, I don't know if I believe her, but what I do know is that Jim is not the one. I hate that for us because there is truly nothing wrong with him, he checks every box…the feelings just aren't there. I've thought about breaking up with him. But he's so darn nice that I always end up putting it off.

So, I'll go to the baseball game with him.

Besides, a couple of other friends are going with us, so it's not like it's a romantic date.

Sighing wearily, I text him back.

Ella: *Sounds good!*

Ella: *Is there a dress code? The last time I went to a major league game was like 10 years ago with my dad.*

I mean, I guess jeans and a T-shirt will be fine, but I just want to make sure.

Jim: *No worries. I've got you covered.*

Jim: *See you tomorrow.*

Ella: *Got me covered? LOL! What does that even mean?*

Jim: *It's a surprise. 12*

Okay, then. I guess I'll have to wait until tomorrow to get my answer, which is fine, because I'm beat and desperately want to take a shower, put on some clean, non-coffee-smelling jammies, and get some sleep. Tossing my phone down, I get up and stretch, then do exactly that—looking forward to sleeping in tomorrow morning.

When Jim shows up the next day, he hands me a bag with my surprise in it. And I have to say, it's awesome.

It's a baseball jersey with the number twenty-two on it.

"I love it! Oh, my goodness! It's perfect!" I examine it closer and turn it around. "Lucas? Who's Lucas?"

"That's Christian Lucas's number, so his name's on the jersey," Jim explains. "I know you're not really into baseball, so I was going for the number and not the player. Personally, I don't know anything about him other than that he wears your number." He winks at me and seems pretty proud of himself.

"Oh, okay," I say, smiling. "I get it. Thank you." I hug him, and it lingers. I'm hugging him like I would my brother, but he's clearly holding on because, to him, it's something more.

I really need to do something about that. After this game, I think I need to break up with him.

When we finally break apart, I excuse myself to change into my shirt. In the bathroom mirror, I fluff my long, blond hair, add a bit more lip gloss, and admire the jersey, genuinely loving having my lucky number on it. I take it as a sign that it's going to be a good night.

When I step back into the room, I pose like a model. "What do you think? Do I look like a fan?"

"You look adorable," he assures me, kissing me on the cheek. "You ready?"

"Let's do this."

I've experienced many things since moving to LA, but going to a sporting event hasn't been one of them until now. Anaheim has a team—the Anaheim Magic—and Jim tells me they're very good. I take his word for it.

At the stadium, we meet up with our friends, and they're all gushing about how great our seats are because we are in the first row, right next to the dugout. Well, now I feel really spoiled, and I imagine all future baseball games will be ruined for me because we have the best seats in the whole stadium.

The game starts, and Jim tries to explain all the plays and what's happening, but I'm only halfway listening. I may not follow baseball, but I'm familiar with the rules. Having him chattering in my ear is kind of ruining the experience.

Our friends keep calling this Christian Lucas guy *"my boy,"* since he's wearing my number. I laugh because, technically, I'm wearing *his* number. Either way, after every play he makes, the dialogue is a bunch of, "Hey, Ella! Your boy just did this," or "Did you see your boy, Ella? He just did that!" It's cute, and I'm having a good time.

Anaheim scores a home run, and one of the players comes out of the dugout to congratulate the hitter. My eyes go wide when I see it's *my boy*. His back is to us, so we can clearly see the twenty-two, but then he turns toward the stands.

My heart races a little because I'm wildly curious and want to put a face to the name and number. To my surprise, he looks right at me—almost as if he knows I'm there. He looks familiar, but with his hat on, I can't be too sure. All I know is that our eyes lock and hold for like five seconds, and it feels as if everything else around me fades away. No noise. No cheering. No chattering.

I blink, and he's gone. I seriously wonder if it happened at all. Did I imagine it? But…I feel a little flustered, so it had to be real, right? I want to ask if my friends noticed, but as I glance around, no one's paying any attention to me; they're just enjoying the game. I guess I should, too.

The only difference is, now I'm a little more invested and actively watching what *my boy* is doing.

His team plays a great game, and by the time it's over, I'm caught up in the excitement of it all and know that number twenty-two seems like a very skilled player.

And he looks good in his uniform.

Jim drives me home. We kiss goodnight, but I know this is it for us. It has nothing to do with the baseball player and everything to do with me. It feels wrong to lead Jim on when there's no hope of him being my forever person. The only fair thing to do is rip off the bandage and be honest. But when I go to say it, he gushes about what a great time he had and how glad he is to have experienced a baseball game with me.

Ugh.

I do break up with him, though.

Just…the next day.

It's all very cordial, and yes, I play the whole it's-not-you-it's-me card because…well…it *is* me.

Naturally, he asks for another chance, promising he can be whatever I need him to be. But he's missing the point. I'm not looking for someone to morph into something they're not. I do that for a living. That's what acting's all about. I don't want that in my real life. I want to be with someone authentic. The concept is lost on Jim, though, and our breakup conversation goes on for almost an hour. Fortunately, in the end, he finally gets it.

"I wish you nothing but happiness in life," I tell him. "And you're going to find the perfect woman who loves you for exactly who you are."

"I wanted it to be you," he says sadly before walking away.

If it were a TV show or movie, it would have been the perfect gut-wrenching scene: the heroine watching her ex walk away as the screen fades to black. But even the audience knows she's doing the right thing.

I'm doing the right thing.

So, where does that leave me?

Auditions during the day and the coffee shop at night.

Until…

I get the role. I'm filming a TV movie!

While I didn't get the part I auditioned for, I'm playing the best friend. It's still an amazing opportunity, and my character has just as much screen time as the one I wanted to play. I'm so happy. Filming starts immediately, so I prepare myself for long days, very little sleep, and doing everything I can, because every role gets me closer to my dream.

On one of the few nights that I'm not on set, I meet up with my friend, Whitney, for a late dinner. We became friends after meeting at several auditions—never for the same roles—and I love having someone to talk to who understands the business.

"I can't believe you finally broke up with Jim. Yay, you!" she says, raising her glass of water to me. I raise mine right back.

"Thanks. It was time. We could have kept going, but…" I shrug. "It just wasn't there. We went to a baseball game, and when he took me home, I knew it was time."

"Wait, you went to a baseball game? I thought sports weren't really your thing."

I shrug. "I mean, I enjoy going to games. I just don't follow sports. Jim had some complimentary tickets from work for the Magic game, and a bunch of us went."

I take a sip of my water, thinking about that night. I glance at Whitney, and before I can stop myself, I blurt out the whole eye-contact thing with Christian Lucas.

"I know it's crazy, but it felt really intense," I tell her. "Like it was an important moment. And his number is twenty-two! Don't you think that's crazy? What are the odds that he's the one I made eye contact with?"

"Were you trying to make eye contact with him?" she says with a suspicious laugh.

"What? NO!" I huff. "It just felt…it seemed like…" Another huff.

"Use your words, Ella," she teases.

"I don't know how to explain it. It was like there was a force pulling us to look at each other. And then it felt like no one else was in the stadium but us."

She takes another sip of her water. "Do you want to meet him?"

"Who?"

"Christian Lucas. Isn't that who we're talking about?"

"Yes, but…why would you ask me that?"

"Because my husband, Ryan, knows him…well, kinda." She pauses. "Ryan played baseball with him in college. Small world, right? They've since lost touch, but Ryan loves to watch him play. Since Christian signed with the Magic, Ryan and I have been going to games a lot—or we watch them on TV. I was probably at the same game you were."

"Wow, what a small world! I'm guessing we never talked about it because you knew I wasn't exactly into sports," I reason.

Wait, am I suddenly into sports now?

Whitney whips out her phone, types something, then puts it back down. "Your name has actually come up a time or two in my conversations with Ryan."

"Christian's from Central Florida, too. Any time that comes up, I mention that you grew up there, and we always joke that we should fix you two up. How wild is that?"

"Um…very."

She studies me for a moment. I don't know why, but I squirm under the scrutiny. "I think the two of you would really hit it off.

Besides the whole Florida connection, you seem to have the same… what's the word…moral compass? You're both super sweet, very driven, and would give anyone the shirts off your backs. We really should have tried to fix you two up by now."

"So, why haven't you?"

"Ella, come on. Between auditions and working, you're always on the go. Now, you're shooting a movie—which, by the way, I am so excited for you! I haven't landed anything in months. Pretty soon, I may have to go back to working at The Cheesecake Factory," she murmurs.

"Oh, stop. You'll get something soon. I just know it. And while this movie is great, it's almost over. I'll be back at the coffee shop again any day." I sigh. "I really wish someone would spot me on the street and just gush that I'm exactly the type of person they need for their major motion picture and hire me on the spot."

Whitney sighs, too. "Yeah. That's the dream. Unfortunately, the only time things like that happen is in the actual movies."

"I know."

"Back to setting you up…the baseball schedule is really intense. Christian is either in training, playing here, or traveling to play somewhere else. I don't know how easy it will be for him to find free time for a date, but it's worth a shot, right?"

We're quiet for a moment, then she asks, "So? What do you think? You get zero percent of the chances you don't take. What if you made eye contact for a reason? He could be your person. Look, the worst he can say is no."

"But Ryan doesn't have his number, and that seems like a lot of work to find a way to get in touch with him." It's tempting, but…I don't commit. "I'll think about it."

We enjoy the rest of our night and promise to get together again soon. I finish filming two weeks later, and then I'm right back to serving coffee—just like I said I would be.

A month later, my publicist calls to talk to me about the movie premiere. Ava Mitchell has been my publicist for almost two years. She and my agent are all about getting me seen, and I'm thankful for that. The movie will have a limited theatrical run, but they're still doing a red-carpet thing for it that I'm looking forward to.

"Okay, so, the premiere," she says excitedly. "Who are you bringing as your date?"

"My date?"

"Oh, sweetie, you need to have a date for something like this. Aren't you dating anyone?"

"Um…no?" I squeak.

"We need to find you someone," she says. "Anyone you're interested in? Someone you've maybe gone out on a date or two with? You know LA is filled with guys who would love to go to a movie premiere and network with the cast and crew."

Not any of the guys I know, but I don't tell her that.

"My friend Whitney was trying to convince me to let her fix me up with this baseball player guy," I say with a small laugh. "I saw him at a game, and his number is my lucky number. We're both from Central Florida…"

"Ella, that's perfect! You need to go out with him."

"Ava, I can't. I've never even met him, and I don't think a movie premiere is the sort of thing you do on a blind date."

"But it's not a blind date. You've seen him, so you know who he is. And…wait. Who is he?"

"Christian Lucas. He plays for the Magic. But…"

"If I put in a call to their PR team and hook the two of you up, will you go out with him?"

Oh, Geez. Would I?

Should I?

"I don't know, Ava. How *Hollywood* is it of me to have my publicist call his publicist? He's going to think I'm some sort of stuck-up actress."

"This is how things are done," she states. "Now, should I reach out to his team or not?"

"Um…"

"It would make a great story, Ella."

I can't even believe I'm considering this, but…I trust Whitney's opinion, and if she thinks this is something I should do, then I should go with that, right?

Before I can second-guess myself, I say, "Okay, I'm in. Make the call."

Two

I'm semi-blasting my favorite song, "The Middle" by Jimmy Eat World, and dancing my way around the apartment. I'm in a great mood, and there's nothing like a little dance party to keep me there.

The living room doubles as everything—office, dining nook, movie theater, and dance space. A cozy, blue couch faces our small, wall-mounted TV with a thrifted coffee table barely wide enough for a laptop and two mugs. The floor is faux hardwood, clean but creaky, and a woven rug adds a splash of personality.

Plus, it acts as a decent buffer for our downstairs neighbors, since we're not exactly quiet sometimes.

"What about red? You would look *sexy* in the red dress," my roommate and BFF, Jen, asks as she pops her head out of her room. Right now, she's trying to help me figure out what to wear to the movie premiere. She's a hair and makeup artist, and I absolutely adore her style. But so far, nothing is really grabbing me.

"I don't know if I'm going for sexy," I explain as I twirl a bit. "After all, it's a premiere. And potentially a blind date. I don't think that's the vibe I want to be giving off."

The song ends, and another comes on, but I lower the volume and follow Jen into her room, hopping onto her bed.

We've been roommates for almost two years, and I am so grateful we met. When I first moved to LA, I rented a teeny-tiny studio apartment that wasn't ideal. Plus, I was lonely. It was my first time really living on my own, and it was hard going home to that little place by myself every night to stare at the four walls. I mentioned to some people that I wanted to find something a little bigger and have a roommate, and Jen's name came up. We agreed to move in together without even meeting first, so it's awesome that it not only worked out, but we also ended up becoming such great friends.

Our current apartment is on the second floor of a modest stucco building tucked between palm trees and buzzing power lines. Inside, the space is compact but bright, thanks to the big sliding glass door that opens to a narrow balcony just wide enough for two chairs and a cactus.

I don't have a green thumb, and neither does Jen. A cactus is the only thing we can keep alive.

I wasn't picky about what I wanted in an apartment, as long as it was in a safe part of town, and we could each have our own bedroom. Luckily, it worked out. It's small, but it works.

Jen's bedroom has a full bed pushed into one corner, with just enough room for a nightstand and a small desk that doubles as a vanity. She calls it "Glam Central."

"Fair enough," she says while rummaging through her closet. It's shallow but crammed with LA-style essentials: colored jackets, vintage tees, and sneakers. We always start with her stuff because she has a much more impressive wardrobe than I do. I prefer to dress for comfort, while Jen makes a statement almost everywhere she goes.

She pulls out a blue dress because that's my favorite color, and then a yellow one, even though it may clash with my blond hair. Then, she pulls out a long, black number that looks a little too goth for me. I'm about to say as much when she beats me to it.

"Um, no, right?" she says with a laugh. "You're all cute and sunshiny. This is way too…I don't know…Wednesday Addams."

We both start laughing because I cannot even imagine myself in something like that. Or Jen.

"Why do you even have that dress?" I ask. "It's totally not your style either."

Tilting her head, she studies it for a moment. "I want to say it was for Halloween one year, and then I wore it to a New Year's Eve party because I literally couldn't find anything else that I wanted to wear. It was a big hit."

"Oh, well…that's awesome. Good for you!"

She puts the dress back and starts flipping through all her clothes again. "How do we feel about green? It matches your eyes."

"Depends on the style."

"I could braid your hair and style it in a fun updo, and I can do your eye makeup to be a little sparkly and…" Before she can finish the thought, she shakes her head and puts the dress back. "Nope. It's not the one. I know you, Ella, and none of these dresses is speaking your name."

"That's a new one," I say, thoroughly amused. "I didn't think dresses could talk."

She grins at me over her shoulder. "You know what I mean. Whatever dress we choose has to be perfect. It's a big night on multiple levels. It's a lot of pressure for a dress. Of course, everything looks good on you, so you wouldn't think this would be so difficult. But I know we haven't found *the one* yet." She closes the closet door with a dramatic sigh. "Come on. Time to check your closet. And if that doesn't work, we'll hit the thrift store. You know we'll find something there."

I hop off her bed. "I know, but I'd love it if I didn't have to buy anything right now. Between the two of us, there has to be something that will work."

My bedroom is slightly smaller than Jen's, but I've got the same amount of furniture tucked inside. My bed hugs the wall beneath a window that faces the building next door, and some old plastic crates act as makeshift shelving.

It isn't fancy, but it's home: sunlit, a little cramped, and alive with the hum of traffic, neighbors' music, and the drone of the occasional helicopter overhead.

"Yeah, but if we go to the thrift shop, we both get to play dress-up. And how fun is that?"

"I do enjoy it when we get to try stuff on…" I sit on my bed and watch as she starts going through my closet.

Honestly, it's a bit funny to me that I'm enjoying this.

I was a tomboy when I was younger.

Like…a soccer, getting dirty while playing in the mud, not caring one bit about my appearance, sort of thing. If my mother wanted me to wear a dress, she practically had to chase me down to get it on me.

Thinking about that now, it's really kind of cool. I mean… sometimes, people think you're the person you're going to be from a very young age. Like if you were a girly-girl at five, you'd always be a girly-girl. Or if you enjoyed eating PB&Js as a kid, you'd always love them.

That was definitely not the case for me.

Well, except for the PB&Js. They're still delicious.

But other than that, I have always marched to the beat of my own drum. Even if it didn't make sense. It didn't matter what was expected or trendy; if it didn't suit me at the time, I didn't do it. Some might look at a child not doing what all the other kids are and call them odd, but I never cared about what other people thought.

Even as a little girl, Ella Rose Holt became synonymous with *unconventional.*

For a while, I was obsessed with the *Karate Kid* movies and would wear a karate uniform—a gi—all the time. I even wore it for my school pictures, despite my mom desperately wanting me to wear a dress.

I was the only girl on the boys' soccer team. In my mind, I wanted to play, and the fact that the rest of the team was all boys didn't stop me. I didn't mind getting sweaty, running, or playing in the dirt. It was exhilarating and challenging, and I loved proving to people that I could do it. I wasn't the best player, but I worked really hard and vowed to always be a great asset. I was driven, even at a young age.

So, besides being unconventional, I was also very determined.

Of course, none of that would have been possible without the best parents in the world. They were always supportive and encouraging, and they never did anything to deter my ambition.

There were four of us kids, and we all had different hobbies, interests, and dreams, but my parents were always there, cheering us on. It was a strict parenting rule for them to never say no to our dreams.

However…

That didn't mean we were all running wild with no boundaries or discipline. They were strict when they needed to be, but each had an incredible work ethic and wanted that for us, too.

So, they taught by example. But they never did the work for us.

I'll never forget the Christmas they gave me a hat with *Dream It. Be It* on it. They used that hat as a teaching tool and told me that all my dreams were possible, but they wouldn't just fall into my lap. I had to put in the hard work to make it happen.

That became my personal motto: Dream it. Be it.

Then, I started singing and acting in the fourth grade because I knew I wanted to be an actress. It was obvious to me that it was more than a phase. It was *going* to happen, and I was willing to put in the work.

"Ella? Hello? Earth to Ella?" Jen says, and I realize I've been in my head for a little too long.

"What? Oh, sorry," I say with a nervous laugh. "My mind wandered for a minute."

She sighs with a hint of drama, leaning against the closet doorway. "Look, I get it. All the dressing-up stuff isn't your thing."

"I don't mind dressing up," I counter. "And I'm having fun *thinking* about all the possibilities. I'm just…I don't know. I think I have a lot on my mind. Maybe I'm just not in the right frame of mind to decide on a dress today."

"Um, no. I think you're a little overwhelmed because there are so many moving parts connected to this particular dress, that's all. Like we said, it's a movie premiere *and* a potential blind date." She pauses. "Blindish? Is that a better word? I mean, we still don't know if you're even going with that Christian guy. Or *any* guy, for that matter." Laughing, she shakes her head. "Either way, you're straddling the line here on what direction to go in with the dress, and it's got you stumped."

I don't exactly *love* that analysis, but unfortunately, she's right. I *am* stumped.

If this were just a movie premiere, I'd be fine.

If it was only a date, I'd be okay.

But combining the two?

And on top of all that, my golden birthday is coming up. I believe something special is going to happen on my actual birthday, but I stop my mind from getting ahead of itself. Is all of this connected?

Ugh, this is too much. As an actress, I prefer when everything is scripted. All of this feels very unscripted, and I cannot control it. So, yeah, I'm stumped.

"Fine. Let's just say, for argument's sake, that I'm stumped. What am I supposed to do?"

Jen studies me, and I know she's really thinking about it. It's one of the things I love most about her. She listens, cares, and we have yet to find a problem she can't help me solve.

"I'm so lucky you're my friend," I say.

Her head tilts, and her expression softens. "Aww. What made you say that?"

"Because I'm spiraling, and you're always there to help me. And it's real help, not just empty encouragement." I shrug. "I really appreciate it and wanted you to know."

Stepping away from the closet, she sits down beside me on the bed. My head immediately falls to her shoulder, and her arm comes around me. When her head rests against mine, I'm overcome with gratitude.

"I feel the same way," she says after a moment. "And you know there isn't anything I wouldn't do for you."

"I know."

"And you also know that I will always be honest with you."

I nod. "It's another one of your amazing perks."

"Okay, then." She lets out a soft sigh. "You need to get out of your head and pick something to wear. It doesn't have to be about the premiere or even the date. It has to be about you. What do you want to wear that's going to make you feel good? Pretty. Special."

Lifting her head, she pulls back a bit, making me look up. "You're right. I'm overthinking this, and I need to stop."

Easier said than done.

I've been waiting for this birthday for so many years, I think I'm trying to manifest something great. I don't want anything to go wrong. But maybe I'm getting in my own way. Even though the movie premiere isn't *on* my birthday, it's my birthday week, and anything close to the date is going to weigh heavily on my mind. Can I leave something *this* special to chance?

Jen slowly stands, watching me with an almost comical level of caution. "I'm going to go through your closet, and we are going to discuss the pros and cons of all the possibilities. And if we can't find anything…"

"We'll go to the thrift shop," I finish for her. With a sigh, I wave to the open closet door. "Okay. Let's do this."

Thirty minutes later, we've discussed every pro and con of pretty much every article of clothing I own, but nothing has inspired either of us.

"Before we go anywhere," Jen announces, "I'm going to call Penny. You know she has some amazing vintage clothes, and the two of you are around the same size. I want to see if maybe she has something that could work. Hang tight."

She practically skips out of my room as I flop back onto my bed, mentally exhausted. I'm contemplating a quick nap to deal with phase two of the perfect dress search when my phone rings.

I'm practically giddy when I see my mom's name on the screen.

"Hey, Mom!"

"Hey, sunshine. How's my girl doing?"

"I'm good. How's everything at home? How's Dad?"

"Oh, everyone's fine," she assures me. "Your sister was just complaining that she wishes we were still in Florida so she could go and spend the day at Wonder Land like we used to."

"I get that."

"It's been almost two years, and we all miss it. But…it is what it is. So, what's new with you? Any exciting auditions?" she asks.

"No, but I'm filming a guest spot on a sitcom next week. And today, Jen and I are trying to figure out what I'm going to wear to the movie premiere in two weeks."

"That's right. I remember you telling me it was coming up. What are you thinking of wearing? Have you found anything yet? Jen has such great taste and style, I'm sure she'll find the perfect dress for you."

Sighing, I tell her all about how our afternoon has gone so far, but I leave out the whole Christian angle. I don't know why. Usually, I tell my mom everything, but for some reason, I'm being vague. "I don't know, I'm being really indecisive."

"Hmm…that doesn't sound like you. What do you think the problem is?"

"I'm not sure."

"Ella…" And yeah, her tone tells me she's not buying it.

"Ugh, fine. I might get set up with someone to go as my date to the premiere."

"And?"

"And…he's a baseball player. Sort of a friend of a friend."

"Okay, so then you have someone to vouch for him," she reasons.

"Do you want to go out with him, or are you doing it because you need a date? Because if you're not really interested in going out with him, then I don't know why you're making yourself crazy about a dress. Don't overthink it."

"It's still a movie premiere, Mom. I want to look my best," I explain. "And I want to go out with him. He intrigues me, but I don't know why."

"Wait, is he the baseball player you were telling me about? Number twenty-two? You made eye contact with him at the game you went to last month, right?"

"That's the one."

"Now this is all making sense."

"Does it?" I ask with a small laugh. "Because I still don't get it."

"Ella, you are the most confident girl I've ever known. Just be yourself. He's either going to like you for you, or he's not the one."

"Um…yeah. I'm not sure where you're going with this," I murmur.

"Ella, I know you like to control everything, and you don't like surprises, but you know what I've always told you. When you meet the one, you'll just know. I think this is just unfamiliar territory for you."

I fight the urge to roll my eyes, even though she can't see me. "I've gone on dates before, Mom."

"Not with a famous baseball player. You've always been the one in the spotlight—the famous one."

"Well, that's where you're wrong. I'm definitely not famous. Not yet."

"Ella," she says with a hint of admonishment. "It's okay to be nervous about this date. It's okay to try something new. And it's even okay if you go out with him, and it doesn't exactly work out. But it's not okay for you not to try."

I sit up so fast that I have to shove my hair out of my face. "What do you mean? I am trying! I'm looking for the perfect dress and everything."

"Yes, yes…you're looking, but you're being wishy-washy. At least, that's the way it sounds to me. Treat this like you would treat any other audition. My Ella would have already picked an outfit and would have Jen working on the perfect accessories for it."

"We just started this like an hour ago…"

"But you've known about the premiere for weeks. This isn't

brand-new information, that's all I'm saying. You need to be the confident and decisive girl you were raised to be."

Would Christian like that girl?

My eyes instantly land on my hat sitting on one of my makeshift shelves. The one my parents gave me for Christmas that has *Dream It. Be It* embroidered on it. It's old, and I don't wear it anymore, but I display it as a reminder that I could be anything I wanted, but I had to work for it.

And right now, it is the perfect reminder of all the things I've dreamed of and how I made so many of them come true because I was that confident and decisive girl. So, why am I not confident about this date? If it's meant to be, then it will happen no matter what I wear. I need to get out of my head, just like I said to Jen only minutes ago, and it's time to find the darn dress.

"You're right," I finally say. "I am feeling a little out of my element. The whole thing with having my publicist call his just seems so weird to me."

"It's Hollywood, Ella." She laughs. "That's the way things are done. If anything, it's like the universe telling you you've made it. It's not weird. It's exciting."

"I guess I never looked at it like that."

But I still think it's weird.

I wonder if Christian thinks it's weird, too.

I'm about to say more when Jen comes running back into my room with an armful of garments. "I've got the best idea!" she announces. "Remember in *Cinderella,* when the mice gather up all the little odds and ends and help create her dress? What if we create your dress? I've got my sewing machine and all kinds of cool pieces we can play with. And Penny's going to bring over some stuff, too. What do you think?"

I'm a little speechless, honestly. But my mom chimes in with her two cents.

"I love that idea. Hi, Jen!" she says loudly.

"Hey, Mrs. Holt. We'll send pictures when we're done."

"I think I need to go, Mom," I say as I climb off the bed. "I promise to send pictures when we decide on a dress. But…maybe not the one that's potentially being constructed."

Laughter is her initial response, followed by a reminder of everything we've been talking about. "Be brave, be bold, be confident, sunshine. Wear something that makes you feel that way. Even if it's not what your talented and helpful friend is trying to create for you."

I'm looking at the things Jen is currently laying out all over my room and, for the life of me, I can't envision what she's thinking.

"Thanks, Mom. I love you, and we'll talk soon. Give Dad and everyone my love."

"I will, sweetheart. Take care. Love you."

Putting the phone down, I try to find something to say that won't offend Jen.

"Why don't we hit the thrift shop before we start taking apart your clothes?" I suggest. "Not that I don't appreciate the sacrifice. But it would be a shame to start deconstructing stuff when we might find something already made."

She pauses as she turns to look at me. "You hate it, don't you?"

It wasn't a question.

"Of course, I don't hate it. I don't even know what it is yet. I'm just saying that we were all excited about the thrift shop, and after talking to my mom, I know I'm being difficult—but not on purpose," I quickly clarify. "I'm just nervous about this date."

"Well, duh. Yeah. We all know that, Ella."

"We? Who's we?"

"Me, Penny, and Freya" she throws out, like it's no big deal.

"When did you all even talk about this?" I'm not really accusing her of anything, but thinking of my friends all talking about me behind my back sort of gets my hackles up. I know it's crazy—call it childhood trauma—but I don't like it.

"Yesterday, when we were all at the coffee shop, remember? That's when I first asked if you wanted to look for a dress today. And even though you were off the clock, you had to jump in and ring up that guy with the tattoos and purple hair. By the way, while I think it's awesome that you help them out in a pinch even now that you're starting to make a living from the roles you're getting, you shouldn't have to work when you're not even on the schedule."

"I know. But everyone was busy helping other people, and it just felt wrong to leave that guy standing there."

She rolls her eyes. "Anyway, while you were gone, the girls and I were talking about dresses, and we all know about your whole eye-contact-with-Christian story and figured you were nervous, that's all."

"Oh."

I didn't have many friends when I was growing up, so this whole dynamic is new to me. I'm still learning about healthy friendships.

Does Christian have a group of friends that he's talking to about me and our maybe-date?

"So? Are you ready to admit it?"

"Admit what?"

"That you're nervous about Christian calling?" she asks, but then stops and gasps, her eyes going wide. "Or maybe you're nervous that he *won't* call." Another gasp. "That's it, isn't it? You're worried that his publicist is going to put this idea to him, and he won't be interested."

"Um…"

"Oh. My. *Gosh!*"

Jen sounds way more concerned about this than I think she should, but she could be right. Is that what my deal is? Am I secretly afraid that he won't call me?

I slowly sink down onto my bed—on top of a bunch of the stuff Jen put on it—and let this new information sink in.

Meanwhile, Jen flits around my room, offering words of encouragement, but it's all white noise to me. I mean…is a dress really leading to all this self-discovery?

Obviously, I've dated guys before. And while that was more of an adult-Ella thing than a teenage one, I've still gone out with men. I've never had issues like this, where I'm obsessing over things.

And I've never had butterflies in my stomach when thinking about it as I do now.

So…am I? Obsessing? Sure, I'm overthinking it a little, but that's only because I want to look nice. That's not a crime, right? Even if I knew that the person I was going out with wasn't *the one*, I would still want to look my best while we were out.

"You've never been this picky before," Jen's saying, but she's also smiling—and still enjoying this way more than I think is necessary. "But why? Why this guy? What's so different about him?"

I wish I knew…

"Any other day," she continues, "I could have pulled out a dress or two, and we would have had you accessorized and ready to go. Or we would have been at the thrift shop already."

"We can still get to the thrift shop if we stop discussing it," I say calmly. And that's when I decide that I'm done thinking about this.

Which is what I tell Jen.

"No more psychoanalyzing," I say, forcing myself to smile. "Call Penny and tell her we're going to shop a bit and to hold off on bringing things over. Say she can come over later, and we'll order pizza or something, okay? I'll try on her stuff then if I need to."

Luckily, Jen agrees, and I help her gather up all the clothes that are scattered around my room.

"Let me go put all this stuff back, and then I'll text Penny while I touch up my makeup," she tells me.

I don't even question her multitasking skills because I know she can basically do it all.

But while she's doing that, I decide that maybe I should freshen up a bit, too. Not that I've been doing anything that requires it, but it seems like the thing to do while I'm waiting.

So, I apply some lip gloss and fluff my hair. I consider putting it up in a ponytail but decide against it.

Then, I look at what I'm wearing—jeans and a sweatshirt—and think about whether or not I should change. If I'm going to be trying on dresses, is this the best choice? Does it even matter?

Does Christian like a jeans-and-sweatshirt kinda girl?

"I really hope we leave soon because I'm starting to annoy myself," I mumble before grabbing my purse and phone and walking out of the bedroom.

There's no sign of Jen yet, so I grab a bottle of water and sit down on the couch.

"You almost ready?" I call out.

"Two minutes! I decided to get changed. The thought of peeling myself out of these jeans more than once was enough to do it for me." She laughs. "You know, just in case we end up at more than one shop."

Dang it. Now I'm second-guessing things for like the hundredth time today.

Sipping the water, I tell myself I don't have to change, but now I feel like I really want to. I stand up just as Jen comes out of her room, looking adorable in a pair of comfy yoga pants and a cute top.

"Sorry about that," she says. "Oh, good call on the water." She grabs a bottle for herself before heading out of the kitchen. "Let's do this."

I guess I'm not changing.

I'm halfway to the door when my phone rings. We both pause. When I look at the screen, I don't recognize the number.

"Who is it?"

I shrug. "No idea." I look at her. "Should I answer it?"

She waves it off. "Just let it go to voicemail. Penny's going to meet us at the thrift shop over on Westwood."

I go to put my phone into my purse, but my curiosity gets the best of me. "Just give me a sec," I tell her before tapping the screen. "Hello?"

"Hi, I'm looking for Ella Holt," a deep, masculine—and completely unfamiliar—voice says.

"That's me. Who's this?"

He clears his throat. "Um, hey, Ella. This is Christian Lucas. Your publicist gave me your number. Is this a good time to talk?"

Three

My heart is hammering so hard, I seriously think it's going to beat right out of my chest. I reach out and frantically grab Jen's arm to get her to stop without saying the words. I know my eyes are wide, and she has no idea why I'm acting this way. So, I quickly blurt out, "Oh, hi, Christian. Sure, yes, this is a good time to talk."

Jen starts excitedly jumping up and down, even as she steps around me and unlocks the apartment door, silently ushering me back inside. I don't know whether I should stand or sit, so I end up pacing.

He doesn't say anything for a moment, and I wonder if he's still there.

"Christian?"

He lets out a small laugh before speaking. "So, um…this is a little strange. It's definitely an interesting way…to meet someone."

Sitting down, I smile. "I agree. I was afraid that doing things this way would be a deterrent to you. Please know I'm not the kind of person who does the whole 'have your people call my people' thing." Then I'm not sure what to say because it's obvious we're both a little nervous.

"That's a relief," he murmurs with a hint of amusement.

And then he's quiet again. I'm trying to come up with something witty to say, but he continues.

"I'll be honest with you, Ella, my publicist mentioned us going to a movie premiere together, and…well…that's not really my thing. I'm sure you're a very nice person, and I didn't want to *not* call, but I'm not really comfortable with a blind date on the red carpet."

"Then let's go out before it," I blurt. "It doesn't have to be anything big. Just coffee or something. And, for what it's worth, I wasn't particularly comfortable with our first date being at the premiere, either. It didn't seem like a great way to get to know someone."

"Exactly," he replies, and I think he's starting to relax. "I don't know many actresses, but I'm guessing your schedule is potentially as busy as mine."

"I'm shooting an episode for a sitcom this coming week and will be on set for several days. What about you? What's your schedule like?"

"This is the last week of the season. We didn't make the playoffs, so our final game is on Sunday."

This isn't as simple as I thought it would be, but I'm determined to find a time for us to at least meet. Even if he doesn't want to, or can't, go to the premiere with me, I feel like I need to meet him.

"How about dinner Monday night?" he suggests. "I've got a game, but you can come and watch me play, and then we can go out to dinner after the game."

I'm so ready to say yes, but…Monday's my birthday.

My *golden* birthday.

It's the one I've been waiting for since the fourth grade. Is Christian Lucas the great thing that will happen to me? *For* me?

Do I even mention that it's my birthday? Or would that totally scare him off?

Talk about pressure, right? I'm not sure I'd want to go out on a first date with someone on their big day.

"Are you still there, Ella?" His uncertainty is back.

"I would love to go to dinner with you on Monday," I tell him. "Just let me know the details, and I'll be there."

"Oh, great. Yeah, that's great," he says, clearly relieved. "The game starts at six. Will that work?"

"Absolutely."

"I'll text you all the details, tell you where to park, how to get around the complex, and where to pick up your tickets. It's not too hard to find your way around, but…"

"I've actually been to a game recently," I tell him, feeling a little proud of myself.

"Really? That's awesome. Did we win?" He chuckles.

I can't help but smile. "You did." I almost blurt out that we made eye contact, but I decide to keep that to myself, too. It's like I'm holding in all these details and coincidences until I get to know him.

"Well, all right. Good for us." He laughs softly.

"Sounds good. Monday at six. Okay."

"Okay," he agrees in that deep voice of his, and I wish he'd say something else so I can hear it again.

But now we're both silent. It somehow feels wrong to be saying goodbye already, even though I know we should.

"I'm really looking forward to this," I say. "Thank you for calling and for even considering us going out."

"Like I said, it's not the most conventional thing I've ever done, but I'm looking forward to meeting you, Ella." It sounds like he means it. "I'll see you Monday at the stadium."

"See you then. Bye!" I can hear how high-pitched my voice is, but I can't help it. I hang up quickly and hope he won't hold it against me.

Jen is casually hovering a few feet away. When I turn and face her, I know I'm still smiling, but now I can jump up and scream, too.

"You're going out with a baseball player! You're going out with a baseball player!" she chants, our hands clutching each other's arms as we jump around.

"We're going to dinner Monday night. Gah!"

More jumping. Clearly, we're both super excited, so when Jen stops and stares at me with wide eyes, I'm confused.

"Now you need two outfits."

Oh, my goodness, she's right.

I step away and pick up my purse, phone, and water, then announce, "And now, we shop."

It's my birthday, and my friends have gone out of their way to make my day wonderful. Jen picked up coffee and freshly baked cinnamon rolls for us for breakfast, and now we're meeting up with Penny and Freya for lunch.

"Are you ready for tonight?" Penny asks.

We're crammed around a tiny table at Café Mosaic. It's one of my absolute favorite places to eat. It's very boho chic with exposed brick, lots of bold, jewel-toned colors, and tons of local art and photography hanging on the walls, framed in mismatched wood and metal. The furniture leans toward functional, but it's artsy: small, round café tables with wobbly metal bases, mismatched wooden chairs, and a couple of couches in the corner with slightly worn upholstery. The vibe isn't polished. It feels lived-in, like a place where you could spend hours reading or talking.

It's the perfect hangout for when you're with friends. There's so much to see, and there's a chalkboard menu behind the counter with all the daily specials and drinks in slightly smudged handwriting. They serve some of the best sandwiches and salads, and we've ordered a plate of sweet potato fries for the table.

The only drawback is that it's super crowded. That's not unusual, but it seems like there are way more people filling the space and sitting on every available chair today.

We opted for a table that is essentially for two and squeezed a few extra chairs around it. Otherwise, we would have been waiting for at least an hour.

"I think so," I tell her. "I have three different outfits picked out, all casual, but I haven't been able to decide which one I like the best yet. It depends on my mood later."

"I have a favorite," Jen chimes in around a bite of her turkey and brie on ciabatta. "But I'm keeping it to myself until you're ready. And of course, I'm going to do your hair and makeup."

"Just make sure you leave super early," Freya says, shaking a fry at me. "You know the traffic is going to be a beast. Plus, it's always smart to take your own car when you're going on a blind date."

Trust me, I've watched enough episodes of *Dateline* to know how to be safe.

I'm happily picking through my lunch, an Asian chicken salad with the yummiest crispy wontons, but every time I try to take a bite, someone asks me something.

"Are we still calling it that?" Jen ponders. "I mean, you've seen him, he's kind of seen you, you have mutual friends…"

"I'm still calling it that since we haven't met face-to-face," I state, longingly looking at my forkful of chicken. "But I can't wait to finally meet him. Between him being number twenty-two, the whole thing when I went to the game, and then finally talking to him, I just feel this…connection, you know? And he has *such* a great voice."

"Seriously? A great voice?" Freya asks. "Is he British? Because anyone with a British accent has a great voice. Other than that, I'm not usually impressed."

"What about Australian?" Penny tosses out. "I'm a sucker for a good Aussie accent." Then she proceeds to imitate the accent. Badly.

"He doesn't have an accent," I clarify. Even now, I can still hear his voice: rich, steady, and husky in all the right ways. I can't wait to hear it again. "He just…he sounds kind."

I don't think I've ever thought about anyone's voice before, unless it involves singing, but something about Christian's seems nice. And I'd be lying if I didn't add—hot.

Ugh. I seriously have it bad. I hope I'm not building things up too much in my head. It would be a real bummer if we didn't connect after all of this. And there is nothing worse than sitting through a bad date when all you want to do is pack up and go home.

There's finally a lull in the conversation, so I quickly take a bite of my lunch. Sweet ginger dressing, crispy goodness. I sigh happily.

"Do you know what you're going to talk about tonight?" Penny asks. "Do you think he's only going to want to talk about baseball? Or that he'll want to know all the famous people you've worked with?"

I hold up my finger so I can finish chewing. At this rate, I may never finish my salad.

"I really haven't thought about it. I'm hoping we won't only talk about our careers. Personally, I'm very curious about what his life is like when he's not on the field. And, you know, *he's* famous, so I seriously doubt he's going to be impressed by anything I've done so far."

"Okay, but that's like…sports famous," Penny reasons. "I don't think it's the same."

I disagree. If anything, I'm pretty sure he's been around way more famous people than I have.

"Have you gone online and looked him up? You can probably find out everything about him before you go. This way, you'll have some guaranteed conversation starters." Freya looks at all of us. "What? That's what I'd do."

"Believe it or not, I haven't. I don't want to read about Christian because we all know you can't trust everything you read online. When I meet him tonight, I want it to be authentic, you know? I don't want to go into this with random facts or preconceived notions. Is that weird?"

By the way they're all looking at me, it is.

"Don't be upset, but I looked him up," Jen says as she picks up her drink. "And I won't say anything except that he seems like a genuinely nice guy. A decent human being. And from everything I've read, I can see this being a thing."

"A thing?" I ask. "Like…me and Christian?"

"Uh-huh. But, like I said, I'm not going to say anything to sway you in any direction. Just know this all has my seal of approval."

She's grinning, so I know she's teasing, but deep down, I kind of love that she did the digging. Jen may say she won't share what she found, but I know she would have told me right away if there were any red flags. The fact that she's been quiet tells me that Christian Lucas is one of the good guys.

I know my bestie would never let me down or allow me to go out with a creep, so I'm feeling even better about tonight.

But first, lunch.

"Jen, tell the girls whose hair and makeup you're doing this weekend," I say, hoping to shift the subject from me to someone else for a few minutes.

Luckily, it works, and I listen as she enthusiastically tells us all about the up-and-coming actress she'll be working with.

I am seriously happy for my friend. And so proud of her. I call myself Jen's hype friend, and she is mine. She works incredibly hard, and I never realized how challenging both our careers can be. I'm out there hustling to find roles, and she's doing the same to find clients. She works at a salon, but I know her dream is to have a place of her own someday.

I happily munch on my salad and smile at how we all hype one another up.

This is a good group.

Some days, I let my guard down and truly embrace the circle of friends I have. I was bullied as a kid, and I know what it feels like to be lonely. I met some good girlfriends in middle and high school, but I barely knew anyone when I moved to LA and had to start all over again. But as I sit here on my birthday, I realize that one of the best gifts I ever received is the women sitting around this table with me. They are true friends, and I'm so grateful.

The owner of the café, a lady named Gwen who's the sweetest, appears. Clearly, she knows it's my birthday, because she's carrying a plate with a giant cupcake topped by a candle.

"Hey, Ella, we have a special birthday treat for you. I baked them fresh this morning. Here's one of my famous chocolate cupcakes," she says, looking for a spot to put it down.

"Hang on." Jen wipes her mouth. "I'm done with my lunch. Let's move some plates."

Everyone joins in, and I'm glad I'm nearly finished with my salad. I'll gladly skip the rest in favor of a cupcake. I don't know why, but cupcakes make me ridiculously happy.

Christian still doesn't know it's my birthday, so there's likely zero chance of more cake tonight.

Once everything is cleared, Gwen puts the cupcake down and lights the candles as my friends all sing "Happy Birthday" to me.

"Make a wish, Ella," Gwen says.

Wish-making is quite possibly my favorite thing. And not just on birthdays, but in general.

It all stems from one of my favorite movies, *Pinocchio.* I love the song "When You Wish Upon a Star." It played a huge part in my childhood.

When my dad started working for Wonder Land, it meant that our family had free passes to go anytime we wanted. But if anyone asked me which part of it all I most looked forward to when we walked through the park's gates, I would say the fireworks.

They were my favorite.

Many times, we'd go to the park just to see them.

We had a routine on those nights. As we waited for the show to begin, we'd get hot chocolate or ice cream, and my mom would talk about how your dreams would come true if you wished on a star. So, whenever we were outside at night, she encouraged us to make wishes.

I can feel everyone around the table looking at me and waiting, so I close my eyes and make my wish.

I wish this date with Christian Lucas ends up being the start of something amazing.

Then I blow out the candle.

When I open my eyes, everyone's smiling and clapping, and I have to admit, so far, turning twenty-two is pretty darn great.

I'm a confident woman.

You have to be in the business I'm in.

But as I drive across the city to the Magic's stadium in my old Toyota Corolla, I've got butterflies in my belly, and I'm second-guessing everything. Should I have borrowed Jen's car? I love my Toyota, but it's very old, has significant rust, and my rearview mirror is being held up by duct tape.

I'll bet Christian drives something sleek and sporty.

I smooth a hand over my thigh and wonder if I should have gone with something dressier. Or more casual, since I'm going to the game first. The white capri jeans are comfortable, my pink top has a little bit of bling on it, and I feel super cute, but…is it *too* cutesy? I glare at my Hello Kitty purse, and even though it's like my signature thing, I fear I should have toned things down for tonight. I probably should have gone with Jen's suggestion of black jeans and the coral sweater. It's too late now. I'm halfway to the stadium, and this is what I'm wearing.

Please don't let him think I look too young.

That's a crazy thing to wish for because I *do* look young. Heck, it's been a huge perk for my acting career. Looking younger than my age is the reason I still get parts on the Storyteller Channel. I typically play a teenager, and I love it. I lean into it. But this is the first time it might be a deterrent.

I need to get to the stadium and get this date started, because the longer it takes to get there, the wilder the scenarios playing out in my head get.

I can't explain it, but I somehow know this date with Christian is important.

And it has nothing to do with the premiere and everything to do with my heart.

I'm a grown woman. I've met hundreds of people and have dated a few men, but I've never had this kind of…anticipation.

Maybe I'm putting more pressure on this meeting because it's my golden birthday. Maybe it's all in my mind, and it's making me spiral.

Or maybe this is just a date. I'm just a girl, and Christian is just a boy, and we're just going to dinner.

It doesn't feel right even thinking about it like that.

"Okay, I need to get out of my head for a few minutes." I turn on the radio and nearly squeal with excitement when I hear Whitney Houston singing about how she wants to dance with somebody. One of my favorite songs.

Maybe it's a sign.

The rest of the drive is spent singing along to one song after another. When I see the stadium in the distance, the butterflies in my belly take flight again, but I ignore them. Instead, I follow Christian's instructions for which entrance to pull into and then follow the signs to the premier parking area. There are so many people and cars that parking takes just a little longer than I expected, but I finally pull into a spot and close my eyes, letting out a long breath. This is it.

This is happening.

It's just a date, and everything's going to be fine.

When I open my eyes again, I still feel a bit nervous, but mostly, I'm good. Perhaps even a little excited. I turn off the car, toss my keys into my purse, and climb out. The door creaks loudly as I shut it, and I cringe with embarrassment.

It is what it is I remind myself as I follow the throng of people and make my way up to the ticket office.

Here we go.

Four

I see him in the distance.

At least I *think* it's him.

When I head toward the clubhouse after the game, he walks my way, and I just know. I smooth a hand over my hair and then along my hip as I walk, giving him a small wave.

The corner of his mouth curls into a smile. He slows his pace, his eyes never leaving mine, and for half a second, I swear he's fighting back a grin.

My stomach flutters. That subtle, knowing smile—like he's both happy to see me and amused by me all at once—makes my pulse skip. I bite back a grin of my own, suddenly hyperaware of how my heart is hammering, and think, *OMG, he's even better up close.*

I suddenly wish I had taken everyone's advice and looked him up online so I would have something to say, because right now my mind is completely blank.

Well, except for the part focused on how handsome he is. Blond hair, a lean, athletic build, and the closer we get, I notice his smile more and more. My heart skips a beat.

Is this what it's like when you meet your person? The one?

"Ella?" he asks when we're close enough.

I nod. "Hi, Christian." Not sure whether we should shake hands or hug, I go in for the hug and say, "I'm a hugger." We embrace, and I notice that he smells good. He's not wearing any cologne as far as I can tell, but just his natural scent is worth bottling and selling.

"I'm glad you made it. I know stadium traffic can be brutal."

We step apart, and I miss the feeling of our closeness immediately. "It wasn't too bad. I made sure I left early so I wouldn't be late."

"Would you like a tour?" His smile seems genuine, and I am instantly lost in his bright-blue eyes.

What did he ask? Oh! A tour.

"Sure. That sounds great." I answer, and his eyes crease in an almost smile.

For the next few minutes, I get to experience the Magic's complex with my own personal guide as he gives me a behind-the-scenes tour. His hand lightly brushes mine and lingers, and I do my best not to sigh dreamily.

There's only a handful of people lingering after the game, and it's cool experiencing this without all the noise and crowd.

"Do you want to go onto the field?" he says, his voice carrying a hint of excitement. He puts his hand on my lower back and guides me toward the outfield gate. When he touches me, I instantly get full-body chills. I wish he would keep his hand there and pull me in for another hug. "There's no better view in the entire stadium than when you're standing on the field. I've played in hundreds of games, but this view never gets old."

We walk onto the outfield grass, and the view is beautiful. "It takes your breath away," I say, in complete awe of the stadium around me and also the man standing right in front of me. We keep walking toward center field, and he pulls out a baseball.

"I heard it was your birthday, so I wanted to give you a game ball to remember this special date. I hope it's okay that I signed it to you."

I am truly speechless in this moment and cannot get over how sweet and thoughtful this man is. I look at the baseball on which he wrote: *Happy 22nd birthday, Ella. Best wishes, Christian Lucas.*

I look up at his blue eyes and give him a big hug. "Thank you so much, Christian. This is such a kind gift. I didn't tell you it was my birthday because we were already meeting under unusual circumstances, and I figured if I threw the whole birthday thing out there, you'd probably run away as fast as you could," I joke. "I didn't want to add any additional pressure to our date."

"Well, my sister googled you, and she gave me strict orders not to show up empty-handed," he says with a slight laugh.

Suddenly, there's silence between the two of us, but it's not awkward. There's a palpable energy, as if the rest of the world has paused and we're the only two people in it.

I break the silence. "Remember when I mentioned how I was here for a game a few weeks ago?"

He nods.

"Well, we were sitting right behind the dugout. You stepped out and looked out at the crowd, and…"

"And…?"

Ugh. I hope I don't regret admitting this.

"And it felt like you looked right at me," I blurt.

He stares at me for a moment before his eyes go wide. "You were sitting in the first row, right? There was a guy to your left and a girl to your right. And you were wearing my jersey."

Now, *my* eyes go wide. "I was!"

Holy crap. I cannot believe he remembers that.

"You see, I am so focused during the games that I never look at the crowd. That was the first time in my professional career that I had ever looked in the stands during a game. I remember you because I couldn't believe I had broken my focus. I didn't realize you were a Magic fan.

"Oh, I'm not a fan," I quickly correct, and then realize how bad that sounds. "I mean, I don't really follow baseball. I was wearing your jersey because my…um…my friend got it for me. Twenty-two is my favorite number, and he thought it would be fun to get me a jersey for the game with that on it."

"Twenty-two…?" His eyes narrow, and I have no idea why.

"Mr. Lucas?" someone calls out, and we both turn to see one of the bat boys running out onto the field. "Sorry to interrupt, but you left your cell phone in the clubhouse."

"Oh, wow, I didn't realize I left it. I guess I was rushing too fast to get out of there. Thank you so much, Jake."

As Jake runs off, Christian looks at his phone. "We should actually get going so we have plenty of time for dinner before the restaurant closes."

I feel Christian's hand come to rest low on my back again as he gently guides me back to the outfield gate. My knees practically go weak.

"My car's parked in the players' lot, so…"

"Would it be okay if I drove myself to the restaurant?" I ask, feeling a little nervous. "No offense or anything. I just figured for later on, after we're done eating…"

"It will be easier for you to head home." He smiles. "Not a problem. I'll drive you around to your car. Mine's closer."

"Oh. Okay."

We stroll along quietly, and I'm not sure if it's because there isn't anything to say, or if we're so close to his vehicle that he doesn't want to start a conversation. Still, I'm not a fan of the silence.

This really would be a good time for me to pull some random internet facts out, but I've got nothing.

"I'm parked right over here," he says, and I'm mildly surprised—in a good way—when I see that he drives an older car, too. Suddenly, he's a little more relatable.

He opens the door for me, and I'm about to climb in when I see a beautifully wrapped box on the passenger seat. Christian leans in and grabs it before holding it out to me. The paper's white, with little pink flowers on it, and it has a big pink bow.

I'm seriously twinning with this box, and it's awesome.

"I had to get you a real present," he says shyly.

"Oh, my goodness, Christian," I say, smiling so hard that my cheeks actually hurt, but it's worth it. "You totally didn't have to do this but thank you."

"Why don't you sit down so you can open it a little easier?"

That's a great idea, because it would be awkward while standing.

As I'm taking a seat, he jogs around to the driver's side and joins me in the car. We're both grinning, and I honestly can't believe he did something this sweet.

I carefully tear open the wrapping paper because I don't want to seem too eager. When it's off, and I open the box, I cannot even believe what I'm looking at.

A Hello Kitty purse.

Is this man the sweetest or what?

My eyes go wide as I take it out of the box and hold it up. "I love it!"

"Are you sure? In my sister's research of you online, she said that she saw several pictures of you carrying these kinds of bags, so I thought it was a safe bet." Then he nods at the one I brought with me and grins. "I'm glad I was right."

"Are you kidding me? This is amazing. And so thoughtful of you." Without thinking, I lean in and kiss him on the cheek. I inhale a little bit of his natural scent because he smells so good. When I pull back, he looks a little stunned, and I know I am because I can't believe I just did that. But rather than address it, I simply thank him again.

"Happy birthday, Ella," he says before starting the car. The way he says my name, with his voice low and husky, sends a shiver down my spine. It feels like…a promise.

"Thank you. It may seem silly, but I collect Hello Kitty purses. I have over thirty bags, but I don't have this one." The bag is really cute, pink with a quilted design, silver stitching, and, naturally, Kitty's adorable face. It makes me happy.

We take the short drive around the stadium parking lot to my car. "I'm honored you're spending your birthday with me, but I'm sorry that I took you away from celebrating with your friends."

"You're not. I promise. I went to lunch with some of them today, and we're going to have a party next month."

His brows furrow in confusion. "Why next month?"

"Because it's also my friend Freya's birthday in a few weeks. We thought it would be fun to have a joint party. Plus, we've all got crazy schedules, and it was the first date we could all agree on that would work."

I'm already wondering whether I should invite him.

Maybe get through this date and then decide, silly. Don't be pushy.

We round the corner, and I know I don't have to point out which car is mine because it's literally the only car left in the lot. I had been a little self-conscious earlier about my old, rusty vehicle, but knowing that Christian's isn't in much better shape makes me feel better.

He pulls up beside it, and I quip, "This is me." We both laugh.

"The restaurant is only ten minutes away, and a straight run from the stadium." He gives me the address in case we get split up in traffic, and before I know it, he's getting out of the car to walk me to mine.

Which is three feet away.

Is he perfect?

He opens one door for me to get out and then opens the other so

I can climb in. We're both smiling, and now I almost hate that we're driving separately.

"I'll see you in a few minutes," he says. "Follow me as best you can."

"I will." Then I wait for him to get in his car and pull away before backing out and following him across the parking lot, then out the exit.

The radio is on, and Taylor Swift's "Love Story" comes on the radio, and I sing at the top of my lungs. Is this a sign? I am in such a great mood. I wish I could dance around right now, but since I can't, I do my own little moves behind the wheel. When I pull into the parking lot of Oak & Iron, I let out a fortifying breath because I feel like I've been waiting for this moment for such a long time. I know that's not accurate—it's only been a few days—but I'm just so ready to be on this date.

I've never been to this restaurant before. The sign claims the Oak & Iron is a bistro known for upscale comfort food with a gourmet twist, and I am here for it.

Christian's suddenly at my door and opening it for me, and I smile as I put my hand in his and climb out. The best part? He keeps holding it as we walk inside.

"They rarely take reservations, but I called ahead and asked about having a table held for us." With a casual shrug, he adds, "I almost played the celebrity card, but that's not something I'm comfortable doing. Tonight is about getting to know each other, so I was hoping we'd get a table in a quiet corner."

"And what did they say? Do you think they'll accommodate your request?"

Now, he grins. "I eat here a lot, and the manager knows me, so…yeah. He's the one I spoke to."

"So, you didn't have to play the celebrity card. He already knows you're a big deal."

"Well, I don't know about that, but…"

The hostess interrupts to let us know our table is ready, and I guess she knows who Christian is, too, because she calls him by his name, and they chat as she leads us to a table in the far back corner. It's cozy and semi-private, and I'm a little giddy as I slide into the booth.

She places our menus down, promising that our server will be over shortly.

I look around, loving the decor—it's very rustic-modern with dark wood tables, wrought-iron details, and dim Edison-bulb lighting. And sitting here in the corner, it almost feels like we have the place to ourselves.

Within minutes, we have our drinks, and I order the coq au vin. Christian orders the steak. As soon as our server takes our menus, it's like we both audibly relax, and then laugh softly because we did it in sync.

"Okay, I have a question," he begins, his voice lowering just a bit. The deep timbre of it makes me shiver. I never knew a voice could be so…sexy. His hands are folded on the table, and I'm fascinated by them, too. "Is Ella Holt a stage name or your real name?"

"It's my real name. My full name is Ella Rose Holt, but no one ever calls me that."

He studies me, his head tilted, his expression thoughtful. "It's a beautiful name. Ella Rose. It totally fits you." The intensity of his gaze and the way he says my name practically have me on sensory overload.

Oh, my…

I can feel myself blushing, and I duck my head for a moment to compose myself. When I look up, he's still watching me, and everything around us fades away.

We talk about our lives and how we both grew up in central Florida and how it was such a coincidence that we only lived thirty minutes apart. It's a little wild how many similar experiences we've had. It almost feels like we should have met at some point long before this, but obviously, we didn't.

Our families are alike, as well. Christian has four siblings, and I have three. Both of his parents were schoolteachers. My mom is a teacher, too, and we were both very passionate about our prospective careers from a young age.

"Did you always want to act?" he asks.

I nod. "Definitely." I tell him about how my dad worked for Wonder Land when I was a kid, and how going to the parks so frequently made me want to be a part of it all. "I knew from the time I was young that I wanted to be on a Storyteller Channel show. Like, it had to be that specifically. I remember taking singing lessons, dancing lessons, and then acting lessons. I can't think of a time when this wasn't the dream."

"And you're clearly doing it," he says. "You're on one of their shows right now, aren't you?"

I nod before taking a sip of my water. "It's a recurring role, so I'm not in every episode, but people recognize me for playing the character."

"What's that like?"

For a moment, I'm not sure if he's being serious or not because I'm pretty sure he gets recognized everywhere he goes, too. But when he just continues to look at me, I guess he genuinely wants to know.

"It's actually very exciting," I admit. "I mean, it's not like I've got a mob of people chasing me, but I always love it when someone sees me and their expression changes, and…" I gasp and mimic the look. "It's just so cool."

"It can be exciting," he agrees. "So, how did you end up here in LA? You're from Florida, and I know you said you were chasing the dream of starring on one of Storyteller's shows, but I'm sure there's more to the story."

That's putting it mildly, I silently muse.

Leaning back a bit against the cushions, I know I want to give him the abbreviated version of my journey. The last thing I want to do is dominate the conversation and have him think I'm one of those self-absorbed people who only talk about themselves.

"Well, like I said, I took all the lessons while I was growing up. I knew I had to start making a name for myself regionally and build my resume. In the beginning, it was being an extra on a Storyteller television special. Then the choir I was in was cast for one of their holiday specials. You can still see it on YouTube."

He grins. "Really?"

"Oh, yeah." Pausing, I take another sip of water. "I was part of my high school theater department and the community one, as well. I did some local commercials and some modeling, but…"

Christian holds up his hand to stop me. "Okay, I have to ask this. Did you ever get to work at Wonder Land? It seems like such a logical step for you, especially with your dad working there, and would offer the most opportunities. At least that's my take on it."

"Funny story. I applied to work there on my sixteenth birthday and got the job."

His brow furrows. "And that's funny…why?"

"Well, in my head, I was going to be this amazing performer in shows and parades. I had memorized all the songs and choreography from all my years at the parks. It just seemed like that was what I would do."

"And it wasn't?"

I shook my head. "Not even close. I was essentially a handler for the characters, and my job was to stay in the background. Then they put me in a troll costume. I mean, you just look at me and think troll, right?" My eyes roll before I can even stop them, and then I'm laughing.

But so is Christian, and it turns into an exceptional moment.

"I did eventually get to be in a parade, so that was exciting."

We pause as our dinners arrive, and for the next few minutes, the conversation is all about the food, which is fine with me because it all looks and smells delicious.

"Did they cast you in the TV show because of your work in the parks?" he asks, and for a minute, I'm confused because I didn't expect him to want to go back to my story.

"Sadly, no. My dad left his job at Wonder Land and took a position with a company in Tennessee. Our family moved right after I graduated high school. Then, I got accepted to the University of Cincinnati College-Conservatory of Music."

He looks very impressed, and I can tell he wants to know more.

"It was an incredible opportunity, but…" I shrug. "It wasn't a good fit for me. The program was geared more toward actors looking to perform on stage, and I wanted to be on TV and in movies."

"That makes sense."

"I got the opportunity to star in an independent film in Italy during my first semester."

His eyes go a little wide. "Wow, that's pretty incredible. Was that part of the program?"

"No. It was through a connection I'd made earlier, and I had to take time off from school to go and film it. By the time I got back, everyone was wondering why I was even going to college for acting when I was already landing roles." Another shrug. "That's when I had to decide if I was going to stay in Cincinnati, go home to Memphis, where my family was, or take the risk and make the move to LA."

"And here you are," he says with a smile.

"And here I am." I smile back. "What about you? How did you end up playing for the Magic?"

If I thought I worked hard and had my share of setbacks, they're nothing compared to what Christian's journey was like.

He's short for an athlete. Like, not ridiculously short, but at five foot seven, he's definitely shorter than the average player. Because of that, he was underestimated from the beginning. As I listen to his story, I find I'm angry for him. Time and again, he was passed over or just flat-out overlooked. And that's even after he won the World Series. If I thought getting turned down for a role here and there was depressing, I can't even imagine what it's been like for him.

"How do you keep going?" I ask. "Did you ever just want to walk away and be done with it?"

Shaking his head, he confidently says, "Never. This has been my dream, and all those disappointments just make me want to prove everyone wrong."

"I know exactly what you mean."

And right there, there's a connection that goes beyond any physical attraction. There's something deeper, more profound, and it's on a whole other level. I already know that I like this man. But now, there's more to relate to than the fact that we both grew up in the Sunshine State. The more I learn about him, the more I want to know. And given how he keeps asking me questions, I think it's the same for him.

We finish our dinner as he tells me more about his career.

"What was it like to win a World Series? Your family must have been so proud of you. I'll bet you celebrated like crazy." I can only imagine what something like that—a career high—must feel like, and I'm practically on the edge of my seat waiting to hear all about it.

He doesn't answer right away. And when he does, I'm a little surprised by what he says.

"Winning a World Series was a dream come true." His voice is calm, not at all excited like I thought it would be. "The team worked hard for it, and no one believed we'd make it."

Okay…

"Was your family there to celebrate with you?"

He nodded. "Almost everyone. They all stayed in my apartment, my sisters slept on the floor in sleeping bags, but it was great to have them there."

"Who didn't make it? I would think something that huge would have every member of your family there to support you."

He shrugged. "My father wasn't there. He had to work, so…" Another shrug. "Winning the World Series was the best night of my life. We celebrated as a team, and my family got to celebrate with us. But every season you play, you expect to win. I was just doing my job. It's what I've trained for." He's looking at me and can probably tell that I'm a little shocked by his answer.

Unable to help myself, I reach across the table and place my hand on top of his. "Christian, you know what an amazing achievement that was, right? What you did, even if you *did* train for it, was still such a tremendous accomplishment." I pause, caressing his hand, both to comfort him and because I can't seem to help myself. "It's a big deal, and I bet some players play their entire careers and never win a World Series. I'd still be celebrating if I were you."

For a moment, he looks uncomfortable. Turning my hand in his, he studies them. "That's not the way I grew up. In my family, we acknowledge the victory and then move on to the next thing."

I need to process that statement, but before I can say anything, our server comes over to ask if we're ready for dessert. The awkward mood is broken, and I'm not sure if I'm relieved or not. Still, we order dessert, because it's my birthday and he insists, and he changes the subject to the sitcom I'm filming this week.

By the time we're done, the restaurant seems quieter, emptier, and when I realize it's after midnight, I almost can't believe it. I know we've eaten and talked, but I had no idea it had been over two hours. I have to be on set early in the morning, and I still have a bit of a drive back home, but I don't care. My mom always said, "You can sleep when you're old." And I feel twenty-two years young.

Yet I'm hesitant to leave because I'm having such a great time.

"I could sit here and talk to you all night," Christian says, interrupting my thoughts, "but I've got another game tomorrow, and I'm pretty sure filming starts early for you, too."

"It does, but I'm having such a wonderful time that I kind of hate to leave."

Why deny it, right?

"We'll just have to continue this Thursday night at your movie premiere," he says confidently, but then immediately frowns.

"What? What's the matter?"

Before he replies, he laughs softly. "Do you realize we've talked about pretty much everything under the sun *except* the premiere?"

Did we?

And then I'm laughing, too. "Oh, my goodness, you're right. And that's the reason we're here tonight."

"I know." Shaking his head, he grins. "There were just too many other things to talk about. And I still feel like I'm forgetting something. Like…there was something I kept telling myself that I needed to ask you, and now I've completely forgotten it."

"You can always call me or text me when you remember," I tell him. "And now I'm super curious."

"It'll come to me." He waves our server over, apologizes for us staying so late, and pays the check, and within minutes, we're sliding out of the booth. His hand rests low on my back again as we make our way across the restaurant, and I love that he's comfortable enough with me to do it. It's such an intimate gesture, and it makes me want to lean into it—into *him*—and savor the touch.

But not in the middle of the Oak & Iron bistro.

Christian holds the door for me as we step out into the cool night air. I shiver slightly, and he moves closer as we make our way to my car. I'm parked under one of the outside lights, and when we stop, it feels like there's a spotlight on us. I had been hoping for maybe a romantic kiss under the stars, but the brightness is killing the mood.

I stop next to the car and face him with a soft, happy sigh. "I had a wonderful time tonight. Thank you for being willing to come out and meet me like this."

"I'm the one who should thank you. I was nervous about meeting someone under these circumstances, but I'm glad I didn't let it stop me." He pauses, his expression thoughtful. "I'm glad I left my comfort zone and came out to meet you, Ella Rose."

I can feel my cheeks heat. No one's ever called me that. At least, no one but my parents, and they haven't called me by my full name since I was a little girl.

And it never made me feel quite so…swoony.

"And I'm *really* glad you left your comfort zone to come out and meet me," I tease lightly.

Then we're just standing there, staring at each other, and I'm wondering if there will be a kiss or if it's too soon. I hope it's not, but I also don't want to be the one to initiate a kiss just in case he thinks I'm coming on too strong.

Ugh…why am I still like this? I've never been indecisive in my entire life. Why now?

The next thing I know, he's reaching up and caressing my cheek and then…he stops. His thumb gently brushes against my face one last time before he pulls away.

"Make a wish," he whispers.

"Um…what?" Is this man seriously asking me, the girl who lives to make wishes on stars, to make a wish?

He nods at his thumb. "You had an eyelash on your cheek. You're supposed to make a wish and blow it away." He smiles. "Come on. Make a wish."

My heart feels like it's ready to explode because, if ever there was a confirmation that Christian Lucas is my person, this is it.

I lightly bite my lip and meet his gaze, right before I close my eyes.

I wish for Christian to kiss me goodnight.

Then, I delicately blow on his finger and secretly pray the eyelash blows away.

When I open my eyes, he's studying me intently, right before he reaches up again to gently cup my face. I feel myself leaning in, hoping I'm not misreading the situation. But then he tenderly presses his lips to mine in a kiss that is somehow both chaste and perfect.

And, unfortunately, over too soon.

"Goodnight, Ella Rose." He reaches around me to open my car door and holds it until I'm seated. "Text me when you get home so I know you made it there safely."

I can't take my eyes off him, even as I nod and promise, "I will."

He closes my door and takes a step back, but he doesn't move until I pull out of the parking spot and then turn out onto the road.

I'm smiling, even though I feel like I just left part of my heart back there under that bright light.

I guess my fourth-grade teacher was right. Something special *did* happen on my golden birthday.

I know this is the beginning of something big.

Five

I'm having a tea party.

Sort of.

So, fun fact, I love tea parties. Like, I'm seriously obsessed with them and have been ever since I was a little girl. When I'm happy? Tea party. When I'm sad or stressed? Then it's a pit-tea party.

I'm hysterical, I know.

Right now, I'm happy. Jen is doing my hair and makeup for the movie premiere tonight, and I'm wearing my fluffy pink robe, sipping tea, and letting her do her thing.

"I got home late last night and heard you talking to someone, but I didn't want to disturb you," she says as she begins curling my hair. "Did Christian spend the night?"

"What?!" I cry, choking on my tea. "No, Christian didn't spend the night! He wasn't even here. We were on the phone. Sheesh."

She steps in front of me with a wink and a grin. "Just checking."

With a nervous laugh, I defend myself. "Why would you even ask such a thing? We just went out the one time."

"Yeah, I know, but you've been talking about him nonstop ever since."

"Um…"

"When you got home Monday night, how late did we stay up talking about the date?"

Oh. Right.

"They had to use extra concealer under my eyes when I got to hair and makeup Tuesday morning."

"Because it was easily 3:00 a.m. when we finally crashed. And when you got home Tuesday night, you were still gushing about him."

"He's very gushable. What can I say?" I quip before taking a sip of my chai tea. "He called me last night. That's who you heard me talking to. We were on the phone for three hours, and I didn't want to hang up."

"Mm-hmm…"

"I hope this premiere doesn't freak him out or make him think I'm a weirdo or something."

"Why would you even think that?"

"I look very different in the movie and act completely differently."

"Yeah, it's called acting, Ella. He knows it's not real." She steps in front of me and continues to wield her curling iron. "So, you play a punk rock chick and look a lot less like your usual Pollyanna self. It's just a role. And if he freaks out over it, then that's a tiny red flag."

"I don't want there to be any flags," I murmur, feeling myself pout.

"Look, from everything you've told me about him, it won't be an issue. He knows what you do for a living, and he knows this is just a movie, so stop looking for trouble."

She's totally right. I think I'm feeling this way because Christian isn't in the entertainment business. I've spent so much of my life surrounded by people who are like me. We all had a fairly common goal and shared hobbies and interests. So, I'm completely focusing on what I *think* he's thinking, and I shouldn't be. I know we've spent a lot of time getting to know each other this week, but there's no way I know everything about him.

Not yet.

But I desperately want to.

"You didn't act like this when you were dating Jim," she says, interrupting my thoughts.

"That's because I wasn't really invested in the relationship. He was a nice enough guy, but I didn't have romantic feelings for him, and I could never see myself marrying him. I knew he wasn't the one."

"That's fair. And I already know you have them for Christian. I've never heard someone describe a brief kiss with quite so much intensity."

I can feel my face heat, but she's not wrong. That one little kiss felt more powerful than any other kiss in my life.

And I really hope we can kiss again tonight. He's picking me up, and we're driving to the premiere together, so it feels like a traditional date scenario, where it would totally be the norm to share a goodnight kiss when he brings me home.

"Are you almost done with your tea?"

Looking up at her, I nod. "How come?"

"Because I want you to go and brush your teeth so we can start on your makeup. I don't want you to sip anything or have to wipe your face or mouth. By the time I'm done, your beautiful face will look like a work of art."

I quickly finish my tea and hand her my cup. "A work of art? Really?"

She preens. "I'm that good."

I stand and stretch before hugging her. "Yes, you are."

Within minutes, I'm back with minty fresh breath and a clean, spray-tanned face for her to work with. I've done this so many times, both on set and here in the apartment with Jen, that I'm completely at ease.

"Did you decide which outfit you're going with tonight?"

"The green tiered skirt with the black top," I tell her, careful not to move my lips too much.

"Ooh…interesting choice. I would have thought you'd go with the pink sundress."

"Considering I'm a punk rock girl in this movie, and the whole thing is about the not-so-glamorous side of the rock world, I thought the pink would be a little too light and sunny. The green and black sort of fits the mood."

"No, I totally agree," Jen says as she applies my foundation. "You just didn't seem overly enthused with that combo when we talked about it."

"You were right. I was so hyper-focused on finding the perfect dress that I wasn't finding anything I actually wanted to wear. And the skirt is so cute."

"It really is. And it looks good on you, too. Christian's going to love it."

Will he?

"So, it's the movie and then the after-party tonight, right?"

"Yup. Don't wait up," I tease, and she laughs.

"Are you kidding me? I'm going to want all the details. But I've had a really long day already, so maybe I won't wait up. We'll see."

We talk about clothes, makeup, and Christian while she finishes my makeup. My hair is still curled and sprayed, but she hasn't brushed it out yet. That comes after I get dressed.

Which is what I'm doing now.

Jen follows me into my room with the rest of her hair tools and sits on my bed while I get dressed. I grew up with sisters, so it's not a big deal that she's hanging out while I change. I slip on the skirt, then the sleeveless top, before stepping into my sandals. No sooner am I done than Jen's on her feet and fussing with my hair.

I'm standing in a cloud of hairspray when she tells me to twirl.

So, I do.

"Perfect!" she declares. "Your hair, the makeup, the outfit…everything. Yay!"

I move to check my reflection in the mirror, and I feel good. Confident. Pretty.

"So?" she asks. "Are you ready for it?"

Am I?

Grabbing my little black purse, I nod. "I am so ready for tonight. This is going to be the first chance for Christian to experience my world."

"Well…really?" Jen asks hesitantly. "I mean, he's already a big deal, and he's on TV all the time because of baseball."

"That's true, but he's never been to a movie premiere before, so it's kind of nice that I get to share that with him."

"He's either going to enjoy it, or it will scare him off."

"He doesn't strike me as the type who scares easily," I assure her.

In the distance, our doorbell rings.

"And he's punctual."

"That can be a good thing," she says, following me out of the bedroom. "Go and have fun. I can't wait to hear all about it."

I don't think I've made a mistake, but…

My on-screen self is a punk rocker, and it's a little jarring seeing how different I look. I've got black-and-green-striped hair, and I'm pretty much rebelling against everything and everyone. I'm rough around the edges, and the total opposite of who I am in real life.

I keep glancing over at Christian, and every once in a while, I find him looking at me like, "*Who is this person*?" I don't know what to make of it. Still, when the movie's over and the theater lights come on, he's nothing but positive.

"Great job," he says. "You were amazing, Ella Rose."

"Thank you. It was fun to play someone *so* different from my usual self…"

Which is my way of assuring him that I am *not* that girl with the multicolored hair.

Even though she was pretty badass.

The after-party is at a nearby venue, so we opt to walk there because LA traffic is always a beast.

"How do you choose the roles you audition for?" he asks, and it's a legit question.

"A lot of times, it's just if I fit the age and physical description. I like the challenge of playing unique characters—you know, to push myself. This role was like night and day, compared to my parts on Storyteller's shows. I can play the cheerleader and the popular girl, where my looks are always bright and perky and cute. This was a chance to be a little grittier."

He nods. "You were definitely believable."

"Thank you."

We walk in companionable silence for a minute or two, but the noise of the city is all around us: traffic, music, and the buzz of downtown filling the momentary break in our conversation. I'm hugging my clutch close, my eyes darting from the bright marquees to the clusters of people spilling out of restaurants. There's so much to see and do, and the energy is palpable.

"So, this after-party," he says, smiling. "On a scale of one to ten, how sure are you we'll actually find it?"

I can't help but smile, too. "A solid seven. Maybe an eight. But I promise if we end up in the wrong place, I'll buy you pizza on the way back."

Shaking his head, he laughs. "That's not the worst backup plan, but I'll be the one doing the buying. My mother would have a fit if she heard I let my date buy me dinner."

"Well, it's just pizza," I counter, playfully nudging his shoulder with mine, even as he continues to shake his head.

"It doesn't matter. I was raised with traditional manners, and if there is pizza—or any food tonight—I'm buying."

Unable to help myself, I loop my arm through his and rest my head against his biceps for just a moment as we keep walking. He's so incredibly sweet—almost too good to be true.

We stop at a crosswalk, the red hand blinking above us. Christian leans a little closer, lowering his voice as if sharing a secret. "Honestly, I wouldn't mind if all we did was walk around the city tonight. I know you need to make an appearance at the party, and I think it'll be fun, but…this is nice too."

I lean my head on his arm again and can't fight the smile. "I think so, too." The light turns green, and we step off the curb together, the city carrying us forward for another few blocks until we finally reach the venue.

You can almost hear the music before we even see the building—bass notes humming through the sidewalk, laughter spilling out onto the street. There's a red carpet, and part of the area is roped off. Bouncers and PR people stand at the door, checking the guest list to make sure no one gets in who isn't supposed to.

We pause on the corner, and my eyes widen at the rooftop lights strung like stars above the tall, brick building. I knew the party was being held on the roof, but it's still such a pretty sight, even from down on the street level.

Christian gently nudges me, and I can tell he's been watching my reaction. "Found it. And no pizza required."

"Well, that sucks," I tease. "I was kind of looking forward to it."

He lets out a breath as he stares up at the building. "You ready for this, Ella Rose?"

I give his biceps a quick squeeze as I nod. "Let's do this."

I spot a few photographers, and as Christian and I approach the red-carpet area, we stop and pose for a few pictures.

"Hey, is that Christian Lucas?" I hear someone call out, but Christian only waves and smiles, politely acknowledging his question but avoiding the spotlight. When we step into the building, I ask him why.

"Tonight's your night," he replies, gently brushing a strand of hair away from my face. The touch of his hand makes me shiver ever so slightly, and I'm starting to get addicted to it.

I almost want to ask someone to pinch me because this feels a little like a dream. Not the movie premiere, but this man. This incredibly sweet, considerate, and selfless man. I've dated actors, and they never missed an opportunity to promote themselves. So, the mere fact that Christian is willing to take a metaphorical step back for me feels weird.

Nice, but weird.

Inside, the elevator smoothly carries us up with a low hum. I'm not a fan of enclosed spaces. I wouldn't say I'm claustrophobic, but I secretly hope it's a quick ride to the roof. I grip the rail just a little tighter for good measure.

Christian notices my unease and steps in front of me, forcing me to focus on him—his piercing blue eyes filled with tenderness and maybe a hint of something else. "Don't worry, if it breaks down, I'll keep you entertained with my questionable dance moves."

I know he's going for funny and distracting, but my eyes still go wide. "That's supposed to make me feel better?" I ask with a nervous laugh.

The doors open before he can answer, revealing the lighted rooftop filled with the buzz of voices. The smell of food drifts to us from the buffet tables. Music plays, something lively but not too loud, and clusters of people stand around chatting with glasses in hand.

Christian gestures ahead, stepping back so I can go first. "After you. Let's make an entrance."

I hesitate for just a beat, then walk forward, taking his hand in mine. Christian falls into step beside me, lowering his voice as if we are the only two people there. "Okay, so…what do we do first? Do we need to let anyone know you're here? Or do we mingle?"

"Mingling is fine. We just need to make sure we say hello to a few key people," I explain. "But we're not in any kind of rush." I glance around and wave to some actors I know. "Do you want to get something to drink? Or maybe check out the buffet?"

He grins. "Or are you ready to see just how questionable my dancing is?"

"Um…I'm gonna take a hard pass on that for now," I say lightly, patting his chest. Our laughter mingles with the music, light and unguarded, as we step into the glow of the party.

We weave our way through the crowd toward a bar tucked under a string of lights. I order a glass of sparkling punch, while Christian gets water with a lime wedge balanced on the rim.

When we're a few feet away from the bar and find a semi-quiet little pocket, he raises his glass toward me. "Second date, first toast. Do we toast to you? The movie? The success of the movie?" He laughs softly before his expression turns thoughtful. "I think I want to propose a toast to you. You played an awesome punk rocker, and your talent blows me away. So…to you."

I know I'm blushing even as I whisper, "Thank you." After we touch glasses and drink, I'm already wondering how long we have to stay. I know this is where I'm supposed to be, and it's important for me to make connections and promote the movie, but what I really want is to find someplace quiet so we can just sit and talk until the sun comes up.

"Ella! There you are. I thought I saw you come in." My publicist, Ava, is suddenly at my side, and we do air-kisses before she turns and positively gushes over Christian. "Christian Lucas, look at you. No wonder Ella's friends wanted her to go out with you. I'm so glad your publicist convinced you to make the call."

Then she's got her arm around me as Christian and I exchange awkward grins.

"And seriously, how impressed are you with our girl here?" she goes on. "Did she do a fabulous job in this movie or what?"

Before the poor man can answer, Ava's talking again.

"Listen, you need to work the room a bit. I want there to be pictures of the two of you all over the place tomorrow." She takes a step back and studies us. "You're gorgeous together. Absolutely and completely gorgeous! People are going to both hate and love you because you're so adorable together."

I try to get her to maybe ease up a bit, but she's already doing another round of air-kisses before disappearing into the crowd.

Christian looks a little dazed, and I feel like I need to put his mind at ease. "She's only like this at events, I swear."

"That was…wow. She's a lot."

"I know. I know, and I'm sorry. If you want, we can leave and—"

Taking my hand in his, he just holds it. "We're not going anywhere. Apparently, we need to work the room so people can love *and* hate us." He chuckles. "I'm not exactly sure what that means, but I think we can pull it off."

Tilting my head, I stare at him and wonder if I need to explain it or if he's teasing. "How do you feel about doing a little gushing while you're plastered to my side?"

He's instantly beside me, one arm banded around my waist, his hand resting on my hip, and his breath is warm against my ear. "You are fabulous. I'm thinking Academy Awards." Pulling back slightly, he winks, clinking his glass gently against mine. "What do you think, will that work?"

"It's a little over-the-top, but…I like it." I kiss his cheek without thinking. His freshly shaven skin is so smooth, and his natural scent is intoxicating. It makes me want to linger and simply inhale.

But I don't.

Instead, I pull back as our eyes meet. I feel like we're asking a dozen questions without saying a word, and for a moment, the rooftop crowd seems to fade into the background.

Why did you kiss me?

Can I kiss you?

If we work the room fast, can we leave?

Do we have to work the room?

Someone bangs into me as they walk by, breaking the moment, and I realize that there's been a photographer taking photos of us canoodling this whole time. Ava is standing behind him and gives me a wink as if saying, "*Good job.*" I look at Christian, completely embarrassed, but he seems to take it in stride.

"Come on," he says, leaning in close to my ear. His breath is warm, and it makes me tremble slightly. "Let's mingle and see what's on the buffet. I think I saw someone with pizza, but maybe it was wishful thinking."

And, just like that, we're laughing again as we step away from our little spot and face the crowd. Then, almost as a unit, we join them and do our best to be fabulous.

It's late.

I don't even know exactly what time it is, but I know it's late.

We stayed at the party for longer than I thought we would, but we ended up having a great time. We ate a little, drank a little—fun fact, neither of us drinks alcohol, but we both enjoy a good mocktail—and danced and schmoozed like we were supposed to. Christian's dancing *was* a bit questionable, but I love that he was willing to get out on the floor with me.

After we left, we stopped at an ice cream shop and split a sundae because I was dying for something sweet. There was dessert at the party, but honestly, I was ready to leave and go someplace with just the two of us.

"I finally remembered what I wanted to ask you the other night," he says after scooping up some ice cream.

"When we went out Monday night and were at the stadium, you mentioned how twenty-two was your favorite number, remember?"

I nod around a spoonful of whipped cream.

"Were you on a flight to LA about two months ago?" he asks, seeming a little hesitant. "And were you drawing the number twenty-two on a piece of paper?"

My eyes go wide. I can't believe I didn't put it together sooner. There's been this feeling like there was something familiar about him since I first saw him at the game a few weeks ago.

"Oh, my goodness. You were sitting next to me!"

It's his turn to nod. "I was."

"You may not believe this, but I really wanted to keep talking to you. After I told you about, you know, the ex sitting in front of us, I got the feeling that you thought I was a little weird and weren't the least bit interested in continuing our conversation."

His face scrunches up a bit. "You're not completely wrong."

"Oh, man, I knew it," I murmur.

"But I was also exhausted. My schedule had been very hectic, and then after I had to run across the airport to avoid missing the flight, I just wanted to close my eyes and rest. Your note about the ex just forced me to nap."

I can't help but laugh. Luckily, he does, too.

The walk back to his car feels like miles, but that's because I'm getting tired. He offers to get us a cab so I won't have to keep walking in heels, but I power through.

Now, we're parked in front of my apartment building, and I'm debating whether to ask him in.

The vehicle's interior is dim and a little warm. Christian's holding my hand, and I know I'm going to miss it when it's time for him to go.

"Do you have a game tomorrow?" I ask.

A soft laugh is his first response. "Today was a rare day off for me, so yeah, I have a game tomorrow. We have games almost every day during the season, but Sunday is our last game for the year."

"Then the season is over?"

He nods. "It is, but not really. Not for me." Pausing, he runs his thumb lightly over my palm. "I'm very disciplined. I'm the guy who practices even when there isn't a formal practice. It's just the way I've always been. I live by a very strict routine. I have to. This season was a little rough, and I'm dealing with an injury that I need to get resolved before next season begins."

"Oh, wow. You'd never know anything was wrong," I say, trying to think if I've noticed a limp or if he winced at any point, but he didn't. "May I ask what kind of injury it is?"

"They think I pulled my piriformis muscle," he says, like that explains everything.

"So, what do you have to do for that? Do you go to physical therapy?"

"Yup," he says solemnly. He's studying our hands, and I can tell he's got something else to say, but he's trying not to say it.

"Christian?"

He looks up at me.

"I feel like there's more to this than you're telling me," I add.

He's quiet for a moment before letting out a long breath. "When I heard about you and the premiere, I wasn't only hesitant because of the whole, you know, Hollywood aspect of it."

I know he's referring to my people calling his people, and he's not being derogatory.

"I guess I wasn't thinking of anything beyond…this."

When he pauses again, it hits me that I could be reading the situation wrong. Am I the only one catching feelings? Maybe he's just a nice guy who gets along with everyone, and I misinterpreted the whole thing. I've never been the type of person who romanticizes relationships, because I know right away if I have those feelings for someone or not.

And I have them for Christian.

But it seems it might be one-sided.

"Oh," I force myself to say. Now, I'm studying our hands and the way he's still caressing my palm. The tenderness of it makes no sense. How can his touch be so gentle if he's already pulling away? I want to pull back and break the connection, but I can't.

With his other hand, he reaches out and touches my cheek. Now, I have to look at him.

"I didn't realize I was going to meet a woman who would turn my carefully disciplined world upside down."

I gasp softly, and my heart starts to race. Is he saying what I think he's saying?

"I don't date a lot because I don't have much downtime," he goes on. "And I've never met anyone who made me want more time away from the field."

The lopsided grin he gives me is endearing, but I don't want to say anything until he's done.

"My career is everything to me. I live, breathe, eat, and sleep baseball. I don't like to take my focus away from it because an athlete has a short shelf life, if you know what I mean. If I don't stay at the top of my game, my career is over." He takes a deep breath. "I'm not ready for that yet."

"O-kay…" I draw out the word. I'm feeling some mixed signals.

Does he want to be with me but can't because of his career? Because that's where I feel this is leading.

"This last week has been one of the best I've had in a long time. And honestly, I didn't see it coming."

I laugh nervously. "Me, neither."

"Here's the thing. This injury requires me to work with the team's trainer. The physical therapy will be pretty intensive if I want to be in top form for next season."

Ugh. He's dragging this out, and I don't even think before I blurt out, "It's okay, Christian. I get it. We had a great time, but the timing's off for us. You need to deal with your injury. Maybe when you're feeling better, we can try again. Or not. I'm not really sure what you're thinking." I let out a small huff. "And now I'm just rambling because I swore I was going to stay quiet until you were done talking. But I feel like you're trying to let me down easy, so you're taking the long way around."

I hate that I can feel tears stinging my eyes, but I force them back and keep going.

"I totally get dedication to your career. Heck, I grew up without any real friends because I spent so much time and energy focusing on every kind of lesson out there that would help me become an actress." I close my hand around his and force myself to smile. "Am I disappointed because I really saw this going somewhere? Yes. But I can honestly say that it's okay." I give his hand a little squeeze. "I promise."

He doesn't say anything, and his expression doesn't change. But when I go to pull my hand away, he holds on.

"Ella Rose, the last thing I want is to disappoint you, and even though I appreciate you saying that you'll be okay, that's not what I was going for."

I'm confused again. "It's not?"

Shaking his head, I catch a glimpse of a smile. "No. What I was *trying* to tell you—in my very slow and roundabout way—is that I have to go to Arizona to work with the trainer."

"Why Arizona? I thought with the stadium being here…"

"Our training facility is in Tempe. That's where most of our staff is."

"Oh."

"I'll be gone for a month, and that disappoints me because, well, I'm going to miss you. I hate that we've had this amazing week, and now I have to leave."

Relief washes over me like a wave, and I'm not sure if I should laugh or cry.

My breath is shaky as I release it. Those tears still sting my eyes, but they're happy tears now.

Sort of.

"Okay, then," I say. "We'll still be able to talk on the phone and… and…" Then I pause. "So, you'll be gone a month?"

"Yes, four weeks. But I'm hoping maybe I can get it done in three."

"Oh. Okay. And when do you leave?"

"Sunday. Right after our last game."

In less than three days.

"Wow. Um…" Another long breath. "This is totally doable. It's not great, but we'll make it work."

Again, he doesn't respond right away, but I know there's more coming.

"You should come with me," he blurts.

"What?" I'm certain my eyes are comically wide as I sputter and stammer and try to think of something to say.

Christian nods. "Come with me," he says in earnest. "I know it's a little crazy."

"Ya think?" I ask with a nervous laugh. "Christian, I…I don't know. I mean…I want to say yes, but we just met. And I'm really an old-fashioned kind of girl. I'm not sure I'm comfortable staying in a hotel with a man I barely know."

"I would get you your own room. And I don't expect anything, you know, in return. I just really hate the idea of leaving when we just found each other."

Oh, my goodness. My heart is seriously going to beat right out of my chest.

I want to be impulsive. I want to say yes. For most of my life, I've acted on impulse because I believed in whatever I wanted to do. But this?

This isn't a role in a play, a commercial, or a TV show.

This is real. And it has the potential to ruin something really great if we don't think things through.

I should lead with my head, not my heart, shouldn't I?

Taking both his hands in mine, I stare at them. I memorize the way they feel, even as I let out a shaky breath. I can't believe I'm going to be logical about this.

"I love that you want me to go with you," I tell him. Slowly, my gaze meets his. "But I can't do it. I'm sorry."

His disappointment is palpable. "Oh."

"We're still going to make it work. I promise. We'll talk every day. And with any luck, it will only be a few weeks."

Mentally, my fingers are crossed.

"Are you sure? I don't expect you to just sit around and wait for me to come back from Arizona. I'm sure you have guys practically banging down your door. I mean…look at you. You're beautiful."

And there are those butterflies. Right on cue.

"You think I'm beautiful?" My voice is so soft, I'm sure he can barely hear me, but he must because he nods. That boyish grin of his melts my heart.

"I do," he whispers as he begins to slowly close the distance between us. When his lips are just a breath away from mine, he pauses. "Is it okay if I kiss you, Ella Rose?"

All I can do is nod.

Then his lips gently touch mine. It's so much better than the first kiss because it lingers and goes a bit deeper. It's the kind of kiss you sink into but are in no rush to end.

I know it will.

But I'm going to savor it while I can.

Six

Sunday morning, I'm lying in bed with my cup of tea.

It's pit-tea party time.

Right now, Christian is on his way to the stadium for an afternoon game, and immediately afterward, he's headed to the airport with an open-ended ticket. I know it's a good thing for him, but selfishly, I want the trainer to be here in LA so we don't have to say goodbye.

"Knock, knock," Jen says from outside my bedroom door. "Can I come in?"

"That depends. Do you have waffles?" I ask miserably.

"No, but I have giant chocolate chip muffins. And cheesecake."

Now she has my attention.

"Come on in." I sit up a little straighter, but I know I don't look my best.

"Hey, you," she says as she carefully opens the door. Holding up a pastry box with a sympathetic smile, she sits at the foot of my bed and gets comfortable. "I figured you were having your sad tea party and decided you needed some cake to go with it."

I glance at the clock and see that it's a little after nine. "It's a bit early for cheesecake."

"Pfft. Why is it too early for cheesecake but not a muffin? Or a cinnamon roll? Or a donut? I mean, why are we relegating the cheesecake to the p.m. time?"

"You make a good point. Hit me with a slice."

"Um, I'll be right back. I forgot the plates." She's on her feet. "And forks." She dashes out of the room. "And napkins!" she calls.

While she's gone, I put my tea on my bedside table before opening the box and inhaling deeply.

Oh, sweet sugary goodness, how I love you.

Before I can profess my love, Jen's back with her hands full of everything we need for breakfast in bed.

I scoot closer to the wall and move the blankets aside. "Join me," I tell her.

She happily climbs in beside me and pulls the covers back up over our laps. I rest my head on her shoulder as she hands me a plate with a slice of cheesecake and a muffin. I take a forkful of cheesecake and hum in appreciation.

"That's the stuff," Jen says after doing the same.

"Cheesecake is always there for you. It never leaves."

"Oh, sweetie…"

I immediately think about last night.

Saying goodbye was harder than I thought it would be.

A part of me can't believe I'm this attached and emotional about a man I barely know. And yet, here I am.

Christian's schedule was hectic the last couple of days, but we managed to squeeze in an early lunch date before his game yesterday. It wasn't ideal, but we wanted to see each other one more time. We talk on the phone every chance we get, but it was nice to see his face.

We met up at the café around the corner from my apartment, and as soon as he spotted me, he walked over and kissed me on the cheek. "Hey, Ella Rose," he said softly, his lips lingering against my skin.

I love it when he does that. The warmth of him, his smooth jawline…it's like a magnet. And as usual, he smelled so darn good.

When he pulled back, he took my hand and led me to a table in the corner that he had secured for us. I sat, surprised to see that he had even ordered a cup of tea and a chocolate croissant for me.

"I remembered you telling me how much you love these," he said as he sat. His blue eyes, the ones that always look so kind and comforting, looked sad.

So, he was feeling it, too.

There were so many things I wanted to say, but I couldn't seem to make myself say any of them. Mainly because it was about how much I didn't want him to go. I'd been torturing myself since Thursday night with the entire situation. I knew it was something he had to do. *Had to.* His future playing baseball depended on it. Which meant I couldn't be selfish, no matter how much I wanted to be.

Instead, I wrapped my hands around my tea, letting the heat seep into my palms and keep me from reaching for him. Across the table, Christian leaned back, his own cup untouched.

"A month," he said softly, almost as if testing the words.

I tried to smile, but it wavered. "It's not that long."

"Feels like it could be."

Something in the way he said it caught me off guard and made my chest tighten. We'd only just begun—had barely scratched the surface of each other's lives—yet the thought of him being gone made the edges of the room blur.

I stared down at the steaming, deep amber liquid in my cup. "You'll be back before I even realize it." But my voice was quiet, betraying more than I wanted it to.

Christian leaned forward, his forearms resting on the table and his gaze steady. For a moment, the sounds of the café faded—no clattering cups, no laughter at the corner booth, just the quiet press of his presence and the space between us charged with something unspoken.

I swallowed hard, a lump rising in my throat. *It shouldn't matter this much already*, I thought. But it does.

"Are you sure you can't come?" he asked, and I could hear the want in his voice. The need.

"I…"

Reaching across the table, he placed one strong finger over my lips. "I'm sorry," he whispered. "I shouldn't have said that. It's hard enough without my putting pressure on you."

Slowly, that same finger gently rubbed my lip before completely falling away. Our gazes held, and I wasn't sure where the conversation could go from there. Fortunately, Christian did.

"My flight leaves tomorrow, right after the game. Even though it's a Sunday, I'm meeting with the trainers right away. We've already talked on the phone several times and have a treatment plan in place, but they want the chance to examine me before we hit the ground running on Monday."

We lingered until our cups were empty and the café began to fill with the afternoon crowd. I kept glancing at the clock, wishing I could make time stall for a little longer. But I knew he needed to get going. He still had stuff to do before the game.

When Christian finally stood, I rose with him, my chair scraping lightly against the wooden floor. We stepped outside together, the sound of the LA traffic a stark contrast to the low hum of conversation in the coffeehouse.

His car was parked at the curb, but I knew he would walk me home. Wordlessly, we headed that way. He was holding my hand, and I loved the connection. As we walked, I looked up at the sky. It was afternoon, and there weren't any stars out, so I had to pretend I could make a wish on one.

I wish this next month flies by so Christian can come home fast.

Even though it was a little awkward, I rested my head on his shoulder as we walked. "So… a month," I said again, my voice almost swallowed by the passing rush of a bus.

Christian gave me a half-smile, though it didn't reach his eyes. "I'm aiming for three weeks."

"That would be nice."

"I'll call you. We'll text and video chat every day. Chances are, you'll get tired of me."

I laughed softly, but it caught in my throat. "That's not even possible."

We walked the rest of the way in silence, and when we finally came to my building, we stopped, finally facing each other.

This was it.

He hesitated, then reached out and tucked a loose strand of hair behind my ear. The gesture was simple, but it made my pulse stumble. "Don't forget me while I'm gone," he said, quiet enough that only I could hear.

My chest ached as I forced a teasing tone, though I knew my smile wavered. "You think you're that easy to forget?"

Our eyes held for a beat too long. Then, before I could say anything else—before I could do something reckless—he pulled me in close. "I'm gonna miss you, Ella Rose." And then he kissed me. It was slow and tender, and my arms went around him, holding him as close as I could. I had no idea how long we stood there, kissing under the bright California sun, but when we finally broke apart, I was shaking and willing myself not to cry.

I failed because, suddenly, he was gently brushing the tears off my cheeks. Swallowing hard, I took a small step back. "Have a safe flight. Text me when you land, okay?"

"I'd like to call you tonight after the game, if that's okay. I love hearing your voice as I'm drifting off to sleep."

I sniffled. "Me, too."

He nodded. "Let me walk you inside."

I shook my head. "I'm fine. Really. You need to go."

"Are you sure?"

I forced myself to nod. He kissed me one last time, soft and lingering, before turning and walking away. I stood there on the sidewalk, the hum of the city around me, already feeling the emptiness of the space he left behind.

My cell phone rings, jolting me back to reality. To today. I can tell from the ringtone that it's my mom. Jen recognizes it, too, because she carefully scrambles from the bed to grab it for me.

"I'm taking my cake," she whispers before blowing me a kiss and leaving the room, closing the door behind her.

"Hey, Mom," I say as I answer the phone, and I almost cringe at how depressed I sound. "How are you?"

"Oh, my goodness. What's wrong? Is it bad news? Did you lose a role? Are you sick?"

I surprise myself by laughing a little. "I'm not sick, and all of my roles are safe."

"Hmm…okay. Are things going okay in general? Are you homesick? Did you and Jen have a fight? It's okay, you can tell me."

I laugh a little more. "Mom, everything's fine. I promise. I always miss you, Dad, and everyone. Jen and I were just having breakfast in bed, so…"

"Breakfast in bed?" she repeats, and I can hear the confusion in her voice.

"I'm a little sad today, and Jen was trying to cheer me up. She went and got us muffins and cheesecake, and I was drinking tea and—"

"Ah. The sad tea party. Okay. Okay." She pauses for a second before I hear her gasp. "Oh, sweetheart, why? Did your date to the premiere with Christian not go well? I was trying not to bug you, but you have to know I've been dying to call."

"You know you can always call me. I love talking to you."

"So, tell me what's going on."

I gingerly maneuver around on the bed, placing my plate next to my teacup on the bedside table before fluffing my pillow and getting comfortable. And then I tell her all about the last week. The first date, all the conversations and phone calls with Christian afterward, the premiere, his injury, and his going to Arizona for physical therapy.

"Oh, wow. That poor boy. You know he's got to be a wreck worrying about getting better. This is his livelihood. You know what that's like, Ella. You know if there was something you needed to do to keep acting, you'd do it. And you have."

"I know that," I say.

"And it isn't always convenient. It isn't always easy. But when you're passionate about your career, you do what needs to be done."

I nod and try not to get frustrated because I'm ready to snap, *"I know that, Mom!"*, but she's only being helpful. It's not her fault that I'm in a miserable mood.

"We just really hit it off, and now he's going to be gone for a few weeks—maybe a month—and, you know, that's why I'm sad."

"Obviously, you'll be able to talk to him," she reasons. "He won't be in physical therapy all day, every day, so there's that. And he can fly back on the weekends. Is that an option? I know it's not cheap, and it might not be completely practical, but maybe you two can trade off, him coming home one weekend and then you visiting him the next."

"He actually asked me to go with him," I murmur.

"And you turned him down?" she asks incredulously.

If I were sipping my tea, I would have spit it clear across the room.

"Um, excuse me? Are you telling me I should have followed a man I just met to another state and stayed in a hotel with him?"

"Well, I'm not saying you need to share a room with him," she says primly.

I'm honestly in total shock right now because it *sounds* like my sweet, little, Southern, Christian mama is encouraging me to go and stay with him.

Well, not *with* him, but, you know, with him.

Ugh. When did my personal life get this crazy?

"Mom, come on. You can't be serious." I laugh nervously again because I think she's joking, and yet, she's not.

"Ella, sometimes you have to claim what's yours," she says with complete confidence. "If you feel this strongly about him, and he feels the same about you, then you need to be with him."

"But…"

"No buts. If you were anybody else, I would not encourage this at all. But you, my sweet girl, are the most levelheaded person I know. You dream big, and you always go after what you want. Why shouldn't it be Christian Lucas?"

I have no response. She's left me totally speechless.

"What's your schedule like for the next few weeks? Are you filming anything you need to be in town for?"

I think about it for a moment. "No. I just finished filming something last week, and my schedule's clear for a little while. I typically spend my downtime looking at what's being cast and then meeting with my agent so she can get me auditions."

"You can still do that in Arizona. If there's something you have to audition for, you can easily fly back to LA. It's not like you're stranded out there or even have to stay for the entire time he's there. For all you know, you may hate it. Or maybe you and Christian won't feel as comfortable as you think you might."

"I doubt that, Mom. He's…" I sigh. "Do you remember when I was little and would just *know* what I wanted to do? The lessons I wanted to take, the roles I wanted to play? I know Christian's not a lesson or a role, but a part of me, something deep in my heart, knows he's meant to be in my life."

For a moment, neither of us says a word. My heart's racing because I'm essentially saying that I'm in love with this man without actually saying the words.

"I have always believed in you," my mother says, her voice gentle and soothing. "You were never a girl who chased after the boys, and you were always very selective with the ones you dated. If your heart is telling you that this man is the one, then why wouldn't you go to Arizona?"

"Because it sounds crazy to jump on a plane and stay with a guy I just met, especially a famous baseball player," I say with a laugh. This time, it's humor and not nerves. "I don't want to give anyone the wrong idea. You know, there are women out there who chase after professional athletes, and I certainly don't want anyone accusing me of that."

"Anyone who knows you, knows you wouldn't do that."

"You and Dad raised me to be responsible, practical, and level-headed. And I have been."

"Going to Arizona won't change that, Ella. I think this is something you have to do."

And it is.

"I know this is crazy," I say, because I need her to know that I realize it. "But he's a good man, I promise. We've talked for hours, and I feel like I've known him forever. It's just…different. There's a connection I've never felt with anyone else."

"That's how it is when you meet your person. The one. I always told you that when you met 'the one,' you'd just know." She goes quiet for a moment. "You're sure about this?"

I hear the concern in her voice, and I wish she were here so I could hug her. "I really am, but it means everything to me that you support my decision." I pause and laugh. "Well, you're basically the reason I'm doing this. Without your encouragement, I would have played it safe and hated every minute of Christian's time away."

"I'm glad, sweetheart. It's my job to encourage you and to be your biggest cheerleader. That will never change, no matter how old you get."

Tears sting my eyes, and I realize I've had that reaction more lately than I ever have in my life. I guess this is my emotional era. I wipe my eyes and smile. "I can't believe I'm really going to do this."

"I don't know why. You've always had a fearless streak."

She's right. And hearing her say it makes my heart ease even as a mix of relief and giddy excitement starts to bubble up. "Oh, my gosh. I'm really doing this. I'm really going to get on a plane and go to Arizona to be with Christian." The little squeal of excitement that comes out sounds a bit restrained for me, but I also don't want to hurt Mom's ears. "And you promise you're okay with this? You're not, you know, just doing that supportive thing, even though you think it might be a mistake?"

Her soft laughter is her first response. "Ella, I'm your mother. I'm always going to worry. But if you believe in this, then I believe in you."

"Thanks, Mom. I love you."

"I love you, too. Now, go and make your plans, and be sure to let me know what they are. It's important that I know your flight info and where you'll be staying."

That makes me smile. "I know it is. And I promise that I'll either call, text, or email as soon as I have all the details figured out."

"Okay, then. Go. And good luck."

"Thanks, Mom. I'm gonna need it."

We hang up after another round of I love yous, and then I'm all alone as the enormity of the situation hits home.

I've packed up and moved for things I believed in before, like going to college in Cincinnati and then moving here to LA. So, what makes this any different? It's not like I'm moving there. I'm just going for a few days, tops.

Glancing at the clock, I know Christian's already at the stadium getting ready for the game, so I can't call him and let him know I've changed my mind. Now, it's a matter of seeing when I can get a flight and how fast I can leave.

Jumping off the bed, I take a quick bite of my muffin before grabbing my laptop. Once I'm back on the bed with it and all the cake, I call out to Jen.

A minute later, she's standing in the doorway. "What's up?"

"I'm going to Arizona," I firmly state, right before she starts asking about a thousand questions.

"How long will you be gone?"

"Um…"

"When are you leaving?"

"I'm just looking…"

"Does Christian know you're coming?"

"He's at the stadium getting ready for the game right now, but—"

"What made you change your mind?"

"My mom said—"

"Where are you going to sleep?"

"Um…"

"Do I need to come and be a chaperone?"

On and on it goes, and I do my best to answer them all. When she's finally okay with all of it, we sit side by side as I research flights, and we look up the hotel he's staying at.

Things start to fall into place, and I decide to wait a couple of days before joining him, so he can get settled at the hotel and meet with his physical therapist. I'm sure once he has a schedule, it will make things easier for us.

I just hope Christian hasn't changed his mind about my being there with him.

Late Wednesday afternoon, I land in Phoenix.

I waited until Monday night to tell Christian I was coming. It was important to me that he meet with his trainers and see what they had in store for him, then let it be his decision if he still wanted me to come.

Luckily, he was completely on board with my plan. I'm staying through Sunday. Hopefully, by that time, we'll have a clue as to how long he'll need to stay.

I'm walking out of baggage claim and looking for the car he said he was sending for me. He offered, even though I said I didn't mind getting a cab. I take out my phone and re-read his earlier messages.

Christian: *The driver will be there when you land. He has your flight information.*

Christian: *When you step outside, follow all the signs for rideshare.*

Christian: *It's a black SUV, and there's a Magic logo on the door.*

Christian: *Text me when they pick you up. I can't wait to see you!*

I realize that I'm standing and waiting in the wrong spot and quickly follow the signs to the pickup area. It's a lot farther than I thought it would be, but luckily, I spot the Magic logo and notice a man standing beside the SUV with a sign that says *Ella Rose*. I just love how he calls me by my first and middle names. I am going to kiss Christian silly when I see him.

"Good afternoon, Miss Holt," the driver says as he steps forward to help me with my bags. "How was your flight?"

"It was good. Thank you," I say with a smile.

He loads my luggage into the back and then holds the door open for me to climb into the back seat. Once he's behind the wheel, he informs me that there's water waiting and even adjusts the temperature of the vehicle for me.

I thank him again, and before I know it, we're on our way. Taking out my phone, I quickly tap out a text to Christian.

Ella: *In the car and on my way.*

Ella: *I'll text you when I'm settled in my room. See you soon! xoxo*

It's only a short drive to the hotel, and I feel a bit guilty for making the Magic send a car for me.

Well, not the Magic. Christian.

We pull up to the hotel, and I suddenly feel guilty for an entirely different reason. When Christian mentioned paying for my room, I wasn't entirely okay with it, but he wouldn't budge. But the hotel I'm looking at right now is a bit swankier than it looked online, and I don't know how I'm supposed to be okay with the whole thing.

The driver helps me out of the car, and a bellman is immediately there to assist with my luggage. I'm not used to this level of service, and I have no idea who I'm supposed to tip or how much.

I'm no country bumpkin, but I wasn't prepared for *this*, and I'm second-guessing my decision to come without setting some boundaries first.

Too little, too late, Ella. You're here now.

I reach into my purse to tip the driver, but he politely declines and wishes me a wonderful stay. With nothing left to do, I follow my luggage into the hotel and go to check in. At the front desk, I pull out my ID and credit card and quickly find out that my room is ready, and they don't need my card. They simply hand me my room key and a resort map and, once again, wish me a wonderful stay.

I smile, but it feels awkward.

All of it.

I don't make small talk with the bellhop on the way to the room, but that's only because he's giving me the whole spiel about the hotel and its amenities. I smile and nod, feeling utterly relieved when we arrive at my room. This time, I make sure to tip. Once I'm alone, I think I may be a little overwhelmed.

Is Christian's room next door? I don't see an adjoining doorway, but that doesn't mean anything. Does everyone on staff know I'm here with him? Do they know we barely know each other? Are they talking about it?

"Okay, get a grip," I mumble. "We're not that newsworthy."

Stepping farther into the room, I walk over to the window and look out at the view of the mountains. It's breathtaking. I instantly relax and give myself a few minutes to admire the scenery. I don't know much about Tempe, but I'm sure I'll learn all about it over the next several days.

My phone rings, and I realize that I never let Christian know I arrived at the hotel. Or my mother. But when I look down, I see it's Christian.

"Hey," I say when I answer. "I'm here."

"That's great. I figured you needed time to get checked in and up to your room. I really wanted to meet you in the lobby, but I just finished my session, and I'm heading back to the hotel now."

"How did physical therapy go today?"

"Long and painful," he says with a laugh. "But we can talk about it, or not, over dinner. I made reservations at the rooftop restaurant."

"Oh, wow. You didn't have to do that. I would have been fine just grabbing some sandwiches or something." I don't want him spending all this money on me. It's something we'll have to discuss sooner rather than later.

"I thought it would be nice for our first night together in Tempe," he says easily. "I should be there in about fifteen minutes. I'm in the room across the hall from you."

"That's great. I was wondering if we were on the same floor or in completely different parts of the hotel. Either would have been fine, but I was just curious, and it's all so unfamiliar to me. But the hotel is great. Very nice. Much nicer than I thought it would be. And this room is amazing, and the view is spectacular. I'm going to take pictures and send them to my mom and Jen. They'll be so envious, and—"

"Ella Rose?" he says in that deep, masculine voice that I'm getting very accustomed to. "You're rambling." I can hear the amusement in his voice, but he's right. I'm definitely rambling.

"This is just…" Pausing, I sigh. Loudly. "This is just so much more than I was expecting, and I guess I'm nervous."

"The last thing in the world I want is for you to be uncomfortable."

"I'm not. I swear. But it's all new to me." The nervous laugh is out before I can stop it. "I'm fine. Really. By the time you get here, I promise I'll be my normal self."

"As long as it's how you feel," he says, and I can already feel myself calming. "You don't need to pretend with me. It's okay if you're nervous. I am, too."

For some reason, that thrills me.

"Really? You're not just saying that?"

He laughs. "I believe in being truthful at all times. Even when it might not make me look great. The thing is, this is all new to me, too. All I know is that I'm glad you're here, and I can't wait to see your face. It's been too long."

"It's been four days. Barely," I tease.

"Still too long."

Aww…this man…

"My ride's here. I'll see you in a little bit, okay?"

"Okay."

"Do you need anything?"

Just you.

"I'm good. But thank you. I'll see you soon."

"Yes, you will."

We hang up, and I spring into action. I unpack a few things and quickly freshen up. The flight wasn't long, but I still dressed casually, and I'd like to look a little more put-together—especially if we're going to dinner at the rooftop restaurant.

I change out of my leggings and sweatshirt and put on a pair of black jeans and a turquoise sweater. My hair is up in a ponytail, so I remove the scrunchy, shake my head, and brush it all out. Studying my reflection, I touch up my makeup a bit and reapply my lipstick. By the time Christian knocks on the door, I'm ready.

More than that, I'm both excited *and* relaxed.

This is it.

The start of everything.

When I open the door and see his handsome face, my heart tells me I have nothing to worry about. I made the right decision.

Our future starts right here, right now.

Seven

At this point in my life, I've taken a lot of risks. Some have panned out, others haven't. But this trip? It has more than panned out—it's everything.

Coming to Tempe put us in our own little bubble. There are no distractions, except for the few hours a day when Christian is at physical therapy. Once he's done, we literally have the entire day to ourselves. We've packed so much into the five days we've had, and he's made every moment so incredibly magical. I had no idea relationships could be like this.

We did a bit of sightseeing; he took me shopping and bought me a couple of outfits and shoes, and we even found a Hello Kitty purse I didn't have.

"You know, you're sort of a good luck charm for my little obsession," I tease.

Laughing softly, he looks at me. "Um, I'm not quite sure what that means, but it sounds like a good thing."

"You are two for two in the Hello Kitty department. The one from our first date and now this, so…" Leaning in, I kiss his cheek. "Thank you."

"You are very welcome, Ella Rose. I enjoy spoiling you." He gently runs his fingers down my arm in the softest caress before taking my hand in his. His smile is both adorable and sexy.

It's such a sweet thing to say, and clearly, he's very good at it, but a part of me wishes there was something I could do for him. Which is what I tell him as we enjoy a fabulous dinner later that night.

"Okay, so I know that we're not keeping score and all that," I begin casually, "but you've been so incredibly generous, and I wish there were something I could do for you."

He holds my hand, caressing it with his strong fingers, and the look on his face is beyond tender.

Seriously, he could be the hero in a romance novel.

"But you've already given me something more valuable than anything I've given you," he says in that low timbre that I'm seriously getting addicted to.

"I haven't given you anything," I say lightly, feeling myself blush.

"Ella Rose, you dropped everything and flew to Arizona just to be with me. Do you have any idea what that means to me?"

All I do is shake my head. I'm mesmerized as I listen to him.

"Material things are all fine and well, but you're here with me, giving me the gift of your time. There are probably a dozen other things you could be doing right now. I know how important your career is to you, and every day is a new opportunity for you to be out auditioning or looking for a new role. But you hit pause on that because you wanted to be here with me."

The emotion in his tone is raw, and even if he didn't expand on that thought any further, I know exactly how much my being here means.

Turning his hand in mine, I gently caress it. "I hated the thought of us missing out on the time together almost as much as it bothered me to think of you being here by yourself."

His lopsided grin is positively charming.

"I wouldn't have been by myself. There are trainers and—"

"And when you were done with your sessions, you'd be alone at the hotel," I finish for him. "Eating by yourself, not having anyone to talk to…" I shrug. "Plus, having all this time for just the two of us with no distractions is kind of amazing. Back home, we would see each other, but not for these all-day kinds of dates. We may have only known each other for a little over a week, but it doesn't feel that way."

He nods. "I know. I think I've told you more about myself than I've ever told anyone. The only people who know more about me are my family."

Christian's family is very close.

A part of me is super excited to meet them, but the other part is terrified because I'm a little worried they'll see me as an outsider who isn't welcome. Although Christian is such an incredible person, I like to think the rest of the family will be as warm and friendly as he is.

"Then I guess I should say thank you for wanting to share so much with me," I say softly. "And believe it or not, it's the same for me. I have a lot of friends, and so much of my life is an open book, but I think I've shared more about me—the *real* me—with you than anyone else."

That seems to please him, because that tender look is back. I swear I could look at him like this forever. His kind eyes, his smile, his hand in mine…

It's magical.

Tonight's my last night with him before I head back to LA, and I don't want it to end. We're eating at the hotel's rooftop restaurant again because it's so good. There are twinkly lights outside by the bar, the part that's actually outside, and once we're done eating, we head out there for dessert and to enjoy the view.

Not that I wasn't loving the view inside, but this is equally spectacular.

The night feels suspended, like the city itself has paused just long enough for us. Tempe stretches out below, a shimmer of lights and movement, but up here on the rooftop, everything is still. The music is soft and bluesy—the exact tone for my mood.

We sit at a small bistro table with a candlelit centerpiece, and I let out a happy sigh. It doesn't seem possible for the night, our surroundings, and pretty much everything to be so perfect, but it is. Our server takes our dessert order, and as soon as he's gone, Christian stands, holding out his hand to me.

"Would you care to dance?"

Is this moment even real? My heart melts. Placing my hand in his, I nod and get to my feet. "I would love to."

I fit perfectly in Christian's arms. It isn't new anymore, the way he draws me in, but it still makes my heart flutter. His hand rests on my lower back, his thumb tracing idle circles that send warmth curling through me. My hand lies flat against his chest, and I feel the quiet rhythm of his heartbeat beneath the cotton of his shirt. I am the exact height for him to cocoon me in his embrace. I could stay here all night long.

"Remember when you said you couldn't dance?" I softly tease, reminding him of the night of the movie premiere.

His smile curves, slow and sure. "I do, and I still can't," he says. "You make me look better than I am."

The quiet laugh is out before I can stop it, the sound muffled as he leans down and presses a kiss to my temple. It isn't rushed. None of it is. Over the last several days, we've learned how to move together—not just in rhythm, but also in silence. In understanding.

The twinkly lights overhead cast everything in gold: the curve of his jaw, the shimmer in his hair, the faint glow caught on everything around us. I feel his breath against my cheek, his words barely a whisper.

"I'm going to miss this," he says. "Miss *you*."

My throat tightens. "You're not allowed to say things like that when I'm already trying not to melt."

He chuckles, low and warm, and I can feel it rumble through him. "Then I'll stop talking." He pulls me closer.

And we sway. No more words, no more teasing. Only the slow press of his hand low on my back, and the sound of the music blending with the city noise far below. The world feels wider from up here, yet somehow smaller, too, like it's narrowed to the space between us. We're in our own little world, and I want to stay here.

But I know I can't.

When I finally look up, I find his gaze waiting—steady, familiar, and full of something that both scares and soothes me.

Under the canopy of lights, with Tempe glittering below us, I realize that this, this quiet, effortless closeness, is what falling in love feels like.

We dance, we have dessert, and yet I keep my feelings to myself. It may feel like we've known each other forever, but I have to remind myself that it's still early in our relationship. The last thing I want to do is scare him off.

I steal a glance at him as we walk to the elevator, and I know in my heart that nothing I say will change what we have. I can't exactly explain why I'm so sure of that, but I am. Christian Lucas is my person, and that's all there is to it.

But I still opt to keep it to myself for now, my confidence wavering like a seesaw.

We're quiet as we ride the elevator down to our floor. Holding hands in the comfortable silence works. I rest my head on his shoulder, and when the doors open, he releases my hand and rests his on my lower back again.

I love it when he does that.

Every night that we've been here, we kiss goodnight at my door. He never asks to come in, and he's such a gentleman that I can't believe he's real—or that some other woman hasn't scooped him up already.

Though that works in my favor, so…

We reach my door and pause. This is basically it. My flight and his physical therapy session are early in the morning. I knew this moment was coming, the goodbye, but that doesn't mean I'm ready for it. Or want it.

"I had a wonderful time tonight," I say dreamily. "Everything was amazing. Just like this entire trip. You really made everything special."

I can tell that he's not entirely comfortable with the compliment. His ears turn a little red, and he looks down briefly before meeting my gaze again. "You're special, Ella Rose. I want to make sure you know that. It was important to me that you were comfortable being here with me." He pauses, taking both my hands in his. "I'm not used to anyone doing things like this for me. Other than my family."

"I wanted to be here. I just needed to let myself acknowledge that and give myself permission." Then I giggle because the conversation with my mother immediately comes to mind. "Well, that and knowing my mother approved."

He smiles because I already shared that story with him.

"I don't want to say goodbye. I feel like we did that barely a week ago. But I know we have to."

"I'll be back in Anaheim in three weeks, tops."

"Really? I thought you weren't sure?"

"I didn't want to say anything and get your hopes up, but earlier today, I confirmed it with the trainers. I planned on telling you at dinner, but we were talking about so many other things that it didn't cross my mind." He gives my hand a gentle squeeze. "And that's only because I didn't want to think about this moment."

I nod because I know exactly what he means.

"I know we just spent the entire day together, well, several days, but…how attached are you to sleeping?"

By the shocked look on his face, I know I worded that wrong.

"I mean…I *meant*…that we could stay up and talk," I quickly clarify. "You know, you can come into my room, and we can watch TV or just stay up and talk some more." I practically hold my breath, waiting for his response.

He releases my hands, only to reach up and cup my face. Before I know it, he's kissing me. It's soft and sweet, and I melt against him. There's nothing rushed about it, and there's no urgency. He's kissing me simply to enjoy the kiss.

Which is great because I'm enjoying the heck out of it, too.

When he pulls away, we're both a little breathless and dazed. He slowly smiles. "I'd love to stay up and talk with you all night, Ella Rose."

So, we go into my room and talk until the sun comes up. In the morning, he leaves to shower and get ready for his session while I pack and prepare to head to the airport.

We ride down in the elevator to the lobby together, and an Anaheim Magic driver is waiting for me. He handles my luggage as Christian and I enjoy our last minutes together.

"Three weeks," he tells me, his forehead pressed to mine. "Sooner if I can. I want to be back for your big birthday bash."

With this whirlwind of a relationship, I haven't even thought about my party. I mean, I'm looking forward to it and celebrating with my friends, but I'd especially love it if Christian could be there with me.

However…

"Only if your trainers tell you it's okay. You need to make sure you're ready. I don't want you to rush back on my account, only to end up reinjuring yourself."

"I'll be smart about it. I promise."

And I know he will. He's so passionate about his career that I know he won't do anything foolish. But I also say a little prayer that his therapy works so fast it's miraculous.

"Call me when you land back in LA," he tells me before kissing me soundly.

I cling to him, framing his freshly shaven face with my two hands, memorizing the way his lips feel. I take a deep breath of his intoxicating natural scent. When we break apart, I feel like crying, but I don't.

Not yet.

He opens the car door for me, and I reluctantly get in. When I look up at him, I force myself to smile. "I'll call you when I land." My voice trembles, and I quickly clear my throat, so I don't sound quite so needy. "Go and have a good session. Make sure to tell the trainer that your hamstring is feeling tight today. And be sure to use the foam roller. You said it really made a difference. Maybe stay at the team facility longer since you don't have to rush back for my sake. And—"

"Ella Rose?" he says softly, effectively stopping my rambling. "Don't you worry about a thing. I've got it all under control. And now that you're heading home, I'm extra motivated to get better." He crouches until we're at eye level. "I'll be there with you before you know it."

All I can do is nod.

Last night, we promised that we wouldn't do one of those long, drawn-out goodbyes. I swear I'm trying to keep that from happening, but I know that Christian's going to shut the car door any second, and the driver will take me away from him. I just need to savor the sight of him for a little longer.

The alarm chimes on my phone—a reminder that it's time to leave for the airport. I hate that it ruins the moment.

Christian leans in and kisses me. This time, it's quite thorough and full of all the pent-up emotion and frustration we're both feeling. One powerful hand holds my face, and I want to grab his shirt and drag him into the car with me. Unfortunately, before I can even try, he's breaking the kiss and backing away from me. When I blink him into focus, he's standing and holding the door.

"Have a safe flight. We'll talk when you get home." Without another word, he shuts the door, and the car is moving. Taking me away.

It's only temporary, I tell myself.

It's only temporary, and I immediately start to cry because I already miss him.

Two and a half weeks later, Christian's back, and I am beyond giddy about it. He put in the time with his physical therapists and flew home today, just in time for my party.

I'm in my bedroom relaxing when Jen pops into my doorway. "Hey. Do you have a minute?"

"Sure. What's up?"

"Okay, so I was talking with the girls about all the final party-planning stuff, and something sort of fell off all our radars."

My mind races to what that could mean. "What did we forget? The decorations look great, and we've got the food covered, so…"

She looks mildly uncomfortable. "Oh, all the physical stuff for the party is great. It's all under control."

"So…what, then?" I prompt.

"Please don't be upset, but…when we first planned this party and sent out all the invites, we invited Jim." She pauses. "As in your ex-boyfriend, Jim."

Laughing, I ask, "Is that it?"

She nods.

"Jen, I don't think we have anything to worry about. I highly doubt he'll show up. We haven't spoken since the breakup, and I can't imagine him wanting to be there."

The look on her face tells me I'm mistaken.

"You know how we're all like this big friend group?" she asks. "Well, he's also good friends with Freya, so…"

"Oh." And then it hits me what she's really saying. "Oh! So, he's definitely going to be there."

"That is correct."

"Well, I guess that makes sense," I murmur, even though I know it has the potential to be super awkward.

"Your face is getting scrunchy," she tells me before sitting on the bed beside me. "Tell me what you're thinking."

"I'm thinking that it's going to be really awkward introducing Jim to Christian. Especially after he bought me a jersey with Christian's number on it."

"Oh, my gosh. I forgot about that." She laughs a little too hard and then realizes I'm not laughing with her. Clearing her throat, she forces herself to be serious. "I mean, okay. Yes. That *is* going to be uncomfortable."

"And you really think he'll show up?"

"Freya mentioned it, so…"

"Shoot." Unfortunately, there's nothing I can do about it now. The party's tonight. I'll just have to deal with it.

"Are you going to be okay?" she asks.

I glare mildly at her. "Do I have a choice?"

"Sorry. But there'll be a lot of people at the party, so hopefully it won't seem like he's right in your face, or that you're in his, you know?"

"Maybe." I pause. "Should I call him? I should probably call him just to cut down on the potential weirdness later."

"That's totally up to you. If it would make you feel better, then I think you should." She gives me a quick hug before getting up. "Sorry to have been the bearer of bad news like that."

"It's fine. I appreciate the heads-up."

With a small wave, Jen leaves the room. I sit there for a solid few minutes, second-guessing whether I should reach out to Jim.

But I know.

Calling him is the right thing to do.

Reaching for my phone, I don't give myself time to think. I pull up his number and call. When he answers, I can hear the surprise in his voice.

"Hey, Ella. How are you?"

"Hey, Jim. I'm good. And you?"

"Great. I'm looking forward to the party tonight. I wasn't sure you would want me there after…you know…we broke up, but Freya said it was cool."

Reminder to talk to Freya about this. She must've felt pressured.

"So, listen…I wanted to talk to you before the party because, of course, I'd like you to be there," I begin carefully. "But I also wanted to let you know that I'm seeing someone now."

I let that hang there for a moment, and he doesn't reply right away.

"Um…"

"It's okay," he says, but he sounds a little deflated. "I appreciate you giving me the heads-up. I know you said when we broke up that we weren't really a good fit, and you're such a beautiful girl, I knew you'd be dating again in no time."

I'm not sure if I find that flattering, so I opt not to comment on it.

"As I said, I'd like you to be there tonight, but I didn't want you to find out when you got there."

"That was very nice of you, Ella—to be concerned for me. But then again, you're always kind." He sighs. "You're really a one-in-a-million kind of girl. I only wish I were the guy lucky enough to be taking you to your birthday party tonight."

"Right…so speaking of the guy taking me to the party. Funny story. Remember when—?"

"It's okay," he quickly interrupts. "I'm fine. It's fine. Really. I'll see you tonight, okay?"

"Um…"

"Thanks again. Bye."

I've never had anyone hang up on me so fast in my life.

Jim's a good guy. A good friend. And really, I wanted us to *stay* friends. But when he started talking about wishing he were taking me to the party, it felt a little uncomfortable. I was trying to tell him about Christian, but I guess he'll find out tonight.

I handled the situation like an adult, and hopefully, we can all celebrate at the party without anything being too awkward.

At least that's my hope.

Christian is picking Jen and me up at six so we can go over to Freya's to finish decorating. I'm so excited that he's back from Tempe and will complete the rest of his physical therapy in Anaheim. It's so much easier for us to see each other when he's only forty-five minutes away instead of a six-hour drive or a ninety-minute flight.

I have my outfit ready—my favorite faded jeans, a new, hot-pink sequined top, and hot-pink sandals. Earlier, I went for a mani-pedi, so even my nails are pink and sparkly. Freya and I are going to wear matching tiaras, and we're leaning heavily into an '80s theme for the party. So, really, I'll fit right in. I tried to convince her to wear a sequined top, too, but she said she wasn't feeling sparkly. Which is a shame because we would have looked amazing.

At least we have the tiaras.

Jen and I each take our turn in the bathroom, doing our best to stay out of each other's way. When Christian rings our doorbell promptly at six, I am just putting on my lipstick.

"I'll get it!" I awkwardly call out before quickly blotting my lips. I'm still barefoot, but I don't care. I run to the door and nearly yank it open in my haste to see him. "Hey! You're here!"

Before I even know what I'm doing, I'm jumping into his arms and kissing him. We're both kissing and laughing and carefully maneuvering through the doorway. I kick the door closed and go back to kissing him. When he finally puts me down, I just look at him because I'm so happy to see his face.

Which currently has a lot of my lipstick on it.

"Hey, Ella Rose," he says in that sweet voice, and I swear he's blushing a little. "You didn't really give me a chance to greet you properly."

"Sorry about that."

But I'm not.

"I'm just so excited that you're back."

"It was only two and a half weeks, and we talked every day," he reminds me with a wink.

"True, but it's not the same as you being here in person."

"Hey, Christian," Jen calls out from the other room.

"Hey, Jen." Then his attention's back on me, and he gives me a very thorough look. "You look beautiful."

Now, I'm the one blushing. "Thank you. I just need to put on my sandals. Make yourself comfortable. I'll be right out." I'm halfway to my room when I stop and grab a handful of napkins and race back to him. "Here. Sorry about all the lipstick."

But then I kiss him one more time. Because I can.

Jen and I pass each other in the hallway, and she assures me that she is ready to go. In my room, I slip on my shoes and grab my purse before checking my reflection again.

You look beautiful.

I can't help but study myself and try to see what Christian does. I don't ever see *beautiful* because being an actress in Hollywood can really destroy your confidence. Agents, casting directors, producers…sometimes, it feels like they aren't even considering the fact that I am a person with feelings. They critique everything about me. I am too short, not thin enough, not pretty enough. Gosh, if I had a dollar for every time a casting director said I wasn't "Hollywood pretty," I would be the richest actress in LA.

It was enough to make me feel like maybe I shouldn't be walking the runway in elegant dresses and instead be hidden away in a bell tower like Quasimodo.

"Don't you listen to them, Ella," Mom would always say. "You are so much more than a pretty face."

"But they just said I didn't have a pretty face."

"You are a naturally pretty girl. You're the girl next door. Someone everyone can relate to. And that's better than being someone who needs all that hair and

makeup to make them pretty. Remember, beauty fades. It's what's on the inside that counts."

I love my mother, and I love how she always has words of encouragement at the ready. Sometimes, it's just hard to hear negative things said about me.

Especially right to my face.

In my mind, I know I'm not a supermodel, but I also know I have more talent than many of the girls I compete against. It's pointless to wish I were taller, thinner, curvier, or had bigger boobs. Sure, those things would be nice, but it isn't my focus. I don't want to be known only for my looks. I want people to look at me and remember my name because I'm talented. Because I put on a performance that touches them.

I want to be the best Ella Rose Holt I can be.

You look beautiful.

But when Christian looks at me and calls me beautiful, while I know I don't see it, he *does.* And that's really incredible.

"Ella?" I hear Jen calling my name. "We're gonna be late if we don't leave now."

"Coming!" And with that. I dash out of my room with a smile on my face, ready for a great night.

The room is already buzzing before the song even starts—music pulsing, laughter spilling over the fizzing sounds of soda cans being opened and the hum of conversation. Strands of colored lights are draped across the ceiling of Freya's loft, making everything look fun and festive, and everyone is in party mode.

We're an hour in, and my cheeks hurt from smiling. Someone insisted on a round of karaoke—my friends never need much convincing—and now I'm standing center stage, mic in hand, eyes sparkling with the mischievous confidence that comes from pure joy and adrenaline and turning twenty-two.

The opening chords of "I Will Survive" blast through the speakers, and my friends erupt in cheers.

"Oh, this is one of my favorites!" I shout with pure joy.

Laughter echoes around me, and I am living my best life right now. I spot Christian sitting at a table near the front, leaning back in his chair, grinning. His gorgeous blue-eyed gaze never leaves me. It's like he is completely transfixed. Like I'm the only thing worth seeing in the crowded room.

I am in my element, all energy and light, twirling my free hand in the air while singing into the mic with unapologetic joy. This is what I'm good at. This is what I was born to do.

"At first I was afraid …"

The crowd claps along, and I throw myself into the performance, half-singing, half-laughing, but feeling completely alive. When I catch Christian's gaze and take in his soft, proud smile, my heart does a little somersault.

And then, midway through the second verse, the door opens. I'm looking right at it when it does, and it feels like a pathway appears out of nowhere. The energy shifts. Just slightly, but enough. And then I see him.

Jim.

He's standing framed by the doorway, hands shoved into his jacket pockets, that familiar half-smile on his face as I'm singing about how I'm somebody new.

My breath hitches for a second, because…come on. How ironic is that?

Maybe it's muscle memory, or something braver, but I keep singing. Louder this time. My chin lifts a little higher. The words that have always felt like a fun karaoke anthem suddenly hit with weight, truth pulsing through every syllable.

Christian's eyes are still on me. I can feel it. I wonder if he noticed the hitch or saw the change in me, the sudden renewed energy, and how I'm standing a little straighter, even as my hand holding the mic trembles slightly. I dance and twirl so I can find him again in the crowd. When I do, his expression is soft, and I can see pride and protectiveness mingling in his eyes. It's all I need to turn around and finish the song.

That's when I notice poor Jim still standing near the door, clearly unprepared for what he walked into.

Meanwhile, I spin toward my friends, who are cheering even louder, clapping and dancing along with me. When I belt out the final line, laughing through it, I almost wish there were a few more verses.

But when the song ends, I drop into a playful bow. The applause is deafening.

And then Christian is there, already moving through the crowd, reaching me just as I step down from the little stage. His hand finds mine, warm and sure.

"You," he says quietly, with that smile that makes my knees a little weak, "were incredible."

I squeeze his fingers, breathless and laughing. "Thank you," I say, throwing a quick glance toward the door where Jim was. "I've always loved to sing, and that's a fun song to do." When I look a second time, Christian gives my hand a gentle tug.

"What's going on?"

"What do you mean?"

"You keep looking at the door," he says. "Is everything okay?"

Ugh…

Taking his hand, I lead him to a quiet corner. "Okay, so remember the game I went to when I was wearing your jersey?"

He nods.

"Well, I was there with a guy I was dating. He's the one who bought me the jersey."

Another nod.

"He's friends with all of *my* friends and, he's here."

"Okay…"

"I already called him to let him know I'm dating someone, but he doesn't know it's you." I pause, waiting to see if he'll react, but he doesn't. "I'm just a little…I don't know. It feels a little surreal that he brought me to an Anaheim Magic game, bought me your jersey, and now you and I are dating." The words fly out of my mouth so fast that even I can barely understand what I'm saying. Somehow, Christian gets it.

"Ah. Okay. I guess that is a little bit of a coincidence, but you weren't dating him when you and I went out for the first time, right?"

"No. I had already broken up with him."

"Then I don't see an issue. It's a coincidence, but that's all it is. And maybe a little funny." Then he tugs me in close. "And you and I were going to meet, whether or not you were at that game. We had to. Our friends were already talking about it. You being at the game just added a little more, you know, luck to our story."

Our story.

I like that we have one.

But I love that Christian knows it, too.

Eight

If I thought those five days in Tempe were magical, they were nothing compared to this new chapter of our lives.

Now that Christian is back in California, we see each other constantly. He often drives to LA during the week to see me, and then I go and stay with him in Newport Beach. I always associate him with being in Anaheim because he spends so much time at the stadium, but his home is right by the ocean, and it is incredible.

You wouldn't think it'd be a big deal, given I'm from Florida, but I grew up in the middle of the state. The beaches were over an hour away, so it wasn't like I saw them regularly. Being able to spend the weekends walking hand in hand along the sand with the man I love is wildly romantic.

We have a favorite spot where he takes me to watch the sunset overlooking the ocean, and I can't help but marvel, again, at the fact that he was single before we met.

"Do you have any idea how amazing you are?" I ask in pure wonder as the sun sets.

Christian turns his head, and I wish I had a camera because he looks so handsome, relaxed, and happy. The boyish grin he gives me makes my heart flutter.

"I don't think I'm amazing," he replies, playfully nudging me with his shoulder. "But I guess I do okay."

"Are you kidding me? These last weeks have been like something out of a Hallmark movie. You put so much thought into everything we do, and you make it all so romantic." I sigh happily. "It's still a little hard to believe that there aren't women chasing after you."

That makes him laugh. "Ella Rose, I don't think I'm doing anything so special. Last night, we got Slurpees from 7-Eleven after having pizza. I'd hardly call that romantic."

Silly man.

"But it is," I say. "I think we're all a bit trained to believe romance means fancy and expensive dinners, flowers, and jewelry. But I think it's romantic when you put thought into doing things you know the other person really loves."

"Like pizza and slushies?" he teases.

Laughing, I nod. "Like pizza and slushies. Don't get me wrong, I love going to dinner at a fancy restaurant once in a while, but I'm really more of a simple girl. I enjoy taking these walks on the beach and watching sunsets and eating food that doesn't cost more than my rent."

He nods in agreement. "Then it doesn't bother you when I cook for us instead of going out?"

Oh, yeah. You read that right. He cooks.

"Are you kidding? I love it. You're really good at it. It's impressive."

"Well, growing up, my mother made sure we could all cook. Life skills are important. Plus, living on my own, it's a necessity. Takeout is fine once in a while, but I couldn't do it every night. I grew up with meals that I now make for myself. That's the true meaning of comfort food, right? Just sitting down and eating a dinner that makes you feel closer to your family."

It's sweet, and yet I feel a little sad for him. I miss my family, but I can hear in his voice that he *really* misses his. That's how close they are. If anything, it only adds to his appeal. A good-hearted man who works hard, is wildly romantic, and loves his family? It's a little like seeing a unicorn hanging out with Santa Claus and the tooth fairy.

"I love that," I tell him. "Your mom must be an amazing cook because everything you've made for me is delicious."

"I'll be sure to tell her you said so."

It's on the tip of my tongue to ask if maybe there will be a time when I can tell her myself, but I don't say anything. I know we're heading in that direction, and I can be patient. Just because so many things between us have been fast-tracked doesn't mean all of it has to be. For now, I'm very content with the way things are.

There are moments like this—quiet and romantic. And then there are others where we're just ridiculously goofy. Somehow, it all fits. It's incredible to be on the same page with someone, to be able to show up exactly as you are without worrying they'll think you're strange or too much. I don't think I've ever felt this comfortable with anyone in my life.

With my family, I've always been able to be myself, but outside of them, I usually keep a small part of me tucked away. With Christian, nothing feels hidden. I let it all spill out, and the best part is, he does, too. With me, he lowers his guard, and we're suddenly just two people talking about everything from world events and politics to the absolute disaster that is bad reality television.

We love to discuss all things pop culture, and ever since my birthday karaoke performance, we have started singing more.

FYI, Christian is not a good singer at all.

And yes, he knows it.

Still, we both love music from the eighties and nineties, and that's all we play when we're in the car. I made us a playlist—well, several of them—with all our favorite songs. And while that should have been enough to thoroughly entertain us for sing-along purposes, I upped our game with some inflatable microphone party favors. We keep them in the car and sing to each other while we're stuck in all the California freeway traffic. Jen says we're adorkable, but I know she means it as a compliment. We are living our lives as our genuine selves. And isn't that really how it should be?

But being genuine doesn't always mean our best, you know?

Spending so much time together while we were in Tempe was awesome because we were away from our regular lives. It was like being on vacation. But now that we're back home and have returned to our semi-normal schedules, at least until baseball starts up again, there's more room for some of our not-so-best sides to come out. I know it happens in all relationships, but not every quirk is cute.

Or relatable.

Christian has a hard time with how unpredictable my career is. Don't get me wrong, even with all the time we're spending together, I am still auditioning and actively pursuing roles and taping the shows that I have recurring parts on. It's just not a rigid schedule like his.

Even though baseball season is over, and he is still undergoing physical therapy for his piriformis injury, he trains every day. He goes to the gym every day. He is beyond regimented. I admire his dedication to his sport, but there are days when I'm a little like, "Dude, you can take a day and relax, right?" But it's rare that he does.

For as many ways as we are completely in sync with each other, there are equally as many things that make us total opposites. I'm laid back. He's structured. I'm an extrovert. He's more of an introvert. I am ready to pick up and go on a moment's notice, but he needs a little more time to get mentally prepared. He hates the way I drive, and I'm not really a fan of the rules and restrictions he puts on his life.

We balance each other out, and I know that's the way most couples are, but I'm worried that we're going to hit that bump at some point, that quirk or trait that will make us question what we're doing.

"How about we start walking back home, Ella Rose?" Christian asks, and I realize I've been in my head, lost in my own thoughts instead of enjoying the sunset.

So, I smile and place my hand in his. "Let's go."

Fall comes to an end, and before we know it, the holidays are here.

I love Christmas. Like seriously love it. Unfortunately, as much as we want to spend them together, we are both very much about our families, and we end up agreeing to spend the holidays apart.

Sort of.

"I want you to meet my family," he says. "But I don't want you to miss out on spending Christmas with yours."

"I feel the same way. So, where does that leave us?" His family is still in Florida, and mine is in Tennessee. I really wish my parents still lived in Florida because it would be so much more convenient.

"Come to Florida with me for a few days before Christmas, and then I'll fly to you and meet your family afterward. And then we'll fly home and spend New Year's with our friends. What do you think?"

"I think that sounds wonderful."

We fly out of LAX four days before Christmas to spend two days with Christian's family, and I still believe our plans are great. Am I nervous? Definitely. But I know it will go well because Christian is so easy to get along with, and I'm confident the rest of his family will be the same.

And they are.

Sort of.

From the moment we walk through the door, I can sense that things aren't going to go quite as well as they did in my mind.

Everyone is very friendly, kind, and polite, but I can tell that A.) they're not used to Christian bringing a girl home to meet the family, and B.) they are super protective of him. Most people I meet are interested in my career and ask about the famous people I know, but the Lucases just sort of smile and nod as I talk about myself.

I can't remember the last time I was this nervous, and I'm relieved when the conversation moves away from me.

Christian has two sisters and two brothers, all of whom are incredibly chatty and eager to tell me every detail about Christian's life. His mother keeps putting food out for everyone to eat, but his father just watches me. It's not like he's glaring or frowning, he's just… observing. I make a mental note to spend a little time talking to him so I can win him over.

"Ella, did you know that Christian was voted most helpful in school?"

"Ella, did Christian ever tell you about the old car we all used to share?"

"Christian, tell Ella how you started learning how to throw by aiming for the stop sign on the corner."

"Did you tell Ella about the time you got hit by a ninety-five-mile-per-hour fastball?"

When he doesn't answer fast enough, his oldest sister, Marie, explains.

"It was crazy, and he let the ball hit him so he could get on base. Can you imagine? And this was while he was still in college, mind you. The ball deflected off his arm and hit his ribs so hard he had an enormous bruise there the next day." She shakes her head, even as she smiles at Christian. Note to self: *I really like Marie, but I can tell she's very protective and considers herself like another mom to Christian. I need to make sure she trusts me.*

He grins. "We won, so, it was worth it."

I just smile because that seems a little excessive. I've wanted roles before, but not enough to physically hurt myself. I've worn different makeup and changed my hair, but nothing painful. Then again, sports is an entirely different animal from acting.

I learn so much about Christian over the next two days and thoroughly enjoy myself, but I never get the time I wanted with his father. When it's time for me to leave for the airport, and I'm saying goodbye to everyone, I save his dad for last.

"It was a pleasure meeting you, Mr. Lucas. Thank you for welcoming me into your home." I smile, my voice soft and sincere, but he doesn't return it.

"Nice to meet you, Ella," he says stiffly before turning and walking away.

It isn't until Christian and I are alone in the car that I ask if I did okay.

"Why would you even ask?" he says, sounding totally amused. "Everyone really liked you."

"Except your dad," I murmur.

He studies me for a long moment. "My dad's just…stoic."

Every time we've talked about his family, I got the impression that his father was strict, but I thought it was when Christian and his siblings were growing up. The man I just said goodbye to seems like maybe he's still that way. And it makes my heart ache for my man. He deserves to have a dad who gushes over him and everything he's accomplished in his career.

But I keep that observation to myself.

I do that a lot in this relationship, and I'm not sure why. I talk a big game about how we are free to be ourselves and how great it is, but am I lying to myself? Shouldn't I be able to voice these feelings instead of mulling them over and keeping them to myself?

It's something to think about.

Later.

Now, I focus on what things will be like after Christmas. Our families are very similar, but I know my dad will be a lot easier on Christian than Mr. Lucas was on me.

At the airport, he doesn't walk me in. Dropping me off at the curb is easier, and I know he's eager to get back to his family.

"I'll see you next week, Ella Rose," he says, right before he kisses me.

I'm getting better with these goodbyes, but I'm still going to miss the heck out of him.

Meeting the Holts is filled with as much enthusiasm and as many embarrassing stories as Christian's siblings had, and I'm cringing a little when my mom puts in a VHS tape, because we are probably the only family that still owns a VCR, of the Wonder Land Christmas Special that I sang in when I was twelve.

Christian is smiling from ear to ear, and I know he's enjoying himself.

Maybe because it's my turn in the hot seat.

After the video comes the pageant scrapbooks. I haven't seen them in years, and now that I'm looking through them with Christian, I'm curious what he thinks.

So, I ask.

"That is a *lot* of makeup," he says with a laugh. "I didn't think young girls wore that much."

"They don't, but it's a necessity when you're competing." We joke about my hair and some of the dresses, and even though it's all in good fun, I know this is something Christian would never let our kids do.

Oh, my…

Where on earth did that thought come from?

I quickly push it aside and sigh with relief when we're done with my pageant era and move on to my acting one. At some point, we stop for dinner. My mom and dad made the equivalent of a Thanksgiving feast to impress my boyfriend. Bless Mom's heart. And while we're in the kitchen putting the finishing touches on everything, she gives me a knowing smile.

"What?" I ask, fighting my own grin. "What's put that look on your face?"

"I like him," she whispers like we're best friends sharing a secret. "I really like him. I'm so glad you went to Tempe and claimed what's yours."

"Mom," I hiss, but end up laughing. "Don't say that out loud."

I already told Christian the story, but I think it would embarrass him to no end to hear her telling it to the rest of the family. It takes a little extra begging, but she finally agrees not to bring it up again.

As we eat, my dad asks Christian a million questions about baseball, and I am more than happy to sit quietly and listen to him talk about the sport he loves. He's so patient as he talks and listens to everything Dad asks, and as I look around the table, it's a little like the last piece to a puzzle.

He fits.

He completes our family.

We've talked about the future—our future—without really pinning anything down, but this trip and meeting each other's parents is a big step. When we get back to California, I know we'll start taking our plans more seriously. Especially since spring training will be here in no time. He's already talking about it like he's trying to prepare me, but I'm confident that it won't be a big deal. I'm already looking forward to watching him play and cheering him on, even though I know he won't be as accessible as he's been since he returned from Tempe.

But it doesn't matter. Whatever it is, whatever the schedule turns out to be, I'll be there. I am one hundred percent in this relationship. It's not just the romantic times, it's the boring, everyday times, too. The grouchy times, the sad times, the challenging times. I'm in.

I want to show Christian that I am here not only to support him and be his biggest cheerleader, but also to be there for him.

Like physically, in person, be there.

I know his family really loves him, and he calls them every day, but he doesn't see them that much. His mom still teaches, his siblings work and have kids, and his dad is the city commissioner. The more I get to know him, the more I realize how lonely his life is, and it makes me sad. One of Christian's favorite songs is "Here I Go Again" by Whitesnake. A song that is basically about a man who feels like he's a drifter, born to walk alone.

Well, that will never happen on my watch. I want to hold Christian's hand and walk beside him down every stretch of that road he's dreamed of. I don't ever want him to feel lonely again. I want to be the person who eases his worries, helps carry the weight when things fall apart, and stands there cheering him on when everything goes right.

This isn't a role I'm playing or a version of myself I'm trying on. It's deeper than that. It's real and lasting, and it feels like something I was always meant to be.

New Year's Eve gets off to an uneventful start. We returned home late last night, and Christian kissed me goodbye after helping me bring my luggage into the apartment, promising to pick me up for the party tonight.

I sleep in, and then Jen and I meet up in the kitchen to eat cinnamon rolls and drink tea while we talk about our holiday trips.

Hers was a lot of the same old, same old, with only a hint of nagging from her mother about when she was going to find a nice guy and settle down.

"Typical guilt-trip kind of trip," she jokes. "How did meeting the parents go?"

I tell her all about my observations of Christian's family—especially his dad.

"I can't believe you didn't win him over. You're usually so good at that sort of thing."

"I know. He's a tough nut to crack," I say. "But it will happen. I know it."

We laugh about Christian having to watch my Wonder Land videos and seeing all the scrapbooks, but it's all in good fun.

"Okay, what are you wearing tonight?" she asks. "Are you dressing up? Going more casual? A dress? Jeans? I bought a little black dress that I can accessorize in a bunch of different ways."

"I was thinking of the turquoise dress and pairing it with a denim jacket." It's really all just coming to mind now. I've been so wrapped up in traveling and the holidays that I haven't even considered what to wear tonight. Ugh.

"That one is super cute. We'll do your hair with some soft curls, and maybe we can find a clip or headband to go with the dress." She pauses and thinks for a moment. "Ooh! I have something that will work perfectly."

And then she's running from the room while I relax and finish my tea. I know that whatever she finds and decides to do will be fabulous. I consider making myself a second cup of tea as I pop the last sweet bite of cinnamon roll into my mouth.

My relaxation is cut short, however, when she calls out to me from her room. That's when I know I'll have to start getting ready and making wardrobe decisions sooner rather than later.

Good thing I know she only has my best interests at heart.

"Christian is going to love this," she gushes as she pulls out some hair clips, purses, and costume jewelry.

I still wish I were sitting with my feet up and sipping a second cup of tea, but this is fun, too.

"I have to go and help a few clients with their hair and makeup, and I'll be out of here around four, so I'll meet you guys at the party. What time is Christian picking you up?" she asks.

"The party doesn't start until eight, but we're going to grab an early dinner first, so he'll be here at six."

"Ooh, where are you going? Someplace fabulous?"

I shake my head. "Well, I wouldn't say fabulous, but I think our apartment is pretty darn cute."

Pausing, she stares at me. "You're eating…here?"

"Yup."

"Why?"

Shrugging, I experiment with a headband as I look at myself in the mirror. "Because we wanted to have a pizza date before the party. There's going to be food there, but we were both talking about how we were in the mood for pizza."

"I've said it before, and I'll say it again, you guys are adorkable."

We are, and I am here for it.

The party is at our friend Will's place. He shares a massive, top-floor loft in the city with two other actors in the industry, and it is the perfect party space.

It's also decorated nicer than some movie sets I've been on.

Fairy lights are looped across the apartment ceiling, casting a warm glow over the crowd of friends crammed into every corner. There are streamers and signs everywhere you look, and the party vibe is palpable. Someone set up a countdown clock on the TV, and the music pulses, low and steady.

Christian has met and hung out with my friends enough times to know them, and he is comfortable talking to them without me at his side. Right now, I'm chatting with Will, and he's standing across the room, chatting with a group of people—some I know, others are unfamiliar—but when he turns his head and catches me watching, he smiles, and I'm mesmerized.

"I'm so happy for you, Ella," Will says. "You've found your Prince Charming."

"I still can't believe it. I never would have predicted this; it's truly fate. My mom always said that when you met *the one* you'd just know, and she was right."

"And the fact that you had your first date on your golden birthday, and he's number twenty-two? You are living a real-life fairy tale," Will marvels. "I'm beginning to think that I'm destined to be alone for the rest of my life because every guy who enters my story turns out to be a villain."

"Don't worry, Will, your Prince Charming is out there, and he'll find you. Don't give up on love." I give Will the biggest reassuring hug before he runs off to start passing out champagne for the midnight toast.

My gaze goes right back to Christian. I begin to think of every small thing that has led to this moment: our first date, the movie premiere, meeting each other's families over the holidays, the quiet drives, the laughter, the singing, and just knowing how it's only the beginning. This new year holds so much potential, and I almost can't wait for midnight so it can start.

I can tell he's wrapping his conversation, and his blue eyes are on me as he makes his way over, weaving through the partygoers. Everything else blurs around him. He stops at the bar and asks for two drinks. It's getting close to midnight, so I know he's getting something for us to toast with. We're not drinkers, and my friends know that, so there's sparkling cider especially for us. Drinks in hand, he continues his way across the room. When he gets to me, his gaze is soft and tender.

"Are you having a good time, Ella Rose?" he asks, his voice low and close to my ear, as he places a glass in my hand.

I lean in, smiling, trying to position my body perfectly into his. "I am." I turn my head so I'm speaking close to his ear. The music's loud enough that we almost have to shout to be heard, but in our own little pocket of the party, it feels like an intimate conversation.

"You were looking pretty intense a moment ago. What were you thinking about?"

I don't even hesitate. "Us, and the incredible path we've taken to get here tonight. Between movie premieres, out-of-state physical therapy, and hundreds of phone calls, it feels like a lifetime, but it's not." Pulling back, I give him a sweet kiss on the lips. "Plus, we met each other's families and survived. I think we can handle anything the new year throws at us."

He laughs and brushes a strand of hair from my face. "Have I told you how beautiful you look tonight?"

I nod just as the clock on the TV starts its countdown.

Ten… nine… eight…

The noise in the room swells, friends shouting, glasses clinking. But right here in our cozy spot, everything feels still.

Christian takes one of my hands in his. "Ella Rose," he says quietly, like he doesn't want to lose the moment to the noise. "I love you."

My breath catches. All the laughter, the chaos, and the sparkle falls away. My heart feels ready to burst. We've said I love you in every way except with those three wonderful words.

Until now.

I look up at him, my heart full and steady. "I love you, too."

Three… two… one!

The room erupts in cheers, confetti, and the pop of corks, but we barely notice. Christian kisses me, deep and sure, as fireworks light up the night outside the window.

When we finally pull apart, the noise feels far away. He rests his forehead against mine as we both smile.

"Happy New Year," he murmurs.

"Yeah," I whisper, my voice catching. "It really is."

I have no idea how long we stay like that. All around us, the music swells, and laughter fills the room again. It's a celebration, after all. But not just for the new year. It's a celebration for all the new beginnings.

Nine

The new year is off to an amazing start.

January is a lot of life as usual, but I ultimately land a role as a series regular on *Workin' for Laughs*. It's a sketch comedy series celebrating everyday folks doing what they do best—finding humor in the hustle. Several well-known male stand-up comics headline the series, and it's heavy on Southern humor. I'm one of the few full-time female cast members. It's a huge deal, and I am so excited about it. Shooting won't start for a couple of months, but it's the sort of thing I've been working toward.

Meanwhile, Christian is gearing up for spring training. With my new TV role, I can't go and stay with him for the entire time, so we'll have to do the long-distance thing. We sit down with our calendars, but I plan to fly out to see him as much as I can. The decision comes after a conversation that really solidified the direction of our relationship.

Christian is getting into baseball-season mode. I already know how hard he works, and he's shared everything he puts into his training with me, but now, he sits me down to fully prepare me for it.

We're at his place near the beach, and he's grilled us some steaks for dinner. Christian is a grill master, and I'm ready to dig in when he reaches for my hand.

"Ella Rose, I love you so much, and I still can't believe you're mine."

Aww…

"In any other situation, I would have been down on one knee already and putting a ring on your finger."

"Christian…"

"I need you to understand why I haven't," he says somberly. He gazes at our hands briefly before looking up again. "I have always been honest with you about my work ethic and how I spend the season."

I nod, because he has.

"But it's very important to me that you experience a full baseball season with me. I need you to get to know *me* during a baseball season before we fully commit to each other."

He's a little emphatic on that point, but before I can argue that I already know him and that nothing will surprise me, he goes on.

"My daily routine is very strict. It has to be. You've seen a little of that side of me, but once spring training starts, it's on a whole other level."

"That makes sense, but…"

"An athlete's life is hard. Being an athlete's wife is even harder. So, I need to make sure you know what you're getting into."

"Christian, I can handle it. I promise." I realize I may sound like I'm really angling for a ring, but that's not it at all. I want him to know that I can be patient. I don't want him putting any unnecessary pressure on himself.

But he's still hesitant, like he doesn't think I'm capable of understanding. "Okay, here's the thing. Most people only see the fun and glamorous side of the game. They think it's all sitting in the stands and cheering with the wives and girlfriends and families, then hanging out and celebrating after. But it's not. It's a long season, especially if we make the playoffs, and sometimes, it will be very lonely for you. Once spring training starts, all the time we've been spending together will be over."

I don't want to jump all over that statement because I *do* get what he's telling me. However, I *also* have a career that isn't always conducive to being in a relationship. My time isn't my own, and it's hard to maintain a life outside of filming.

Which is what I tell him. But he's still frowning.

"Just know…I will always put you first and do everything I can to set you up for success. In baseball, I put my teammates first, and you are now my most important teammate."

Okay…

"We're a team now. Me and you." Pausing, I see him swallow hard. "I've never let anyone into my life before. Not like this. There's no blueprint. In my heart, I see this season as something that will confirm that we are meant to be together."

"But…?"

"But I can't help but be a little nervous, because this may not be the life you want. Like I said, it's not glamorous. Our time together won't be what it has been, and—"

I silence his worries with a kiss. When I gently pull back, I caress his jaw. "I want *you*, Christian. And baseball is a part of who you are, so I'm going to want that, too. I get that it won't be easy, and there will be some adjustments, but at the end of the day, we get to be together, so…I'm in."

Now, he looks hopeful—but not too hopeful.

"Your career is really starting to take off. You have this new TV show, and everything you're doing is in Hollywood. Everything will be in constant motion. Flying back and forth, living out of suitcases, late-night phone calls, and possibly long stretches of time where we're apart." He pauses for a moment. "All I want is for you to be happy. That's what means the most to me. But with all of these…I don't know…obstacles, I guess I can't help but worry a little."

I'm glad I'm not the only one.

"I think we can both agree that this wasn't something either of us planned for. Like, a year ago, I wouldn't have believed anyone who told me I'd be in love and dating a Major League Baseball player."

"And I certainly wouldn't have believed I'd be dating a Hollywood actress."

"We've got this," I assure him. "We're a team, and we are going to make this work. I'm up for the challenge if you are."

That boyish grin finally appears as he nods. "I am. For you, Ella Rose, I am all-in."

I'm a pretty awesome and understanding girlfriend, if I do say so myself.

At least, I think I am.

When it's time for Christian to leave for spring training, I'm excited and supportive, and we have a schedule in place for the times I will be there, and when I can't. During the baseball season, there's no time for him to fly to see me, so if we want to see each other, I have to travel to him. We are as prepped and prepared as we can be.

Still, I think he's surprised by how smoothly it's all going. I was fine handling my own travel, dealing with routine, his intense schedule, his eating habits, the rituals he's imposed on himself, and being supportive by not trying to take his focus away from his job. I understood all of it because it is the same for me, and Christian has been that way when I'm the one filming for different roles. So, it's not only me doing it. He's done it, as well.

Our biggest challenge, honestly, is time. We both want more of it together, but we're sacrificing it right now because we each have dreams. Careers that we have spent our entire lives working toward. And he was right; it *is* lonely at times. I miss him like crazy, even though we talk every night, but I do my best not to let it show. Because as much as we're alike in our drive and ambition, I'm an actress. Even when I'm not okay, I can pretend I am. So, even though I miss him and wish things were different, I never let him know that because I don't want him to feel bad or guilty or anything negative.

I want him to know that I can be a good teammate, even when my heart's a little sad. You know, sometimes you've got to fake it till you make it. So, I do.

My first few visits to Phoenix were quick weekend trips. There weren't any games, so we had some time to be together.

After he practiced.

My first proper introduction to his world is a team dinner reception. I'm supposed to meet all the coaches, his teammates, and their wives or significant others, and I am extremely excited about it. The thought of finally getting to experience being Christian Lucas's girlfriend at a team event is a major step. He was already a plus-one for me at a movie premiere. To me, this is the baseball equivalent.

The dinner is being held in one of the ballrooms of our hotel, and as we ride down in the elevator, I grip his hand tightly.

"Are you nervous?" he asks.

"No." But then I realize that's a lie. "A little."

He kisses my hand. "You have nothing to worry about. Everyone's going to love you."

I'm a people person, so I'm not afraid of talking to anyone. Unfortunately, I'm not very familiar with this world, and I don't want to do or say anything to make Christian look bad. This isn't just about me. I'm here as his plus-one, his girlfriend, his teammate.

"Just be yourself," he says gently.

When we step out into the lobby, several of his teammates are already there with their wives, and we quickly join them. He makes all the introductions, and my head spins as I try to keep up and remember all the names.

We walk en masse to the ballroom, and I relax. I've got this.

The night passes in a blur. I lose count of all the people I meet, but everyone's interested in my career, who I know, and what movies and shows I've been in.

"Who's the most famous actor you've ever worked with?"

"How many movies have you starred in?"

"Do you get to keep the clothes you wear on TV?"

"Who's the hottest actor you got to kiss?"

This is typical of any group setting when people meet me for the first time. So, really, I'm right at home. I exchange phone numbers with several people, and we plan to see each other when I'm in town next time. Overall, I would call the night a success.

The following day, the team manager's wife hosts a luncheon for just the wives and girlfriends.

I'm a little nervous because I won't have Christian standing right beside me. This will be me on my own. I don't know why I'm nervous. Everyone was super friendly last night, so why wouldn't they be today, right?

However, before Christian left for practice this morning, he sat me down for a little pep talk.

Somehow, it felt a little like a warning.

"Okay, I know you met many of these ladies last night, but this will be way more one-on-one. You should be friends with everyone, but close with no one, because players move around and get traded all the time. Girlfriends come and go, and they don't really treat you as though you're here to stay until you have a ring on your finger or are married. It's like they want to make sure you stick around before they let you into the fold."

"Um, okay. Wow. I guess that makes sense." I pause, nibbling my lip. "How do you know all this?"

He chuckles. "I've been doing this for a while, and even though I've never brought a girl around, I've heard the stories. I told you I would always set you up for success. So, if there's anything I know, I want you to know it, too." After a very nice kiss, he says, "I don't think you have anything to worry about. Everyone's going to like you, and I hear these luncheons are a lot of fun. So, go and enjoy yourself. I'll see you tonight for dinner."

I replay those words in my head as I make my way down in the elevator.

You should be friends with everyone, but close with no one.

Maybe that's just him being overly cautious. This is just a first meeting. No one's going to do or say anything I need to be worried about.

You should be friends with everyone, but close with no one.

But what if they do or say something? What should *I* say? What should I do?

I don't have the answers. When the elevator doors open in the lobby, I put on my most confident smile and make my way to the luncheon.

It's all very nice and elegant, and held in a smaller ballroom than we were in last night. We have assigned seating, so it kind of forces you to get to know those at your table. The centerpiece lists ten questions we can ask each other, and I realize fairly quickly that I'm sitting with women who've been here before. I'm the new girl, so they're all primarily looking at me.

I suddenly have a flashback to the panel interviews I used to have during my pageant days. My palms are a little sweaty, and my smile feels forced. Before I can even begin to relax, the questions start.

"When did you and Christian start dating?"

"Christian has never brought a woman to any of the team events before."

"Were you a baseball fan before the two of you met?"

"So, did you meet him through someone on the team, or was it like a random thing?"

"Has Christian warned you about how crazy the fangirls get?"

"You'll learn. It's a *very* different world dating a ballplayer."

I'm only halfway through my glass of orange juice, and my head is already spinning. The questions come at me in rapid-fire succession. They're all smiling, but I can already tell that they're sizing me up and trying to decide whether or not I'll fit in.

"And you're an…*actress*? It's going to be really tough for you to see each other if you're working."

I don't miss the hint of disdain in that question.

My smile never falls, but I'm completely relieved when I'm done answering their questions and can finally sit back and listen to who they are. By the time lunch is served, I'm mentally exhausted and just want to go back to my room and cry. Christian is at practice, so I need to have my mini meltdown before I see him. There's no way I'm going to burden him with this. Maybe I'm being overly sensitive, but I get the feeling that I won't make any lifelong friends here.

Even *with* a ring on my finger.

I know he warned me it could be like this, but I really thought he was overreacting.

Now that I've experienced it firsthand? I don't know if I'm good enough of an actress to pretend I'm okay with it.

It's a completely different world, and I'm utterly out of my element.

I think I'm totally pulling off the I-had-a-great-day vibe when Christian and I meet up for dinner, but he takes one look at me and immediately knows something's wrong. We don't even make it to the elevator before he turns us around and heads back to my room.

"What happened?" he asks gently.

"What do you mean? Everything's fine," I lie, but he sees right through me.

"Ella Rose?" And then he sits down on the corner of the bed like he's got all the time in the world to wait.

Ugh…

"Fine. I got the feeling that…" I groan, totally aware of how this sounds like I'm whining, but I do it anyway. "It felt like I was under the microscope, and no one really liked what they saw."

He doesn't say anything, so I go on.

"I'm used to people asking me all kinds of questions about myself, and I don't have a problem with it. But this time, it was like…"

Another groan. "I don't know, Christian. Maybe I'm wrong, but…" I sigh and sit beside him, waiting for his response.

His expression is fierce. "Were they mean to you?"

"What? No. No, everyone was very nice. Everything they said, they said with a smile. I can't really put my finger on it. It was the *way* they asked the questions. I felt like I was on the witness stand and they were the jury. I could feel their judgment."

He nods.

Pulling me into his embrace, he holds me. "I'm sorry, Ella Rose. I was hoping it wouldn't be that bad."

"Me, too." We stay like that for a while, in our little cocoon, away from the outside world. This is where I want to stay. I'm done socializing for the day. All I want to do is order some room service, curl up, and watch TV—just the two of us. That's our thing, our safe space.

Unfortunately, I know that's not going to happen. He made dinner reservations at a fabulous restaurant, and up until a little while ago, I was really looking forward to it.

Maybe it won't be so bad to get out.

That's what I tell myself as I look up and meet his gaze, kissing him softly on the lips.

"Do you feel better now?" he asks.

I nod, even though I'm not really sure.

Christian stands and gently pulls me to my feet. "Come on. Let's go and have a nice dinner. It'll be fun."

It isn't until we're in the lobby that he mentions we're not going alone.

"Sorry, I was going to say something sooner, but I could tell you were upset. Now, I hope I'm not making things worse."

I want to be annoyed, but this is part of his job, and I know I have to get used to us socializing with his teammates and their wives. Smiling, I ask, "Who's joining us?"

"Matt Taylor and his wife, Jessica. I can personally vouch for Jess. She's very nice, super genuine." Then he pauses, frowning. "I hope she wasn't one of the girls at your table today."

Relief washes over me like a wave. "I don't remember meeting a Jess, so I think we're good."

And we are.

Dinner is a lot of fun, and I can already tell that Jess is a good person. She doesn't have that tone, her questions about my life seem sincere, and over the course of the evening, she gives me a few tips on how to survive a baseball season.

"Never take it personally when Christian's a little distant," she says. "Players just completely immerse themselves in training, playing, wins, losses…just all things baseball. It's hard for them to think about anything else. I'm sure it's a lot like when you're preparing for a role in a movie, right? You need to get into the character's head, and any distractions can really mess with you."

She's not wrong.

"A lot of WAGs see everyone as competition."

"Um…WAGs?"

She nods. "Wives and girlfriends. Even though it's a team sport, everyone is only concerned with how their man plays, and they take it very personally. Do not talk or comment about how another player is doing because you never know if their wife, girlfriend, or family member is sitting right next to you. Obviously, one person cannot carry the weight of the entire team. Each one is only a small part of the whole, you know? But you'll figure out pretty quickly which ones think they're higher on the chain." She laughs softly. "And there will be times you'll have to bite your tongue, but don't let anything they say get you down."

I nod, but that wasn't exactly the vibe I got today. She must sense it because what she says next hits home.

"Then there are the ones who've been around the longest and make everything feel like we're back in high school. The more seniority your man has, the more popular you are as a WAG. There are cliques. I'm sure you must have noticed that already. Unfortunately, they're everywhere. Every team has them. You can either accept it or not, but it isn't going to change." She laughs softly. "I was really looking forward to making adult friends as an adult, but some people never got the memo that we're not in high school anymore."

"Today was a little eye-opening. I felt like I was being interrogated." I try to say it lightly, but my nervous laugh gives me away.

"It's like that when you're the new girl. Everyone wants to know all the details and gossip. Many players have women chasing them and have a new girl with them at every game. It's kind of funny. But I think everyone's interest in you today was more because you're the first girl Christian has ever brought to an event. Now that they've met you, know who you are and a little about your relationship, they should be fine."

I sigh with relief. "Okay. Good. Thanks."

"And don't take it personally if they don't all cozy up to you. Until you've got a ring on your finger, they don't know if you're going to stay, so they don't truly engage."

"Christian basically said the same thing, but I figured he couldn't really know since he's not hanging out with the…well…the WAGs."

She smiles, and it truly puts my mind at ease. "The players talk, too. If anything, they're just as gossipy as the girls. But if there's anything you need to know, you can always ask me. Here, let me give you my number."

We exchange information, and the conversation turns to the training schedule, how often Jess visits, and how often I'll be here. Luckily, there are some dates when we'll be here at the same time, and I already know I'll be a bit more relaxed on those weekends.

But moving forward, I stick to Christian's advice and don't sway from it. I was friendly with everyone, but I wasn't close with anyone.

Except Jess.

It felt good to have at least one friend in my corner.

As spring goes on, I start rehearsals for *Workin' for Laughs* in Atlanta. When I accepted the role, I knew it wouldn't be filmed in Hollywood, but I still kept my apartment in LA. Filming a season would only take two to three months, and I had recurring roles on other shows that filmed in Hollywood, so it just made sense. But during it all, Christian and I tried to see each other every two weeks. Especially while I was filming. It was a lot of traveling for me, and the lifestyle wasn't ideal, but we knew it was temporary.

At least, that's what I thought.

As time went on, however, all the traveling started wearing me down. Early in my career—like as a kid back in Florida—I spent a lot of time in the car with my parents driving me to auditions, or to acting, dancing, and singing lessons. I am someone who typically thrives on keeping busy. But between traveling for the TV show in Atlanta, more in LA, and then meeting up with Christian, I have enough frequent flier miles to take me around the world.

Twice.

Plus, living out of a suitcase was getting a little old, and once baseball season was in full swing, the time Christian and I had to spend together was very routine—just like his schedule. We spent most nights just sitting in front of the TV. We were both exhausted all the time but determined that we could do this. We could make it through.

And it wasn't only the traveling that was weighing heavily on me. It was the WAGs.

No one was ever mean to my face, but there were plenty of times when I caught the looks or heard the whispers. And none of them were flattering.

I grew up in a middle-class family, and we didn't have much extra money. I'm not someone who cares about designer labels, and I'm so proud when I can DIY something instead of paying a premium price. I can be very frugal. I'm a small-town girl who is comfortable in blue jeans, T-shirts, and my Hello Kitty purses. They make me happy, and anyone who really knows me knows that.

These women live in a completely different league…the big leagues.

So, when I went to games and sat with everyone, they were all there in their designer clothes and Louis Vuitton bags, and there I was, sporting Hello Kitty.

The snickering was hard to miss.

Outwardly, I didn't let it show that it bothered me, but it did. And it took some of the fun out of flying out to watch my man play. Every time my feelings wanted to be hurt, I remembered Christian's words to me.

You should be friends with everyone, but close with no one.

And I refused to change just to fit in. That's not who I am. If a purse was going to be the thing that made people not like me, it said more about them than me.

You should be friends with everyone, but close with no one.

There was another dynamic within the WAG group that had nothing to do with designer labels. I was new to the group—the team—and I was just a girlfriend. It was also different for me because I didn't have any children. Many baseball wives are moms with young kids. So, I didn't fit into that group either. There was no meanness to it; it was just a fact. We didn't have anything in common. And it added to my loneliness.

You should be friends with everyone, but close with no one.

Whenever Jess was at the game, I would sit with her. I always felt more comfortable when I did, but when she wasn't there, I usually sat by myself in the family section.

Summer came and went, and we were still in that frenetic pace of trying to see each other as much as possible but giving our all to our careers at the same time. The Anaheim Magic made the playoffs, which meant that Christian was deep in baseball mode.

If I thought the regular season was intense, it was nothing compared to playoff mode.

They're currently in Boston, and things aren't looking good. When we were on the phone last night, my heart broke just listening to Christian recount how badly the game had gone and how he blamed himself for the loss. They have to win game three. Otherwise, their season is over.

I hadn't planned on going to any of the games in this round because my schedule is tight, but tonight is a make-or-break game, and I know I need to be there for him. And who knows, maybe surprising him, and him knowing that I'm in the stands will be a good thing and boost his spirits?

I book my flight on my way to the Atlanta airport and make arrangements with the assistant in charge of seating for the team's families. I nervously wonder whether I should text him and let him know I'm coming but decide to wait for him to call me like he usually does in the morning. It's super early, but this puts me on the ground in Boston by 9:30 a.m., which is when he is typically done with his first game-day workout. I wish I could just show up and be like, "Surprise!" but throwing something like that at Christian when he's in his hyper-focus mode might not be the best.

The man lives by a schedule, and you can't deviate from it.

When I land in Boston and check my phone, I see a missed call and text.

Christian: *Hey, beautiful. I know you're probably busy, but I really wanted to hear your voice. Call me when you get a chance.*

Aww…

Lugging my carry-on, I head out to get a cab and don't respond until I'm on my way to the hotel.

Ella: *Are you free to talk?*

My phone rings almost immediately.

"There's my girl," he says with relief when I answer the phone.

"Hey, you," I coo. "What's going on? Bad day?"

"I'm still frustrated because of last night. There's a lot of pressure on tonight's game, and the overall mood here is really intense. Everyone was quiet at breakfast. I needed something to perk me up, and the sound of your voice always does that for me."

That is so sweet. I've always felt that way about his voice, too.

"What if I said I can do better than just the sound of my voice on the phone?"

"What do you mean?"

"I mean…what if I told you I'm in Boston and on my way to the hotel?"

"Are you…are you serious? You're here? Really?" I can hear the controlled excitement. Like he's afraid I'm joking.

"I'm really here, and I can't wait to see you. Are you at the stadium or…?"

"No, I'm still at the hotel. We're not leaving for the stadium until two, and I already worked out down in the gym. That'll give us a few hours before I have to go. How far away are you?"

"We should be there in less than twenty minutes."

"I'll meet you in the lobby," he promises, then pauses. "How did I ever get so lucky? I can't believe you took time off to be here, Ella Rose."

"I wanted to be here," I tell him. "Now, go do whatever it is you need to do. I'll see you in the lobby. I love you."

"I love you, too."

We hang up, and I lean back with a sigh. I'm mentally and physically exhausted from my schedule and being up so early for the flight, but I take a few steadying breaths. This is the balancing act I'm still learning—showing up for work, for my relationship, and for myself—sometimes all at once. Sometimes at the expense of sleep and sanity. I need a few minutes to regroup so I can be everything he needs me to be to help him get through this game tonight.

Christian is waiting for me as the cab pulls up, and as soon as I put my feet on the ground, he has me in his arms, spinning me around. I can feel all the tension in him, and I hate it for him. I know my being here is a comfort to him, but no pep talk will make things better right now.

When he puts me down, he takes my small suitcase in one hand

and holds my hand with the other. We make small talk on the way up to the room—how's filming going, how was my flight, did I eat breakfast? His concern is sincere, but I can't tell if he's just making conversation or if he's trying to keep me from asking about the game. So, I simply follow his lead.

"How long are you here for?" he asks.

"Just tonight, unfortunately. My flight back to Atlanta is tomorrow afternoon, but it's all I could manage before I need to be back on set."

In the room, he puts my bag down before gently pulling me back into his embrace. "I still can't believe you're here." He's fresh from the shower, and I wrap my arms around him and breathe him in.

We gently sway to imaginary music, and I have to admit, I needed this, too. I long for a time when we can be in the same place for more than a day or two and have at least semi-normal schedules. I cherish these moments when we're together. Where I can not only see his face but also can feel the warmth of his skin. Be comforted by his gentle touch. I can smell the soap he uses, and I inhale deeply. Every bit of this is like a feast for my senses but in the most calming of ways.

When we both pull back, I can see that this has helped him, too, but I'm still at a loss for words. I don't want to say the wrong thing or do anything to get into his head, breaking his deep concentration about tonight.

As if reading my mind, he smiles. But it's a little sad. "You don't have to walk on eggshells around me. We can talk about the game and all that. Right now, I'm just thankful that I have your beautiful face to look at instead of being here by myself, obsessing about the game tonight."

Away games have a way of feeling claustrophobic. Hotel rooms are smaller, kitchens are nonexistent, and there's no slipping into the ballpark early to settle into a familiar routine. Instead, you sit and watch the clock, waiting for time to move. I'm glad I'm here to break that stillness for him, even if it's only for a few hours.

"Did you call SJ and let him know you'll be here and need a ticket?"

"I did, and it's set. I'll be right there with all the other WAGs."

He chuckles softly as he glances around. "I don't see any Hello Kitty purses anywhere."

I know he's teasing, and it makes me feel better because, even though it's silly, he's able to think beyond the game. Even if it's only for a little while.

"I didn't have time to grab one. I've been taking this big, boring one to the set every day so I can throw everything I need into it. It just made sense to bring it today."

"Well, I personally love it when you have your favorite bags with you, and I wanted to make sure you didn't leave them behind on purpose."

So, yeah, I told him about all the whispers about my purses, and he was completely on my side about not letting anyone change who I am or dictate what I love.

He asks about the show as he gets ready, and I tell him about some of the funny sketches we're working on. I notice him wince more than once, and I can't tell if he's in physical pain or if what I'm saying is bothering him. I can admit that the humor in some of the sketches is a little more risqué than we like, but I'm sure that's not going to be how it is all the time.

"They're really playing more on my looks right now, but once I'm more comfortable with the writers and the cast, I'm sure I'll get more of a say."

He just nods.

We have lunch together, talking about everything and nothing, and before we know it, it's time for him to get ready and head to the team bus. I wish he were already in his uniform so I can tell him how cute his butt looks or something flirty to make him smile, but I already know he's getting into the *zone*. He's quiet as we head down to the lobby together, but all I get to do is give him a quick kiss before he joins his teammates.

The stoic baseball player is back, and I respect it, even as I call out, "Good luck! You've got this! Go Magic!"

I watch him leave and say a silent prayer that things turn around and the night ends on a positive note.

Unfortunately, it doesn't.

And I'm so focused on the loss and seeing the utter devastation on Christian's face that I don't even pay attention to the people around me. But then again, I doubt they're focusing on me either. Except… we're all silently united in a state of mourning for the men we love, whose playoff dreams ended tonight. This is the first time I feel like I am truly bonding with these women, and it stinks that it's because of a major loss. We're quiet as we leave the stadium, and I have no idea what Christian's state of mind will be in when he gets back to the hotel. All I know is that I'm glad I'm here for him.

On the ride back to the hotel, I can't help but remind myself that…we did it.

We made it through a baseball season.

I made it as the girlfriend of a Major League Baseball player.

That was our goal before spring training began. This was my test. *Our* test. We needed to see how I could handle Christian and all his structured routines.

Personally, I call them superstitions, but I learned early on not to use that word.

So, they're routines.

However, his *routines* are intense and quite lengthy. He has his game-day routine scheduled down to the minute.

Except for today, when he handled my showing up and interrupting everything like a champ.

He eats the same thing every day, he always has to wear clean clothes—he couldn't wear anything twice without washing it. That one was fairly normal. But that did not apply to pajamas. Because if he had a hit streak…he would *not* wash his pajamas…otherwise, it would break the streak. He could not step on a line or a crack… *Ugh*, so many rules!

And I know we spent more time apart than together this season, and that at some point, these rules will be a part of my everyday life. But now, I can be prepared for when that time comes.

Still…we made it.

Tomorrow we'll have to say goodbye again, and I'm already dreading it. I'm going to fly back to Atlanta, and he'll head home to Anaheim. We're officially in the offseason for him, so we'll have more time together, and things will go back to the way they were.

Weekends in Newport Beach.

Less flying.

Starting to maybe put down some roots and really begin planning the future we've both been dreaming of.

I'm already looking forward to it. It's finally within my reach. It makes me smile and fills me with hope.

Only I had no idea it wasn't going to happen.

Ten

We got through the rest of the fall after the Magic were eliminated from the playoffs and settled into a routine I was comfortable with. I still had to fly back and forth to Atlanta a bit, but filming was wrapping up, and I was looking forward to three months of living a normal life.

We spent Thanksgiving with Christian's best friend, Terry, and his girlfriend, Dana. Terry is in the US Army and just got back from being deployed overseas for the past nine months. We have so much to be thankful for—especially his safe return. Christian's friends have become my good friends now, too. I love how our separate lives have blended so smoothly. There is so much laughter and joy, and things are good. Better than good.

Christian and Terry have been best friends since kindergarten, and I love how the pressure from both of their jobs melts away when they are together and how they have such childlike fun wherever they go. I get along great with Dana, too. It's like we were all destined to be in each other's lives.

Christian is finally out of his funk from last season, and we're already looking forward to the new year. But as we're getting ready to jingle some bells and celebrate the holidays, things take an unexpected turn.

Since, there has been zero *fa-la-la-la-la*-ing this holiday season.

At all.

Because the Magic don't renew Christian's contract.

He gets the call as we step off the plane in Florida to spend Christmas with his family. Actually, there's a text from his agent, urging Christian to call him back. When he does, his agent breaks the news. There's no warning, no heads-up, just a cold call saying they weren't resigning him. He's devastated, and the timing obviously isn't great. Like…couldn't they have waited until after the holidays to pull the rug out from under him?

"It's going to be okay," I say, but honestly, I don't know that. I don't know anything about what happens when you're an athlete who doesn't get signed. He's a free agent now, but I don't know if that's a great situation to be in either.

He's tense, and all he does is nod as we grab our luggage at baggage claim.

We pick up our rental car, and his phone rings. It's the Magic's general manager. Christian addresses him by name instead of a greeting, and I swear I'm holding my breath, afraid of where this conversation will go.

But I'm so proud when he takes the high road and doesn't raise his voice or get angry. I have no idea what the GM says, but after several minutes, Christian ends the call with, "I wish you all the best."

It's said through clenched teeth, but still…

We make the drive to his parents' house in total silence. I know it's what he needs, but I hate it for him. And the worst part is, I can't get a read on him. I almost always can. I know he's angry and disappointed, but the whole situation is foreign to me. What is he thinking? This is a side of him I've never seen before. I've seen the casual, laid-back man, I've seen the injured athlete, and I've seen the professional baseball player through a season. But this is new.

I want him to open up and confide in me, but I think he's partially in shock and trying to wrap his head around everything before he shares it with me. Still, I want to help, and right now, that means staying quiet.

Thankfully, it's only a thirty-minute drive.

When we pull up to his childhood home, he finally looks at me.

"I'm not ready to tell anyone about this news."

I nod.

"I just need some time to process everything." He lets out a long breath. "Hopefully, we can still enjoy our holiday."

"That sounds good." I'm spending Christmas with him and his family because his dad has been ill lately, and it is important for me to be here with him. We'll fly to Memphis to see my family the day after Christmas, and then, like last year, we'll be back in LA for New Year's.

It's like speed dating with the holidays.

We get out of the car, and I can see that he's struggling. He's close to his family, and he usually tells them everything. So, the fact that he's *not* going to tell them what just happened must be weighing on him. Still, I think this visit is exactly what he needs right now.

Until we walk through the door.

One look at his mom, and I know something's not right.

"It's your father," she says quietly. "He's…it's…he's in the ICU with stage four kidney failure."

Kidney disease runs in the Lucas family. Three of his siblings have had transplants. It's heartbreaking. Now, unfortunately, it's his dad's turn.

All of this happens in the span of an hour. I practically have whiplash from it all, so I can't even imagine how Christian is processing it.

Naturally, we head to the hospital immediately. I'm not sure I truly understood or appreciated the closeness of this family until now. I do my best to stay in the background, grabbing snacks and drinks, and I'm there for support. Over the next several days, I see an entire community come together—people getting tested to see if they can donate to Mr. Lucas—I even get tested. Sadly, none of us is a match.

And during it all, Christian is still talking with his agent, trying to find a team. He's so strong, balancing this nightmare with his career while struggling with the possibility of losing his father. He doesn't crumble. There's never a moment when he throws up his hands and says he can't handle it.

But me? I'm having a hard time keeping it together. I'm not very close to Mr. Lucas, but it's devastating to see him like this. I'm an emotional person, but none of the Lucases are. So, I keep my fear and sadness to myself. I've snuck off more than once to allow some tears to fall. But when I rejoin everyone, my smile is firmly in place, and I'm there to help wherever I'm needed.

Meanwhile, Christian starts receiving offers, but they're not what he's looking for. I can relate. Just because you're offered a role doesn't mean you have to take it. Is the money right? The terms? Is it something you can live with? It's no different with a baseball contract. I'm seriously impressed with Christian's business side. He knows his worth, and he's unwilling to settle. Ultimately, he gets a career-changing deal that he is very excited about. It's for three years, and he's getting the respect he deserves.

However…

It's in St. Louis.

All of my hopes and dreams of us starting a life in California are suddenly gone.

My career is in LA. I know I'm filming *Workin' for Laughs* in Atlanta, but everything else is in Hollywood. I geared my entire life toward that goal. That dream. I made sacrifices. I left my family when I was nineteen. I battled loneliness time and time again. I handled the trial of living through a season as a baseball girlfriend. And it was all about California. The West Coast. Movies. Acting. Sunshine. Beaches.

Selfishly, I want to run away and cry again about how unfair it all is. I know I've experienced disappointment before. And I know things don't always go my way. But I was so darn sure that it was heading in that direction this time that I can't help but feel the heaviness of disenchantment.

When Christian and I met, it felt like the universe *wanted* us to meet. There were too many coincidences. Too many signs. My lucky number. My golden birthday. And from that first moment, I just *knew* we were meant to be together. That's why it is beyond devastating that the same universe that put us together is trying to keep us apart.

It was all starting to fall into place, and now, it's all up in the air again. This means long-distance dating again. It means flying back and forth all the time and living out of suitcases. It means Christian living in one place, and me living in another.

It means a balancing act that will leave me feeling like I'm failing and letting everyone down.

Internally, I'm having a complete meltdown, but when Christian looks at me—his eyes shining with hope—and asks, "What do you think, Ella Rose?"

What do I think? *What do I think?*

My inner voice screeches in near hysteria at his question. There are dozens of comebacks on the tip of my tongue just begging to be said:

I think I hate this.

I don't think it's fair.

I think I deserve something to go my way.

I think you need to find a team that doesn't disrupt our entire lives.

I let out a quiet breath as my raging thoughts settle. He's still looking at me with the same expression—all hope and love. And in that moment, I know I would follow this man anywhere in the world. And if our roles were reversed, I know he'd do it for me, too.

"I think it's too good a deal to pass up," I say with complete honesty. I smile, and I'm genuinely happy for him. He deserves a contract like St. Louis is offering him. And after the way the Magic crushed his spirit, I'm glad the Archers see his potential.

If only it was the Magic going to St. Louis and the Archers coming to Anaheim.

"Are you sure?" he asks, breaking into my thoughts. "This will be a big change for us. And this move isn't just about me. It will affect you, as well. This last year and a half that we've been together, we've been happily settled in Southern California. It was convenient for both of our careers. And now, I'm turning everything upside down."

The fact that he sees it cushions the blow a little.

Swallowing hard, I nod. "I know. I was looking forward to not having to do the long-distance thing any more than we have to, but…"

"I know you have your career, too. You've worked so hard to get where you are, and I would never ask you to give it up. I just need to know that you're okay with this."

I love that he's asking, and that he respects my opinion and my career.

Just like I know and respect that this is something he has to do.

"It's a tremendous opportunity for you. You've worked so hard to get where you are, and I will follow you wherever you go. We'll make it work."

Because we are one. We're a team.

I could whine a little and maybe get some of the frustration off my chest, but it's not necessary. My life has been a series of crazy schedules and inconveniences while following my dream. What makes this any different?

So, I say the only thing I can.

"Let's book our flights to St. Louis and see our new home for at least the next three years."

We have a very subdued Christmas with the Lucases, and his dad officially gets on the transplant list. I tried to tell Christian that we didn't need to go and see my family. I called and let them know what was going on, but he insisted because he could tell I needed it.

And I did.

I do.

The first chance she has, my mom takes me by the hand and sits me down in my old bedroom.

Far away from the rest of the family.

And Christian.

"You have a very expressive face, Ella," she says. "I already know about Christian's dad, and I know that's very upsetting, but I can tell something else is wrong. Your father noticed it too, so…out with it."

I don't even pretend that I don't know what she's talking about and blurt out the whole thing about the Magic not re-signing Christian, all the offers he received, and the one he accepted.

"So, you're moving to St. Louis?"

"Kind of."

"What do you mean, *kind of*?"

"Mom, my job is primarily in Hollywood and Atlanta for now. I can't move to St. Louis full-time." I pause. "And don't think I don't know what you're thinking."

She smirks. "Okay, what am I thinking?"

"You're thinking I need to go after what's mine. And I am. Just not…I can't quit my career," I say firmly. "I won't. I love Christian, and we know we want to get married, but…"

"But your career is just as important as his."

"Exactly." Even though he's making way more money than I could ever fathom making, that doesn't mean my dream is less.

"This isn't exactly what you signed on for," she says softly. "But you, more than anyone, know that if you want something, you need to work for it." Then she smiles. "Or maybe I should remind you of a

Christmas gift we gave you when you were a little girl."

The baseball hat with *Dream It. Be It* embroidered on it.

"Mom…"

"You can be anything you want to be, Ella. You can be an actress. A singer. A dancer. You can even be the wife of a Major League Baseball player. But…"

"I have to work for it," I finish.

"Exactly."

She hugs me, and I hold on for longer than usual because I need this. Tears sting my eyes. So much is changing, and I thought my life would be more settled by now.

She gives me one last squeeze before stepping back. "When do you leave for St. Louis?"

"January second. We want to celebrate New Year's with our friends. Plus, we have some shopping to do. Neither of us even owns winter clothes. I'm not sure I've ever seen actual snow. I'm used to the fake stuff they use on movie sets. Or at Wonder Land. Remember the way they would make it snow for the holiday parties?"

"I do. And I remember seeing the look on your face the first time you saw it. You were enchanted by it and looked like an angel." She sighs softly.

"It was magical," I say, remembering how I would twirl under the flurries that were just fake snow made from a soap product called SNOAP. Even when I got older and knew it wasn't real, I still liked to pretend it was. "I'm guessing St. Louis gets a lot of snow."

"I'm sure! I think you're definitely going to see it in January," she teases. "Is there anything I can do, sweetheart?"

"You've already done it. You listened and let me get everything out that I've been keeping inside."

Like so many other things.

"Christian needs to know how you feel. Relationships don't work if you don't communicate."

"I know, and I'll tell him. I just didn't want to do it while we were in Florida. There's so much going on with his dad. I didn't want to add to all the stress. But…we'll talk about it. I promise."

"Good girl. Now, come on. I made all your favorite holiday dishes."

"You didn't have to do that. You just made it all two days ago."

"Nope. We haven't had Christmas yet. We were waiting for you."

And then I'm hugging her again, and even though I can hear the kitchen timer going off, I hold on to her for a long time.

"What have we gotten ourselves into?"

Christian's reading my mind again because that's exactly what I'm thinking.

We landed in St. Louis an hour ago, grabbed our luggage at baggage claim, and then picked up our rental car.

It's a little like déjà vu.

We went from the warmth of the California sun to the ice and wind of a St. Louis winter. I think my body's in shock.

Now, we're driving through the frigid January wind that's whipping through the streets. Everything is gray, wet, and gloomy. And then it starts to snow. It's like when Dorothy woke up in Oz, except we went from Technicolor to black and white.

Of course, that's a bit dramatic, but it was that drastic a change.

We'll be here for a week. The Archers have several events they want Christian to take part in, but that doesn't start for another two days. We wanted a few days to ourselves to get acclimated.

And from the looks of things, we are going to need it.

We check into our hotel, and it isn't until we're in our room that I start to warm up.

Literally.

I sit on the bed, and Christian's immediately there beside me. "So? What do you think so far?" He takes both of my hands in his larger ones to warm them up, a lopsided grin on his face. I look up into those blue eyes I love and want to pretend we're anywhere but here right now.

But that won't help anything.

"Um, it's…cold," I say with a laugh. Luckily, he laughs, too.

"Yeah, that one's going to take a while to get used to. Although I'm already looking forward to spring training being in Florida." He grins. "But it's not bad, right?"

"It's hard to tell anything about the city yet," I reason. "Once we go out and explore, I'll share my opinion." I playfully nudge his shoulder. "But I think I'm going to need to wear more layers if we walk anywhere."

He laughs again. "Same."

When he gets up and shrugs off his coat, I sigh with appreciation. I don't make a habit of openly ogling him, but…come on. The man has a very attractive physique, and I can't help but sit back and admire it when the opportunity presents itself. He stretches and goes over to the windows to look out at the city, and I follow. "What about you? What do you think so far? You know, other than the cold. Do you think this could feel like home?"

"It has to. The contract is signed, and this is home for the next three years." He's very casual about it. Like it's no big deal.

"Oh."

When he turns his head, I realize what I did.

"Ella Rose?"

That's it. Just my name. In that deep timbre of his.

"Okay," I begin after letting out a shaky breath. "I'm not…I'm not *loving* this. Not right now. I'm sure I will in time, but this truly rocked our world, Christian. It popped our perfect bubble."

He leads me back to the bed to sit down. "Believe it or not, I feel the exact same way. This wasn't part of the plan, but everything got ripped out from under me. This is something I have to do. Maybe I should have discussed it more with you, but I thought you were okay with it. I hate that I've upset you."

"I'm not going to lie, I was devastated. Everything I thought we were working toward changed." I sigh. "Plus, there was just so much going on between everything with the Magic, your dad, and the holidays. It was a lot to take in." Another pause. "But I know change can be good. It's all about how we look at it, right?"

He nods, his expression tender. "I'm hopeful that after this week—once we meet the team and tour the stadium and find an apartment—all our anxiety will be gone. If you think about it, it's kind of exciting."

Is it?

"When we met, we were both established in California. You had your life in LA and Hollywood, and mine was in Newport Beach and Anaheim. It was easy to slip into each other's lives because everything was there. But this? This, we're building together. We're making a home here. You and me."

"I love the sound of that. But…I'm not going to be living here a lot of the time."

"It doesn't matter. This will still be our home. Not me moving in with you, or you moving in with me. It'll be *ours*."

I feel the first twinge of excitement.

Ours.

Not his place. Ours.

Maybe this isn't the worst thing that could happen to us.

Maybe the long distance will work out just fine.

After all, if it means coming home to Christian whenever I can, to a place that belongs to both of us, how bad can it be? I'm beginning to thaw from the frigid temperatures outside, but Christian can tell that I am still frozen. He takes my jacket and scarf off and pulls me onto the bed and under the covers. He wraps his warm body around me like a heated blanket, and the cold reality of our situation melts away. We cuddle, and he gently kisses my face all over until he meets my lips. Then, he reassures me that everything will be okay. I guess St. Louis isn't so bad…

We find an apartment on the first day we go out looking, and I already have big decorating plans for it. At least, I do in my head. It's not something I can commit to right now. It doesn't feel like something I should do until we're more settled in our relationship. I don't want to say that I won't decorate until we're married, but it's more like when I have the proper time, and not just when I'm here for a weekend.

The cold weather is completely rude, but we both grin and bear it as we explore the city.

The closer we get to meeting up with the Archers, the more I can tell that Christian's pulling a little away from me and turning into the professional athlete guy. I don't take offense. This is essentially a job interview, even though he already has the job. So, I let him have his space to get mentally prepared.

The event we're attending is for charity, and we can both tell right away that it's a totally different vibe than anything we ever did with the Magic. From the moment we walk in the door and start meeting the management, I know it's an environment that will be good for Christian.

And me.

We meet his new teammates and a ton of fans. At one point, they call Christian up onto the stage and introduce him to the masses. The cheers from the crowd are deafening. I watch with pride as he takes it all in. They're cheering for him—not the team, just *him.*

I'm happy. I'm truly happy. This is where he's meant to be.

Even if it is ridiculously cold.

But hey, it's not winter year-round, so…that's a plus.

Once I stop looking at this change as being all about me and what I'm losing, it's easy to see what I'm gaining.

Right now, it's Christian's time to shine, but I know there will be room in the spotlight for two when the time's right.

Spring training doesn't start until March, but there are so many things we need to do before then. When we get back to California, I have meetings with my agent about some potential roles, plus production is starting again for *Workin' for Laughs.* Meanwhile, Christian prepares for his move. He no longer needs an apartment in Newport Beach, and whenever he comes to LA to see me, we'll just stay at my place. Still, it's bittersweet when we pack up his apartment. It's where we fell in love. We have so many memories that we will cherish forever.

Things are happening, and we're busy. One afternoon, Christian surprises me by stopping by the apartment unannounced.

"Hey, Ella Rose," he says, kissing my cheek.

"Hey, you. What are you doing here?"

I lead him to the kitchen to get us something to drink when he completely shocks me.

"How would you feel about going to Wonder Land for a week?"

Spinning around, I bang into the refrigerator door, nearly falling on my butt. "Um…what?"

"Wonder Land? You know, the place in Florida that you love so much." He's teasing, and his smile is absolutely adorable. "I was thinking maybe we could take one last vacation before life gets chaotic. And since you're the one making most of the sacrifices, I wanted to go somewhere that's special and meaningful to you. So? What do you think?"

"Oh, my goodness! Are you kidding me? I love this idea!" But I don't know if my schedule will. "Hold that thought," I tell him as I run to my room to grab my planner. I find him sitting on the sofa and immediately join him. "Okay, when are you thinking?"

"You tell me what dates work for you, and that's when we'll go. I'll handle all the arrangements."

Seriously, could I love him more?

We look over my calendar and realize we need to do it sooner rather than later. "What can I do to help?"

He kisses me, caressing my cheek as he does, and it makes me all gooey. I just melt against him. "Not a thing. I've got it all under control."

I have a feeling he's got something up his sleeve, but I'm not going to let myself think about it and possibly ruin whatever it is. Christian may not think he's romantic, but he seriously is. So, I will be patient, sit back, and enjoy the plans he makes.

And hope my curiosity doesn't get the best of me.

Two weeks later, we land in Orlando, and I'm shocked when a limo picks us up.

"Christian. What in the world…?"

He's smiling, clearly enjoying my joy.

My next surprise is when we pull up at the most deluxe hotel of the Wonder Land Resort. "Are you kidding me?" I ask excitedly. "We're staying at The Grand Brightwater?" I cannot hide my wide-eyed wonder.

This is like…top tier. It has always been my dream to stay here, but it's completely out of my budget. I've come here to just walk around so many times, dreaming of the day I'd be able to afford to stay. I can't believe I'm going to be staying here.

We walk into the lobby, and it's just as magical as I remember. The Grand Brightwater blends Victorian romance with storybook elegance. I feel a little like royalty as I walk in. The decor is all soft blush and champagne tones, antique gold filigree, creamy marble floors, and cascading chandeliers shaped like floating glass petals. The architecture feels grand but intimate, less *palace* and more *enchanted lakeside manor*.

The hotel's signature scent of white magnolia and vanilla musk with a faint note of honeyed amber greets guests in the lobby. I already know they sell candles and lotions with the scent, and I will want to take them all home with me. I'm already wrapped up in the ambience and feeling right at home.

But one of the coolest things about this resort? At night, the entire lobby glows in rose-gold light from hundreds of tiny sconces designed to look like fireflies in glass.

It's magical.

And I'm staying here!

I think I know what Christian has planned for us, but I don't want to jinx it and even say the words to myself. This is wildly romantic, and he's making one of my dreams a reality.

By the end of this trip, I have a feeling that one of my *biggest* dreams will have also come true.

He gets us checked in, and we walk through the atrium—a sweeping glass-roofed conservatory at the heart of the resort, filled with living greenery, a trickling fountain, and moonlight that spills in after dark. A pianist plays soft instrumental Wonder Land and Storyteller classics that I recognize from my childhood. The music drifts up through the balconies of the guest floors.

Magical.

Our suite is positively decadent and has a perfect view of the storybook castle right in the middle of Wonder Land's signature park. I open the door that leads out to the balcony, feeling like a kid on Christmas morning. I don't think anything could be more perfect than this.

Then I turn around and find Christian down on one knee.

Oh, my goodness…

My hands immediately fly up, covering my mouth as I look down at this incredible man who clearly knows my every wish.

He lets out a soft breath. "I never thought my hands would shake like this." Then he seems to relax. "Ella Rose, I've played in front of forty thousand people. I've stood on fields where every breath feels like it matters, and every mistake echoes for miles. I've faced pressure, expectation, noise…and somehow, this moment is louder than all of it. Because it's you."

His lopsided grin is so freaking endearing that I don't even let him say anything else. I'm instantly in his arms, saying, "Yes! Yes!"

We're both laughing, but then I realize he probably planned to say more. I sit back on my heels, holding his hand, and smile.

"When I met you, I thought I was pretty solid. I had my career. My plans. My future mapped out like innings in a game. But then you walked into my world, and somehow everything—*everything*—got better.

Brighter. You turned the spotlight into something warm instead of blinding. You made all the miles, all the airports, all the games feel like they led me somewhere worth arriving.

I've always talked about being a team. That's how my brain works. Wins. Losses. Commitment. Showing up. Pushing through the slumps. Celebrating the victories. And I realized somewhere along the way that every time I thought about the future, it wasn't just me on the field anymore. You were there, too."

I reach up and caress his powerful jaw as he continues.

"You, laughing in the stands. You, singing in the car into an inflatable microphone. You, reminding me I'm more than what I do. You, being home…no matter where we are."

Tears sting my eyes, and my heart feels ready to burst.

"I don't want us to be two people trying to balance separate worlds. I want us to build one. Together. I want to face the noise with you. I want to come home to you after the great games and the terrible ones. I want to cheer for you when you shine and hold you when the world gets unfair. I want every chapter, every season, every impossible, beautiful, ordinary day…with you. So, this is me, right here, heart wide open, doing the scariest and easiest thing I've ever done all at once."

I know what's coming, and yet I still hold my breath.

"As I look into your eyes—the same eyes I saw for the first time by chance on a plane and then at a baseball game while you were wearing my jersey—I see the same ones I want to look at for the rest of my life." He pauses. "Ella Rose…will you be my teammate for life? Will you marry me?"

Christian's a man of few words, but when he uses them, they're powerful.

Tears stream down my face as I nod and whisper, "Yes."

That's when I notice he's not holding a ring box, but a cute Hello Kitty purse—another I don't have. I look at him, and he nods at the purse. "Look inside."

I spot a little blue box and pull it out. I think I'm a little in shock that all this is happening.

"Don't you want to see the ring?"

Oh, right. I do! I open the box and slip the ring onto my finger, twirling it in the light. "It's a perfect fit," I whisper, and he smiles.

"Just like you're a perfect fit for me," he says, and he's right. We're a perfect fit.

Then we're kissing, and I feel like I'm in the middle of a fairy tale. When we break apart, my eyes immediately go back to the ring. I can't wait to call my family and friends and show it off. There are like a million things I suddenly want to do, but I don't know where to begin.

"This is the best day of my entire life, Christian. You gave me the proposal of my dreams."

"The day's not over yet," he says with a mischievous grin.

If the baseball thing doesn't work out, I swear he's got a future in romantic event planning.

Because he knows how much I love tea, he made reservations at The Grand Brightwater Tea Room for us. I swear I'm walking around with eyes wide like a cartoon princess. Everywhere I turn, it's more magical than before. We sip tea and eat cake, and just when I think, *Nothing can top this*, he does.

"Our families are meeting us for dinner. And tomorrow, we have an appointment with a wedding planner here at Wonder Land. I want you to have the fairy tale wedding of your dreams, Ella Rose, and I couldn't think of a more perfect place for it."

I'm pretty sure I black out for a moment because…just because.

"I want you to have the wedding you always wanted," he tells me. "But after the baseball season is over. Please. All the planning is up to you. I won't be able to help you with any of it, unfortunately, because my focus needs to be on the game. Especially since I'm starting with a new team."

It's not ideal, but I get it. He's hyper-focused when it's a regular season, but starting fresh somewhere new? Yeah. That will take one hundred percent of his time and energy. And I respect that.

Plus, it's not like I'll be planning our wedding completely by myself. My family and his will be involved—and the actual wedding planner. So really, I'm confident that we can do this.

Then I remind myself that I'm also working on multiple TV shows, traveling, and still auditioning. It won't be as easy as I just thought. But hey, I can do it. I know I can.

I will.

It's just one more thing for me to balance. But I'll make it work.

After tea, Christian and I stroll around the resort grounds, making plans for our future. They range from career goals—another World Series title for him, and an Oscar for me—to having our dream home back here in Florida, where we'll live with our kids. The thing is, I can totally see it. We're on track for all of it.

"I'd accept an Emmy," I say after a moment. "Since I'm working primarily on TV, that's the most likely scenario. And at some point, I'll get that big break in a movie where I get an Oscar nomination."

"I know you can do it." He kisses my cheek as we walk along.

"What time are we meeting everyone for dinner?" Before he can answer, I realize I never asked the obvious question. "And how did you manage to get everyone here?"

"Everyone except my father," he reminds me. His dad is still in the ICU, awaiting his transplant. "When we were visiting your parents after Christmas, I talked to your dad and let him know my intentions and asked his permission to marry you."

And the sweetness keeps flowing.

"Even then, I knew this would be where I proposed, so they were just waiting for me to tell them when to be here. And my family is only thirty minutes away, so it's no big deal for them to join us." We walk along quietly for a minute before he adds, "Family is the most important thing and should always come first, so it's only right that they're all here with us as we celebrate."

"Absolutely."

Dinner is positively beautiful, and having both of our families with us makes my heart so happy. This is the first time everyone's meeting each other, yet it doesn't feel that way. Everyone's laughing and talking and joking about how Christian and I had to move across the country to meet, even though we grew up only thirty minutes apart.

"It's like a real-life movie," my mom says. "A real-life fairy tale."

She gets it.

All the movies I grew up watching…I am *living* them.

We have dessert, and we're getting ready to wish everyone a good night, when Mrs. Lucas's phone rings. I can't speak for everyone, but I know my heart stops. I grip Christian's hand tightly and can feel the tension rolling off him.

She steps away from the table, speaking softly. No one moves. No one follows. We see her shoulders sag, and all I can think is, "Please, God. Please don't let this be bad news."

It feels like forever, but when she turns to face us, she's crying. Christian lets go of my hand and rushes to her, followed by his siblings.

And then she smiles.

"Tori is approved to donate her kidney. Your father has a donor," she says through the tears. "He's going to be okay. It's a miracle!"

Tori is married to Christian's brother, Karl. She had to go through a bunch of tests to make sure she could donate, and now that we know she can, this is an answer to all our prayers. The relief is palpable, and then we're all laughing and crying and hugging before we sit back down to celebrate all over again.

It's a great day, and it just reinforces my thoughts from earlier today.

Magical.

Eleven

The next ten months are an absolute whirlwind. There were days I wasn't sure I could survive it. Planning a wedding is stressful enough, but when you add in a fiancé who plays Major League Baseball and has a heavy schedule, *and* a bride-to-be who is busy filming a hit TV show, flying from LA to Atlanta to St. Louis almost constantly while regularly doing press and red carpets, I'm not sure when I was even getting any sleep.

However, my publicist gave me a fabulous idea. I talked about the engagement and our upcoming wedding a *lot* while promoting *Workin' for Laughs* and other projects, and it really paid off in some fun ways.

I was on the cover of not one but *two* bridal magazines. I was sponsored by a wedding dress designer, and we are even going to be featured in a couple of magazines on our honeymoon.

Work smarter, not harder, right?

The night before the wedding, we have our rehearsal dinner with our families and a few close friends. I am just so happy to have everyone here and all the planning and work finally over. Christian's dad had his kidney transplant three months ago, and he's here to celebrate with us. Everything feels complete.

I'm standing alone, having a contemplative, quiet moment to myself to admire how beautiful the room looks, how perfectly everything came together, and watching everyone enjoying themselves, when his dad comes to stand beside me. I smile at him, marveling at how good he looks after being sick for so long.

"Having a good time?"

He nods.

"How are you feeling?"

"Fine."

Okay…

"Tell me, Ella," he says as if it's a test. "Ninety-five percent of actresses' marriages fail. What's going to make this one different?"

Um…wow. That's not a question I expected. I get that he's not the warm-and-fuzzy type, but this pushes me too far. I know that he's just being protective of his son, but he clearly doesn't know me, and I don't appreciate the implication. I don't know what comes over me, but I suddenly get a warm rush throughout my body, and words fly out of my mouth.

"Interesting. I've heard that ninety-five percent of baseball players' marriages fail, so what's going to make *this* one different?"

We stare at each other in a silent battle of wills, and then I walk away. I cannot believe I just did that. It feels like he's been putting me through a probation period to see if I'm worthy of his son. However, we are getting married tomorrow, and I love Christian more than anything. When I first met him, I wasn't looking for a husband—I was focused on my career. But my mom told me that when I met "the one," I'd just know. Christian is "the one," and we've both made so many sacrifices to be together. Mr. Lucas needs to accept that I'm here to stay, and we *will* be in the five percent of actress-athlete marriages that succeed.

The following day, on November 26, I can honestly say I have the wedding I've dreamed of since I was a little girl.

It's a fairy tale wedding from start to finish. From the ceremony in the Catholic church that Christian went to while growing up, to the reception at The Grand Brightwater Resort. The theme is "When You Wish Upon A Star," and the number twenty-two is incorporated throughout. Over three hundred of our friends and family came to the wedding, and it's a big party with lots of food and dancing.

Every little detail has been thoughtfully planned out. I made sure to take everyone into consideration for the menu, the music…all of it. We even give away miniature baseball bats as our wedding favors. It's a celebration of love—not just mine and Christian's, but the love we have for our friends and families, as well.

As the day goes on, however, I realize that I made one crucial mistake. My new husband is a very shy and private person, and I planned a very over-the-top event with tons of publicity. ESPN did a feature, and our wedding will be in a bridal magazine. It's all been way too big for Christian.

And because we invited so many people, we don't really get a chance to *enjoy* the day because we're too busy meeting and greeting the guests. So, ultimately, while I got everything I wanted, and it was a gorgeous wedding that everyone said was one of the best they'd been to, we don't get to take it all in.

Now that it's done, I know that if I could do it all over again, I would have a much smaller event.

Still, I will always treasure the memory.

And the pictures.

Never have two people needed a vacation more.

Two days after the wedding, we board a plane to Hawaii. I don't think either of us lets out a calm breath until we're taxiing away from the gate.

Alone.

Just the two of us.

Finally.

Even though we had plenty of time over the last ten months where we were technically alone, it was like the wedding plans, baseball, and acting were third wheels at all times.

But now, they're all gone, and it's just my husband and me.

Husband.

Gah! I'm married! I don't think it's fully set in yet. Christian's holding my right hand, so I'm free to study the sparkly new ring on my left. It's so pretty, and I love everything it symbolizes with its circular shape, having no beginning or end: love, commitment, eternity. It represents unending devotion.

I sigh happily, resting my head on his shoulder.

"I like that sound," he says. "That's your happy sigh."

"Yes, it is, and I am."

"Me, too, Ella Rose. Me, too." Now, *he* sighs. "I was beginning to think this day would never come."

"You mean the wedding?"

"No, leaving for the honeymoon." I hear the amusement in his voice, but I know he's serious. He talked about the honeymoon the way I talked about the wedding for the last few months. "This is going to be exactly what we need after all the planning, playing, acting, and traveling. I'm ready for us to be away from everything."

"Mmm, that does sound good."

"Just the two of us on the beach, like we used to be back in California…"

"I'm pretty sure the beaches in Hawaii will be way nicer than that. Plus, we're staying at a beautiful resort, so we'll have some privacy, too. Maybe even have the beach to ourselves—or at least a portion of it."

I know that part is very important to him after the spectacle of our wedding. He was seriously such a good sport about all the media coverage, so having this time for it to be just the two of us means he will be completely back in his comfort zone.

Except for the one afternoon photoshoot that my publicist committed us to for a magazine article.

"Don't be offended, but I'm probably going to nap for part of this flight," he tells me right before he yawns.

"I'm not offended. I'll be right here snoozing beside you." And I will, because it's a long travel day. But once we arrive, we will have ten glorious days to ourselves, and I am so ready for it.

Three days later, we're sitting in our private cabana, loving life. Everything so far on this trip has been at a level of luxury I didn't know existed. It's close to everything we had at The Grand Brightwater, but with a lot more personalized attention.

I'm seriously getting spoiled.

"So, what do you think? Is it worth it?" he asks out of nowhere.

"Um…what?"

"We're here and having this incredible break from reality after almost three years together. I guess I was just curious if all the sacrifices…the ones we had to make, the ones you had to make—and will probably still have to make—as a baseball wife are worth it."

I study him for a long moment before I reach for his hand. "Christian Lucas, I would do it all again in a heartbeat."

He looks relieved. "Really?"

I nod. "Really. Although, maybe with a smaller wedding."

We both laugh at that one. "You wouldn't get any argument there from me."

I catch him looking at our hands, even as I do the same. "Does it feel weird wearing a new ring?"

"Sort of. But not in a bad way. To be fair, other than my World Series ring, it's the only ring I own, and that ring is too big to wear every day."

We're quiet for several minutes as we enjoy the view and each other's company. It's serene and beautiful and comforting.

I'm the one to break the silence. "You know, I didn't get to experience your World Series win with you," I begin carefully. "So, I would appreciate if you would win another one, just so we can experience it together." I say it jokingly, but I'm sort of serious. I would love to be with him and see him reach that career high again. I know it's something he talks about every season, but I hope it will happen again sooner rather than later.

Grinning, he winks at me. "I'll see what I can do."

Twelve

One of my favorite things about fairy tales is how they always end, with the prince and princess riding off into the sunset, all smiles and full of love, their happily ever after guaranteed.

For a while, ours looks like that. Perfect. Magical. Everything we've ever wanted.

But the truth? Behind the scenes, the fairy tale is starting to crack.

Dramatic much?

Okay, it isn't our *relationship* that's cracking. Not exactly. But the pressures from both of our careers suddenly feel heavier than they ever have before.

I'm getting ready to start filming *Workin' for Laughs* again, and things aren't exactly great.

It's a sketch comedy show in prime time, so while we're not pushing the envelope like they do on *Saturday Night Live*, there *are* a lot of innuendos and implied things that I'm getting uncomfortable with.

And so is Christian.

My recurring roles on Storyteller are much more wholesome. I'm still able to play a teenager because of my looks, so on one network, I'm essentially a child, and on the other, the humor is…well…very adult.

And not so wholesome.

I'm conflicted.

Essentially, I was cast because I was the cute girl who should be seen and not heard. Look cute, but don't be too funny. The arm candy.

That's not to say I don't have speaking parts—I have plenty. But it's nothing compared to the men's roles.

But like I'll never tell Christian how to play baseball, he's never tried to tell me how to act. We share our experiences, listen to each other, and show support. But as I'm getting ready to fly to Atlanta, I can't help but gripe a bit.

"I just wish they would let me spread my wings a little," I say as I start placing clothes in my suitcase. "I'm not new to the business, and I've worked on several successful TV shows."

"Have you tried talking to the writers? The producers?"

I shrug. "Every once in a while, I go rogue during rehearsals and try something, hoping they'll like it, but it's like getting reprimanded in school. I'm told to stick to the script."

He nods, but I know he's choosing his words carefully. "Okay, but that's not really talking. You need to have a conversation with them and let them know how you feel."

It's sweet that he's trying to help, but he doesn't understand how things work in the entertainment business. There's a chain of command, and I am the lowest person in it.

"It'll be fine," I say, but even *I* can hear the weariness in my voice.

The next thing I know, Christian's leading me over to the bed to sit down.

"You know we've always been honest with each other, right?"

"Right."

"And you know that I would never tell you what you can or can't do."

"I know that."

He pauses, and I'm not sure where he's going with this.

After another moment, he lets out a long breath, taking my hand in his. "I'm not comfortable with some of the…the characters you've been playing on *Workin' for Laughs*. It feels like they're…they're…" Another pause. "Okay. I'm struggling with seeing you being objectified on national television," he blurts out. "I know it's just acting and it's not real, but it's something that's getting harder and harder for me to deal with."

Oh.

Oh…

Some of the sketches I've been in have really pushed me out of my comfort zone, but I'm not taking into account how they make him feel.

Wow.

"I'm not saying I don't want you acting or that you have to quit *Workin' for Laughs*, I'm just saying there's nothing wrong with speaking up when things don't sit right with you."

"It's not that easy, Christian. Writers can be very sensitive when you mess with their work, and they don't appreciate the actors—the ones who aren't also writers—telling them how to do their job."

"But you're not…"

"Trust me. It's how they take it."

He caresses my hand. "Okay. Okay."

But now he has me thinking.

"What if I speak up and they put me in fewer sketches? What if I end up only being the girl in the background? This was supposed to be my big break. It was finally my turn on a major network in prime time. People are getting to know my name."

He doesn't say anything, but that's okay. I do.

"The Storyteller shows are kids' shows. My characters are really funny, and I get to showcase a wide range of acting—I can have fun with it and show off my acting skills. But on *Workin' for Laughs*, only the guys get the funny stuff. I'm only supposed to stand, pose, smile, and be cute."

"You are far too talented to only have to pose and be cute." He laughs softly. "Although you do it well, and I personally love looking at you. Still, that's not what you've worked so hard for. It's not what made you move across the country at nineteen."

"I know. I just don't see any scenario where this will go well."

We sit in companionable silence for a bit before he gives me something to seriously think about.

"I guess the question is, can you be happy with things staying the way they are? Is it worth not making waves just to have your name on a show?"

I want to say that it's worth it, that this is the kind of thing every actor dreams of. But now I'm not so sure. Is this the kind of thing *this* actor is dreaming of?

Is this what I trained and sacrificed so much for?

Right now, I don't have an answer. All I can do is finish packing, catch my flight, and show up on set in Atlanta.

Then, it's anyone's guess.

Spring training is over, which means Christian is fully immersed in baseball season while I'm in Atlanta, staring at my calendar and realizing I still have a full month of filming ahead of me. Time is flying yet somehow dragging all at once.

I'm surrounded by people every day on set—constant noise, constant movement—but I've never felt more alone. I'm a newlywed living out of a suitcase in one city while my husband builds his life in another. I eat takeout more nights than not, talk to Christian through a phone screen, and fall asleep alone.

We're both chasing the lives we worked so hard for, trying to meet in the middle where we can. Since the wedding, the longest stretch we've had together is two weeks. More often, it's a handful of days before one of us is back at the airport, promising it won't be long this time.

I know the season won't last forever, but knowing that doesn't make it easier to live in. Balance sounds simple in theory. In practice, it feels like learning to walk a tightrope while missing the person meant to steady you.

And on top of that, I am struggling with my role on *Workin' for Laughs*. I show up every day, but I'm starting to notice a pattern. After several more attempts to give my input on the characters I'm playing, I'm getting less and less speaking time. I'm practically a piece of the scenery now.

Is it worth not making waves just to have your name on a show?

That question comes back to me more times than I can count, and I'm fighting hard to say that it's worth it. Is it?

I mentioned being bullied a lot when I was younger. As I've said, I always marched to the beat of my own drum, and that started at a young age. While I was growing up, my classmates used to do all kinds of mean things to me, from name-calling to stealing my homework. It's something that's never gone away. Obviously, I don't think about it obsessively, but I'm thinking about it now because it's kind of how I feel on this production.

Bullied.

Bullied into submission.

Bullied into not making waves.

Bullied into being someone I'm not.

Is it worth not making waves just to have your name on a show?

No. No, it's not.

And that's when I know it's time for me to stand up, say my piece, and let whatever happens, happen.

If I were a writer, I would have written the scene like this:

A talented, underused actress walks onto the set. She reads her lines and delivers them as they're written, but then…she realizes the scene needs a little something more.

"What if I wore something a little less revealing, and instead of just lying down on this workout bench and showing how this exercise machine works, I use my physical comedy skills, just like Lucille Ball, and turn it into a whole bit. I can take something simple and make it hilarious. Can I show you?"

The writers listen to her great idea, let her try it, and then all collaborate to make it the funniest sketch possible.

It *went* like this: I walked onto the set, read my lines, made the suggestion, and was told to just read what was written—the scene didn't need anything else.

Once rehearsal wraps, I'm summoned to the executive producers' office—Max and Aaron. They have last names, but they're always together, and everyone calls them by their first names, like a matched set. I try not to lean into stereotypes, but they do very little to disprove the Hollywood-producer variety—the kind who prefer women who are agreeable and quiet. They like me well enough…as long as my ideas stay unspoken.

Apparently, I've been a little too generous with my opinions.

Standing outside their office, I draw in a slow breath before knocking. When they call me in, I'm no longer sure what I'm feeling. I only know that whatever this is, it won't be simple.

"Won't you have a seat, Ella?"

I smile even as I shake my head. "I'd rather stand."

They give each other surprised looks, while Max sits on the couch and Aaron takes the chair behind the desk. "Listen, we understand that you've had a lot of opinions about your scenes, but the writers are fantastic at what they do, and they understand the tone of the sketches we're doing. Every time you offer a suggestion, you're undermining their work."

"I'm not trying to undermine anyone. It's about wanting to make a sketch the best it can be, and I know I have more to offer."

"Everyone here really likes you, Ella. You're a great girl, but…we're almost done with the season, and we don't want an actress with opinions. We just want an actress who will do what we tell her to do."

"But I *have* been doing what you tell me to do. I just think I can *enhance* what we're doing without it being seen as undermining anyone."

At first, they just stare at me like they don't understand what I've just said. Like they can't grasp that I genuinely want to contribute to the show with more than my looks.

But I keep talking. "I'm a talented actress, and I've never had any complaints on any other show or movie I've done. I deserve to at least have my ideas listened to rather than immediately dismissed." My heart is pounding so hard I'm almost sure they can hear it. I'm trembling and starting to sweat.

"Ella, look, you're a pretty girl and a good actress," Max says. "No one's debating that. But on this set, our writers are the ones writing, okay? Not you, not anyone else on the cast, just them."

It's a lie. All the male actors make changes and suggestions all the time, and none of them gets called into the office for it.

I go to comment, but Aaron holds up a hand to stop me, his huff of annoyance a clear sign that he's done listening.

"Bottom line is," Aaron says firmly, "you're holding up production. We still have several episodes to go to wrap up the season, and we're done with your distractions. You're fired."

For a moment, I only stare at them, unsure whether I should laugh, be angry, relieved, or try to convince them to change their minds. The decision is made for me when they turn and start talking to each other as if I'm no longer in the room.

And with that, I leave.

Everyone on the set, from the other actors to craft services, heard me getting called to the office, and I swear everyone's still standing around waiting to know the outcome. But I walk with purpose back to my dressing room, pack up my belongings, and head out to my car. Naturally, by the time I get there, someone's waiting to take my security badge, so I can't get back onto the lot tomorrow.

I hand it over with a smile.

As I get into my rental car, I realize I'm still shaking. I grip the steering wheel so tight that my knuckles turn white, and I can't see a thing in front of me because tears are waiting to fall.

So, I let them.

Only…I'm not sure why I'm crying. I'm not sad about getting fired. It's genuinely for the best. But I know I'm disappointed that it came to this. That I was essentially forced—no, bullied—out of a job.

Oh, how I hate bullies.

I want to yell, scream, and cry at the unfairness of it all. I don't understand why people are the way they are or why they do the things they do. All I wanted was to do the best job and make the show better. Make it something I could be proud of. And where did it get me? Nowhere.

Swallowing hard, I shake my head before wiping away my tears. This is not the way I want anyone to see me or how I want them to remember me. So, I give myself a few minutes to calm down. When I finally pull away from the lot, I realize I'm not just leaving a sound stage, I'm leaving the dream of this show being my big break.

Now, it's over.

I want to call Christian, but I know he's at the stadium right now. I'll have to wait until our call later tonight to tell him what went down today. He's deep in baseball mode, and I hate the thought of burdening him with this. He's spent so much of his life hyper-focused on his game and career, I'm not sure how he'll handle having to worry about someone else.

Even if that someone is me.

I want to call my mom, but I know I'll turn into a blubbering mess and shouldn't be driving when that happens. She'll try to tell me how it's all for the best, and that something amazing will come along, but right now, I know I won't believe her.

Even though she's usually right.

And I want to call Jen and let her know that I'll be coming back sooner rather than later. I need to decide whether to go to LA or St. Louis first. I have to let my agent know what happened and have her start looking for roles and auditions.

Suddenly, my to-do list is a mile long, and I'm overwhelmed all over again.

But I push it all aside as I drive to the hotel. I turn on the radio and find something upbeat to sing along to. The universe must know my pain because my favorite song, "The Middle" by Jimmy Eat World, comes on, and I take my first calm breath since things went sideways earlier.

There's a slight shift in my mood, and as I start singing, I believe in the words.

I sing like no one could hear me, because no one could, letting the words push the ache out of my chest. It is a reminder I cling to every time things fall apart: that it takes time, that being stuck doesn't mean being finished, and that somehow, things will straighten themselves out.

I'm not fully there yet, but I know this role, this TV show isn't the end for me. Leaving *Workin' for Laughs* is just a temporary speed bump. I'm going to bounce back from this, and even without hearing it directly from my mom, I know in my heart that something else will come along.

So, I sing loudly as I maneuver through the Atlanta traffic, thankful for everything I have instead of focusing on the loss.

Because, as the song says, everything'll be all right.

I end up going to St. Louis first because I feel like I need the time with Christian more than anything else. My agent is lining some things up for me, so I know my career is being handled, and having time with my husband is what matters most.

I want us to have time to live like a married couple. And really, the timing is perfect because Easter is next weekend, and I want us to start making our own traditions.

Although I'm not quite sure how that will go since the Archers have a game on Easter Sunday. Still, I'm hoping we can go to brunch before Christian has to leave for the stadium. It'll be fine. We'll be together, and that's all I want.

Well, that and a normal life where we're together more than we're apart.

That's not too much to ask, right?

My first week in St. Louis is wonderful.

Mostly.

It's a lot of working around his schedule—and his schedule is brutal. To say that my husband lives, breathes, eats, and sleeps baseball is an understatement. And because we are living together now, I'm seeing things I didn't see before.

For one, he's a much pickier eater than I ever realized. I'm literally learning exactly what he eats—down to the brands he prefers—so I can cook for him. I even reach out to his mom for some recipes.

On the flip side, he makes us breakfast every day, so... Who can be mad when you get pancakes every morning?

Pancakes aside, the conversation Christian and I had right before I experienced my first baseball season comes to mind.

"Okay, here's the thing that is...well...most people only see the fun and glamorous side of the game. They think it's all sitting in the stands and cheering with the wives and girlfriends and families and then hanging out and celebrating after it. But it's not. It's a long season—especially if we make the playoffs—and sometimes it's going to be very lonely for you. Once spring training starts, all the time we've been spending together is over."

It was different when I was filming, and we were together for only short periods of time. Now that I'm here—and I know I'm going back to LA for some auditions soon—I truly understand what he was trying to tell me.

Every day is like *Groundhog Day*. We sleep in for as long as Christian can because he needs to rest his body as much as possible. When we get up, he makes us pancakes and bacon, and we watch TV for about an hour. Then he begins his game-day routine with an Epsom salt bath and stretches. Then he cooks the lunch he will take to the field with him to eat later. He leaves for the field no later than 1:00 p.m.

After he leaves, I go to the grocery store and get something to cook for dinner, then I go to the stadium for the game. I usually eat something at the ball field and then again with Christian after the game, so he's not eating alone. The post-game time is really important to us. It's our time. He plays every day, except for one or two days a month. Those days are precious, but Christian needs to get his rest on those days, too. So, if we are lucky enough to be together on an off day, we just stay at home, watch TV, and cook or get carryout from one of our favorite restaurants. Our life during the season isn't glamorous. It's a grind. However, there is no one I would rather sit on a couch and do nothing with.

It's Easter Sunday morning, and we're walking out of church. The game starts at one o'clock today, and Christian likes to get to the field early for day games. In my mind, I'm like, *"But it's Easter Sunday, so maybe he can get there a little later today. I mean, it's only 8:30 in the morning, right?*"

I keep waiting for Christian to suggest that we do something special, but when he doesn't, I ask, "Hey, what would you like to have for brunch before you head to the field?"

At the very least, I expect him to suggest our pancakes or maybe a trip somewhere to eat, but he quickly dismisses the suggestion. "Ella Rose, I have to go straight to the stadium. I'll just eat something when I get there."

My mind immediately freezes because this was *not* the plan. Easter is my favorite holiday, and I've been thinking about having Easter brunch with my husband all week. Did I tell him that? No, but I assumed we would do something special.

I literally don't say anything else on the drive to the stadium. If I do, I fear I will start crying, and that's the last thing Christian needs right before a big game. He's doing so well here. He loves his team, we love the city, and the city loves Christian, so I'm not going to ruin his positive mood this morning. We only have one car in St. Louis, so if I go to the game, I need to drop him off. We pull into the players' lot at the stadium, and he's smiling.

"You'll be at the game, right?"

I nod. "Of course."

"Great. I'll see you there." He kisses me. "I love you, Ella Rose."

"Love you, too."

As soon as the door closes, and Christian walks into the stadium and out of view, I burst into tears. This is not at all what I thought today would be like. I want to call my parents, but they're at church. I want to call Jen, but it's too early in LA. Being a baseball wife can be really lonely, and right now, I'm at my loneliest. I pull myself together enough to drive home safely, but I'm hungry, and I don't want to go back to the apartment to cook anything.

I drive around the city with no actual destination in mind. When I see something I want, I'll stop. However, as I drive, I see families pouring out of church in their Easter Sunday best, laughing, smiling, and taking pictures. They're probably heading to Easter brunch, and I cannot be the party of one eating by herself in the corner.

Cue the waterworks again. It's now 9:30, so my options are limited, but then I see it. Like a black, white, and red beacon in the distance.

Steak 'n' Shake.

Yeah, not a traditional breakfast, but that doesn't even matter. Nothing does. Not right now. Traditional doesn't exist in my world. Not in my career, my marriage, none of it.

I pull up to that drive-thru and order the most ridiculous thing I can even imagine for breakfast: a Chili 5-way, French fries, and a cookies-and-cream milkshake. I can't even make eye contact with the cashier because I'm a mess, and I'm sure I'll see pity in her eyes. Instead, I pay, grab my food, and then pull over to the edge of the parking lot.

And eat the saddest Easter Sunday breakfast ever.

I'm crying so hard between bites of spaghetti, chili, cheese, fries, and gulps of my shake that I'm thankful no one can see me.

Or maybe they can. My vision's blurry, so I can't tell.

"This is not what I signed up for!" I cry. "Why can't anything just be normal? Why can't we just have a regular life?"

More sobbing, more eating.

I don't know why this is the thing that breaks me, but it does. The thing is it *is* what I signed up for. Christian was always honest with me about it. It's my own fault for thinking I could handle it.

There's a good chance that I'm overly emotional after getting fired from *Workin' for Laughs*, but right now, I'm going to blame my meltdown on not being able to go to Easter brunch. I'll be much calmer and reasonable later when I get to the stadium, but for now, I'm going to eat this super-sized mistake with extra cheese.

I'll deal with the fallout later.

As I'm eating, I realize I really should have stayed home, made some tea, and enjoyed a pit--tea party in my pajamas.

"There's still time for that," I murmur around a mouthful of fries.

Something's got to give. Clearly, I was a ticking time bomb that just detonated. I don't like feeling like this. And as much as I know I'll be better when it's time for the game, it's not. Not really. I'm friendly with the wives, but I'm close to no one…

Ugh.

Same song, different verse.

Yeah. Something's gotta change.

Thirteen

I manage to survive what will forever be known as The Worst Easter Ever.

But I don't tell Christian how I feel.

Why?

Because he's so darn happy.

So, I push my feelings down and chalk it up as a lesson learned. I now know I need to set more realistic expectations for plans during the season.

It also helps when my agent calls the next day to tell me about a fabulous opportunity.

"Ella, how fast can you get back to LA?"

"Um…that depends. Why?"

"Something interesting just came across my desk that I think you would be perfect for," she says. "I know you've been wanting to do voice-over work, and this might be your shot."

She's right. Most of my work has been on camera, but voice-over work has been very elusive. I've gotten close several times, but I've never booked a job.

"How exciting! What's the role?"

She doesn't respond right away. "I don't have all the details in front of me at the moment, but I would love to talk to you about it in person. So, how soon can you be back here?"

"Tracy, come on," I say with amusement. "You have to know a *little* something about the role. I don't want to waste your time or mine if it's not something I want to do."

Another pause. "Let's just say this is something you're going to want to do, but no one knows about it yet. So, legally, my hands are tied. I can't say what it is." Then she laughs. "That sounded dramatic, right? Oh, my goodness. What I mean is, the showrunner isn't giving out many details. It's very hush-hush. But that tells me it has the potential to be huge!"

Okay, now I'm getting excited.

"I can be there by the end of the week. I can't wait to tell Christian."

"Oh. Oh, no, Ella. You can't."

"I can't?"

"I mean, you can tell him you're going to audition for a voice-over role, but other than that, you can't talk about this."

I'm not excited anymore.

"Tracy…"

"You have to trust me on this. Come to LA, and we'll talk. I've also got a few other auditions lined up, so even if the voice-over thing doesn't work out, it won't be a wasted trip, okay?"

My curiosity is wildly piqued, so I reluctantly agree.

"I'll see you Friday," I tell her. As soon as I hang up, I realize the timing couldn't be better.

It's not that I'm happy to leave St. Louis—and Christian—especially after crying about how much we needed more time together, but I'm looking forward to having part of my life back.

One that comes with a regular schedule and only one dinner per day.

"I hate that you're leaving already," he says a few days later as we're getting ready for bed. He had a game today, so we ate a late dinner, and now, it's time to relax with a little TV. "I feel like we haven't had much time together."

You're not wrong…

Obviously, I don't say that, but I do think it.

"I know, but my agent got me this audition for some voice-over work. She's being super secretive about it, but no matter how much I ask, she won't tell me what it's for."

"That's strange, isn't it? I mean, how can you prepare if you don't know what the part is?"

"It's one of the reasons I'm heading back early. The audition isn't until next week. It's super top secret, and she can only share the details and the script with me in person."

He frowns. "I don't like the sound of this. What if you fly all the way back there and it's something weird or crude that you don't want to do?"

I laugh softly. "I think we both know I wouldn't take a role like that. Not after the way things went down with my last stint."

He pulls me into his embrace. "It wasn't all bad."

Hugging him back, I agree. "It wasn't. But it definitely wasn't what I thought it would be." When I pull back, I smile. "Now I know the questions to ask so that it never happens again. Besides, I feel like I'm due for something good—a good role. And if it's not the voice-over one, maybe it'll be on one of the other auditions."

"It's gonna happen, Ella Rose. I know it. You're far too talented."

"Thank you. I need to record you saying that and play it on repeat before my auditions. You are my ultimate hype friend."

We crawl into bed and get comfortable. His arm slips around me, and my head fits against his shoulder like it was always meant to be there. I love moments like this—the simple ones, where nothing is required of us beyond being close. His warmth seeps into me, our legs tangled beneath the covers, familiar and reassuring. I trace idle patterns on his chest, memorizing the feel of him, the steady rise and fall of his breathing.

I wish these precious moments were all my heart needed. I wish I didn't yearn for anything else. At this point in my life, I'm very happy, but sadly, the truth is that I know I'll be happier if I can get my career back on track.

And it really hasn't gone off the rails, I know that. I know I'm being hard on myself. But that's why I need to go and see Tracy and have the auditions. I know I'll feel better about myself, and I'll be able to handle things better when I feel like things in my universe are a little more under control.

He kisses the top of my head, and I hum softly.

This is good.

Things are going to turn around for me, and then I can be a better wife and a happier woman.

I'm claiming it.

I just hope this voice-over thing isn't something strange.

I get back to LA, and Tracy tells me that the audition is for a new *Galactic Wars* animated TV show.

Um… *WHAT?*

Galactic Wars is one of the biggest movie franchises in history, but I thought they had wrapped up the whole saga. Six movies, that was it. Now, they are making an animated show? This is going to be huge! I want this so badly, but everything is so top secret, and none of the lines even make sense. It's all very generic, and there is only a brief description of the character. It's really hard to prepare.

After sitting in a lobby, waiting to audition with all the top voice-over actresses in LA, it's finally my turn. I get settled in the studio and say my first line, "You don't have to carry a sword to be powerful. Some leaders' strength is inspiring greatness in others."

"Okay, that's good, Ella. But we need more of an accent. Can you try something different?"

"What kind of accent?"

"We'd like an Icelandic accent," the casting director says.

So, I try to say the line with an Icelandic accent, and I know immediately that he doesn't like it. The audition is taking place in a studio. I'm in a small recording booth with padded walls for sound, a microphone, and a large panel of glass. On the other side of that window are ten people, all gathered in the studio just watching and listening to me. Intimidating much? Yes, very! After I say my line, I see a collective frown.

"We're going to give you some new lines. Can you try it again?"

"Of course," Internally, I'm panicking because I have no idea what an Icelandic accent even sounds like, and I'm just guessing. I don't even have time to practice the new lines. I have to read them cold, in an Icelandic accent, for a group of strangers I really want to impress. This audition is *not* going well, and I can feel myself spiraling. I try my best.

"Welcome to the *Galactic Wars*."

I see all their heads drop and shake again. I don't think I have ever bombed an audition so badly.

"Try it one more time. This time with more of an Icelandic accent," says the casting director.

I don't even know what accent comes out of my mouth, but it definitely isn't Icelandic. It seems to be a mix of Russian and Irish. Now, I'm completely sweating, my heart is pounding, and I'm beyond frustrated because I can feel this opportunity being ripped away. And I want it *so* badly! I don't know what comes over me, but all of a sudden, I raise my hand on the other side of the glass in the recording studio, and the words fly out of my mouth. "I'm sorry, but I don't know what you want. However, I *do* know that I really want this role, and if you give me the chance, I promise I won't let you down."

"Oh, my gosh…that's it," the casting director says. "What you just said? That tone? That's the voice."

I hold my breath, waiting to see if everyone agrees.

I don't want to point out that I started with my own voice, and they kept directing me away from it.

"You had a little more of a snippy tone, and it works," says the casting director. "It's perfect. Can you read the rest of the scene?"

So, I do, and while I don't fully understand the world this character is set in, I do my best to focus on my voice and not on anything else. By the time I'm done, I'm left facing ten sets of eyes, all of which are staring at me in awe.

I nailed it.

I *know* I nailed it.

I only need them to *tell me* I nailed it.

They all exchange looks before the casting director speaks. "Ella, that was perfect. It's exactly what we were hoping for. You truly embodied the character. Of course, we do have a few more actors to meet with. Thank you so much for your time. We'll be in touch."

I tell everyone thanks before leaving, and I have to admit, I am wildly curious about who this character is and which part of the franchise they'll be added to.

I leave feeling confident, but it's not like I know the part is mine. Now, I wait and hope and pray that I get a callback.

I call Tracy as soon as I get in the car.

"But they loved you, right? They sounded positive?" she asks after

I tell her how it went.

"They seemed interested, but they have more actors to audition, so…"

"Typical, but I wish these casting people would just go with their gut for once. From everything you just described, you tried multiple accents until you found the one they liked. Why wait? Why go through the process of other interviews when they found the voice?"

I love how outraged she is on my behalf.

"Okay, now that that's done, are you ready for more auditions? I have a few single-episode roles, four commercials, another ensemble sketch comedy…"

The groan is out before I can stop it.

"Ella, don't let what went down on *Workin' for Laughs* make you jaded. Besides, they got canceled. So, if you ask me, they got what they deserved for being so closed-minded."

I don't want to be happy about it, but I am.

"I'm sure they'll all bounce back," I murmur.

"And so will you." She pauses. "So? How long do I have you for? Do you need to rush back to St. Louis?"

"No." It's out of my mouth, and I gasp with shock. "I mean…I can stay if you need me."

"Mm-hmm…"

"What? Why are you making it sound like…?"

"Like what?" she says coyly.

The last thing I want is for anyone to speculate about my personal life. Tracy and I have known each other for years, so I don't have a problem speaking frankly with her.

"Look, Christian is having an amazing season, and it's really important for me to balance everything. Being there for Christian, being an actress, managing our lives. I'm going to make it all work. Just let me know when I need to be in LA, and I'll be here."

And that is the absolute truth.

"But…?"

My shoulders sag. "But I'm going a little crazy, okay? Like…I know getting fired from *Workin' for Laughs* was truly a blessing, but *That's So High School* is ending, and I'm feeling a little lost."

"And I totally get that, and we're working on stuff for you." Another pause. "I just need to know that you're okay and happy."

I hesitate. "I'm…okay," I finally say. "And I know I'll be happier once I feel a little more settled in my career again."

Luckily, she doesn't push for more. I'm not about to burden her with my tales of woe—about how I'm not close with any of the other WAGs, how quietly depressing Easter was, or how being a baseball wife isn't nearly as glamorous as people think. Mostly, I don't want to admit how lonely it's been.

I'm not someone who likes to complain.

And I don't want to.

That's not the person I was raised to be.

I know I've been incredibly blessed. I've had opportunities that many others haven't. So, if being a little lonely—or a lot—is what I have to deal with right now, I should be able to handle it. Plus, I know it's temporary. I only have to get through the season.

And the next.

And the one after that.

There's no retirement strategy for athletes. You play until you can't. In the grand scheme of life, the period of time that an athlete can play in the major leagues is short. It's a moment in time that won't last forever.

But if I could have an acting role during baseball season, I'd probably feel a lot better than I do right now.

Ugh, I sound so ungrateful.

"Come by the office, Ella," Tracy says, interrupting my thoughts. "We'll talk strategy to get you out there more."

It's on the tip of my tongue to clarify that I am a very happy person who doesn't need to be coddled, but I don't.

Right now, maybe a little coddling would be a good thing.

I land a few single-episode roles and read for a major motion picture while in LA. Spending time with Jen, Penny, Freya, and Will feeds my soul in a way I can't even describe. I had hoped to hear about the *Galactic Wars* role before heading back to St. Louis, but I don't.

"Don't fret about it," Tracy tells me. I'm on my way to the airport and just touching base with her one last time before I go. "I've been in contact with them, and they're still auditioning people."

I don't take that as a good sign.

"Oh."

"Ella, I'm telling you, it's all happening like it should. Just because it's taking longer than we thought doesn't mean it's a bad thing. Now, go back to St. Louis and cheer on your husband. It looks like he's having an incredible season."

He truly is.

And it isn't just Christian, the Archers are having an amazing season so far, too. And maybe I'm biased, but I know my husband is a big part of that. His stats have never been better, and all the analytics prove it, even though he doesn't know it because he doesn't pay attention to any of that during the season. It breaks his focus and routine.

"I'll be back next month to film my last episode of *That's So High School*." I sigh. Tiffy was such a fun character to play, and I know I'll miss her.

"And hopefully we'll hear back about *Galactic Wars* by then."

I don't want to get my hopes up, but I *really* want the part.

How cool would it be to be a character in that universe? I've been a fan since I was a little girl.

"Safe travels, and go Archers!" she says before hanging up.

When I arrive at the airport, I quickly text Christian to confirm that my flight is on time. He's got the night off, so he'll be the one picking me up. I can't wait to see him. I think this time away really refueled me.

But I don't want it to become necessary.

What if this pattern—only spending a few weeks together at a time—becomes the only way for us to survive?

Us, or *me*?

Ugh.

No. I refuse to accept that.

As I sit at the gate, I decide to call him. I know I just texted him a few minutes ago, but I really want to hear his voice.

"Hey," he says in answer. "Don't tell me your flight got delayed."

"What? No. I'm just sitting at the gate and thinking about you. I wanted to call and hear your voice."

"I know the feeling. I always look forward to hearing yours. Especially when you're not here, and a phone call is all we have."

"How'd the game go today?"

"It went okay."

The man never gives himself the credit he deserves. He's one of the hardest-working athletes in the entire league, and I wish he knew just how impressive he is.

"What's on the schedule for tomorrow?"

"Well, I thought after we have breakfast together—I went grocery shopping and got all the ingredients for pancakes—we could spend the day relaxing, just the two of us."

"Really?" I already knew there wasn't a game on the calendar for tomorrow, which is why I chose to fly back to St. Louis.

"Yup. Ask me why?"

I laugh softly. "Okay, why?"

"Because I miss you, Ella Rose. I hate it when we're apart. I know it's necessary, and we knew things would be like this, but I really want us to have a day with nothing to do except be together."

Aww…

"That sounds perfect. I missed you, too."

"Plus, I'd love for us to look at your calendar and see what you have going on next week."

"Next week? Um…how come?"

"I'd like you to come with me to Pittsburgh," he says, like it's obvious.

My first thought is that I wish he were asking me to go somewhere romantic or tropical. But I guess Pittsburgh is fine, too.

"Oh, uh…why? What's in Pittsburgh?"

"I got voted into the All-Star Game. So, naturally, I'd love to have my wife and family with me."

"Christian!" I say far too loudly, making everyone around me stare. "That's amazing! I'm so proud of you!"

"Thanks. It is pretty exciting."

I roll my eyes with amusement because only my husband could be this low-key about such an honor.

"It doesn't matter what's on my calendar. I will be right there with you in Pittsburgh, cheering you on. There's nothing more important than that."

"But what if you get a call for an audition? Or you're filming? Or…?"

"It will all have to wait. I wouldn't miss seeing you play in the All-Star Game for anything. I love you."

"Love you, too, Ella Rose. I can't wait to see you tonight."

"Mmm…I can't wait to see you either. Soon. I'll be home soon."

We talk for a few more minutes, and when we hang up, I go and grab myself a snack and a magazine. It won't be an excessively long travel day, but it's certainly not a short one either. So, I settle back into a seat at the gate and get comfortable again.

Only…I'm not.

I'm a little twitchy, and even though my conversation with Christian was all good, I've still got this…I don't know, a niggling of something I can't quite put my finger on in the back of my head. If I had to describe it, I'd say it's like a feeling of impending doom, and I don't like it. But I don't know if it's about me and my career, Christian's, or something about our families.

His dad is still waiting for his transplant. Even though he has a donor, his health hasn't been great, and the doctors need him to get stronger before they do the surgery. So, maybe that's on my mind?

Sighing, I pull out my phone and call my mom. Maybe she could distract me and put my mind at ease.

"Hey, there's my sunshine."

I love my mom's greetings. They always make me smile.

"Hey, how are you? How's Dad?"

"We're all fine. Where are you calling from? I thought you were flying back to St. Louis today."

"I'm at the airport, and boarding doesn't start for another thirty minutes. I was restless, so I thought I'd call and say hi. So…hi!"

She laughs. "You know I always love to talk to you. How are you doing? How did the rest of your auditions go?"

"They were fine. Nothing new to report. Now, we play the waiting game to see if I book anything."

"You just have to keep moving forward, Ella. Your father and I are so proud of you."

"Thanks, Mom." No matter how old I get, I will always appreciate my parents' praise.

"And how's Christian? Your father said his game the other night was one of his best."

"He got voted into the All-Star Game this year. I'm so happy for him."

"Oh, my goodness! That's incredible. Tell him we're proud of him, too."

Smiling, I nod again. "I will."

"I know you weren't thrilled with this move at first, but it seems like this was the right one for his career."

"It really has been. He's having a great season, and he's so…, he's just so deep in baseball mode. He's so focused, and he never lets his foot off the gas. He just keeps pushing himself harder and harder."

"We all felt that way about your acting career. When you were growing up, you were so fixated on learning everything you could—the singing, dancing, and acting lessons—you never really just let yourself be a kid. You know, the two of you are both intensely driven. That's why you're a perfect fit for each other."

I know this, but I guess I never considered how my drive looked to other people. Christian and I have talked about it, but not quite to this extent.

"Did you ever think I was wasting my time or…?"

"Nope. You were passionate and so determined," she says. "And you were naturally talented. If you were doing all those things and didn't have any talent, your father and I probably would have found a way to point you toward something else. But you put your heart into everything, and that's what Christian's done, too. He's a gifted athlete, and right now, this is his moment." She pauses. "And it's important that you're there to support him. Because you know he would do the same for you."

When I don't respond to that right away, she continues.

"That's one of the things that's been so impressive about the two of you. The balance. You spend so much time apart because of your careers, but you make it work. Everyone who knows you can see how you support each other. I love that you've found someone who gets you. And clearly, Christian does."

Now, I'm speechless. The sigh that slips out is the kind only a mom would notice.

"What's going on, Ella?" I hear the concern in her voice, and I'm not even sure how to put what I feel into words. There are things I obviously wouldn't and didn't share with Tracy, but this is my mother. Shouldn't I be able to talk to her about how I feel without fear of judgment?

When she repeats my name, I know I have to say something.

"Lately, I've been feeling like…like I can't keep that balance. I'm trying so hard to hold it all together, but it's like I'm walking on a balance beam and keep falling off. Am I selfish for still trying to have my acting career? Is that hindering our marriage?"

"Oh, sweetie, why would you even think that?"

Tears sting my eyes, and I huddle in a corner by the gate, trying to hide. "Because I couldn't wait to leave St. Louis and come to LA," I say miserably. "Easter was awful, I'm exhausted from trying to keep up with Christian's schedule and routines, and…and eating two dinners, and…"

"Wait, wait, wait…two dinners? Why on earth would you eat two dinners?" I can tell she's mildly amused and curious.

So, I explain the home-game schedules, and how I eat at the stadium because it's dinner time and I'm hungry, but then we get home, and I make dinner for Christian because he's hungry.

"I don't want him to eat alone, and I feel weird having something small after I've made him a complete dinner. Plus, with all the work it takes to make the meals he specifically enjoys using only the brands he explicitly eats, I'm not about to let any of it go to waste."

"Hmm."

"That's it? Just…hmm?"

"I'm not exactly sure what you want me to say. We all have our quirks, schedules, routines, and what have you. And while, yes, Christian's seem to require a little more work and understanding, they're not so wild that they're ruining your life." She pauses to laugh a little. "But I don't think this was really the issue you were talking about. You're upset because you were excited to leave St. Louis."

"Yup."

"To be fair, you were having your own personal crisis and were trying not to burden your husband with it."

"Exactly. He's having such a great season that I don't want to bring him down or break his focus."

"And I get that, but…you're wrong."

"Excuse me?"

"You're wrong, Ella. If you don't tell Christian what is going on and what you're feeling, then you're essentially lying to him. The man is walking around thinking you guys are living a fairy tale, when the reality is, you're not. You're miserable, and he has no idea."

"Okay, but to be fair, *he's* not making me miserable. I love Christian more than I ever thought a person could love someone. Our relationship is strong, but…"

"The careers are the issue."

"Exactly. Am I crazy to even be entertaining the possibility of taking on a role that has the potential to be long-term?"

"Don't you think he deserves to know? Or have a say in it?"

"I do, but…just not right now. I need to figure this out on my own. What if I talk to him and it stresses him out, and he starts playing badly? That would totally be my fault, and I am not going to be the reason Christian breaks his streak or goes into a slump. I need to be a supportive wife and keep everything running smoothly for him."

"Sunshine, you can have both," she gently reminds me. "It shouldn't be that you're only happy and supporting him when things are going great for you. Marriage is twenty-four-seven. Not just on the good days, you need to be all-in, even on the bad ones."

"I am, but sometimes…it's lonely. And…well, lately? It just feels overwhelming. We were planning this amazing life, and so far, it's been a lot harder than I imagined."

"Oh, darling, marriage is hard. And these hard times will make the two of you stronger, as long as you lean on each other. When your father and I moved to Florida, we had three kids under the age of four. Your dad worked two jobs, and he was barely ever home. I was a young mother with a newborn, two toddlers, and no help. I always felt overwhelmed and off balance, but we made it through. You kids turned out pretty darn great, and your father and I are still happily married. But we made it through because we're a team."

Wow, no one can drop a truth bomb like my mom.

"But not telling your husband how you feel is wrong. I get that you don't want to distract him because he's in baseball mode, but just like you're having to learn how to be a wife to a baseball player, he needs to learn how to be a husband to an actress. Again, marriage is twenty-four-seven. It doesn't have a season."

Dang it. She's right.

The announcement comes over the intercom that my flight is boarding shortly, so I need to get ready.

"That's the call for my flight, Mom. I love you. Thank you for the advice and for listening to me."

"Always, sweet girl. Always."

"I love you."

"Love you, too. Have a safe flight and give Christian our best."

"I will. I'll text you when I land."

"That's my girl."

We say our goodbyes, and then I'm standing, stretching, and gathering up my stuff. I'm a pro at traveling now. I almost never have to check a bag, and I carry only the necessities in my carry-on. Still, I've got my snacks and magazines, and I'm good to go home.

Home.

I guess I'm starting to look at St. Louis as home. Christian's contract is for three years, and who knows where we'll go from there?

Suddenly, I realize I don't know either. It hits me that I'm almost afraid to think in terms of where I want us to be because it can all change at a moment's notice.

Will they extend his contract? Will he get traded somewhere else? Do I have a preference?

Nope.

At least not one I'm allowing myself to entertain. There's no need for me to get my hopes up.

But no matter where the future takes us, I see myself with Christian.

I just hope I find the right time and the courage to talk to him about all the things I'm struggling with.

Fourteen

Christian picks me up at the airport, and he looks tired. Like more tired than I've ever seen him. I didn't notice it when I got into the car because it was dark out, but once we step into our apartment and I really take a good look at him, I know something's wrong.

"Are you okay?" I ask, my hands gently caressing his face, my heart filled with concern.

"What? Yeah. I'm good. I've just got a headache."

Two days ago, he played a game in Philly, and as he was sliding into second base, the second baseman's knee accidentally smashed him in the head, hitting him hard on the right temple. I didn't see the game, but he told me about it when we spoke that night.

"Do you think it's from the game the other night? Have you gone to the doctor?"

He waves me off. "It's fine. Nothing a good night's sleep with my beautiful wife next to me can't cure. You know I sleep better when you're here with me."

He's a sweet-talker, but I know a distraction when I hear one.

Probably because I've been doing the same thing for a while.

Still, this is serious. A head injury shouldn't be taken lightly.

"Christian, I really think you need to see a doctor. Or at least talk to the trainers."

He gives me a patient smile. "Ella Rose, I know my body, and I'm fine. Trust me." He kisses me softly before carrying my suitcase into the bedroom. Naturally, I follow, but I'm watching him like a hawk.

And not just because I find him incredibly attractive and we haven't seen each other in a few weeks.

It's late, and we're both ready to crawl into bed and watch some TV. I want to do nothing but relax, I'm not sure I can. If this is a concussion, he shouldn't be sleeping, right? I think I need to wake him up every few hours. But he hit his head two days ago, and he's obviously slept through the night since then. So, maybe he *is* okay.

Ugh…I really wish I knew more about sports injuries.

As if reading my mind, he gently murmurs, "Relax, beautiful girl. I'm fine." He holds me a little closer, kissing me all over as he talks.

I love it when he does that. Love how safe, secure, and loved I feel in his powerful arms. It's the best place in the world to be.

"I missed you. Missed this," he murmurs gruffly, and that voice… it makes everything better.

"Me, too."

We settle in with the TV on, and after a few minutes, we shift a little to get more comfortable. His arm curves around me until my back fits perfectly against his chest, and I love how easily our bodies find each other now, how my legs slip between his and stay there, warm and certain. I breathe him in and close my eyes, grateful for this moment, for the way he holds me without thinking, for the quiet intimacy of being here together after so much time apart. No words—only the comfort of his body against mine and the simple, overwhelming relief of having him close.

I find his hand and hold it close to my heart, and that's how we fall asleep.

The next morning, Christian leaves for the field, but he's back a lot sooner than usual.

"I have a concussion," he says miserably, tossing his hat onto the sofa, his frustration palpable. "I'm off for the next three days."

"You need to see a doctor," I say firmly, almost hating that I was right.

"I saw the team doctor. He's the one who diagnosed me." He collapses next to his hat, raking a hand through his hair, leaving it all askew.

"Okay, but maybe you should see a specialist." I sit beside him, smoothing his hair back into place. I can't help myself. I want to comfort him, soothe him.

"No, I'm okay."

It's his standard response, but I'm not buying it. Unfortunately, he is beyond stubborn, and as soon as those three days are over, he goes right back to the stadium and plays.

I am beyond frustrated because I can see that he still isn't feeling well, but the man will not listen to anyone. He is determined to play, and that is all there is to it.

And as if that weren't enough, the night before we're set to leave and fly out for the All-Star Game, Christian's dad collapses. He is literally only a month away from the transplant, but a complication with his kidney dialysis caused his lungs to fill with fluid.

"Do we need to fly to Florida?" I ask. Because this seems like something we should all be there for.

"No. My dad would hate it if I missed the All-Star Game." He keeps in constant contact with his siblings until we get on the plane and is back on the phone with them as soon as we land. Fortunately, the doctors got him stabilized, but it is still terrifying how close the poor man is to death.

My husband is like a rock, however. He is as cool and calm as can be, and I honestly don't know how he does it. If it was my dad, I would be an absolute mess and flying home, no matter what.

But I have to remind myself how this is just part of life when you live with chronic kidney disease. The Lucases have learned to become very matter-of-fact about it. And it's not a bad thing; it's just different for me.

In Pittsburgh, we barely have time to check into our hotel before we need to head out for the red-carpet event to kick off the weekend. We're all smiles and excitement—even more so when Christian's brother, sister, and brother-in-law show up. It's like a mini family reunion. No one would ever guess we'd just dealt with a life-or-death family crisis.

Again.

The American League beats the National League in the All-Star Game the next day, but we still have a great time. Plus, I love having family in the stands with me, so I don't feel so alone. It isn't like a regular game. The two teams are comprised of the top players from all the different teams, so I barely know any of the other WAGs. Still, everyone I met is super nice.

We head back to St. Louis, and with all the excitement of the weekend over, I notice that Christian's still not quite himself. I don't know how much longer I can let him pretend that he's fine.

The reality is that he's not playing like he used to. He's making mistakes and missing plays that should be easy for him. I try not to harp on it, but I'm not quiet, either. His game is changing. His thoughts and reactions are slow, and he's striking out constantly. Christian never strikes out. He has excellent vision and can make contact with the baseball no matter where the pitcher throws it—it's what he's known for. Now, the balls are flying past him, and his bat isn't even coming close. But the scariest part is that his memory isn't the same. Christian has always had a photographic memory. He can recount each game, pitch by pitch, with exact detail. But now, his memories aren't as sharp. They're even fuzzy at times.

"Christian, this has to do with the concussion," I state, hating that things have gotten to this point. "We need to get you to a specialist. You can't keep going like this. All of these symptoms have to do with that injury."

With his ever-patient smile, he replies, "I'm fine. Every day, I feel a little better."

But it's a lie. He's getting worse each day, and he's completely in denial about it. I understand being passionate about the game and your career, but to what end? Is it worth dying for? Because that's all I can think about. That something more traumatic than anyone realizes has happened to his brain.

Needless to say, I'm terrified, and I can't understand why no one is doing anything about it. Like...how can his coaches and trainers keep letting him play? How can I make them listen?

As luck would have it, someone finally—*finally!*—realizes it isn't going away.

Christian comes home from a Sunday-afternoon game looking incredibly defeated. I was at the game, and it was impossible to overlook how poorly he played. I would never say that to him. I always try to be positive, but it was getting harder and harder to find the right words.

"Hey," I begin cautiously. "Is everything okay?"

"The trainers brought me into the office after the game," he begins miserably, tossing his hat onto the sofa again. "They said they think I have post-concussion syndrome."

I do my best to keep my expression neutral. "And what did you say?"

"What *could* I say? I told them, I don't think, I *know*." Raking a hand through his short hair, he lets out a ragged breath. "You've been saying it for weeks, but I didn't want to believe it." He collapses onto the couch, his head thrown back.

I'm immediately beside him. "So, what happens now?"

He looks tortured, his blue eyes dull and without their usual sparkle. "Now, I don't get to leave with the team for Cincinnati for our next game. I have to stay here and see our team's eye specialist tomorrow. Take some sort of an exam." Another sigh. "I hate this. I can't believe this is happening."

It would be wrong not to point out that injuries are common in sports, and that he's had them before—and will, more than likely, have them again.

Or the fact that this was inevitable, considering how long it has been going on.

Instead, I take one of his hands in mine and place a soft kiss on his palm. "Now that we know this is something, we'll get you the help you need. Head injuries really need to be taken seriously, Christian."

He glances at me only briefly before carefully pulling his hand from mine. "Is that your way of saying I told you so?"

"What? No! That's not what I'm saying at all. All I've wanted all this time is for you to be okay and to give yourself time to heal. I worry about you. Don't you get that?"

"What you don't get is how bad it is to be on the injured list. The Archers are having a great season, and I don't want to miss out on any of it."

It's on the tip of my tongue to remind him, again, that if he had taken the time off right after he hit his head, he might not have to *be* on the injured list again.

But I keep that commentary to myself.

Hopefully, we'll get proof tomorrow that he needs to take this seriously, and he'll stop playing until he's fully healed.

I can tell he's upset and that talking about this won't help, so I do the only thing I can. "Are you hungry? I made your favorite—fried chicken, Southern-style green beans, mashed potatoes, and those dinner rolls you like. They're in the oven right now."

Turning his head, he gives me a weak smile. "I'm sorry, Ella Rose." His voice is soft, barely a whisper.

"For what?"

"I'm sure you think I'm just being stubborn, and I know I've been in a surly mood. I don't mean to be. I'm sorry I snapped at you. I'm just frustrated with the situation. But that doesn't give me the right to take it out on you." He picks up my hand and mimics my earlier move, kissing my palm. "I love you."

I caress his jaw with my free hand. "I love you, too." He tugs me in close, his arms going around me, and we stay like that for several minutes until the oven timer goes off. Lifting my head, I smile. "Let's eat."

We spend the rest of the evening pretending everything's normal. I have a lot of anxiety about his appointment tomorrow and what they'll find. I'm supposed to fly back to LA next week for an audition, but if the doctor finds something seriously wrong, I'm not going anywhere.

Just breathe…

I'm already expecting them to find something, I just don't know how serious it will be.

The eye doctor clears him to join the team in Cincinnati.

Their big test for post-concussion syndrome? A standard eye exam—reading letters, checking depth perception, and asking him a few questions, which I'm pretty sure he did *not* answer truthfully. I can tell he doesn't feel well. He's pale and wincing, and I know he's in pain, but did he tell the doctor that? No.

We leave the office, head home, and then I'm driving him to the airport so he can play with the Archers tomorrow.

I'm absolutely heartbroken.

"Please, don't do this," I beg as we head to the airport, my voice cracking.

"You heard the doctor, Ella Rose. I'm fine."

"Pfft. That wasn't an accurate exam," I say, my frustration making my voice rise. "That was a standard eye exam, Christian. You need to be seen by a specialist."

He pats my hand. I'm sure he doesn't mean for it to be condescending, but that's how I take it. My head is ready to explode.

"I would think you'd be happy they didn't find anything. That means you can stop worrying."

"How could they find anything when they barely did an exam?" And yeah, I'm heavy on the sarcasm.

"Please, don't be upset. I've got this under control, okay? It's going to be—"

"Fine. Yeah. Got it. You've said it enough times that I'm sure you believe it. But I don't. And you know what? I don't have to. You may not want to take this seriously, but I do."

"I *am* taking it seriously," he counters calmly. "I take my career very seriously."

"Mm-hmm…"

"Ella Rose…"

"Look, we'll just have to agree to disagree right now." I'm taking the exit for the airport, and there's no point in continuing the argument. I don't want to send him off angry, and personally, I don't want to be angry either. So, we drive to the terminal in silence. When I pull up to the curb and put the car in park, I do my best to compose myself.

"I'll text you when I land," he says before leaning over and kissing me.

I want to clutch him close and beg him not to go, but it won't matter. I know it, and I hate it.

"Have a safe flight. I'll talk to you tonight when you're back at the hotel." I kiss him again, but neither of us lingers. He gives me a lopsided grin as he gets out of the car. Once the door is shut, he turns and waves, and I watch him walk into the airport. Neither of us ever pulls away until the other is out of sight.

The airport doors close, and I force myself to look away.

I cry the entire way home.

Four days later, I'm back at the airport to pick Christian up. Not because he was due to come home, but because he's injured, and everyone's taking it seriously.

Finally.

I'm a nervous wreck, but that's nothing new. I've been living on pins and needles and walking on eggshells ever since he got the concussion. But this is a fresh injury, and he needs an MRI. As soon as he walks out of the airport, I nearly burst into tears. He's walking slowly, like every step is agony, and I don't know how to help him. I don't want to jump out of the car, take his bags, and risk embarrassing him or hurting his pride, so I wait for him to join me so I can look him in the eyes and tell him it's all going to be okay.

But I don't know whether I believe it.

Christian gingerly gets into the car, and I can tell it even hurts for him to smile. "Hey, beautiful. Thanks for picking me up."

I don't wait for him to lean over to kiss me; I'm the one moving. I kiss him, hold his face, and will myself not to become a big, weepy mess. Resting my forehead against his, I let out a shaky breath. "It's going to be okay," I whisper.

"I don't know," he says quietly. It's the first time he's ever sounded less than confident. "I just don't know, Ella Rose."

I kiss him softly before straightening in my seat. "Let's get you to the doctor." The trainers already made arrangements for him to get the MRI as soon as he got back to St. Louis, and I'm beyond relieved that they're finally doing something that may actually help my husband.

As I pull away from the curb, I glance over and see that his eyes are closed, his head fully back against the cushion, his baseball hat slightly askew. As much as I want to talk to him, because it's one of my favorite things to do, I don't want to disturb him. He needs the rest.

He's needed it since the concussion.

Ugh…stop harping on it.

Besides, I already know what happened. Yesterday, the Archers were playing in Chicago, and during a play that had Christian sliding into home plate, he collided with the catcher. His body bent at an unnatural angle, and the trainers think he did some damage to his oblique muscles. So, essentially, an entire side of his torso. They pulled him from the game and taped his whole midsection to stabilize it, but even without knowing about the play, anyone with eyes can tell he is in pain.

So, I drive in silence. By the time we reach the medical complex, I can tell he's asleep.

"Christian?" I say softly. "We're here." I place my hand on his thigh and squeeze it gently. Fortunately, he wakes up right away.

"Let's get this over with."

I get out and race around the car because now I don't care what anyone sees or thinks. My husband is in pain, and I'm going to help him, even if he doesn't think he needs it.

But he leans on me and lets me support him. We awkwardly make our way inside, and they take him back immediately.

Now, all I can do is wait.

Guess who's back on the injured list and has to stay there for four weeks?

I don't do a victory dance or say, "I told you so," but for the first time in ages, I finally feel like I can breathe.

Christian completely detached his oblique from his ribs. I don't know how he could stand the pain from it, but the only way for him to heal is to rest and do absolutely nothing for a month.

And guess what the best way to heal from post-concussion syndrome is?

Four weeks of doing nothing except resting.

Relief doesn't even begin to describe how I feel, but I also have to cancel my audition in LA. There's no way I can leave Christian right now. Not because I don't trust him, but because he seriously has to rest, and I don't want him to have to do anything for himself. I want to take care of him and make sure he knows that he's the most important thing in the world to me.

My agent and publicist aren't happy with me for bailing on the audition, but they both know Christian and know how traumatic this last month has been.

"So, what does this mean, Ella? Are you taking the entire month off?" Tracy asks. "Am I supposed to just hit pause on pitching you until Christian's better?"

"I think that's best," I tell her. "We live so far away from our families. There's no one close by who can stay with him."

"But he's not completely helpless. Surely, he'd be okay for a few days. Or you can hire someone to stay with him. Like a home health person or something."

"That's not the point." And yes, I'm a little annoyed at what she's implying. "I've been so worried about him. I need to be here with him for my own peace of mind."

She sighs. "Why don't you call me when he goes back to playing? That way, I'll know when I can start actively looking for roles for you again."

"Thanks, Tracy. I appreciate it."

"I hope so. That movie role could have been amazing for you. It wasn't some low-budget indie deal either. It was with a major studio."

"Then I guess I need to hope they don't find anyone else for the part before I can come back and audition." I say it lightly, but it's the truth. Landing a role in a major motion picture is the dream, but it's not more important than being here for my husband.

Tracy makes a noncommittal sound. "Give Christian my best and wish him a speedy recovery. Hopefully, we'll talk soon. Bye."

I hang up and let out a long breath. A part of me has serious FOMO about the movie and audition. Could I call one of Christian's siblings and ask them to come and stay for a few days so I can go to LA? Sure. But how selfish would that be?

No. My place is here. I'm a good teammate.

A good wife.

I try not to fixate on the fact that to be those things, I'm being a lousy actress. I'm really beginning to believe that finding balance is just a myth.

At least according to Hollywood's standards.

But I'll focus on that later.

For the next four weeks, everything is about getting Christian better. He goes to rehab and has all kinds of therapy—ultrasound treatments for his side, heating, stretching, acupuncture, and anything else needed to stabilize his oblique.

But four weeks turn to five, and he's still not cleared to play. I don't know how to feel about it.

"I don't know how much more of this I can take, Ella Rose," he says after another round of physical therapy. "It's never taken this long for me to get over an injury before. The team's not playing well, and I know I can help them. Something's got to give."

He's pacing, and even though I can tell that he's moving better, he's still not moving as he did before the injuries. His hat's on backward, he's a little unkempt, and it's absolutely not the time to be thinking about how sexy he is, but I can't help myself. His body needs to heal, but I still enjoy checking him out.

"You need to be patient," I say, pushing my wayward thoughts aside. "You need to trust what the therapists are doing so that when they do clear you to play, you know you'll be going back at one hundred percent."

He doesn't look convinced.

"What did they say today? I'm sure you asked about when they think you'll be ready."

When he doesn't look at me, I know something's wrong.

"Christian?"

"They say what they always say. 'These things take time.'" Tossing his hat off, he lets out a huff of frustration. "I'm tired of hearing that. I know my body, and I think I'm ready. I know I'm not one hundred percent, but I still believe I can play and be an asset to my team."

"Um…" I immediately snap my mouth shut. The last thing he needs when he's this worked up is me offering my two cents. Especially when I already know I agree with the therapists.

His head snaps around to look at me, his gaze narrowing. "What? Tell me what you're thinking."

My shoulders sag, and I can feel my face scrunching into a frown. "Okay. You have a history of ignoring the fact that you're injured and then playing through the pain. That's why you're in this position. I get that you're frustrated and hate being on the injured list, but you have got to listen to the professionals. You all dropped the ball with the concussion and look where that got you. So, maybe trust that they're being cautious with you. You're not going to be any good to the team if you go back too soon and end up injured again."

I may as well have slapped his face because the look he gives me is one of utter disbelief.

Without a word, he walks away. His silence is palpable, and maybe he just needs my support right now… Ugh, I feel terrible.

Or…do I?

Coddling him won't help him in the long run. Right now, he needs tough love. He needs someone to tell him no and that he can't have his way.

If only everyone in the Archers organization felt that way…

The next day, they clear Christian to play.

He is elated.

I'm miserable.

I call Tracy the following day when he leaves for the stadium and tell her to put me back on her schedule. She is positively giddy because, as luck would have it, that major motion picture role hasn't been cast.

There is still hope.

I didn't make the call to be spiteful or because I need to get away from my husband for a few days because I am so stinking frustrated with the situation, but I can see how it might look that way to other people.

I just choose not to think about it.

It's just time for life to get back to *normal.* To try to find some balance. And my career needs my attention, too.

Christian is leaving to meet the team in Houston, and I'm leaving for LA. We're both smiling and giddy for our own personal reasons as we kiss goodbye at the airport.

"Break a leg, Ella Rose," he says, and I know he means it. "You've got this. I believe in you." He looks so handsome, and his blue eyes are sparkling again. He's back in his element.

Unable to help myself, I giggle and smooth my hand over his chest. "Please don't break anything while you're gone," I tease before kissing him senseless. When I pull back, he's grinning, so I know he didn't take offense. "Good luck in Houston. But seriously, be careful."

"I will. I promise. I'm feeling good, and I've got this." He caresses my cheek. "Go and knock their socks off in Hollywood. This could be your chance at an Oscar."

I love his faith in me. As we go our separate ways in the terminal, I turn and watch him get swallowed by the crowd.

Please be safe. I love you.

Fifteen

I don't get the major motion picture role, but I land a part in a movie that is filming right in St. Louis.

Talk about fortuitous.

I'll admit that it will be nice to be working so close to home. No living out of a suitcase, and I get to sleep in my own bed every night next to Christian.

When he's not on the road with the Archers, that is.

He's playing, and the team is on the road to the World Series, but since his last series of unfortunate injuries, he's added a pulled hamstring and a strained shoulder to the list.

As much as I want to wrap him in bubble wrap and keep him from further hurting himself, the team is steadily climbing the ranks, and there's no way he'd agree to miss out on being part of the story.

So, I bite my tongue and do my best to be supportive.

Even though his body is literally being held together by tape. He's usually wrapped up from his shoulder to his knee to keep things stable while he's playing. When he gingerly climbs into bed beside me, I can't help but sigh.

"Everything okay?" he asks.

"Can I ask you something?"

He chuckles softly as he tries to get comfortable. "Are we answering questions with questions now?"

"Christian…"

"Okay, okay. Sure. What's up?"

"Is it worth it?"

His brows furrow a bit. "What do you mean? Is what worth it?"

I twist slightly so I can face him fully. "All of…this." I motion to where he's usually all taped up. He doesn't keep it on twenty-four-seven, but I don't know how he stands it. "The injuries, the physical rehab, the constant wear and tear on your body, the pain, the tape…is it worth it?"

He doesn't answer right away, and I know he's truly giving the question some thought.

"For most of my life, I was told I wasn't good enough to be a Major League Baseball player," he says, his voice a little somber and gruff. "I wasn't big enough, I wasn't fast enough, I wasn't strong enough. If I had listened to the critics, I would have missed out on an amazing career."

He picks up my hand and places it on his chest, right over his heart.

"I've never been a quitter. All I need to be is just enough. You may look at all the injuries this season and wonder why I keep going, but I look at them as stumbling blocks. None of them is career-ending."

"The concussion could have been," I whisper, but I'm unable to meet his gaze. I almost feel guilty for saying it out loud.

"But it wasn't. Looking back, yes, I should have taken it more seriously, but I eventually got the rest I needed."

"I know, but…"

"Athletes have a short shelf life, Ella Rose. There will come a time when I can't play the game anymore. But until then, I'm going to give it my all. Every injury, hardship, and bit of life I've missed out on is worth it to me. I'm doing what I love."

I swallow hard and nod because I get it.

Although my career doesn't have me doing things that can cause permanent damage to my body. When I sigh again, Christian squeezes my hand and gazes at me until I look at him.

"I hate that you're this upset again. And I hate knowing I'm the reason for it."

My heart races, because this is the point where I usually back down. The time in the discussion where I accept things for what they are because I don't want to upset him. So, no one's more surprised than me when I blurt out, "And I hate that you're constantly taking unnecessary risks. I hate that you're being reckless for the sake of a game. You say that you hate upsetting me, but you're not willing to do anything about it. For the last several months, I've been a ball of anxiety, tiptoeing around you. And you know what? That's not how I want to live. I have always taken your thoughts into account with every role I take, and I don't feel like you consider me or my feelings at all where your career is concerned."

His expression turns fierce for just a second, but I see it.

"We talked about this years ago," he says after a moment, his voice completely calm. "It's why I said you needed to experience a full baseball season before I proposed. You knew what this life would be like."

"No," I say adamantly, pulling my hand from his. "No, I didn't. It wasn't like this. I never even imagined it would be like this. I understood and came to accept the loneliness. But seeing you in constant pain and not being able to do anything about it wasn't part of anything we discussed."

Now he's annoyed, but so am I.

"There's a difference between being passionate about your career and being stubborn. I have watched you lie to me, your trainers, and yourself. And for what, huh? You're walking around like an eighty-year-old man when you're only thirty-one. You're being held together by athletic tape and lies, Christian. I feel like the only voice of logic."

He doesn't say a word.

"And what's worse is you expecting me to sit here day after day, night after night, while you destroy your body just so no one can say you're a quitter. I'd rather have you retire and know we can live our lives the way we always dreamed instead of the possibility of you being permanently injured because you refused to listen to reason."

"I would never ask you to quit acting," he says quietly. "Even when I haven't agreed with some roles you played, I never asked you not to act. You've worked your whole life with one goal, and you know that, sometimes, the things you have to do aren't ideal. And they're not forever. I thought we were on the same page with that. I will always support you. No matter what."

For a moment, all the wind goes out of my sails. Like…how do I fight back? I'm not asking him to quit playing out of selfishness; I'm simply asking him to think about all the repercussions.

"The difference is, Christian, those roles aren't destroying my body. They're not physically destroying my health and well-being."

That's it. I've put it all out there. There's nothing left for me to say.

My conscience is clear. I spoke my truth out of love.

He may not realize it, but I'm fighting not only for him but also for our marriage. I've lived by the rules he set for us, all centered on baseball. I've been a good teammate. But that's not all there is to our lives. His wants and needs aren't the only ones. I can't be the only one learning how to balance it all.

I know he's not doing it maliciously. Christian is one of the sweetest and kindest human beings on the planet. But when it comes to his career, he's got tunnel vision.

Without a word, he rolls away from me and turns off his bedside light. With nothing left to do, I end up doing the same. It's the first time in our married life that we don't snuggle together while watching TV until we fall asleep. My side of the bed feels vast, empty, and cold.

Maybe I'm wrong, but I can't cave. And I'm not going to apologize for loving him and being concerned about his well-being.

I most certainly won't apologize for speaking from my heart.

I've made sacrifices.

I've missed out on some amazing acting opportunities.

I've moved away from where I wanted our lives to be.

I've sat in uncomfortable social situations for the sake of supporting my husband.

And now I sound selfish, even though I did all those things selflessly.

How's that for irony?

I love my husband. That's never been the issue. But I want him to be around for our future.

I try my best to get comfortable, willing myself not to cry. I'm tired of crying. But more than anything, I'm tired of crying for things that will never change. Am I fighting a losing battle? Or am I being stubborn and holding on to a version of our lives that I created in my head?

I honestly don't know anymore.

As I'm about to drift off to sleep, I feel the mattress dip, and Christian moving in close. One muscular arm comes around me as he places a soft kiss on my cheek.

"I'm sorry, Ella Rose. I'm so sorry," he whispers before settling in behind me.

I don't reply, but I do gently pull his arm more snugly around me.

The apology means a lot, but I know it doesn't mean what I want it to.

He's going to keep playing.

And I'm going to keep worrying.

What happened to our fairy tale?

The Archers are in the World Series. I'm not surprised. They had one heck of a season, and Christian is on the field with them.

Since the night of our confrontation, for lack of a better word, there haven't been any more injuries. At least none that I know about. But I feel like it's only a matter of time before something happens.

Right now, however, we're here in Game 5, and I'm literally on the edge of my seat. If they win this game, the Archers are World Series champions.

Then my phone vibrates in my pocket.

I don't have a choice but to look at it, and I'm surprised when I see Tracy's name on the screen. Feeling completely conflicted, I answer.

"Hey."

"Ella! You're never going to believe this. They want you."

"Who?" I ask distractedly, even as the play on the field gives the Archers a significant lead.

I'm only half-listening to her because there is so much going on around me. All the WAGs and families are on their feet and on the move.

"This is the role of a lifetime, Ella. They need an answer tonight so they can get their shooting schedule rearranged. You're their first choice, but if they don't get an answer tonight, they're making their second choice an offer."

"Wait. What?"

Tracy sighs loudly. "… the actress had to back out of the role… they want you…in production, and I told them you're finishing up in St. Louis, and…"

I can hardly hear what she's saying. A restless flutter stirs in my chest. I'm staying in my seat and doing my best to focus on the game.

On Christian.

The stadium roars to life around me—an electric, relentless hum of cheers and chants. It's almost deafening, but you can't help but get caught up in it. Bright lights bathe the diamond in a surreal glow, catching every glint of sweat, every blade of grass, every nervous twitch in the players. In my head, I'm cheering just as loudly as everyone else. It's like I'm trying to telepathically say, "*You've got this*."

But sitting in the stands, in a pocket of solitude amid the chaos, I am alone.

Literally.

My husband is mere seconds away from winning the World Series, and minutes ago, security came to get all the players' friends and family to bring them down so they can run onto the field when the big moment arrives.

But I stayed behind.

I never should have looked at my phone.

Heck, it should have been turned off. But I'm in the middle of shooting a movie here in St. Louis. I already know I need to be on set in the morning. The producers were kind enough to work around the playoff schedule, but I need to be aware of any schedule changes.

Hence, the phone being on.

My heart races, and my hand feels clammy as I clasp my cell to my ear. I'm watching what's happening on the field even as I listen to my agent presenting the biggest role of my career. Remember that major motion picture? Their lead actress had to back out, and guess who they want? This is what I've been working toward since I was a kid. If ever there was a dream part, this is it. Unfortunately, her timing couldn't be worse. Everyone knows I'm here to support Christian.

This is his moment.

I wish she had considered that and simply waited until tomorrow to call.

A tiny voice in my head reminds me, *It's Christian's moment*, but… this is important, too.

Not that anyone understands that.

My husband does. Truly. But the looks I got as all the rest of the friends and family were ushered away—and the snarky comments from some of the players' wives—told a different story. Words like *selfish, self-involved,* and *rude* were whispered.

I'm an actress, and things like that aren't anything new. But this time, the words stung quite a bit more than they usually do.

I look down at my free hand. At my wedding ring, sparkling in the stadium lighting. It represents the promise Christian and I made to each other.

So many promises.

So many sacrifices.

I hear the exuberant announcement: "And the Archers have won the World Series!"

"Ella? Ella, are you listening to me? This is an incredible opportunity. They want an answer from you tonight."

Everyone's running onto the field, laughing, cheering, and hugging their loved ones. I should be down there. But I'm not.

"I'm going to have to call you back," I say. "I need to run."

I hear a loud sigh on the other end. "Seriously? This is the chance of a lifetime. What is there to think about?"

"We'll talk tomorrow, okay?"

"Jeez, Ella." Another sigh. "Are you sure he's worth it?"

I don't even hesitate.

"Yes." I hang up and slide the phone into my purse as I get to my feet.

Now, I can go down to the field and celebrate with my husband.

Reality hits. THEY WON! I don't just run, I sprint through the concourse, weaving through the chaos of thousands of fans, crying tears of joy. Then I head down the stairs and past security.

It feels like it takes forever, but I'm finally on the field, jumping up and down and trying to spot my man. Luckily, he's doing the same as he looks for me.

Then it's like the heart-stopping moment in every romantic movie. We're running toward each other (cue the slow-motion effect), and before I know it, I'm in his arms, wrapping myself around him. I'm laughing, crying, and holding on as he spins us both around.

"You're late," he says with a laugh, but I'm too excited to even think of a comeback.

"You did it! You did it! I love you!"

Then he's kissing me, and I swear this may be one of the swooniest moments of my life. When he sets me down on my feet, he looks positively ethereal. I don't think I've ever seen him look so happy.

"We did it," he states.

"Thanks for winning a World Series for me."

"I wouldn't be here without you, Ella Rose. You asked me to win another World Series, and here we are."

"Oh, Christian…" He gives another thorough kiss.

"I was late because security came and got the family and friends early before the final out. I refused to leave."

I didn't stay in my seat because of the phone call. I stayed because my husband is very superstitious.

Even though he hates that word.

Christian can't step on a crack before a game. I've made him the same two meals every single day for the past two seasons. He sleeps in the same shorts and T-shirt every night and has the same routine every day, down to the minute.

I needed to stay in my seat until the end of the game. It's important to him. So, it didn't matter that the game was almost over. Anything could happen until the last out. I knew I needed to stay where I was until the Archers were the World Series champs.

No matter what, I wasn't moving.

I'm not a diva.

And I'm certainly not selfish, self-involved, or rude.

No matter what anyone else thinks.

I was being a good partner. A good teammate.

A good wife.

We have our moment, but it is utter chaos all around us. Photographers, reporters, Christian's teammates. Everyone's celebrating, and it's like nothing I've ever experienced before. I've walked red carpets, but that isn't even remotely similar to this level of pandemonium.

Everyone's either hugging him or taking our picture. I try to step away and let him have his moment, but his arm is wound tightly around my waist, holding me close. I'm nearly blind from all the camera flashes, and my cheeks hurt from smiling. Still, it's an incredible celebration.

One minute, we're in the middle of the field. The next, we're being led away to a stage. I tug on Christian's hand as I lean in close to his ear to be heard over all the noise. "What's going on? Where are we going?"

"They named me the World Series MVP!" he says loudly, carefully leading me through the crowd.

When we get to the stage, he lets go of me and steps up. The team owners and management are all up there, and I swear I've never been prouder in my entire life. In this moment, I can honestly say that it was worth it—all the injuries, the physical rehab, the constant wear and tear on his body, the pain, the tape…it was worth it. Seeing the sheer joy on his face and knowing everything he went through to be standing up there?

Worth it.

Tears stream down my cheeks as the MLB Commissioner—with a trophy in his hands—turns to Christian and says, "I would like to congratulate the World Series MVP, Christian Lucas!"

The entire stadium erupts in cheers as Christian hoists the trophy over his head. He poses for more pictures before giving his speech. I can barely hear what he's saying over the roar of the crowd, and I know how uncomfortable he is with this kind of focus on him. Still, he gives a very inspirational acknowledgment to all the people who helped him get here: the coaches, the fans, his family.

"And through it all," he says, "I've been blessed to have my amazing wife standing beside me. I know this season was a little rough, but you never gave up on me. Even when things weren't looking great. I love you, Ella Rose. Thank you for your faith in me."

More cheers from the crowd.

More tears from me as I cheer along with them.

The next thing I know, I'm being ushered closer to the stage, where Christian immediately joins me. They hand him the keys to a brand-new, canary-yellow Corvette. Neither of us has ever owned a new car in our lives, so it's wild that it's happening. We pose for more pictures, and then it's back to celebrating with the team.

I have no sense of time as we go from the field to the clubhouse. There's no time to talk to Christian right now, but I know we will later. Seeing him like this makes my heart so happy. There hasn't been a whole lot to celebrate lately, and that makes this all the better.

When things finally wind down, and it's time to leave, it almost feels odd when we step outside, and the volume level goes down so drastically.

"Do you think we're supposed to drive the Corvette home?" he asks with amusement.

"Um…"

He laughs, shaking his head. "I don't think I ever imagined a bright-yellow Corvette being my first new car."

"It certainly *is* bright," I add, laughing, too.

When we reach the car and have time to study it, we laugh even harder.

"Ella Rose? Any chance you know how to drive a stick shift?"

"Nope."

"Neither do I." he says around a fit of laughter.

Now what are we supposed to do? How are we supposed to figure out how to drive this car home?

Thankfully, the dealership's owner walks over. "Congratulations on the big win, Mr. Lucas," he says, shaking Christian's hand. "That was one heck of a game."

"Thank you." He pauses. "Um…are we supposed to take this home or…?"

Relief washes over me as the man responds, "Oh, no. This was just for show. You can come down to the dealership anytime, pick out the actual one you want, and we'll ship it to you. I believe I heard you'll be living in Florida for the offseason?"

"That's right. But we'll be in touch before we go."

Now, we're finally ready to leave.

We drive home in our old, clunky Toyota. Christian calls his dad, and in a rare moment, I hear Mr. Lucas give praise.

"Congratulations, son. I love you, Christian," I hear him say.

"I love you, too, Dad."

Now I'm ready to cry again.

Back at our apartment, Christian carries his trophy in, holding it close.

I imagine I'd be the same way if we were coming home after I won an Emmy or an Oscar.

Looking around, I wish there were somewhere fitting for it—a mantel with a light to shine on it, or even a nice table. But there isn't. The whole minimalist thing feels crazy obvious right now. It also feels almost too quiet. After such a loud and eventful night, coming home to our silent, barely furnished apartment feels anticlimactic.

"Do you want something to eat?" I ask. Now that the season is officially over, I know we can let go of some of the strict routines.

Shaking his head, he puts the trophy down on the sofa like it's no big deal, before walking over and kissing me.

This. This is what I love. We can finally have our moment.

When he lifts his head, I let out a dreamy sigh. "I know I said it earlier, but there was so much going on around us. Thanks for winning the World Series for me."

"There's nothing I wouldn't do for you, Ella Rose."

I know in his heart he means it. And now isn't the time to dredge up past arguments. This is Christian's night.

"I just want to shower, crawl into bed, and hold you close while we watch some TV. I'm beyond exhausted."

"Then that's what you should do." I give him a playful shove toward our bedroom. "Go and take your shower. I'll join you in bed when you're done."

I think it's sweet that he picks up the trophy and takes it with him.

When I walk into the bedroom a few minutes later, I find it on the floor. "That won't do," I murmur. Looking around, I'm reminded of how bare our bedroom is. We have a mattress on the floor and a TV on a stand but that's it. This trophy needs a place of honor.

Inspiration strikes.

Well, unconventional inspiration.

Within minutes, I've got everything set up, and as I stand back and admire my handiwork, I know Christian's going to love it, too. I hear the shower turn off, quickly change into my pajamas, and climb into bed. When the bathroom door opens, I'm sitting up against the pillows, smiling.

"How was that shower?"

He looks at me with a sleepy smile. "Fantastic. I think maybe tomorrow we can—" He pauses when he spots his trophy. "What in the world?" Grinning, he looks at me.

"It needed to be on display." I shrug. "And this was the biggest spot I could find."

"The ironing board?" And yes, now he's trying not to laugh.

"Yup. I couldn't just let it sit on the floor." He climbs into the bed beside me, and we both laugh in disbelief at this amazing moment. "I'm in awe of you, Christian, and so were all the people watching you tonight. That MVP trophy was awarded to the right person."

"You're just biased."

"I am. But not about this. You deserve that award. I've never seen you play like you did in this series." I wonder how much he's hurting, but I don't ask.

Resting his head on my shoulder, we both get comfortable as we stare at the trophy.

"I know you probably already envisioned winning the World Series. After all, that's been the goal for the entire season. But was it everything you thought it would be?" His hand's in mine, and for the first time in months, he feels like he's relaxed.

"The goal at the beginning of every season is to win the World Series. That's the only reason you play. You expect to win. That's what pushes you through the hard times. Although there were times this season when it felt impossible, we kept on believing. But to win the MVP? That was never on my radar. I never thought I'd receive that honor."

"As I said, it was well deserved."

We sit in companionable silence for several minutes, the kind that doesn't feel empty or awkward—just full. Full of the crowd still echoing faintly in our heads, full of adrenaline slowly fading into something softer, fuller, deeper. He finally lifts his head, his eyes finding mine, and the tenderness there nearly steals the air from my lungs.

"This was the greatest night of my life, Ella Rose," he says quietly, voice rough with emotion. "And not just because of the win or the trophy. Because you were right there with me. Celebrating it. Living it with me."

My heart squeezes—too full, too grateful. "There's nowhere else in the world I would rather be," I whisper, and I mean it with every beat of my heart.

He gives me a small, shaky laugh—the kind a strong man only lets out when he feels safe. "I'm just so glad you could work out your filming schedule for this. I would've been devastated if you hadn't been here. I know you've got lines to memorize, and scenes to shoot, and your world is just as demanding as mine, so the fact that you chose to be here tonight?" He swallows. "It means everything."

I reach for his hand and curl my fingers through his. "Nothing else mattered tonight. Everyone on set understood that. I understood that. I never even thought about the movie once the game started. My entire world was right here. Watching you, cheering for you, being with you. That was the only thing I wanted."

I briefly think about Tracy's call and know I'm not lying.

My focus was where it needed to be.

No matter the cost.

Sixteen

The offseason is off to a great start. We spend three weeks flying from LA to New York, doing press and all the late-night talk shows. Everyone wants to talk about Christian Lucas, the underdog who was named the World Series MVP. I have never been more proud.

However, no one wants to talk about Ella Lucas. I lost the movie role to another actress because I didn't give them an answer that night. Hollywood can't even wait one night for the World Series, apparently.

Filming finishes in St. Louis just as we're ready to make our move to Florida.

Moving in with my in-laws isn't exactly the dream, but Christian and I both believe in being frugal, and it made sense. After all, why find a temporary apartment and pay rent for four months when we don't have to? But I am a little nervous about us living with his parents when I still haven't really bonded with his father. I don't want things to be awkward, but they are.

Honestly, I feel like his dad is constantly testing me, like I'm still on probation in his mind.

Christian and I live on the second floor of the house, and Mr. and Mrs. Lucas live on the first floor. I don't walk on my tiptoes and, apparently, you can hear my steps from above. On more than one occasion, he's said, "You walk like an elephant."

Then, there are my eating habits. I happen to enjoy three meals a day. Nothing big, but I eat breakfast, lunch, and dinner, along with the occasional snack. Mr. Lucas, on the other hand, only likes to eat one big meal a day. So, whenever he sees me eating anything, it's usually met with, "You eat too much."

Needless to say, I'm not feeling very at home in my temporary home. I have to wait until Christian and I are alone in bed at night to whisper my feelings because, along with the long list of my faults, I'm also too loud.

Ugh.

"I'm only saying, I'm trying very hard to be nice to him and show respect, but does he have to criticize *everything* I do?" I whisper.

"I'll admit that he can be a little critical, but that's just the way he is. He doesn't realize how it sounds. Don't take it personally." He says it like it's no big deal, but it is.

"How can I not?" I ask, hating that as soon as I raise my voice even a tiny bit, I begin to panic. Like his dad is going to come through the door and tell me to be quiet.

"This is all temporary. I know it isn't ideal, but we can get through it. He mentioned going fishing tomorrow, so you won't have to deal with him."

Great. One day. Whoopee.

"Can't you talk to him for me? Please?"

"It won't make a difference. Trust me. You just need to ignore the comments."

"Fine."

But it's not.

The next day, I have the house to myself, which feels like a small gift. Christian is at physical therapy, his mom is at work, and his dad is out on the lake somewhere with a fishing pole and a quiet determination. One undeniable bright spot is the view. His parents' house sits right on the water, and the lake is stunning in the late-morning light.

I decide to treat myself to a sub from the local Publix They're famous for them. Everyone knows exactly what you mean when you say you want a Pub sub. Back at the house, the day is too beautiful to ignore, so I settle at the kitchen table with my lunch, the lake stretched out in front of me. I'm starving, and the first bite of my turkey and cheese sub with extra sub dressing is every bit as glorious as I hoped it would be.

And then I see him.

Mr. Lucas is walking up from the boat dock—back much earlier than I expected.

Seriously? Already?

He walks in, fresh off the lake, and I can see that he hasn't washed his hands. Side note about me, I'm a bit obsessive about germs and handwashing. I cannot eat anything unless I've properly sanitized my hands, and I do not share my food with others.

"How was the fishing?" I ask, hoping to have a pleasant conversation.

"Fine. What are you eating?"

"A turkey sub," I answer.

"Is it good?"

"Yes, it's a Pub sub, and it's my favorite."

All of a sudden, without asking, he grabs my sub with his unwashed, fishy hands and takes a bite. We both stand there in silence as he chews.

Are you flipping kidding me right now?

"Yes, that's good," he says before putting it down, turning and walking away. I don't think I let out a breath until I see him walk into his bedroom and shut the door.

For a moment, I'm too stunned to even move. I'm not sure whether I want to scream or cry. Unfortunately, I have no choice. As calmly as I can, I wrap up my sandwich and throw it in the trash before tiptoeing up the stairs.

Something's got to give.

Soon.

Again.

And thankfully, it does.

A week after the sandwich incident, I'm home alone again with my father-in-law. I'm looking over a script for a single-episode spot I'll be filming next week when my phone rings.

"Someone needs a secretary," he mutters. "Five kids, and I never heard a phone ring this much."

I fight the urge to roll my eyes. Instead, I grab my phone and head upstairs to Christian's and my bedroom. It's Tracy. Things have been a little *cool* between us since the night the Archers won the World Series, and I lost the movie role, and every time she calls, I get a knot in the pit of my stomach.

"Hey, Tracy. What's up?"

"Ella, are you sitting down?"

"Um…" I move over to the bed and sit. "Now I am," I say nervously. I can't imagine the movie role being open for a third time, so I'm not sure what this could be about.

"Are you ready to be part of the *Galactic Wars* universe?"

Galactic…?

The gasp is out before I can stop it, and I'm instantly back on my feet. "Are you serious? They want me?" I ask excitedly.

"They sure do! And FYI, I don't know any specifics about the project other than the fact that you'll be playing a new character, and you'll have to sign an NDA."

"That's fine. OMG! This is amazing. You have no idea how much I needed this today."

"Listen, I told them you will be back in town next week for filming and scheduled a time for you to meet with them. I'm sending the contract and NDAs over to you now. Congratulations, Ella. This is a very big deal. The *Galactic Wars* universe has staying power. I think this is your big break."

"This is incredible! Thank you, Tracy. I can't wait to get started."

"I'm also emailing you the calendar for next week's filming and meeting with the showrunners for the *Galactic Wars* project. And I put in a lunch for the two of us."

"That's great. Thanks again. I'll look everything over and get it signed and sent back to you ASAP." I'm practically bouncing on my toes with giddiness, so I don't make too much noise. "I'll see you next week."

But I am so freaking psyched that I can't control myself and I do a full-out happy dance—you know, arms waving, jogging in place, until I hear, "Stop jumping around up there!"

Yeah. I think I'm going to start packing for my trip now.

This is the beginning of my *Galactic Wars* era.

The overall vibe and energy level of everyone involved is contagious. We're all in on this giant secret that the world can't know about yet, and it is so flipping hard not to talk about it to anyone.

Well, I tell Christian I'm voicing a brand-new character for the GW universe, but I am not allowed to tell him anything about my character or the storyline. None of it.

It's killing me.

Ashla Voss is part of a whole new series set in the *Galactic Wars* franchise. When we first meet Ashla, she is impulsive and reckless. She rushes into battle, desperately trying to prove herself to her elders. She's snippy and sarcastic, but considering she's only fourteen years old, those traits make sense. And I love how feisty she is. *The Echo Wars* will be a new series for Storyteller Studios, and we're starting with the first season. Twenty-two episodes.

Twenty-two episodes. That's a sign it will be something amazing, right? Plus, it's like my life has come full circle, and I'm right back where I started. I have to believe it's a good sign.

My biggest issue?

The release date is over eighteen months away.

That means I have to keep this project to myself for a year and a half.

I have no idea how I'm going to do it, but I know I will. It's too big a deal to blab about it and end up ruining everything.

Honestly, I grew up being a fan of the *Galactic Wars* movies. It's been popular for almost thirty years. I had no idea that adding new characters, movies, and series was even a possibility. As I mentioned, we all thought that the creator of the series was done and had closed the book on the *Galactic Wars* franchise. So, this was all a huge surprise, to say the least. My part is a major character no one knew about, and now I have a lot of homework to do as I dive deeper into the universe.

I'm so excited to get started.

"So, tell me more about your character."

"I can't."

"Are you voicing a new character or an existing one?"

"A new one."

"What's her name?"

"I can't say."

And it's killing me.

Christian lets out a long breath. We're video chatting on our laptops, and he's sitting on our bed back in Florida, shirtless, his baseball hat on backward. He's practically catnip, and it stinks that he's twenty-five hundred miles away.

"So, what can you tell me?"

Tell you about what? Oh, yeah…the show. Seriously, my husband is gorgeous.

"I really can't. I'm sorry." Then I sigh. "But you want to know something really cool?"

"Sure."

"This…what I'm doing…is…" Drats. If I tell him it'll be twenty-two episodes, will that violate my NDA? Now I'm not so sure.

"What you're doing is…?" he prompts with a boyish grin.

"I can't say," I reply miserably, my shoulders sagging. "Let's just say my lucky number plays a part in it."

He chuckles. "Great. You're voicing a part you can't tell me about, for a new *Galactic Wars* animated project I don't know anything about, but twenty-two has a significant meaning to it. Awesome." I know he's teasing. Kind of. And I feel guilty all over again.

"You know I'd tell you if I could. But isn't it a little wild that I'm going to be part of such a popular franchise? Like…in a million years, I never thought I'd end up here."

"And where is here?" he asks, still grinning.

"Nice try," I say with a laugh.

"Hey, I can't help that I'm curious."

"I know, and I wish I could tell you more. I don't know how I'm going to last for a year and a half without telling anyone."

"A year and a half? Seriously? Why so long?"

"That's when it will finally debut. They'll probably announce it sooner, but I don't know when."

"Oh. So, how does this work with voice recordings? I'm guessing you can record your part almost anywhere, right? Do they have a place in Florida for you to do it?"

"Actually, all the recording will be done here in LA," I tell him. "I don't have a full schedule yet, but I know I have to record here every other week for the rest of the year."

He doesn't respond right away, and I am tempted to mention how maybe this will be a good thing, considering how awkward it's been living with his parents. But it could also open the door for him to spend more time in California with me.

"Why don't you fly out and stay with me? It will be like old times. Jen really misses you, too."

He laughs softly. "Um, yeah. I'm sure she does."

"Come on, Christian. Think of how much fun it will be. We'll get to see friends we haven't seen in a long time and eat at some of our favorite places."

"You know I'm in training, Ella Rose. I can't take time off from that. Especially not after the way my last season went."

"You're always in training," I murmur. "And there are facilities here you can use. Trainers you can work with."

"Not Archers' trainers."

Closing my eyes, I mentally count to ten. "I know they won't be Archers' trainers, but you can come out for just a long weekend. You know the exercises you have to do for physical therapy, and our apartment complex has a great gym. Spring training doesn't start for another month. Please. Please come to California. It's just a few days."

"I don't see why you can't fly home on the weekends. You won't be recording seven days a week. It makes more sense."

For a moment, I'm speechless.

"Does it? It's just as easy for you to take three days off as it is for me. And at least if you come here, I know we'll *both* be able to relax and enjoy ourselves."

"What is that supposed to mean?" All amusement fades, and he frowns.

"It means…"

Dare I say it?

"It means I understand why we're staying with your parents. I understand that we both agreed to wait to buy a home until we know where your career will land. And I also know that we are trying to be financially responsible. However…" I pause and hope I'm not about to start a huge fight. "Things are extremely awkward in your parents' home. I mean, your mother is so wonderful and welcoming, and you know I adore her, but I feel like I'm always being watched and judged by your dad. And to be honest, I'm tired of it. I've been nothing but nice and appreciative to him, yet he finds fault with everything I do."

He laughs again. "Is that all? Ella Rose, I told you, that's the way he is. You can't take it personally."

"But I do!" My frustration is bubbling over now. "Maybe you're used to it, Christian, but I'm not. That's not the way my dad talks to me. Not now, not ever. I get that it's his way, but I don't have to like it."

"Okay, but…"

"I adore your mother and your siblings, and I can deal with your dad, too, but *living* with him is a whole different ballgame."

No response.

"Look, the last thing I want to do is fight over this. But would it really be awful if, this once, you came here?"

"*This once?* Ella Rose, I've traveled to see you as much as you've traveled to see me."

That's not really true, but I'm not going there.

"And I'm asking you to do this for me this time, okay? I'm so happy about this role and all the possibilities, and I want to celebrate. However, if I fly to Florida, we'll be surrounded by people, and I cannot risk violating my NDA in any way. Plus, I really need some time with just you and me without your dad listening to my every step… literally my *every* step."

He's quiet, but not for long.

"I guess so."

"Thank you."

I'm not sure what to say next because I don't want to be all giddy and start making plans for the weekend, but I also don't want to randomly change the subject.

But that's what I do.

"How was physical therapy today?"

"You know, the usual. My body isn't exactly doing what I want it to do, but it's also not freaking the therapists out, so I'm taking that as a good sign."

"Well…okay. Sure. I guess that could be a good sign. Have you talked to the team doctors? Is there anything more you should be doing?"

"They aren't going to tell me anything the therapists haven't already. I played hard last season, and it takes time to heal. But not the type of healing that requires me to sit at home wrapped in bubble wrap."

"No one said bubble wrap…"

But I've certainly thought about it a time or two.

"You know what I'm saying. You're worried, and I understand that. But at the end of the day, you need to trust me. I've been an athlete for practically my entire life. By the time spring training starts, I'll be ready."

It's not that I don't want to believe him, but I'm not sure I do.

"Maybe you can reach out to some of your old trainers from the Magic while you're here?"

"That's not allowed, Ella Rose"

"Okay," I say, somewhat defeated because I thought it was a good idea.

"So, um…what do you think?"

"About…?"

I try not to roll my eyes, but I do. "Coming to LA this weekend."

"Oh, uh…sure. I'll book my flight and plan on being there sometime Friday afternoon."

"Yay! Do you want to go out to eat anywhere special? I can make us reservations, or we can wing it, or…"

"How about a pizza date like we used to do?"

Aww…

"I think that sounds perfect. I love you, Christian."

"I love you, too, Ella Rose. I'll talk to you tomorrow."

"Okay. Good night."

"Good night."

I hang up and collapse back onto my bed. I love that I still have an apartment to come back to when I need it. It's comfy and familiar, and it comes with one of my very best friends.

That's when I toss my phone down and go in search of Jen. She was out of town when I arrived, doing hair and makeup for a music video, but she should be home by now. Plus, I would love for us to get some takeout and eat dinner in our jammies while we catch up on each other's lives. We talk on the phone a lot, but it's not the same as having a conversation in person.

I hear the front door open and am pleasantly surprised when I see her walking in with a bag of what looks suspiciously like Thai from one of our favorite restaurants.

"You're home!"

"I am," she says with a grin. Once she puts everything down on the coffee table, she hugs me, and I hold on for longer than usual. "I missed you."

"Missed you, too." If I'm not mistaken, she's holding on tightly, too.

When we finally break apart, we both look a little teary-eyed.

"I was hoping you'd want to eat in tonight," she says. "I was going to call and ask what you wanted me to pick up, but I was craving Thai. I hope that's okay."

"Are you kidding? Yes. It's like you were reading my mind."

"Jammies first?" she asks with a grin.

"Absolutely."

"Meet you back here in five."

So, we do, and it's like no time has passed.

I grab the dishes and silverware, she gets our drinks, and we set up everything on the coffee table before getting comfy on the couch.

"So?" she begins. "You got the voice job, huh?"

I quickly take a bite of my dinner before nodding.

"And you can't talk about it?"

"Nope."

"Bummer. But are you excited about it?"

"I am. It's a matter of playing the long game, you know? Like, so much has to happen before it even gets announced."

"But you can still take other roles in the meantime, right?"

"Absolutely. I just have to make sure it doesn't interfere with recording."

"And you'll be recording here in LA?"

I nod around another forkful of food.

She studies me for a moment. "And how does Christian feel about that?"

I keep zero secrets from Jen.

Okay, maybe not zero, but I tell her more than I tell everyone except my mom.

"I don't think he has a problem with my being here. Especially since it's for such a major project."

"But…?"

"But," I begin with a sigh, "our biggest issue right now is whether he'll come to visit me here or I'll fly back to Florida."

"I figured you'd divvy it up. You know, sometimes he comes here, and sometimes you go there."

I tell her about my interactions with his dad.

"Are you kidding me? Still? What is that man's problem? You've been nothing but an awesome wife to his son, and I'm sure you're like the best daughter-in-law in the world."

I relax a little at her praise. "Thank you, you're very kind. Let's just say that positive reinforcement really isn't his thing." I shake my head. "It's tolerable when we go and visit for a long weekend or something, but living in the same house is starting to be a real issue for me."

"So, why doesn't Christian tell his father to ease up?"

"He keeps telling me it's the way his dad is, that he won't change. But it makes it incredibly difficult to relax and have fun when I feel like I'm constantly being judged."

"Ugh, I wouldn't want to live that way either." Then she pauses. "But I can't see Christian being the only one traveling. You guys have always been very fair about that sort of thing whenever possible."

She's right.

But we've never had to deal with a situation like this before.

Finally, I nod. "I know. I just…" Shaking my head, I take another bite of my dinner instead of finishing the thought.

Jen shifts on her end of the sofa and gives me a very knowing look. "You know you have to say whatever you were going to say. You can't leave it like that, so…out with it."

"Fine. I feel so unsettled. I don't know, I guess I thought we'd be able to ground ourselves a little bit after we got married. I thought we'd start to build our life together. But here we are, still traveling like crazy, living out of suitcases, and we're newlyweds living with his parents. This is not at all how I imagined our happily ever after would start." I stop because all of this venting feels wrong. "Christian is the most amazing husband, and I'm so grateful for him and the life we have together. It's just not very conventional. At all."

"Ella, you can't keep things bottled up. I know you. I've lived with you. You are passionate about everything. The good and the bad. When you're happy, you light up like the sun. And when you're mad, you get feisty and a little snippy. It's awesome. And when you're sad, it breaks my heart."

Jen knows me so well.

"You are like a sponge. You hold it all in, but at some point, you have to wring out your sponge. Have a conversation with Christian. He's a very reasonable guy, and he will understand where you are coming from."

"Jen…"

"You have the biggest heart of anyone I've ever known. And yes, we all know Christian loves you, but he needs to step out of his comfort zone, too. Lord knows you have for him."

"I don't know if I'd say that."

She stares at me.

"Okay, fine. I've had to do it a little bit."

"Exactly. You uprooted your life in California, and your apartment back in St. Louis couldn't be decorated because it was temporary. You cook meals based on his needs and not yours. And then you can be friends with the WAGs, but close to none of them. You've sacrificed a lot."

"It's not so bad."

Shaking her head, she doesn't say anything else, and we eat in companionable silence for several long moments. Still, she's saying all the things I've been thinking and then feel bad about.

"Jen?"

"Hmm?"

"Thank you."

A smile tugs at her lips. "For what?"

"For not being afraid to say the things I don't always want to hear."

"That's what friends do. We lift each other up, say the uncomfortable stuff, and do our best to support each other. And I will, you know. All of it. I'm always here for you."

Tears sting my eyes. "Right back at you."

We're precariously balancing our plates in our laps, but we reach out and grasp each other's hands. It's such a simple connection, but it's powerful.

When we let go, I see that impish grin again. "Do I need to visit you in Florida? Mr. Lucas hasn't heard loud steps until he's heard these feet pounding on the floor above."

We break into a fit of laughter, and it's so darn perfect that I feel all the lingering tension leave my body.

And I desperately want the feeling to last.

I need it to.

The next morning, I wake up to a series of texts from my husband. I can't believe I didn't hear the notifications.

Christian: *Good morning, beautiful.*

Christian: *I booked my flight for Friday. I land at LAX at 12:30 and fly home early Monday morning so I can get my physical therapy in later in the day.*

He sends me all the flight information, because that's what we do.

Christian: *I'm off to the batting cages now and then PT. I'll talk to you tonight.*

Christian: *I hope you have a wonderful day.*

Christian: *Love you and can't wait to see you.*

I stare at the phone, smiling, hearing his voice in my head.

I want to feel like this all the time—seeing his texts or hearing his voice and smiling. And I don't feel like it happens as much as it should. Our lives make it difficult. As we gear up for another baseball season, I find I'm feeling anxious. I want to be mentally prepared for whatever happens.

But I also want to focus on me. And this role.

Becoming Ashla.

I can't explain it, but I *know* this will be a big deal for my career. I want to give it everything I have and make it something I can be proud of.

This is the first time I'm technically going to be the lead in a series. It's not happening the way I always imagined it would, but that's not a bad thing. It means I'll have to find the balance of committing to this role—this character—and being there for Christian and whatever the season holds.

Christian's coming off a World Series win and an MVP title, but his body still isn't healed. I have a feeling he'll need more than luck.

I just hope my lucky number turns out to be lucky for both of us.

For both of our careers.

And everything that goes with it.

Seventeen

It's starting to feel like *Groundhog Day* again.

And not in a cute rom-com way.

Spring training is over, and Christian's hurt and not listening to the doctors.

Honestly, I'm starting to spiral. Balance? Non-existent. I can't keep holding everything together for both of us. I can't be a wife, an actress, an advocate, a therapist, and whatever other hats I need to wear at a moment's notice.

Why can't I just be a woman living a somewhat normal life? When will things calm down enough for us to breathe?

We're back in St. Louis in our sparsely decorated apartment. I have to admit, I want to hang pictures or paint some walls, but why bother? It's still just a temporary home, and this is the last year of his three-year deal. We might have to move again. It's just easier to keep it simple. I think I'm finally coming to accept that. This is part of our lives until Christian retires. Right now, we have this place, my apartment in California, and our room at his parents' house. And none of them are ours.

Not really.

I know my apartment is mine, but it's mine *and* Jen's.

I remember Christian selling me on the move to St. Louis and how we would finally have a place that was ours. Technically, that was true, but it was temporary. It wasn't a place we could settle into and make our own. So, I'm choosing to look at this a little like a role when I'm on location. While I'm not living out of a suitcase—not really—it's also not home. I never realized how much I missed having one until it was dangled in front of me and then taken away.

Ugh…I really am dramatic.

On a positive note, I'm still flying back and forth to LA, recording more episodes of *The Echo Wars*. I am so in love with this series, and my character is developing in such a fun way that I always hate it when our sessions end. I leave wondering what will happen next.

I mean, I have the script, but I still want more. I want to see it all come to life.

And that's the other positive news. Ashla is being modeled after me.

Me! Well, sort of.

Not only do they want me to use my own voice, humor, and personality for Ashla, but they also film my face during recording sessions, and the animators are using my facial expressions for the character. It's all so surreal.

I told Christian about it, and while he was excited, he also seemed distracted. I don't know why he thinks I can't tell when he's in pain. Either that or he's simply pretending I don't know, so we don't have to talk about it.

But he's wrong.

After spending time with Jen, I know I need to start speaking up more. I've gotten better about it, but there are still times when I back down because I don't want to argue—or, even worse, sound like a bully.

And how's that for irony? The girl who has been bullied so much in her life is acting like a bully now.

"I'm not a bully," I murmur as I go into the kitchen to start dinner. Christian will be home from the stadium in a little while, and we like to eat close to that time. It makes it easier for him to come home, eat, shower, and then relax for the rest of the night. Since his days are sometimes long, and I'm not here often during the week, we cherish the times when we can crawl into bed, watch TV, and talk quietly about our days.

It's a nice way to end the day.

But when Christian walks in the door a little while later, my entire body tenses up. He's limping and favoring his left side. Plus, he's walking like he's a hundred years old.

Frustrated, I take the pan of fried chicken off the burner and go to him. "What happened?"

"It's nothing. Just a hard game today," he says wearily before slowly lowering himself onto the sofa. I hear the hiss of breath, see the pained expression on his face, and it takes everything in me not to shake some sense into him.

But at this point, I'd probably only injure him more.

"Christian…"

"Ella Rose, please," he says tightly. "It's been a rough day, okay?" He looks miserable, and I feel like if I say anything, it'll be like kicking a puppy.

And that isn't acceptable.

He looks up at me, and I know he can tell I'm trying to hold my tongue. His expression softens.

"Something smells good," he says in a weak attempt at changing the subject. "Is that fried chicken?"

"Of course, it is. You said you were craving it," I say with only a hint of annoyance. "I actually listen to the things you say, and you know I'll do anything to make your day better."

After a long and not-so-quiet huff of frustration, he looks at me. "Whatever it is you feel you need to say, please say it."

Ugh. Please say it. *Please say it?* Obviously, he knows I'm mad, and he's politely asking me to let loose everything that's on my mind? Well…

I straighten, cross my arms, and stare at him, looking right into those cute puppy-dog eyes.

Darn it.

"Am I a bully?" I demand, but there's very little heat behind the words.

"What?"

Nodding, I repeat the question. "Am I a bully? Do you feel like I bully you?"

"Where is this coming from?"

"Just answer the question, Christian."

"No. I don't think you're a bully."

"Oh."

Frowning, he asks, "Why do you think you're a bully?"

"Because that's how you make me feel!" I practically shout with annoyance, my arms loudly dropping to my sides. "You come in here, clearly hurt and in pain, and you lie to my face about it."

"I don't want you to worry, that's all," he says quietly.

"Well, here's a newsflash. I'm going to worry. Every time I see you wince, I worry. When you limp, I worry. When I see you barely able to walk, I worry. So please save us both the trouble and just be honest." I sit beside him, taking one of his hands in mine.

And yes, he winces.

"Why are you still pushing yourself? It's early in the season. You're clearly still dealing with issues from last season's injuries, even after all the physical therapy. We need to get you to some other doctors. Ones who don't work for the team and will actually help get you better rather than tell you you're okay so they can send you right back onto the field."

"The doctors take my injuries seriously," he counters patiently. "They understand that some injuries just take more time to heal."

"And yet they're not telling the trainers or the coaches to put you on the injured list for a little while."

"I'm the one who doesn't want to be put on the list."

"Yeah. I get that loud and clear. But if the entire staff listened to the doctors and took that decision away from you, then maybe you wouldn't be feeling like this."

"I'm getting older, that's all. I'll feel better after a good night's sleep." He kisses my hand. "Can we please just have a nice dinner and relax?"

It's like talking to a wall, and I know I'm not going to win this battle.

At least, not right now.

"Fine. I'm going to go and finish cooking. Dinner should be ready in about fifteen minutes." I move to stand, but he's still holding my hand, stopping me from moving away.

When I turn and look at him, he looks…defeated.

"I get what you're saying," he says. "And I don't take it as you bullying me. But you know how it felt when you were with *Workin' for Laughs*, and they were underutilizing you, right? You were afraid to stand up for yourself because you were worried about the possibility of them letting you go. It's a little like that for me. I'm afraid that if I let them underutilize me, my career will be over."

Oh.

"I've had to overcome so much in my career. No one believed in me. Every day, I fought for respect. I fought to prove everyone wrong."

"I get that, and you should be proud of everything you've accomplished. Every single one of those people who wrote you off or didn't believe in you had to eat their words after you won a second World Series. Not many players can say they did that, Christian. You don't need to keep proving yourself."

But he's shaking his head. "That's never going to end. If I fail? If I don't go out there with my team, you don't think all those same people will say how they knew I couldn't keep it up?"

"Christian, come on. Where does it end?"

"How can I go from being the World Series MVP to the guy sitting on the bench all season? The fans will pity me, my teammates will be disappointed, and the naysayers will get the last laugh. I can't do it, Ella Rose. I just can't."

I sit back down and snuggle close, resting my head on his shoulder. "I wish I had the answers, Christian. I really do. There's no way to please everyone. It's not possible. It's your body. Your life. Not theirs."

"I don't know if I see it that way. I've been given a gift. A talent. Just like you have. Would you be able to walk away at the height of your career? If you won an Emmy or an Oscar, are you telling me you'd be okay with giving it all up?"

"It's not the same thing. If I were sick or injured, then…yes. If I couldn't physically do my job to the best of my ability, then I think I'd accept it and walk away." I pause before I add, "With dignity." But those two words seem wrong to throw out there.

He looks at me, his smile sad. "It's easy to say that when you're not the one facing the decision. My whole life, I've been raised to not be a quitter. Lucases never quit. And that now means me *and* you. You are a Lucas now, Ella Rose…and I wouldn't expect you to quit."

We look into each other's eyes, and I can tell he means that.

"And look at all the sponsorship deals I made after being named MVP? I'd be a joke if the guy on the cereal box went from running the bases and hitting home runs to sitting in the dugout."

"Pushing your body until it breaks doesn't make you a hero, Christian. Wouldn't it be better to be the guy who was the MVP and knew when his body needed to heal rather than the guy who took too many risks and lost it all?"

We sit in silence for several long moments. When he responds, it's not what I expect.

"Honestly? I don't know which is better. I just feel like I wouldn't be able to live with myself if I didn't give one hundred percent to this. Even if it hurts."

And the crazy part is, I get it because…

That's how I feel about this relationship.

I see the first mockup of Ashla and can't help but squeal with pure joy. Sure, she's an alien with orange skin, blue eyes, and white facial markings. And she has headtails instead of hair. But she's so beautiful, she takes my breath away.

She's a far cry from any character I've ever played, but I love her so much already.

So much of my time is spent being in awe of this process. I think about how I thought they were done making more *Galactic Wars* stories. So, being here now, originating a brand-new character, makes me feel like I've won the lottery.

Plus, this role could allow me to leave a legacy like the well-known characters before me. No one will remember me playing the punk rocker in a movie, or any of the characters I played on *Workin' for Laughs*, but this? This really *could* be my breakout role. The one that finally has people knowing my name.

A lottery I can literally tell no one about.

The plan is to record the entire first season before any announcements are made. I'm very lucky that I have understanding family and friends. Jen's made a game of asking me vague questions, hoping to get me to give her even a tiny bit of information, but it never works. She and her boyfriend are huge *Galactic Wars* fans, so I know she's excited for me, but she'd be even more excited if I gave her the scoop.

Gah! I'm so frustrated yet giddy at the same time.

Which pretty much sums up my life at the moment.

When I'm in LA and working on *The Echo Wars*, every day is filled with nothing but positive energy. Everyone working on the series is psyched to be a part of it, and since we can't share what's going on with anyone outside of the studio, we've become like a little family.

Or a really cool and exclusive club.

But when I'm back in St. Louis, I have a lot of anxiety and…well…frustration. I've done everything but tie Christian to a chair to prevent him from going to the stadium, but nothing's worked. He's still playing, still in pain, and every day when he leaves the apartment, he comes home moving a little slower and wincing a lot more.

What else can I do?

"Hey, Ella!"

I turn and see our showrunner, Amy, coming into the studio. I smile. "Hey. How are you?"

"I'm fine, thanks. Listen, we made some revisions to the next episode. Twenty-two pages worth," she adds with a small laugh before handing me an envelope.

I inwardly squeal with glee because…twenty-two.

We get hard copies of all the scripts to ensure nothing gets leaked. People working on the *Galactic Wars* project in the past have had their emails and computers hacked by fans trying to find out what's coming next.

"We really love what you've done with Ashla so far. And now that we've completed the artwork for her, the animators can finally get started."

"I have to tell you, I love how the writers have her developing. Ashla really is such a fun character, and I'm having the best time breathing life into her."

She nods but doesn't say anything at first. I can sense that something else is coming, but I don't know if it's good or bad.

When she doesn't move to leave, I feel a knot forming in the pit of my stomach. Nothing good ever comes when a showrunner—or any of the creative executives—comes to talk to you privately.

"Is everything okay, Amy?" I ask.

She hesitates for just a moment before seeming to resign herself to the conversation.

"Obviously, Griffin Lawson is overseeing this project," she begins.

Griffin is the creator of the entire *Galactic Wars* franchise. He is very involved in this project, but we don't really work with him directly. He works out of his office in San Francisco, and we record the show in Los Angeles. But we hear many stories about what he thinks about the project, and sometimes, we even receive notes about our performance. Seriously, I cannot believe that Griffin Lawson knows my name.

I nod and wait for her to continue.

"He's been listening to the recordings and looking at the artwork we have so far, and he's not sold on some of the voices."

I feel like I'm going to be sick.

Wasn't she just praising me? Didn't she say how they all love what I'm doing with Ashla? And she gave me a script. That has to mean something, doesn't it?

My head starts spinning when I realize this is how the conversation typically goes when you're being let go. You get a heap of praise before they lower the axe.

Don't cry. Don't cry. Don't cry.

But the script…

Swallowing hard, I nod again.

"We all know Griffin is the genius behind the entire universe. It's practically unheard of for a movie to launch an entire saga that remains popular for thirty years," she says with another small laugh.

A nervous laugh? A normal one? Does she find this amusing?

Another silent nod as my lunch feels like it's lodged in my throat.

"The man knows this world better than anyone. So, if he feels a voice isn't right, then we need to fix it."

She pauses, and I swear the room feels about twenty degrees warmer. I may pass out if she doesn't get to the point in the next ten seconds.

I let out a shaky breath. "Amy, am I…am I being fir—?"

She cuts me off before I can even finish the sentence. "What? Oh. Oh, no, Oh, Ella, I'm sorry. I should have led with that." Reaching out, she gives my arm a reassuring squeeze. This time, her laugh is definitely nervous. "Gosh, I'm so sorry. This whole day has been a little wild. We're recasting the role of Lukan Karzen. Griffin insisted."

"Oh, wow…" I murmur. I'm devastated because Mark Andrews voiced that role, and we were becoming good friends. I feel so bad for him. "Do you have someone lined up already?"

"We do. Griffin went over all the auditions and—ironically—we're going with another Mark. Mark Taylor. I wanted to let you know what was going on before you heard it from anyone else."

"Does this mean we're going to re-record the episodes that we've already done?"

At this point, we've only completed four, but I'm curious.

"That won't be necessary. Mark is just going to re-record Lukan's lines, and he'll be in the next cast record for episode five. But rest assured, your role is safe. Griffin's particularly impressed with your work, and we're all looking forward to introducing Ashla to the fans."

Relief washes over me in waves, and I reach for my chair and sit down. "Any chance his plan is to let the fans know sooner rather than later?" I tease.

She laughs again, looking as relaxed as I am. "Unfortunately, no. We're really leaning into the surprise announcement. And considering this is a brand-new series that acts as a prequel to so much of the existing franchise, it's important that we do everything right."

I know it makes sense from a marketing standpoint, but I can't help being a little impatient.

"No one's going to hear it from me," I assure her. "Even if it kills me."

Amy glances around before moving in like she's about to tell me a secret. "For the record, it's killing me, too." With a smile and a wave, she turns to leave. "Keep up the good work, Ella!"

Sighing, I slump down in my chair. The last few minutes have been such an emotional roller coaster.

Much like the rest of my life, so why am I even surprised?

"I can't believe they let Mark go," Christian says. "Seems to me they wasted the poor guy's time."

"Sometimes, you don't know how something like this will turn out until you're underway, you know?"

"I guess."

"I was about to have a total panic attack because I thought I was the one being let go. I feel terrible that I was so relieved."

"Why should you feel bad? It's part of the business."

"I know, but I hate thinking of anyone losing their job. I'm not competitive like that. It's not in my nature."

"I don't think you were being competitive. You're playing completely distinct characters. Haven't you been on shows where roles were recast or cut completely?"

"I have. It's happened to me before. Twice!"

"Okay, then. So, this really isn't anything new," he says lightly. "And from what you said, they're really impressed with you."

I nod. "I just don't want to get too cocky and think I'm irreplaceable. Because everyone is."

"Don't I know it."

Uh-oh…

"What's going on?"

This is where he typically tells me he's fine, that everything's under control, and I have nothing to worry about.

"I've got a tear in my back."

I close my eyes and silently count to ten before I speak. "Okay. What does that mean?"

"Well, it's technically a tear in the middle of my back. I don't know what happened. I was doing my physical therapy exercises when I heard a loud pop."

"So, did they put you on the injured list?"

"No, I'm doing therapy, and they say I can play through it."

"So, you're still playing."

"Yes."

I really want to punch something right now. I have so much anger and frustration built up that I'll have to look into a way to get it all out before I hurt someone.

Karate? Kickboxing?

I know there are studios all over the city for both. Maybe I can look one up and see if I can join, or if I have to wait for a new class to begin, or…

"Ella Rose?"

But first, this.

"I'm here."

He chuckles. "I know you are, but you aren't saying anything."

"I'm not sure there's anything *to* say. You're hurt. You're still playing. And I'm worried. Same song, different verse."

"The trainer assures me…"

"You know what? I can't do this right now." Guilt hits me hard, but maybe part of the problem is that I always cave and listen and believe and hope.

"What do you mean? Do you have to go?" he asks. There's no hint of accusation, only trust and genuine concern that he's keeping me from something.

"No. I mean, I can't do this—this conversation—again. I can't keep listening to you telling me you're hurt and then saying how you're not going to do anything about it."

"But I am doing something. I'm doing the therapy. I'm being careful…"

"If you were being careful, you wouldn't keep getting hurt."

He's quiet for a minute before I hear the sigh.

"What do you want from me?"

"I want you to get a second opinion. I want you to go to a doctor who is impartial and has nothing to do with baseball. I want you to hear it from a medical professional who isn't being paid by the team. And I want to be there to hear it, too."

He's quiet again before he finally agrees.

"Okay. I can do that."

"Would you like me to look for a doctor, or do you want to?"

"I know you're busy, so…"

"We're both busy," I assure him. "Neither of our jobs is more important than the other. But if it's okay with you, I think I'd like to do a little research and find a physician. There must be a back specialist in St. Louis."

"Okay."

I don't dare get my hopes up because going to the doctor and hearing results won't guarantee anything. Even if he's told he should never play baseball again, I'm not foolish enough to believe he'll listen.

But if I'm there and have all the information and not the watered-down version I know I've been getting, then maybe I can advocate better for him.

If he'll let me.

With my current frame of mind, I'm not going to hold my breath.

Eighteen

I find Christian a specialist who can fix the tear in his back. The doctor also tells us that the injuries Christian sustained in the past are the reason he keeps getting injured. Essentially, his body never healed after he tore his oblique, so his core remained weak. It's the heart of an athlete's body. If your core isn't stable, everything is out of whack.

I know it's like that for everyone, but with professional athletes, it's crucial.

Several Archers players were injured this season, and the team did not make the playoffs. A losing season is not how Christian wanted his time in St. Louis to end. His three-year contract is up, and they don't offer him a new one.

It happens just as I finish recording season one of *The Echo Wars*, so it's hard to celebrate a career high when my husband's career is at stake.

All I can say is that, right now, the wheels are coming off.

I have a pit in my stomach because of baseball, and I can't bask in the afterglow of finishing my first season as Ashla. So many things will start happening now, and I want to be a part of it all. I want to focus fully on every minute of this project being introduced to the public.

But how can I enjoy any of it when Christian's a free agent again, and I have no idea where we'll have to move to next?

We're sitting in bed with the TV on, but I can feel the defeat coming off him in waves. He's quiet in a way that has weight. My heart aches for him—for the years he's poured into this and the identity that's been wrapped so tightly around the game.

But beneath the sadness, there's another feeling I don't quite know what to do with. Relief. Not because I wanted this for him, but because his body has been asking for rest for a long time. Maybe now, it will finally be heard. Maybe *now* he can heal without rushing, without pain pushed aside for the sake of staying in the lineup.

Loving him means balancing both truths at once—grieving the loss of what this moment means to him while quietly hoping it gives him the space to mend. I snuggle closer, placing a soft kiss on his chest. This is my favorite part of our day, wrapped around each other, all cozy and relaxed. Soft touches and even softer sighs. But tonight, all of that is laced with sadness, as well.

"Do you want to talk about it?"

He shrugs. "My agent said he's already putting feelers out. But let's face it, who's going to want a player who can barely play?"

Rock? Meet hard place.

I'm completely torn. Of course, I support Christian and his desire to keep playing. But what if no one signs him? As much as it pains me, I know that's the only way to protect his body so it can heal. It will kill him if no one picks him up, but I fear it will literally kill him if they do.

"What about taking a season off?" I suggest and then hold my breath.

"That's not how things work," he says miserably. "If I were younger, and it were a manageable injury, maybe. But if word gets out about all the things that are wrong with me, no one's going to wait. I'll be another year older and definitely past my prime."

"Okay, so then maybe…"

"Don't, Ella Rose. Just…don't. You don't understand. I want to go out on my own terms, and I know I still have more in me. I can do this."

I'm on the verge of letting him believe that, but I can't.

"This is a safe space, right?" I ask, and he looks at me curiously. "I mean…we don't lie to each other, and we can say what we need to if our hearts are in the right place, right?"

He nods, but I can already tell he's bracing for whatever I'm going to say. His entire body tenses, and I know I need to tread carefully.

Twisting, I face him, take both of his hands in mine, and kiss them. "I love you so much, Christian Lucas. From the moment we met, I knew you were my person. You are my best friend, my husband, my greatest love, and my teammate."

He smiles at that last one.

"What if this is the universe's way of telling you it's time to step back? Time to retire. Can you live with that?"

Christian is quiet but mimics my earlier move, grabbing my hands and kissing them. "Of course, I can live with that. You are my world, Ella Rose, and I'll still have you. Baseball is just my job. I don't know what the next step is. I have no idea whether any team will want me. But if one does, we will make it work as we have for the last five years. We'll sit down with the schedules and…"

"I know," I whisper. "We'll make it work."

Once again…same song, different verse.

But I'm the only one who hears it.

I'm just so worried about him.

We sit in companionable silence, maneuvering until we're shoulder to shoulder, watching the TV again. I'm not even focused on what's on. My mind's still reeling with all the what-ifs. All the ways things can go wrong. What if he gets another concussion? The doctors said that it could have life-altering effects. So many scenarios race through my mind.

Christian laughs at something happening on the show we're watching, and when he turns his head and looks at me, I know he can tell I'm distracted.

He shifts again, kissing my shoulder before resting his head there, something he knows I love.

"So, when this series comes out, are you going to dress up like your character?" he asks. "Like…how alien-like are you? Enormous eyes? Tentacles? Will I have to hold the tentacles when we walk the red carpet?"

It's the most ridiculous conversation ever, but it has the desired effect. I'm laughing. And then we're kissing.

And then it's just the two of us—no TV, no baseball, and no aliens.

The quiet is filled with tender kisses, gentle caresses, and a promise that no matter what happens, we'll always have each other.

Just the way it should be.

"We're going to Toronto!"

Rolling over, I blink Christian into focus. "Um…what?" I ask around a yawn.

He looks happier than he has in weeks, and I know I'm going to need some coffee to have this conversation.

Pushing my hair from my face, I sit up. "Toronto? As in… Canada?"

As if reading my mind, a cup of coffee suddenly appears in front of me when he gingerly sits down on the bed beside me. "I know it's not ideal, and it's only a one-year contract, but at least I'll be playing."

Yay.

Or not. I have so many questions, my head is spinning.

"I'm thinking we might fly up to Toronto next week so I can meet with the team, and we can look at apartments. The good news is that we can plan accordingly. We know this is a one-year commitment. The Skyhawks are a good team, but they haven't made the playoffs in a couple of years, and I know I can help them."

"I know you will," I say, so many thoughts racing through my brain. Christian makes every team he plays on better, but moving to Canada is a whole different ballgame that I had not even considered.

"I love you, Ella Rose, and I know we'll make this work," he says with a boyish grin.

I take a sip of my coffee.

"So, uh…you accepted the deal?"

"I did." He doesn't look at me as he says it, and there's a sadness in his voice. "No other offers were coming in. It was either take the contract or not play."

We sit in complete silence. My mind is in overdrive. Selfishly, I had already allowed myself to dream of our life if he retired. I never fully let my mind go there, but with no offers coming in, I began to daydream about what a "normal" life might look like with a healthy husband. And I liked it.

Now, I sit silently, grieving the new life that was within my grasp, while also coming to terms with the fact that we are moving to a different country. Am I even allowed to work in Canada? I know you need a work visa to be an actor there. I have *so* many questions.

Finally, Christian breaks the silence, "Ella Rose, I couldn't go out like that. I just couldn't. To go from an MVP to a has-been that no one wants? I just couldn't do it. I want to leave the game on my terms. I hope you understand."

I don't want to, but of course, I do.

"Please understand that I am just completely overwhelmed at the moment, and I don't know what to think," I say quietly. "We'll go to Toronto, we'll meet with the team, we'll find a place to live, and of course, we'll make it work," I say, sounding exhausted. How am I going to balance everything now? This might break me.

Sipping my coffee, my thoughts remain in total turmoil.

Another move. Another team. Another city.

Another chance for my husband to get hurt.

How am I supposed to sit in the stands and cheer for that?

"I have a surprise for you," he says, interrupting my thoughts.

A mirthless laugh is my first response. "I think you've surprised me enough for one morning, Christian."

Laughing softly, he nods. "Okay. I deserve that. But I thought that since we're already planning to move back to Florida temporarily, maybe we should book a stay at Wonder Land."

I study him hard for a moment. "Say more things like that."

He grins. "I already have it booked. We'll go directly there from Toronto. One week, just us, no family or friends. Just you and me and seven glorious days at The Grand Brightwater."

Maybe I'm weak, but I'm loving that he thought up all of that on his own.

"I've booked spa treatments, dinner at some of our favorite restaurants, and a fireworks cruise. Remember how we never got to do that the last time? Well, I made sure it was included in the itinerary. So? What do you say? Am I forgiven? Maybe a little?"

"Christian…"

"Look, I get it. I'm making life complicated right now. I'm being stubborn—your words, not mine," he adds with a wink. "I'm not ready to let go of the dream."

That's the one that gets me every time.

He playfully nudges my shoulder, mindful of the coffee in my hands. "And I still get to be number twenty-two. That's a good thing, right? It's still your lucky number."

"I guess. I just wish it were lucky enough to protect you from getting any more injuries."

"Okay, but now we know why I keep getting injured. Once I rehab my core, things will improve."

"Let's hope…"

Toronto is a lovely city.

At least, from what I've seen of it.

A lot of work is happening before the launch of *The Echo Wars*, and I'm spending more time in LA than I am with Christian.

I'm not sure if that's a blessing or a curse.

All the time I've been working on the series, it was just that—a series. Twenty-two episodes that would launch on the Storyteller Channel. But then Griffin Lawson came up with the idea of turning the first four episodes into a movie. He said it would be a great way to introduce the new series to fans. And personally, I'm psyched. A movie gives viewers so much more to absorb than having to wait for new episodes.

But this new plan changed the original marketing. Now, we're having an actual movie premiere, and I'm going to walk the red carpet.

Alone.

The Skyhawks have a game the same night, and there's no way Christian can be with me. That's what you sign up for when you become a baseball wife. You're alone a lot. We're both disappointed, and that's all there is to it.

Right now, Jen's doing my hair and makeup, and she is going as my plus-one.

"I can't believe that I get to go to the premiere of *The Echo Wars*," she says, wielding her curling iron like one of the light swords from the movies. "Have I mentioned how much I love all the *Galactic Wars* movies? This is one of those pinch-me moments. And I've met a lot of actors and actresses in my line of work."

"I know you have," I say, laughing at her antics while secretly praying she doesn't hit me with the curling iron.

"Will Griffin Lawson be there? Do you think it would be weird if I casually asked for an autograph or maybe pitched the idea of me doing hair and makeup for the next live-action movie?"

"It might. Maybe just stick to asking for an autograph."

"Ugh. Fine. I'll relegate myself to a simple fan, get his signature, and go." She pauses. "Or do you think he'd be okay with a picture?"

"Um…"

"You know what? Never mind. We'll play it by ear." She goes back to curling my hair. "Did you talk to Christian today?"

"I did."

"And?"

"And what?"

"Come on, Ella. I know you. I know you're upset that he's not here. Even though the two of you have mastered the art of living parallel lives, this is a big deal."

I shoo her hand away, twisting to face her. "What do you mean, parallel lives?"

She looks like a deer in headlights. "I…I just meant that you both have these careers that have nothing to do with each other and keep you apart almost more than you're together. And…I don't know…you still make it work."

"Oh."

She steps in front of me. "Care to explain why you got so defensive?"

"Maybe because I don't particularly enjoy the parallel life? Or because I wish he hadn't taken the contract with Toronto? Or how I wish he could be here with me because this is a big flipping deal. And because being a baseball wife is sometimes no fun at all?"

"Yeah. That's what I thought." That's it. That's all she says before crouching and hugging me.

She doesn't push for more information, doesn't ask me to talk about it, she just leaves it all up to me.

And I kind of love her even more for it.

"I sound like a brat."

She's back behind me with the curling iron. "No, you don't. You sound like someone who is proud of her work and wants the person she loves most in the world to be here to celebrate with her."

"I guess you're right. It's times like these when I really miss him."

"I know you do. Well, I don't have gorgeous blue eyes, and my butt doesn't look hot in baseball pants, but I'm honored to step into Christian's cleats and be your date tonight." Then she's back in front of me. "Do you think you're going to be as popular as the original series cast? Like…in thirty years, will people be talking about Ashla? How cool would that be? And then I can say that 'I knew you when.'"

We both laugh at that.

"That would definitely be cool. I just hope the fans like her. She's new and different, and while I can see her growth, viewers may not understand that from the beginning."

"Oh, please. They're going to get it because she's awesome, and they should know by now that every character has growth and changes as the series goes on."

I let out a long breath. "I hope so."

We finish getting ready, and the studio sends a Town Car to take us to the premiere.

"It's not a limo, but it's still impressive," Jen whispers to me as we climb in.

One of the things I love most about my friend is her nervous chatter. She hates lulls in conversation, so while I'm just absorbing the enormity of the moment, she's talking on and on and on about her favorite *Galactic Wars* movie, her favorite characters, and even recites several lines.

I may have to shoot her with a blow dart to calm her down.

By the time we arrive, she seems to have gotten a lot of it out of her system.

I step out of the car and onto the sidewalk, where handlers are waiting to direct us to where we need to go.

"Oh, my goodness! It's Ella Lucas! The voice of Ashla!" I hear someone call out, and the crowd cheers.

Jen gives me a thumbs up and motions for me to start walking.

Cameras are filming and flashing, and as I step onto the red carpet, I have a feeling my life is about to change.

Nineteen

If this is a dream, no one had better wake me up.

Right now, I'm at Wonder Land for *Galactic Wars* Weekend—meeting fans, signing autographs, sitting on panels, and living the kind of weekend twelve-year-old me used to wish on every shooting star for. And the best part? I get to be in the big *Galactic Wars* parade.

Twelve-year-old me is losing her *mind.*

This is where everything started.

This is where I used to wander as a kid, imagining myself under the lights—dancing, singing, waving from a parade float as if I belonged here. Standing here now feels surreal. Unreal. Perfect.

The crowd is wild. The lines go on forever. And they're not just here for the rides. They're here for *us.* For the *Galactic Wars* cast. For the galaxy that somehow became home not just to fans, but to me.

How is this my life?

This morning alone, I counted over two dozen fans dressed as Ashla, and every single one made my heart squeeze. Knowing that the character I helped bring to life is becoming a beloved part of the GW universe is beyond anything I ever imagined. Especially after the rocky start—Ashla wasn't exactly everyone's favorite in the beginning. But she grew. She healed. And the audience grew with her. Now, with season two coming out soon, she's officially a fan favorite.

I'm her!

She's me!

And somehow…she lives in all of us.

That's become my tagline for her. And honestly? It's catching on. And it feels *right.*

I love the energy of the crowds. It feeds me in a way I've never experienced before. This is a level of fandom I never knew existed, and I wish this were more than a weekend event because I want to *keep* feeling this way. Having a synergy with the fans, where they appreciate me and I appreciate them. I only wish Christian could be here with me. But since he can't, my family came into town, and the Lucases showed up, too. I have a big cheering section.

Baseball season is in full swing for him, and so far, it hasn't been an easy one. He's still dealing with injuries, and my traveling back and forth from LA to Florida to Toronto is exhausting and really taking a toll on me.

But I can't focus on that right now.

Right now, I'm in the middle of something magical, and I want to just fully focus on it and appreciate every moment.

"Excuse me, Ms. Lucas?"

I turn and see a cast member wearing the same uniform I wore back in the day. "Yes?"

"I'm Tara. I'm here to take you to your parade vehicle," she says with a smile. "Will you come with me?"

Nodding, I follow, my smile so wide it hurts. I pass all of my *Echo Wars* co-stars, and we're all a little dazzled by the reception we're getting. Who knew this animated series would garner this much frenzy?

We stop at a red Pontiac convertible with a decal on the side that has my name (my *actual* name) above Ashla's, and which series I'm in, along with her picture.

"This is so cool," I say as I climb onto the backseat and then up onto the trunk area. "Is this where I'm supposed to be?"

Tara nods. "Exactly. This way, the fans can see you and get pictures of you smiling and waving. But don't worry, the drivers go very slow, so this is totally safe. They can only go three to five miles per hour."

"Oh, okay. Wow. That sounds extremely slow," I joke.

"It's all for safety reasons," she assures me. "This will be your vehicle for all the parades—today, tomorrow, and Sunday. The parade starts at eleven, but we'll need you here by ten-thirty, just like you were today."

I nod.

"I know it's a bit early, but by getting everyone here early, we can make adjustments as needed. Is there anything I can get for you while you wait? Water? Coffee? A snack?"

"No, thank you," I say with a smile as I try to make myself comfortable.

"There are two bottles of water on the back seat, just in case you need them. Your driver's name is Jeremy. He's walking over now."

Within minutes, we're introduced, and he explains the speed limit, the water, that he has a first-aid kit, and how I just have to let him know if there's anything I need.

I'm feeling very well taken care of, and by the time we're ready for the parade to start, I'm relaxed and excited.

The official *Galactic Wars* series music score plays, and I brace myself, my heart racing from the thrill of it all. It's like walking the red carpet, but bigger. There are costumed characters lined up, who are actually cast members of Wonder Land. Anyone who is a live actor or voice actor in the GW universe has their own vehicle to ride in.

The car starts moving as I hear, "Ladies and gentlemen. Boys and girls. Wonder Land welcomes you to the *Galactic Wars* Weekend!"

I do a little happy dance in my spot because I'm just so psyched to see the crowds.

"As part of the *Galactic Wars* Weekend, we are proud to present the Legends of the Galaxy, a very special celebrity motorcade!"

"That's you, Ms. Lucas!" Tara says as she walks alongside the car.

"Do you stay with us for the entire parade?"

"No, just until you get past the backstage gates. Everyone walking has to be in costume. But don't worry, you're in good hands with Jeremy."

"Thanks, Tara."

Before I know it, we're through the gates and driving slowly along the midway, and I want to stop and pinch myself.

It's really happening.

I'm one of the stars of a Wonder Land parade.

We go along, and people are calling my name and snapping pictures, and it's so much better than I ever imagined. When we get to a roundabout, I spot my family. They're all here to support me, smiling and waving, and I swear it means more than all the thousands of other people here to do the same.

Mom and Dad give me a thumbs up. My sisters jump up and down and wave, right along with Christian's siblings and mom. My heart is ready to burst with love. I truly have the best hype squad, and it makes my heart so happy that our families get along so well.

I briefly shut my eyes and imagine Christian standing there with them, cheering me on and beaming with pride. One day, I know he'll be able to attend these types of things, but I'm so grateful for my family and friends in the meantime.

As the car continues on, I turn one last time and wave to them as tears gently sting my eyes because…my wish came true.

I finally made it.

The pace doesn't slow down.

In late summer, I'm back in LA, and Christian's up in Toronto. We're spending more and more time apart, and neither of us is happy about it. My trips to see him are long and expensive, and I'm seriously wondering if I can keep it up. As much as I love my role with *The Echo Wars*, I don't know if I want to pursue anything else. My focus needs to be on my marriage. My husband. And trying to do even more with my career is keeping me from him.

I know I can handle all of my work for playing and promoting Ashla, but anything beyond that feels like too much.

And it breaks my heart. But it seems impossible to find balance at this point. The scales are completely tipped.

I'm so tired of traveling, yet here I am, packing my little carry-on for another quick trip to be with Christian. I can't wait to see him and feel his arms around me as we curl up in bed tonight to watch some TV.

I wish he were only a few hours away, but he's not. The flight alone is a little over five hours, and that doesn't include the two hours at the airport or dealing with customs. It turns into an entire day, and I don't love it.

"Hey!" Jen says as she pops her head into my room. "You almost ready?"

She's driving me to the airport. Normally, I take a cab, but she offered today, and I'm thankful. "Almost."

"Uh-oh. You okay?" She steps farther into the room. "You sound tired. Do you feel all right? Can I get you anything?"

"You're sweet. I'm just…" Pausing, I sigh. "I hate travel days to Toronto, that's all. They're so long and…ugh. I can't wait for the season to be over."

"Do you think they'll re-sign Christian?"

"He doesn't think so and mentioned they might trade him, but who knows, right?" I toss my cosmetic bag into my suitcase and then zip it shut. "Ready."

She just stands there studying me.

"What?" I ask after the silence gets awkward.

Her smile is serene. "I don't like it when you're cranky. You've been in such a good mood lately. It makes me sad to see you do a complete one-eighty."

I know exactly what she means. "Yeah, I'm not a fan either, but I'll get over it. I know it'll all be worth it when I see my husband's face later."

"Any big plans while you're there?"

Shaking my head, I pick up my suitcase. "Nope. Just living together." I smile. "He's got one night off, so maybe we'll go out to eat or something. Other than that, we're just going to enjoy living like a regular married couple."

She laughs softly before nodding toward the door. "Come on. Let's get going. The traffic's going to be a beast."

I follow her out of the room. "You know you don't have to drive me, Jen. There's so much traffic for you—coming and going. It really isn't a big deal for me to take a cab."

"I want to do this. Besides, I'm going to be traveling the next time you're in town, so this will have to hold me over until we're here at the same time again. And who knows when that'll be?"

Unable to help myself, I pull her in for a hug. "I love you, friend."

"Love you, too. And not just because you're Ashla Voss and part of my favorite movie franchise. Because you're Ella Holt. The best friend a girl could have."

I go to correct her, and she stops me.

"Don't even," she says with a laugh as she grabs her purse and keys. "I know you're Ella Lucas now, but you were Ella Holt when we met."

Hard to argue with that logic.

The ride to the airport is long, but we don't talk about anything serious. We sing along to one of our favorite playlists and laugh at some of the memories it evokes. By the time we pull up at the terminal, I'm in a much better mood. And when I hug her goodbye, I'm so full of gratitude.

"Do you have any idea how precious you are?" I ask.

That makes her laugh even as she hugs me back. "That's not a phrase I usually hear."

Pulling back with a smile, I nod. "Well...you should. You're precious, like a precious gemstone, and those are rare. Friends like you are rare and hard to find. You completely lifted my mood and my whole mindset today, and it makes everything from this point on seem tolerable. So, thank you."

"That's what friends are for."

I wish I could take her with me, but I can't.

"Tell Christian I said hello, and you and I will talk soon. Text me when you land."

"Will do!"

I get out of the car and head into the terminal, which feels like a second—or fourth—home at this point. It's loud and crowded, and I want to get to my gate and settle in. It takes forever to get there, but when I do, I find a seat and prepare to sit for a while.

When my phone rings, I know it's Christian. He promised to call after his game.

"Hey! How'd everything go today?"

"Good," he says. "But, um...change of plans."

"Excuse me?" I ask with amusement. "What does that even mean?"

"It means, don't get on the plane to Toronto. We're going to Arizona."

"Wait...what?" I'm pretty sure I'm hearing things. Maybe I'm getting interference from someone else's call, or an announcement on the loudspeaker or something. Because he can't mean that I have to fly to Arizona.

But that's exactly what he's saying.

"Yeah. So, we just beat New York 6–2, and as soon as we got to the locker room, I got the call. They traded me to Arizona."

"But…Christian…how? What about all our things in Toronto? Don't you have to pack everything first? Or maybe I should still go and then meet you in Arizona?"

"You and I both know there's nothing overly important that we'll need right away. Plus, the team said they would help us arrange to have our stuff packed and shipped to our new home. Besides, I know how much you hate the trip to Toronto." He chuckles—part amusement, part happiness. "This is gonna be good. Plus, I'm on the roster for the game tomorrow night, and I really want you to be there for it."

Good Lord. My head is spinning just trying to keep up with all of this.

"What do you say, Ella Rose? Are you ready for another adventure? One that'll have us traveling a whole lot less to see each other? It's going to be like when you flew to Tempe. Only ninety minutes instead of this five-hour deal. And no having to deal with customs. Won't that be great?"

Is he kidding? Of course, it's great. But it's not the point.

It's crazy how my wildly structured husband—a man who always has a plan and a routine—is suddenly okay with uprooting our lives on a moment's notice.

Literally.

"Ella Rose? Are you still there?"

"What? Yes. Yes, I'm here. Sorry. This is just a lot to absorb."

Which is putting it mildly.

We *did* love being in Arizona. That was truly where our story began. Maybe it's a good sign that we're going back.

And maybe, just maybe, it's a step closer to us finally settling somewhere. My mind immediately goes back to how much I used to dream of us settling in California, so maybe that's back on the table.

"Look, I need to go," he says. "I've got to get my things together and say my goodbyes before heading to the airport. Management in Phoenix is handling a hotel for us. I'll text you the details as soon as I have them and meet you there. Love you."

"I love you, too." I hang up, gather my meager belongings, and head to the nearest ticket desk.

"How may I help you?"

"One ticket to Phoenix, please."

If I thought the airport experience was a whirlwind, it's nothing compared to arriving in Phoenix. I get there before Christian since it was such a short flight, and when he arrives, we barely have time to say hello before he's whisked away to the stadium to meet his new team.

Leaving me alone.

With nothing else to do, I order room service and immediately begin researching the area so I can hit the ground running on finding someplace to live tomorrow.

He comes back late, and we immediately crash, watching TV even as he tells me about his speedy tour and meet and greet. He sounds so excited. It's infectious.

I want to ask how he's feeling physically, but I don't want to put a damper on the mood. So, we settle into each other's arms and fall asleep.

The next morning, he's on the go again. We manage to have breakfast together before he leaves, but setting up our new life here will be on my shoulders. What would he do without me?

"I left everything you'll need for the game today in the folder on the table. Luckily, it's an afternoon game, so we can relax later," he says before kissing me thoroughly and heading out the door.

My head is spinning again.

And it doesn't stop until the game is over and we're back at the hotel, where we can finally enjoy a little peace and quiet and our reunion. I know we were here together last night, but it was frenzied, and we were both full of anxious energy.

But now? Now is our time. Just the two of us, where we can reconnect without the rush.

As I look around our suite, I don't think I'll ever stop being amazed at how a hotel room can feel like home simply because he's in it. Being in the same place at the same time and under the same roof does wonders for me.

The suite is quiet. The world is hushed beyond the thick windows. Phoenix sprawls beneath us in glittering lights, but right now, all I can see is Christian—showered, warm, and a little tired, but still soaking in that post-win glow as he leans against the couch with a grin he pretends isn't smug. His hat sits abandoned on the table, his new team jacket is draped over a chair, and his arm is lazily stretched along the couch's back cushion, waiting for me. Always waiting for me.

I sink down beside him, and he immediately pulls me in. It's like there's been a him-shaped hole causing an ache under my ribs, and the piece finally clicks back into place.

"First game in Phoenix," I whisper, smiling into his shoulder. "It feels…full circle."

He gives me a soft laugh, the sound low and fond. "Yeah? You thinking what I'm thinking?"

"Tempe," I say instantly.

And there it is. The look in his eyes changes. Softens. Brightens. Like we just unlocked a shared secret.

"That week to ourselves…" he murmurs, shaking his head. "The hotel, the rooftop restaurant, all the shopping and sightseeing. It was a perfect week."

"Mmm…if you don't count the fact that you were injured and were there for physical therapy," I correct, laughing, even though I don't actually care because the memory is warm and glowing in my chest. "You complained every single day."

"I didn't complain," he says, mock offended. "I suffered silently. Bravely."

"Yes, you did." I pat his chest and fight the urge—again—to ask how he's feeling.

He smiles once more, softer this time. "Being with you was the best therapy in the world."

I lean my head against him, inhaling soap and skin and something uniquely him. "That feels like a lifetime ago. We were such babies back then," I murmur. "Trying to figure everything out. Trying to figure *us* out."

He hums in agreement. "Yet somehow, this still feels like that beginning. Like every time we end up somewhere new, life resets a little. Like we get to remember who we were before everything got… big."

I know what he means. Before the flights and the cities and the distance and the schedules. Before the goodbyes that always feel too soon.

"This was completely unexpected," I say. "This move. I know you mentioned the possibility of a trade, but…"

"Yeah." His thumb drags slow circles over my shoulder, the touch grounding and tender. "I think this will be a good place, where we can make wonderful memories. I love all the memories we make together, and I know there's so much more to come."

I close my eyes, breathing that in.

Then, another feeling creeps up—the one I've been pushing down. He senses it immediately. He always does.

"Hey." His voice dips, the tone gentle. "Talk to me."

I exhale. "I just…sometimes, it all hits at once, you know? Another move. Another city. Packing up. Leaving because you left. Leaving because I need to. Leaving because we're always chasing where your life goes next and hoping mine can follow."

He cups my chin, so I have to meet his eyes. There's no hesitation there. No uncertainty. Just steady, unwavering love.

"Ella Rose," he says quietly, "I know our lives are a bit unconventional, but we know it won't be like this forever. I am so incredibly thankful for you because I would simply be existing through all these moves if you weren't here beside me."

"Christian…"

"No, I'm serious. Because you're brave and strong and you're not afraid to build a life instead of waiting for one to happen to you. Everything we have is because of you. You take care of me. Us. I know I can handle any move, any trade, because you're beside me." His thumb brushes beneath my lip, tender. "But yeah… I know it's a lot. I know I ask a lot of you by…existing the way I do. By doing what I do."

"You never ask," I whisper. "And that's almost worse. You never ask, and I still go."

He smiles as if it physically aches. "That's because we're a team. I don't need to ask. You wouldn't for me either. There will come a time when I will blindly follow you. We do things together. Always."

It settles something inside me that's been rattling ever since I got on the plane yesterday.

"I just hate when we have to live in separate places," I admit, my voice small. "I hate missing you."

His forehead presses against mine, and everything inside me quiets.

"Me, too," he murmurs. "More than I'll ever be able to explain. But tonight…you're here. I'm here. We're not missing anything. We're exactly where we're supposed to be."

And just like that, every sharp edge softens. Every tight knot loosens.

He kisses me then—slow, patient, reverent. Not the kind of kiss that says he hasn't seen me in weeks, but the kind that says he intends to keep seeing me forever. The kind that feels like vows without words.

When he pulls back, I'm smiling, and I don't even realize it.

"Welcome back to Arizona, Mrs. Lucas," he whispers.

"Yeah," I breathe, brushing my nose against his. "It's good to be home."

Even if home is a hotel suite in Phoenix.

Even if that home moves.

Because really, home is…him.

Home.

Ha!

Last night feels like a distant memory in the light of day, because we're immediately back to the real world. Christian's at the stadium, and I'm at the hotel, looking at apartments online. I know by now that they don't have to be perfect. They only need to be functional.

They all look the same to me, and I know it doesn't matter which one we pick; it's temporary.

Always temporary.

I'm sipping tea and having a pit-tea party when my phone rings. Seeing Tracy's name makes me smile.

"Hey, Tracy."

"Ella," she begins excitedly. "Are you in LA or Toronto right now?"

"Neither," I reply with a laugh. "I'm actually in Phoenix."

"Phoenix? What on earth are you doing there? Did you decide to meet Christian for a game?"

"No, um…" I guess it's not really a secret since he officially played on the roster last night. "Christian got traded here. So…here I am."

"Oh, my goodness. This is amazing! That means you can get back to LA quickly."

I'm certain she has an audition for me. That's the nature of our relationship, and one of the few reasons she calls. So, she's not surprised when I ask, "What's the role?"

"Sweetie, this is going to be the biggest thing of your career. Bigger than *The Echo Wars*. Bigger than Ashla."

Okay, she definitely has my attention.

"What is it?"

"How do you feel about superhero movies?"

"Um..."

"You know Storyteller just inked a deal with a major franchise, right?"

I nod, even though she can't see me.

"Well, they're casting for their first big movie, and they're looking at their in-house talent first," she tells me. "Your name came up repeatedly. I don't want to say the role is yours, but...this role could most definitely be yours."

"Oh, my gosh..." I'm breathless and shaking, and I immediately get up to pace. "So, this is a major..."

"A major motion picture, Ella. This is everything we've been working for! So, how soon can you get here?"

I can barely remember what day it is. Monday? Tuesday?

Tuesday. It's Tuesday.

"I can be there Thursday, Tracy. I'll text you as soon as my flight is booked."

"Excellent! It's finally happening, and I am beyond thrilled for you. Here's to great things."

I lift my teacup, but words escape me.

"I'm emailing all the information to you now—everything I have regarding the audition—so you know what you're looking at. We'll talk soon, Ella. Bye!"

I hang up and feel overwhelmed. I need to talk to Christian, but that won't happen until tonight. In the meantime, I look at my flight options but don't book anything. I can always text Tracy later. My mind wanders to what a role like this could mean. I stop myself before my imagination goes any further.

I haven't even showered yet, and I feel like I've run a marathon.

But I can't wait to reach the finish line.

Twenty

I sit on the edge of the hotel bed, holding my phone like it weighs twenty pounds instead of a few ounces. Funny how something so small can hold something as huge as a potentially life-changing decision.

And committing to this role would most definitely change my life.

Tracy's email came several hours ago, and I've read it what feels like a hundred times. *Major motion picture. Lead role consideration. Audition on Friday.* Months on location if I book it. Months away from Phoenix. From Christian.

From *us.*

The room is quiet except for the hushed hum of the air conditioning unit. The space feels too still. My mind feels too loud.

I should be excited. This is the kind of opportunity people spend their whole lives hoping for. The type of thing I used to daydream about while sitting on studio floors, waiting for my name to be called. The moment I swore I'd never apologize for wanting.

But now, I'm staring at the email, terrified of wanting it.

Because Christian is here. Because he's still healing. Because he uprooted his entire life—his team, his routine, his identity—and he's still figuring out what all of that means. He's still struggling to figure out what his career looks like at this stage. And after everything he's been through…what kind of wife disappears for months?

I haven't booked my flight or texted Tracy back yet.

Christian and I always like to talk about career opportunities before we accept them.

If there's time. But sometimes, a decision has to be made immediately without us sitting down to discuss it.

Which is why I'm currently in Phoenix instead of Toronto.

But I often have the luxury of time to sit and have a conversation with him about auditions and potential roles. I love getting his input and having us make the decision together. But now, as I anxiously watch the time, I can't quite wrap my brain around what I'm going to say to him.

Or to Tracy.

I'm so torn. It's like I can practically feel myself being torn in two. Do I turn toward the career I've dreamed of and worked toward my entire life? Or do I walk away and embrace being here, where I know I'm needed?

I may not have asked Christian the questions about how he's feeling physically, but I don't need to. I can see it in the way he moves. I know his body as well as mine. And maybe if I hadn't been distracted by my career, I could have been there to advocate for his health when he wasn't doing it for himself.

It would be easy to pick up the phone right now and bounce ideas off my mom or even Jen, but this feels like something I need to figure out for myself before Christian gets back.

I wish having two successful yet challenging careers in one marriage were easy.

I may be his rock in some ways, but he's *my* rock in others. I've always wanted that balance—the kind of partnership my parents have, built on quiet strength and mutual care. The easy give and take. The steady rhythm of a marriage that knows how to bend without breaking. And I won't let anything stand in the way of that. This isn't a role I can walk away from when the cameras stop rolling. This is my life, and it's worth fighting for.

All I know right now—what my heart is telling me loud and clear—is that if I had to choose between my career and my husband? There's no contest.

My husband. Always.

Forever.

I've had plenty of experiences with different roles. I've sung and danced and acted. And while they were all exciting, none of them compares to how I feel when I'm with Christian.

That's the role.

The life-changing role.

Wife. Partner. Lover. Teammate.

I glance at the clock again. They're playing an evening game, and I know I need to be there. I know how much he loves having me at the games. And it's probably a good distraction for me. Well, that and looking for apartments, which I still haven't finished doing. So…I walk over to the sofa and sit back down, pulling up the listings I had been looking at earlier before Tracy's call. I'll make some decisions and follow them up with appointments.

Maybe by the time Christian and I are back here tonight, I'll have made a decision about everything else.

Maybe.

We're back at the hotel, and Christian has been talking almost nonstop about how much he's enjoying the new team's dynamic. It's clear that everyone is looking at him as the valued player he is, along with being a leader and someone with a strong work ethic and experience from two World Series championship teams.

It's an absolute joy to listen to him. I know he takes his role seriously, and I'm honestly thrilled that he's getting the recognition he deserves.

"I'm gonna grab a shower," he says after giving me a quick kiss. "Will you order dinner for us?"

"Absolutely." It's nice having room service, and I'm seriously impressed that Christian's being so flexible with his dietary routine. I know we'll go right back to it as soon as we move into an apartment, but for tonight, I'm happy not to have to be the one preparing dinner.

When the bathroom door opens several minutes later, I don't look up. I'm sitting on the sofa, staring at Tracy's email again. Christian's footsteps are lighter than they used to be. Cautious. Controlled. Like his body reminds him daily that it hasn't forgiven him yet.

He doesn't say anything at first, just walks over and sits beside me, his thigh brushing mine. Warm. Familiar. The most grounding thing in my life. This time, I do look up and offer him a small smile.

"You're quiet," he murmurs. He doesn't ask what's wrong. He waits. He always waits.

I swallow hard and know it's time. "I got an email today."

He glances at my phone. "Audition?"

I nod. "Not just any audition." My voice comes out softer than intended. "It's…big. Like, game-changing big."

He smiles a little. Proud. Automatically proud. It makes my chest ache.

"That's amazing." He reaches up and caresses my cheek with those strong, sure fingers. I lean into them. "We knew it was only a matter of time before Hollywood really stood up and took notice."

There it is. The part of him that believes in me more than I believe in myself.

I exhale, pressing my lips together. "It's going to be months of filming. Some of it is out of the country. And I just…" My throat tightens. "We just got here. You're still trying to get settled. Still healing. I don't want to leave you. I don't want you to feel like baseball has you fighting alone again. I don't want…"

He reaches for my hand, and I fall silent because I always do when he does that. His fingers thread through mine, his thumb brushing slow circles across my skin.

"Ella Rose," he says quietly, "I never want you to shrink your life for mine."

My eyes sting. "It doesn't feel like shrinking. It feels like… choosing. Like I should be choosing you."

He turns to me fully then, his expression soft. "You *are* choosing me. You choose me every day. But your career? Your dreams? Those are *you*, too. I don't get to be the only thing that matters in your world."

I laugh weakly, wiping under my eye. "Yeah, well…you matter a lot."

He leans forward until his forehead rests against mine. We breathe the same air for a moment. Our rhythm, our calm.

"So do you," he whispers. "I don't need you here to know you love me. Being in the same city doesn't define us. We've already done the distance. We've already done the hard work. We've already survived…everything."

I close my eyes. "But what if you need me?"

He smiles faintly. "Then I'll call you. And you'll yell at me for pretending I'm fine when I'm not. And we'll figure it out, just like we always do."

My chest loosens a little.

"You deserve this," he continues gently. "You've worked too hard not to walk through doors when they open. Don't turn this down because you're afraid of leaving me. I'm not something fragile you have to guard. I'm your partner. I'm on your side. Always."

My breath shakes as I exhale, relief and fear tangling together. "You really mean that?"

He lifts my chin, so I have to look at him. His eyes are steady. Certain.

"I love you," he says simply. "And I'm proud of you. And I want to be the guy standing beside you while you become everything you're meant to be. Not the reason you didn't."

The tears spill then, but they're quiet.

I lean into him, and he wraps his arms around me, pulling me into his chest. I breathe him in—warm skin and his natural scent that is better than any cologne and something that feels like home.

For the first time since the email arrived, I feel like I can breathe.

"Thank you," I whisper into his shirt.

"There's nothing to thank me for," he murmurs, kissing the top of my head. "Go remind the world who you are."

I smile, but I'm still not convinced this is the right decision. My gut is telling me it's not. I open my mouth to tell him that, but no words come out.

The light knock on the door interrupts the moment, and Christian is immediately on his feet and going to get our dinner. We set it up on the small dining table in the suite, and once we're both seated, I'm oddly relieved when the topic of conversation turns to apartments.

"I know you've had a lot on your mind with the audition offer," he says as he cuts into his steak. "But did you have any time to research apartments?"

"I did. I even set up a few tours for tomorrow morning so we can look at them together."

The smile he gives me shows how happy he is that I planned it that way. "Awesome. I don't have to be at the stadium until one, and then we fly out on Thursday for our game in Boston." He pauses. "Tell me about these apartments. Do you have a favorite? Any one in particular that you like more than the others?"

We talk about places to live, our dinner, and his game schedule—and we do it as if I'm going to be in LA for the next week or two.

I don't correct him because…well…because I don't.

I can't.

I need to sleep on it.

Yes. That's what I need, to settle everything in my mind once and for all. A good night's sleep will put everything into perspective.

We look at three different apartments and decide the third one is our favorite.

I use that term loosely because it's temporary. Christian believes this move will only be for this season, so we pick the place we like out of the ones we toured and sign the lease. When we get back to the hotel, we arrange to have all our stuff packed and shipped from Toronto.

"Good thing you're going back to LA this week," Christian says with a small laugh as he gets ready to head to the stadium.

"Um…why?"

"So we can check out of the hotel. By the time we're both back, hopefully some of our things will have arrived from Canada. I know you never travel with much, so you'll need more than what's in your carry-on."

He's got a point.

I let out a long breath and follow him across the room as he gathers his bag and gear for today's game.

"So, I was thinking…"

Before I can say more, his phone rings. Pulling it from his pocket, he groans quietly. "I'm sorry, but I need to take this. It's one of the trainers." He absentmindedly kisses my cheek. "I'll see you at the game, right?"

"Why is the trainer calling you?"

He looks at the phone and then at me, but I know where his attention is. "It's nothing, I'm sure, but…"

"Go," I tell him as I sit back down on the sofa. Christian walks away from me, speaking softly into the phone, and I don't take it as a good sign. I watch as he moves around the suite, pacing slowly, and I get a sinking feeling that things aren't any better.

I mean, I know they aren't. I've known it all along. But I keep holding on to the tiny glimmer of hope that I'm being overly critical and that his body is healing.

His shoulders sag, and I hear him say, "I'll be there. Thanks."

I watch as he slides his phone into his pocket before facing me, but his smile is forced as he comes over to kiss me again.

"Everything okay?"

"My medical records arrived, so…" He shrugs. "They want to meet with me."

I don't ask anything else because I can already tell that he's feeling defeated. So, I reach up and give him a reassuring kiss. "I'll see you at the game. I love you."

That seems to ease his mind. "Love you, too, beautiful girl." And then he leaves.

I woke up this morning knowing my decision about the audition, and this little interaction confirms that I'm doing the right thing.

I stare at Tracy's name on my phone for five full minutes before finally pressing call.

It rings twice.

"Ella!" she answers brightly, polished enthusiasm dripping through the speaker. "Please tell me this is the part where you confess you simply forgot to text me your travel info because you're already studying the superhero universe and deciding what color gown you want to wear to your first Oscar ceremony."

I swallow. My mouth feels dry. And honestly, I might vomit.

"Not…exactly."

There's a brief pause. Not long, just long enough for her instincts to flare.

"What do you mean 'not exactly?'" she asks lightly, but the sharpness underneath is unmistakable.

I take a breath. "I won't be coming to LA. I'm not going to audition."

Silence.

Tracy's not the reactive type. She doesn't gasp. She doesn't shout. She goes very still. But I can almost *hear* her brain recalculating.

"I must've misheard you," she says finally, her voice smooth as glass. "Because you cannot possibly be telling me you're turning down a direct lead consideration for one of the biggest films shooting next year."

"I am."

"And why," she asks calmly, too calmly, "would you do that?"

My fingers grip the phone tighter. "Because it would mean months away. And Christian is…he's still recovering. We've just uprooted our lives again. He needs stability. *We* need stability. And I need to prioritize my marriage right now."

Even though he's okay with me leaving—and I truly believe he is—*I'm* not.

"And you can't do that while working?" Tracy replies instantly.

"It's not just work," I say softly. "It's leaving. It's disappearing from our lives again. And I don't want to do that. Not right now. It's just not the right time."

Tracy exhales a little laugh. It's not amused.

"Oh, sweetheart," she says. "You're romanticizing sacrifice like it's some noble calling. He plays baseball. *You* act. That's the deal. You knew what you were marrying into. He knew what he was marrying into. This is the kind of role people wait their entire careers for."

"I know," I whisper, and I do. I seriously do. "But my marriage isn't something I want to gamble with."

Another pause, longer this time.

"You are making an emotional decision," she says crisply. "Not a professional one. And emotional decisions cost careers."

"I'm aware."

"No," she snaps, her patience cracking now. "You *think* you're aware. You think everyone will just…stay interested. That Hollywood waits politely for actresses who choose domestic bliss over opportunity. It doesn't. It replaces you. Quickly. Quietly."

The words sting, not because they're cruel, but because they're true.

"I don't want to disappear," I say softly. "I'm not quitting. I'm just…choosing differently. Right now."

"Right now turns into later," she replies. "Later turns into 'maybe someday,' and someday turns into *never*."

She's frustrated. Agitated. I can picture her pacing. Not heartbroken. Not hurt.

Just…calculating a loss.

"I appreciate everything you have done for me. Every accomplishment in my career is because of you," I say gently, because I do care about her. Or I thought I did. "But this is what I need to do."

There's a sharp exhale.

"Well," Tracy says coolly, "then I should probably be honest, too."

Something in my chest tightens because her tone doesn't even remotely imply that something warm and fuzzy is coming.

"If you're not actively working," she continues, her voice turning crisp, professional, and unforgiving, "you're not making me money. And if you're not making me money, you're no good to me."

My stomach drops, and my lunch slowly rises in my throat.

I blink. "I'm…sorry?"

"I'm not here to hold your hand while you play house and *find yourself* emotionally," she says. "I build careers. I negotiate deals. I make stars. I don't babysit people who decide their husbands are their entire personality."

The room feels like it's spinning. My heart is racing so hard I fear I might pass out.

"Wow," I whisper.

"I booked this meeting. I secured this opportunity. I've invested years into your trajectory. And you're just…walking away from momentum." She sighs as if it's exhausting. "So, I'm walking away, too. But I'll still be collecting my ten percent for everything I booked for you," she adds bitterly.

"You're quitting?" I ask. Even to my own ears, I sound stunned.

"Yes," she says simply. "I'll have my office send the paperwork. Best of luck, Ella."

The line goes dead before I can respond.

For a moment, I can only sit there, staring at my phone in my trembling hand. But my heart? It's still racing but…not in heartbreak, or even in anger.

Just…clarity.

I thought Tracy was in my corner. I thought she cared about *me.* The human. The friend. The woman whose life she was helping shape.

But no.

To her, I was a product. A brand. A revenue stream.

And now, I'm not.

It hurts. Of course, it hurts. But there's something else beneath the sting.

Relief.

Because for the first time in a long time, the truth is clear.

This isn't personal for her.

But it is for me.

And I chose right.

My manager, Alison, calls me an hour after my call with Tracy and also severs ties with me.

For the same reason. I'm useless to her if I'm not working on anything.

If this is rock bottom, I never want to be here again.

I don't tell Christian about my conversations with Tracy and Alison until we sit down to dinner after the game. I expect him to pepper me with questions, but he doesn't. Instead, he gets quiet. We finish our meal in utter silence.

Christian isn't a loud person to begin with, but when something's weighing on him, he gets…still. Thoughtful. It's the kind of silence that hums—both unsettling and comforting at the same time.

I stand and look around, unsure what to do. The Phoenix city lights stretch out before me through the window, and it reminds me of the nights we ate dinner at the rooftop restaurant in Tempe. I remember swaying to the music, admiring the scenery, and just feeling like my world was perfect.

I'd give anything for Christian to walk over to me now so we can sway to invisible music and just push the world away for a while.

Instead, he stretches out on the couch, staring ahead as if he's watching something I can't see.

Unable to stand the silence any longer, I sit down beside him and gently nudge him with my knee. "You've been in your head for the last hour. Talk to me. Please."

He doesn't answer right away. His jaw works as if he's rehearsing what he wants to say. Or maybe fighting it.

"Do you ever feel like," he finally says, his voice low, "like you ended up being more of a…support system than a wife?"

It hits hard, sharp. "What?"

He rubs his hands over his face in frustration. But not with me. With himself. "I mean…everything. Moving. Packing. Adjusting. Waiting. Holding your life in your hands, ready to set it down whenever I need something." He exhales slowly. "Like I'm living my dream, and you're…orbiting it."

My instinct is to deny it. To tell him he's being ridiculous. But he's not asking for reassurance. He's confessing.

So, I wait.

He swallows. "When we first started this, I promised myself I'd do right by you. That I would always put you first and do everything I could to set you up for success. I vowed to never ask you to carry the weight of my career. But I look back and…" He lets out a long breath. "So much of our life revolves around whether I'm playing, whether I'm hurt, whether I'm traded. Whether I'm okay."

His voice cracks on that last word, and my heart aches.

"You've changed cities, changed routines, changed entire *plans* for me, over and over," he continues, softer now. "And you've done it without a pause. Like it's natural. Like you owe it to me. And I don't know when I stopped questioning that. I don't know when I stopped asking if you were okay. When I stopped making sure that you didn't feel like second place to the game."

"You haven't—" I start.

He shakes his head gently. "Let me finish?"

I go quiet.

"I grew up believing baseball was everything," he says. "And for a long time, it was. It was my identity. My anchor. My future. And then you came into my life and, suddenly, it wasn't the center anymore. You were." He breathes out, long and shaky, both hands raking through his hair, making it spiky. "And somehow, I still kept acting like the game had to come first. Like it was a force I couldn't push back against, even for you."

There's grief in his voice, and it's raw and honest.

He looks at me then—really looks—and his eyes are tired, yet so impossibly full of love.

"You've been a good teammate," he whispers. "You've bent when life needed bending. You've sacrificed without calling it a sacrifice. You've stood by me, even when it meant standing alone. I hate thinking about how lonely you've been." His throat works. "And I haven't been able to do the same for you."

Emotion burns behind my eyes, and I will the unshed tears not to fall.

"Christian..." I breathe softly, reaching for his hand.

He threads his fingers through mine but doesn't look away. "I'm not saying I regret baseball. I don't. I love it. I always will. It's changed my life—our life. But I can't keep pretending that the cost hasn't been real. On us. On you. And I don't get to ignore that because the game is comfortable and familiar and safe for me."

His words land, slow and heavy. I know what he's walking toward before he says it.

"This is my last season," he says, his voice low.

The words linger in the space between us. Not explosive. Not shouted. Just truth.

"I'm not asking..."

He places a finger over my lips, silencing anything I have to say.

"I know you're not. You never would. This is completely my decision, and...I'm done after this season," he continues. "I've been so blessed, and I've achieved everything I could ever dream of and more in my career. Before I met you, I never knew a life without baseball, and because of you, I know what I *want* my life to look like after baseball. And it's not measured in innings or stats or how hard I can push my body before it breaks again." His voice softens, steady and sure. "It's you. It's us. It's being the husband you deserve, not the one who keeps asking you to put your world on hold so I can play in mine."

My vision blurs.

He squeezes my hand, gentler now. "And I want you to chase everything. Every role. Every dream. Every version of your life that makes you feel alive. I don't want to be the reason you ever doubt that you're allowed to want more. If you want to call Tracy right now..."

Now it's *my* fingers over *his* lips as I shake my head. "No. That's not what I want. What I want is right here in front of me." I pause, even as the first tear falls. "You. All I've ever wanted is you."

There's a profound quiet after that. The kind that feels sacred.

I lean forward slowly and press my forehead to his, both of us a little breathless and emotionally drained.

He doesn't try to fix the silence. He simply holds me. Steady. Certain. We're both free in a way that we've never been free before. Our careers have dictated our choices for so long, but tonight we made a choice.

And we chose us.

Twenty-One

"This feels weird. Don't you think it feels weird?"

"Um…"

We're at my apartment in LA now that baseball season is over. We packed up most of our stuff and had it shipped to Florida for storage. Why Florida? Because that's where our families are. My family moved back to Orlando, and it's where we've decided to eventually put down roots because family is most important to us.

But this apartment? Well, this is so we have a place to stay when I need to be here to record for *The Echo Wars*. The show keeps growing in popularity, and we're now recording season three. Despite my agent and manager dropping me, my career has been steadily moving forward. Christian and I are moving forward, too. On our terms.

I slowly walk around the space. The living room that doubles as everything—office, dining nook, movie theater, and dance space. I run my hand along the cozy blue couch that faces the small, wall-mounted TV, and smile sadly at the worn, thrifted coffee table that's always barely been wide enough for a laptop and two mugs. The faux hardwood floors still creak, and the battered and worn woven rug that used to add a splash of personality is beyond faded.

Jen and I have lived what feels like many lifetimes in this space, and it seems weird to be here without her. The sad sigh is out before I can stop it.

"You know she moved only fifteen minutes away, right?" Christian teases, reading my mind.

Laughing softly, I shake my head. "I know, but…I've never been here like this without her. Sure, there were times I was here, and she was away, but her stuff was always here. Now, it feels a little…I don't know…sad."

He walks up behind me, wrapping those muscular arms around me before kissing my cheek. "Then we'll just have to fill it with stuff of our own so it's not quite so sad."

That makes me smile.

Plenty of things in this apartment are mementos from my life before Christian, but there are also many from the time since we met. The thought of us being able to put stuff in here now feels like the closest thing we've had to a place of our own. This little apartment has been the one constant since I was twenty, and I honestly love the idea of the two of us making it ours.

Turning in his arms, I smile up at him. And yes, my heart still skips a beat when he smiles back, and I get to gaze into those brilliant blue eyes that I'll never grow tired of seeing.

"I love that idea," I say softly. "Thank you."

He kisses me, and it goes from sweet to a little something more. When we're here, we're usually on alert for Jen to come through the door, so there's something a little freeing about knowing we won't be disturbed. So, we linger a little while longer before slowly pulling apart, breathless and smiling.

"We really should unpack…" I say, not really wanting to as we kiss some more.

"Yeah, I'm getting pretty hungry. We really should go to the grocery store…" he says before we kiss some more.

"Or we can just order pizza and have a quiet date night at our apartment," I suggest. We can always start unpacking tomorrow. Now that the baseball season is over, we don't have to follow any strict routines.

"Are you kidding? That sounds like the perfect night to me." He moves in close again, "Those are always my favorite date nights."

"Mine, too. But now that we're back in California, the walks on the beach to watch the sunsets were pretty spectacular, too."

"Mmm...they were. We'll have to make some time to do that while we're here."

This is the first time in years that we didn't pack up and go to Florida at the end of baseball season, and I feel like we have so many opportunities. I don't even know where to start. I need to be in LA right now for several promo events for *The Echo Wars* and to wrap up some recordings before the holidays. Christian and I have already planned to spend the time with our families before coming back for my recording schedule. The next several weeks are full for me, but they're the complete opposite for him. We haven't talked about it much, but I'm curious what retirement looks like for him. Right now, we're just taking things one day, one moment at a time.

But first, our pizza date night...

* * *

The Galactic Wars have a tremendous presence at conventions, and I go to as many as I can. They are so much fun, and I love meeting the fans and interacting with them. It's mind-blowing that so many people are so enthusiastic about the universe—and specifically Ashla.

I'm in a weird headspace because...well...this is the life I've always imagined for us, but it seemed so far off. It's here now, and I didn't realize how big of an adjustment it would be to live a "normal" life. One not on a strict schedule, or with an exact routine. This is what I've dreamed of, and it's taking me a while to ease up and enjoy the freedom.

We don't really talk about it, but I can tell that we're both working to find our new groove.

It's also remarkable how much Christian's body has healed. He's worked hard at it—at relaxing and giving himself grace. We found a physical therapist with no connections to the league, and they came up with a treatment plan that has seriously worked wonders.

I've always loved watching him move—both on the field and off. He has an athletic grace that makes everything he does look effortless. And now that he's starting to feel better, it's so much better because I know he's not powering through the pain.

"So? What are we doing today?" Christian asks as we sit down for his famous and delicious pancake breakfast.

Because that's never going away.

#Pancakesforever.

"I have a recording session, but I should be home in time for us to drive to the beach for a sunset dinner."

He nods. "What night are we meeting everyone for dinner? Thursday?"

"Yup. Everyone's going to be there—Jen, Penny, Freya, and all their significant others." I look over at him and let out a happy sigh. "Thank you."

"For what?"

"For always being so willing to hang out with my friends."

"To be fair, they're my friends, too."

It's true. He won them over years ago, and they all adore him.

I mean…who wouldn't?

"And this weekend…?"

I grab my phone and quickly scan the calendar because there's a lot on it. More than I ever imagined. There are conventions literally all over the world, and all of us from *The Echo Wars* are riding the wave of our immense popularity. Between events, appearances, and press interviews, I've been very busy.

So, what makes this different from being on a movie set somewhere far away for weeks or even months?

Christian and I are doing it all together.

Because we're a team.

Go Team Lucas!

"Okay, it looks like the only things we have on the calendar this weekend are an *Echo Wars* meet and greet in Anaheim and a brunch with Michael and Jeremy on Sunday." Putting my phone down, I take a forkful of pancakes, humming with appreciation. "So yummy."

He preens, and it's adorable.

"What about your schedule for next week? Anything exciting?"

"You know, PT on Monday, Wednesday, and Friday, and I received an invitation from the Pasadena Little League to come and speak at one of their events. I have a call with them on Tuesday."

He says it casually, so I'm not exactly sure how he feels about it.

Fortunately, I don't have to ask because he's already talking.

"I think I've been so wrapped up in focusing on letting my body heal that I haven't spent a whole lot of time thinking about what my next chapter looks like." He pauses and then keeps talking. "Everyone expects me to go into coaching. My whole career, I was told that I would make a great coach one day. It's the natural next step," he continues with a sigh. "But, Ella Rose, I'm burned out. I don't want the baseball lifestyle for us anymore. The constant grind. As you always say, it's the same song, different verse."

"Oh, Christian, I completely support you, and I don't want to jump back into that lifestyle either. But maybe the Little League thing…" I prompt. Luckily, he visibly relaxes.

"I think about all the incredible people who came into my life when I was young and fell in love with baseball. Coaches, teachers, older players—all of them. What if…what if I'm the guy who can make a positive impression on a kid who's just learning how to play?"

His face lights up, and his eyes brighten.

"Ella Rose, if I'm being honest, I've lost my love for the game a bit. After dealing with so many injuries, free agency, and contract negotiations…I didn't realize how much I needed a break from baseball."

I think we both needed a break from it, but I don't say anything. I just let him talk.

"Whenever I see kids playing baseball, I stop and watch. I love watching the joy on their faces. I want to find that joy again. I have so many offers to work with major league teams. I'm getting calls constantly to come back and play, or to coach or scout. But I need some distance."

All I can do is nod.

"But kids? I know I can help there and make a difference."

"Christian, by helping kids, you might just end up helping yourself and find your love of baseball again. You should definitely go and talk to the Little League team," I encourage, squeezing his hand. "I also think you should go up to the high school. Remember how your friend from the Waves invited you to come and help his local high school baseball team?"

He shrugs and gives me a knowing smile. "I guess so."

"Yay!" Oh, this makes my heart so happy. Then I glance at the time and realize that if I don't finish eating and get ready, I'm going to be late. "I hate to do this, but I need to power through the rest of my pancakes so I can shower and get dressed. Which means I'm leaving you with the dishes. Sorry."

A deep, masculine chuckle is his only response.

"Christian…" I say around a mouthful of syrupy goodness.

"It's not a problem, you know that. No one's keeping score around here. I know you need to get to the studio, so don't worry. I can handle the dishes."

"I appreciate you so much."

"Appreciate?" he teases. "Really?"

"Love. I love you so much," I counter. "But I appreciate you, too. It's a package deal."

"I can live with that." With a boyish grin, he gives me a quick kiss on the tip of my nose.

Spring arrives, and with it a palpable restlessness.

Christian is a little on edge. A bit unsettled. I know it's not physical because he's back to moving around with ease. I've been to every doctor's appointment and have sat in on some of his physical therapy appointments. I know he's healed. Not one hundred percent, but pretty darn close. Still, I know something's on his mind.

It hits me as I'm bustling around our hotel room in Orlando, preparing for another three-day convention. For the first time in close to his entire life, it's springtime, and Christian doesn't have anywhere he *has* to be.

Every other spring, his life would already be spoken for. Flights. Physicals. Practices. Games that don't technically count but somehow feel like they carry the weight of the world anyway. There was always a fast, demanding, and unyielding rhythm.

But that isn't the case anymore.

Right now, he's standing on the balcony of our hotel room, a mug in his hand, staring out over a skyline that's familiar but doesn't belong to any team. He's quiet. Not heavy quiet. Just…unsettled. Like a man who suddenly stepped off a treadmill he's been running on his entire life, and his body hasn't figured out how to stop moving.

I step outside and lean against the railing beside him. "You okay?"

He huffs a small laugh—not mocking, just honest. "I don't know. My brain keeps telling me I'm late for something. Or like I'm forgetting something huge. I keep waiting for someone to call and tell me to get on a plane."

"Well…we were on a plane just yesterday," I tease.

"You know what I mean. You and I have traveled together so often, and it's a completely different experience from traveling with a team. There's an…energy that's not there anymore."

In my mind, it's a good thing because our version is so much more relaxed, but I have to take into account how new this is to him.

"Okay, but," I say, gently bumping his shoulder, "you get to watch me sign posters, take silly pictures with fans dressed as space rebels, and listen to people tell you how much they love Ashla and *The Echo Wars*."

He smiles, and it reaches his eyes. There's a softness there—and maybe a hint of gratitude.

"That does help," he admits. "Being busy. Being part of something. I enjoy seeing you do this. I enjoy being beside you for it." He glances down at his hands; flexes them like they're still supposed to be wrapped around a bat. "It's just…weird. Good weird. Scary weird. But weird."

I slip my hand into his, threading my fingers through his, giving them a reassuring squeeze. "This is your first spring where you're not at spring training. It's going to feel weird. Baseball was your whole life for so long. It doesn't just…stop being a part of your life. It's who you are."

He turns his head and studies me for a moment, then leans in and presses a slow kiss to my temple.

"I'm glad I'm here with you," he whispers. "Even if I don't totally know who I am in this season yet."

I squeeze his hand. "That's okay. You don't have to figure it out right away. There's no rush. We'll figure it out. Together."

Below us, convention banners flap in the morning wind, promising crowds and laughter and chaos. I'm sure it's both familiar and different to him.

But his shoulder is warm against mine. His breath steady.

Maybe that's our new rhythm.

It soon becomes our new normal, and eventually, I notice that he's more relaxed. Happier. At peace.

And his peace is contagious because I'm feeling it, too, even though my life is moving at a pace that's fun, challenging, and fantastic. The fan response to *The Echo Wars* keeps growing, and being Ashla Voss is a full-time job. It's so rewarding.

Over the next few months, Christian and I travel all over the country, plus make stops in London, Germany, and Japan. I'm getting a lot of good press, and it's both exciting and exhausting. The fans' energy really keeps me going, but being able to experience it all with my husband is the biggest blessing.

We decide to take a few weeks off in August, where we're not traveling anywhere. All we want is a staycation to sleep in our own bed, eat at our favorite local restaurants, and hang out with friends. That was my wish, and Christian has made it come true. Everyone who knows us knows how badly we need this time to rest and regroup.

So, imagine my surprise when the phone rings at 8:45 on Wednesday morning. Before I can even answer it, there is an almost continuous chime of notifications.

"What the…?" I sit up in bed and glance over at Christian, whose phone is chiming with notifications, as well.

"That can't be good," he murmurs as he rolls over and picks up his phone. I immediately think of his father. He had the kidney transplant and has been relatively healthy, but anything can happen.

But when I reach for my phone, I see it's my new publicist, Nora, calling.

"Hey, Nora," I say around a yawn.

"Ella! Did you see the announcement?"

"Um…what?" I'm still half-asleep.

"The Emmy nominations were announced this morning!" she says excitedly. "Click on the link I just sent you."

I knew the announcements were happening today, but I didn't really think anything of it. *The Echo Wars* haven't been nominated before, so I didn't want to get my hopes up.

"Oh, my goodness, I can't wait," she huffs lightly. "Ella, you were nominated!"

"What?!" I say it so loudly that my poor husband nearly falls out of bed. I frantically reach for him, our hands immediately linking. "I was nominated? Seriously?"

"Yes! For Outstanding Character Voice-Over Performance in an animated character role. Oh, sweetie. This is huge. Congratulations!"

I'm stunned. And completely speechless.

"Ella? Ella, are you still there? You know we're going to line up some interviews for you, so let me work on that. I'll email you the details in a bit, okay?"

"Uh…sure. Yes. Thank you. Bye." I hang up and realize maybe I shouldn't have. But when I turn to Christian, his grin is the absolute brightest. "Did you hear?"

"That was my mom on the phone," he says. "And then there were about a dozen texts from my siblings. Everyone says congratulations." He hauls me into his arms. We fall back against the pillows, and he kisses me senseless. We break apart, breathless and giddy. "So? How does it feel to be nominated for an Emmy?"

"I don't think I've processed it yet," I say as he loosens his embrace. Beside me, my phone is still blowing up with texts I'm sure are from friends and family. I hate ignoring them.

"How about I make us some coffee, and you deal with your adoring public?" I know he's teasing, and it makes me laugh. He gets up and bows like he's my butler or something, and it's so darn cute.

Boxers and all.

Rolling over, I see texts from Jen, Penny, Freya, Whitney, Will, my sisters, my parents, Christian's family, my co-stars, and even Tracy.

Go figure.

I don't even know who to respond to first, but when my phone rings, and I see it's my mom, I'm relieved.

"Good morning," I say as soon as I answer.

"Good morning, sunshine. Congratulations! Your father and I saw the announcement. Were you watching? Did you know you were going to be nominated? Are you celebrating?"

"Oh, my goodness, Mom. That's a lot of questions." I laugh softly and prop the pillows up behind me so I can get more comfortable. "I hate to say it, but…we weren't watching. I honestly didn't think we'd get a nomination since we haven't in the past. Nora called. She woke me up and told me. Now, I hate that I missed it."

"Well, I'm surprised your father and I didn't wake you up with our screams from all the way in Florida. We yelled so loud we must have scared the neighbors. You can see it online," she assures me. "Don't worry. But I swear, your father and I both screamed when they read your name, and we saw your picture on the screen. It was very exciting."

That just makes me groan.

"I can't believe I slept through it."

"Go online and watch it. It will still be exciting."

"I guess."

"So? What are you going to do to celebrate?"

"Honestly? I don't know. Christian's making me coffee, so…that's a start, right?" I joke. "I'm still waking up. But Nora is working on setting up some interviews, and I have no idea when those will start. I'm guessing maybe today?"

"That makes sense. Well, don't let me keep you. I'm sure you have tons of people to call and talk to. We love you, and we're so proud of you. Give Christian our love."

"I will, thanks. I love you, Mom. Love you, Dad."

After that, I'm replying to texts until my fingers are numb. Christian serves me my coffee in bed before grabbing my laptop. Then we sit and watch the replay of the announcement.

And it *is* most definitely exciting.

"Look at your name up there," he says, his voice full of pride. "That's my girl. I'm so proud of you. And it's about time Hollywood acknowledged your talent."

"Christian…"

"What? I'm serious. I know you didn't write *The Echo Wars*, but your acting—your voice—it has brought Ashla Voss to life. And she is like…she's the true heart and star of the series. *You* are the true heart and star of the series."

I don't know why, but his words, his praise, make me emotional. "Thank you," I whisper with a trembling voice. "In a million years…I never thought…I never expected this role to turn into the breakout it has become, but I am beyond thankful for it. I thought that after I turned down the movie, my career would coast. That playing Ashla would be fun and fulfilling, but I never expected her to bring me this level of recognition."

"No one deserves it more than you," he says, his forehead gently resting against mine. "We need to celebrate." Sitting back, he's suddenly like a kid on Christmas morning. "What would you like to do today? Name it, and I'll make it happen."

"Oh, um…I don't know. I'm waiting to hear from Nora with a press schedule, so…"

No sooner do I say the words than the schedule appears in my inbox, along with a press release she's drafted for my approval.

"It looks like a pretty full morning and afternoon," I murmur. "And a busy week."

"That makes sense. You're a big deal. Everyone's going to want to talk to you."

I love his support so much.

"But it looks like my last interview is at four today, so we can definitely do something tonight."

"Whatever you want to do, we'll do it."

"Really?"

He nods. "Really."

I say the first thing that pops into my head because it's sort of our thing, and it makes me happy.

"I want to go to Newport Beach and get a pizza and drink slushies and watch the sunset." Just thinking about it makes me smile.

Meanwhile, Christian's looking at me like I'm insane. "But…"

"Nuh-uh. You said we'd do whatever I want to do."

He rewards me with a lopsided grin. "Your wish is my command, beautiful girl." He hops off the bed. "Do you have time for pancakes?"

"Always!"

Two months later, I'm dressed in the most beautiful gown—second only to my wedding gown—and sitting next to the most handsome and supportive husband in the world. I'm dazzled by the sea of celebrities. I've worked with some of them, admired many of them, and I'm humbled to be sitting among them all.

How is this my life?

I know my category is coming up, and I feel like I've been breathing wrong for the last five minutes.

That's the only explanation for why my chest feels so tight, and my heart is pounding like there's a drum line inside me. The next thing I know, the category graphic flashes across the giant screen, the camera swoops, the orchestra plays something dramatic and elegant, and suddenly, I am very aware of how small I feel in the giant room.

"Breathe," Christian whispers beside me, his fingers squeezing mine. "You're okay."

"I'm not going to win," I whisper automatically, like muscle memory. Like armor. "It's just…really cool to even be here."

He gives me a look. Warm. Proud. Like he already knows a secret I don't.

"The nominees for Outstanding Character Voice-Over Performance in an animated character role are…"

They start reading the names.

Each one is massive. Legendary. Powerful.

Then mine.

"Ella Lucas as Ashla Voss in *The Echo Wars.*"

The room applauds. A few cheers. I feel heat rush to my face. I smile because I've practiced smiling. I haven't practiced winning.

I've watched this moment millions of times from my couch, but never thought I'd be sitting here waiting for it. I never thought an animated warrior whose voice is mine, and who I helped create, would bring me to this exact second in time where my entire life seems to be holding its breath with me.

"And the Emmy goes to…"

Time stretches, bends.

I feel Christian's thumb stroke the back of my hand, slow, steady, and comforting.

"Ella Lucas, *The Echo Wars!*"

For half a second, I don't react.

Ella Lucas. That's…me. That's my name. They said my name!

Christian laughs under his breath, joyful and stunned at the same time, and then he kisses my cheek. Suddenly, I can move again. People are clapping. A few are standing. Someone behind me screams. I press a hand over my mouth because I can't make my face behave, I can't school it into any semblance of calm.

I'm crying.

Great. Perfect.

Christian stands with me, his hand on the small of my back, steadying me as my world tilts just a little in the best way possible.

"You did it," he whispers, his voice thick. "This is your moment."

The stage is somehow both the longest walk of my life and the shortest. The lights swallow me. The applause sounds like ocean waves.

They hand me the statue, and it's heavier than I expected.

My voice wobbles immediately because…of course, it does.

"I…was not prepared for this," I manage, and the audience laughs softly, kindly, like they all know exactly what I mean. "I didn't grow up dreaming of winning an award for voice acting. I just…fell in love with a character. A stubborn, fierce, snippy, brave girl named Ashla Voss, who taught me how to fight, and grow, and help, and believe I could still get back up, even when life kept knocking me flat."

My breath shakes.

"I want to thank the *Echo Wars* team for trusting me with her. For letting me grow up with her. For letting me share a heart with Ashla." I swallow. "To the fans who show up in costume, who write letters, who tell me she helped them feel seen—you have no idea what that means. I share this moment with you. Ashla lives in all of us."

Then I find him in the sea of faces. Eyes bright, hands clasped as if he's holding the entire moment together for me.

"And to my husband," I say, my voice softer now, more private, even through the microphone, "who has stood beside me in every season, who has lifted me up when I doubted myself, who never once made me feel like I had to choose between love and ambition…this is yours as much as it is mine. Thank you for believing in me, even when I didn't."

Emotion swells again, and I swallow hard.

"I never thought I'd be standing here tonight. I never thought… I'd be *this* person." I laugh a little, the sound watery and overwhelmed. "Thank you for letting me be her."

The music swells, and I lift the Emmy, dazed and grateful, and take a moment to absorb it all. As I walk off the stage, all I can think is how I can't wait to go back down to my seat, sit beside Christian, and hold his hand.

Because this isn't just my dream, it's ours.

And this award is just as much his as it is mine.

Twenty-Two

It's late when we arrive back at the apartment, but before we step inside, I look up at the glorious, star-filled sky. I always have a wish ready. Always. But tonight, I don't. Because all my wishes have come true. All the years of wishes and struggles and what-ifs were worth it. I don't think my feet have touched the ground since they called my name earlier. It's like an out-of-body experience, even though I know I am firmly within mine.

Encased in this gorgeous gown.

I look at Christian. He's got this serene smile on his face, and I know he's patiently waiting for me to make my usual wish upon a star before we go inside.

But instead of a wish, I whisper a simple, "Thank you" to the universe.

Satisfied, I take the hand my husband extends to me and let him lead me into the building and up to our humble home.

I hold my trophy close as we step inside, like I'm afraid it will disappear if I loosen my grip. It reminds me of how Christian carried his MVP trophy after the World Series.

It's so quiet. After an evening full of laughter, music, conversation, and the general hum of celebration, the silence somehow feels louder. I drop my wrap on the sofa and slowly look around, once again reminded of the night of the World Series. There was this magnificent trophy, and nowhere proper to put it.

So, I place it on the old coffee table. My hands feel empty without it already, but I smile lovingly at it.

Welcome home, Emmy!

"I think we need to add a display shelf to our list of improvements to the apartment," Christian teases. We've made some changes since we made this our primary residence, but nothing major. Mainly because we're on the go so much, and we've made what we have work.

However…

"I wouldn't say no to that." Turning my head, I smile at him, happy tears stinging my eyes again. "I think I'm still a little in shock."

Nodding, he slowly makes his way over, his smile full of promise. Reaching up, he brushes a loose strand of hair from my face, his fingers lingering at my cheek. I lean into his touch. He gently cups my face in his hands, and when our lips meet, it's slow, tender, and achingly sweet. There's none of the camera glare or roar of applause—it's just us. A victory all its own. A quiet celebration of long nights, hard work, and finally being here together. I press closer, feeling the warmth and steadiness of him, the gentle rise and fall of his chest, and in that kiss, all the noise of the world falls away. It's just Christian, me, and a triumph that belongs only to us.

We're finally having our moment.

When he lifts his head, I let out a dreamy sigh. "I've been waiting all night for that."

He chuckles. The low, masculine kind that sends a thrill up and down my spine. "All night? I know I've kissed you multiple times tonight."

"Not like that."

The tips of his ears turn a little red as he takes both of my hands in his. "Do you remember the day we got engaged?"

The giggle is out before I can stop it. "Of course, I do. What made you think of that?"

"We walked around the resort grounds, making plans for our future. We made career goals—another World Series title for me, and an Oscar for you. But you said you'd accept an Emmy."

"I remember."

"And now you have one."

"And you got your second World Series title. Look at us. Making things happen." I say it lightly, but his expression is a little more thoughtful.

"You have no idea how proud I am of you. My heart felt like it was going to burst right out of my chest when I watched you walk up onto that stage. I've always said you were beautiful, but up there, you looked luminous—like you were lit from the inside. You took my breath away." He gives me that boyish grin I love so much. "You've always taken my breath away. I don't know how I ever got so lucky."

"I'm the lucky one. Everything in my life changed the moment we met. I always believed in wishes and dreams and luck, but you are every single wish and dream wrapped up in one incredible person." I swallow hard, emotion clogging my throat. "You are my everything. And winning that award tonight with you right there beside me was just…" My heart's racing, and my voice catches. I pause because I'm overwhelmed by how I feel.

Christian steps in close, closing the distance between us again. The warmth of his body soothes me. "I know," he whispers. "I know exactly how you feel because it's the same for me. Getting an award is such a powerful experience. But when the person you love most in the world is there to celebrate the win with you? There's nothing better."

All I can do is nod before he kisses me again. I clutch the lapels of his tuxedo, even as his arms go around me, steadying me. Grounding me. Within moments, I'm boneless, and the exhaustion of the day catches up with me.

This time, when we break apart, I smooth the fabric of his jacket where I wrinkled it. "It's going to take me an hour to get this makeup off," I tease. Jen came over earlier to make me glamorous, and while she outdid herself, it's definitely going to take some work to wash it all off.

He chuckles again, gently turning me around so my back is to him. "Let me get you unzipped so you can do what you need to do. Would you like a cup of tea?"

"Ooohhh…that sounds perfect. Thank you."

He gives my waist a quick squeeze once my gown's unzipped. "I'll make it for you, and you can drink it in bed while we watch some TV. I know you're tired, but…"

"I am, but it'll take me a while to fully unwind, and tea will help."

Looking over my shoulder, I can't help but gaze up at him lovingly. "Thanks for being my date tonight and for being the absolute best husband ever. I don't know what I'd do without you."

Reaching up, he caresses my cheek. "You'll never have to find out because I'll always be here for you. Always, Ella Rose." He leans in and kisses me one more time. "Go. I've got tea to make."

That's all the prodding I need.

I lovingly caress my Emmy as I walk away.

By the time I get to the bathroom, I'm seriously dragging. I just want to shower, crawl into bed, and drink my tea while Christian holds me as we watch some TV.

Although that almost sounds like too much.

Still, I shower, scrub off all the makeup, and get all the products out of my hair. By the time I'm drying off, I feel ten pounds lighter.

Staring at my reflection, I look for signs. Do I look different? Do award winners look different? Am I supposed to? But all I see is me. Little Ella Rose Holt. The girl with the big dreams who worked her fanny off to make them happen.

"We did it," I whisper, wishing I could go back and tell twelve-year-old me the news.

Yawning, I quickly dry off and slip into my pajamas because my bed is seriously calling my name.

I walk into our bedroom as I loosely braid my damp hair and spot Christian already in bed. "How was your shower?"

I hum sleepily as I climb in beside him and promptly rearrange my pillows so I can get comfortable. "Mmm…it was exactly what I needed. Although tomorrow, I may still have to…" I lean back against the pillows and see it.

My Emmy.

On the ironing board.

"I hope you don't mind that I reused your epic display," he says softly. "There was no way I was leaving that award on the coffee table. It's too special."

"Are you kidding? This is amazing." Resting my head on his shoulder, I stare in wonder at the statue. "I love that you did this. Thank you."

"How could I not? I remember how I felt when I came into our room that night, and you had my MVP trophy on display."

"And I remember how I couldn't believe you had just left it on the floor." We both laugh, snuggling closer.

"Well, like I said earlier, we need some proper displays to show off our awards. We worked hard, and we should be proud of our accomplishments."

I have to agree. Right now, his trophy is on display at his parents' house. I always hoped that someday we'd be able to show it off in a home of our own.

Someday.

We sit in companionable silence for several long moments.

"Your tea is going to get cold," he gently reminds me, but I'm too comfortable to move.

"I know. I don't think I have the energy to even reach for it. Sorry."

"Nothing to apologize for." I feel his soft lips at my temple. "We can stay just like this. Or should I turn on the TV?"

"I'm not done staring at her yet."

"Her?"

"Emmy. I mean, look at her. She's a winged woman holding an atom. Her."

"Ah. Got it."

"She's beautiful."

"If you're into golden-winged women holding atoms, sure."

That makes me laugh.

"How are we going to celebrate this?" he asks. "What would you like to do?"

"I know I'm going to have like…a hundred phone calls and texts tomorrow. I really wish our families could have been here to celebrate with us." I'm a little sad they're not. "I know they couldn't have come to the actual awards show with us, but it would have been wonderful to celebrate with them afterward."

He's quiet for a minute. "We still can."

I lift my head, and maybe I'm more tired than I realize because it sounds like he's suggesting we fly our families out here.

"Christian, we can't fly everyone out here. That's crazy."

Shaking his head, he lets out a low, tender chuckle. "That wasn't even remotely what I was saying."

"Oh." My head goes to his shoulder again. "Then what *are* you saying?"

"Maybe we'll fly home and see everyone. You know, spend a few days, show off the Emmy, and then be home in time for your next recording session. What do you say?"

Before I can say anything, I yawn.

Loudly.

"I think that sounds perfect. I just don't know when…" Another yawn. "I'll look at flights tomorrow, and we can…" Yet another yawn.

Beside me, Christian slowly maneuvers us until we're lying down.

"Tell you what, you're going to be busy being fabulous and doing PR stuff along with talking to everyone you know who wants to congratulate you, so I'll handle the travel stuff, okay?"

"Okay," I say sleepily.

He turns off the bedside lamp before gently pulling me into his arms.

"Christian?" I whisper.

"Hmm?"

"Thank you."

"For…?"

"For making all of my dreams come true. For being my person. For just being you."

I want to say more, but sleep claims me before I can utter another word.

But I know I fall asleep with a smile on my face.

I love a man of action.

Christian made all our arrangements and even packed for both of us while I handled endless calls and texts. Nora had several interviews lined up for me, and between them and talking to family, I have almost no voice.

But it's been so worth it.

Now, as we board the red-eye flight to Florida, I'm looking forward to rest.

We've mastered the art of sleeping on planes after so many years of traveling, and I'm relieved we'll wake up in the morning slightly refreshed so we can hit the ground running with our families.

It takes several minutes of pulling out pillows, eye masks, earplugs, and whatnot before we can safely tuck our bags under our seats. It's not like we'll instantly fall asleep, but everything is now comfortably within reach, so we can settle in.

"You're a genius," I murmur.

"Me? How do you figure that?"

"I didn't think it would be possible for us to get on a plane in less than twenty-four hours."

The look he gives me is a little cocky, but adorable.

"Seriously? We've flown on shorter notice before."

"No, I know that, but this trip was trickier because you had no idea how long those interviews would be."

"That's why we're on the red eye. There was no way you would still be talking to any entertainment sites at ten at night. This was the safe choice."

"Brilliant." I sigh happily and secure my seat belt. "I love that our moms are working together to coordinate lunch tomorrow. I can't wait to see everyone, and for everyone to meet Emmy. She's a member of the family now," I say with a giggle. "Oh, I can't wait for Emmy to meet MVP!" referring to Christian's World Series MVP trophy.

She's lovingly packed in my carry-on suitcase in the overhead bin. There was no way I was trusting her in any checked luggage.

"You are going to be celebrated for sure," he says, taking my hand and linking our fingers together. "I can't even imagine how many people will be there."

"The last head count was twenty-seven. Not including us."

"Wow."

"I know."

We sit back and people watch for a few minutes, and I don't fully relax until the pilot announces that we are clear for takeoff.

That's when I know it's almost time to go to sleep.

Only…I don't.

The flight attendants do a quick offering of snacks and beverages, and we decide to eat and drink a little something. I watch a few episodes of a home renovation show to help me unwind, but by the third episode, I've lost interest. Yet I'm still not quite ready to doze off.

Which is weird for me.

It's quiet in that strange way airplanes always are after midnight—dimmed lights, a low hum, shadows of strangers tucked beneath blankets. Christian's hand is warm, threaded through mine where it rests between us, and even though I should be exhausted after the craziness of the last few days, I'm wide awake.

He shifts slightly, tilting his head toward me. "You okay?" he murmurs, voice rough with sleep.

"I'm fine," I whisper back. "I don't know why I'm still awake."

He smiles, eyes barely open. "I promise no one's going to steal your Emmy. They'll have to get through me first. I'm all over it." The words are barely out before he yawns.

I roll my eyes, even as warmth fills my chest. "My hero."

"We don't all wear capes," he says, soft amusement in his voice, but then his eyes meet mine. His expression grows serious. "I'm proud of you. I don't think I'll ever stop being proud of you."

I swallow, trying not to get emotional at thirty thousand feet. "Thank you. I'm still processing it. It feels unreal. Like I borrowed someone else's moment."

"Yeah," he says gently, squeezing my hand. "Except you didn't. You earned it. You worked for it. And I got the best seat in the world, watching it happen."

I lean into his shoulder, feeling the steady rhythm of his breathing. "The next few days are going to be crazy," I whisper. "Family chaos. Pictures. Hugs. My mom crying…"

"Your dad pretending he isn't," he adds with a grin I can hear more than see.

"And maybe yours finally being impressed."

"I don't know. He could surprise you," he says, a quiet laugh beneath his breath.

We fall into a comfortable silence; each temporarily lost in our own thoughts.

"Hey," he murmurs after a moment, softer now. "I'm glad we get this time. Just us. Even if it is in cramped airplane seats."

"Me, too," I whisper. "Right now feels…good."

He turns his head and presses a light kiss to my temple. "Get some sleep, Mrs. Emmy Winner."

I let my eyes close, the world narrowing to his warmth, the muted hum of the plane, and the steady certainty of the man beside me.

"Only if you do, too," I murmur.

"Already ahead of you," he breathes. His hand stays in mine as we finally drift off to sleep.

The airport's quiet as we walk to baggage claim and then head over to pick up our rental car. I wouldn't say I'm well-rested, but I'm mildly refreshed.

Christian loads our luggage into the trunk, and when he's seated behind the wheel, he's all smiles.

He is definitely more of a morning person than I am.

At least today he is.

"Hey, so it's obviously super early, and I don't think I'm ready to jump into the whole family chaos yet. How would you like to stop for breakfast?"

It's not the worst idea.

"Sure. That sounds good. Where do you want to go?"

"I was talking to my brother last week, and he mentioned this new place he said makes the best breakfasts. Like…the best omelets, the best waffles, muffins as big as your head…"

I start to laugh, even as my stomach growls. "Well, now we have to go. The best omelets *and* muffins as big as your head? That sounds too good to pass up."

"Excellent!"

The drive from the airport is familiar, and we can practically do it on autopilot. And while I'm curious about where this restaurant is, I assume it's on the way.

We're going to my parents' house first, and I wonder if I should text and let them know we're stopping to eat before we get there.

"Uh-oh…"

Turning his head, Christian frowns. "What's wrong?"

"You know my mom is probably planning on us eating breakfast with them. I should probably let her know so she's not worried, right?"

"I hadn't even thought of that," he murmurs. "So…yeah, sure. Text her and let her know where we're at."

"Okay." And I do.

The second I slip my phone back into my purse, my eyes start drifting shut. I am feeling the effects of the red-eye flight now.

"How much longer until we're there?" I ask.

"About twenty-five minutes. Don't worry. I'll wake you," he

assures me, and I happily drift off.

It's only when I feel the car come to a complete stop that I open my eyes. "Are we there?"

I sleepily look around, not recognizing anything. We're not in a restaurant parking lot. We're in a residential neighborhood. But not one that either of our families lives in. This one looks like it's still under construction.

"Um…Christian?"

"Hmm?"

"Are we lost?"

"I told you, we're going to breakfast." He says it so casually, so lightly. Like it makes perfect sense.

But it doesn't.

"There's a restaurant in the middle of a neighborhood?" I ask with amusement, straightening in my seat. There aren't many houses, but several are under construction. "I'm so confused right now."

He reaches over and gives my thigh an affectionate squeeze. "Don't worry. We'll be there in like two minutes."

I laugh nervously. "Where?"

The only answer I get is a soft chuckle.

We drive past a few more unfinished homes until we stop in front of one of them.

"We're here," he says, as if it explains everything.

I look at the house and then back at my husband. "Okay, am I still asleep? Because there is no way a house under construction serves breakfast. It's just not possible," I joke.

Beside me, Christian twists in his seat to face me. And, in his typical, loving way, takes my hand in his.

"The other night—after we got home from the awards show—you said something to me that…well…didn't sit right."

All I can do is stare because I have no idea what he's talking about.

"You told me I made all your dreams come true," he said gruffly, his thumb gently stroking my wrist. "That wasn't exactly true."

"What are you even talking about? Of course, it's true. Our entire relationship…all the things we've done…"

"Please," he says quietly. "I need to say this."

So, I sit and patiently wait.

"That first move to St. Louis, you told me you were disappointed because you envisioned our lives in California. It was close to where most of your work was, and if I had stayed playing for Anaheim, it would have been perfect. That move was the first of many, and no matter where we were, we had a roof over our heads, but it was never truly ours. Never truly a home."

"But they were," I argue lightly. "Home is where we both are. It's…"

This time, he puts a finger over my lips, even as he tries to give me a stern look. "May I?"

I nod.

"Thank you." He lets out a long breath. "It was never truly a home. We didn't paint, we didn't decorate, we didn't put down roots. We were a team of nomads, essentially. And I know—even though you rarely said it out loud—that you have always wanted a home of your own. A home of *our* own. So, that's what this is."

I gasp as his words register.

"This is where we're going to put down roots. This is where we're going to decorate and buy furniture and put all our awards on display." I hear the emotion in his voice, and those brilliant blue eyes are shining with unshed tears. "This is where you will forever get to come home to. I know your job can take us all over the world, but when that job is done, you have a house—a home—that is yours."

"Oh, my goodness…" I glance over my shoulder—at the bare bones of a house—in wonder.

Home.

When I look back at him, I can tell he's unsure of how I'm feeling. "What about you? This can't all be for me."

He visibly relaxes. "I'm going to work with a couple of youth baseball teams here." He shrugs. "It just feels right."

I mentally curse the console in the car as I try to climb over so I can hug him properly. "I can't believe you did this for me. For us." I bury my face in his neck, getting as close to him as I possibly can.

"Welcome home, Ella Rose."

Pulling back, I kiss him. I kiss him and pour every ounce of love and emotion and gratitude and just…everything I have into it. And I would have kept kissing him, except we're interrupted.

By my stomach growling.

Ugh…

We break apart, laughing. "Well…you did promise me breakfast," I remind him.

"Yes, I did. And it should be ready."

When he turns to get out of the car, I'm back to being confused. "Um…ready?"

Over his shoulder, he looks at me and winks. "Yeah. It looks like they're serving it now." He nods toward the house. When I turn around, I see our families coming out of—literally—the woodwork.

"What the…oh, my gosh! Look at everyone!"

Naturally, I bolt out of the car and run right into my dad's arms.

"Hey, sunshine!"

I'm actively crying.

Like…ugly crying, but I don't care.

"Hey, Dad." He holds me tightly, and then it's like I'm crowd surfing as I'm handed off from one relative to the next. I lose track of where I am and where I'm going, but it's the best kind of chaos.

It's full of love.

When I'm finally on my own two feet with only Christian's arm around me, I ask, "What are you all doing here?"

"Christian's been working on this for about a month," my mom explains. "We were all just waiting for him to tell us when you'd be here."

I look up at him, and he simply shrugs and says, "Hero."

My bark of laughter is my first response. "Yes, you are."

"We've got all kinds of breakfast foods set up out back," Christian's mom chimes in. "The builder wouldn't allow us to fully set up inside. He's in the house next door keeping an eye on us, so…"

We all look in that direction and wave.

"Let's go eat!" someone calls out.

Before I even get two steps, Mr. Lucas approaches. I brace myself for whatever non-compliment I'm about to get.

"Well done, Ella," he says. "Congratulations." If I'm not mistaken, there's even a hint of a smile on his face. But it's gone before he turns and walks away.

Christian and I stay right where we are.

"I told you he might surprise you."

"Oh, he did," I say.

"Come on. Everyone's waiting, and I know you're hungry." He takes my hand and leads me across the lawn, our moms walking with us, when I notice the building permit sign.

Lot number twenty-two.

I gasp, but before I can say anything, a cardinal flutters down, landing on the sign.

"Oh, my goodness," my mom says in awe. "Will you look at that?"

We all cautiously take a step forward.

"You know, the cardinal is a symbol of hope, love, renewal, and the beginning of new life," my mother-in-law adds. "What a lovely blessing."

The two of them walk away, smiling and chatting about the meaning of this bold little red bird, and I have to admit, it's pretty amazing.

I point to the sign. "Did you know about this?"

"The cardinal?" he asks with amusement. "Ella Rose, I know I pulled off a pretty spectacular surprise this morning, but the bird completely acted alone."

I can't help but laugh. "Not the bird. I meant did you pick this house because of the site number?"

All he does is grin as he slowly leads me away.

"Christian…"

"Like I was going to pass up a sign from our lucky number."

The cardinal spreads its wings and takes flight over the yard before disappearing from sight. Then we're joining the family. I'm surprised at how they've set everything up—tables, chairs, hot food.

I've had many memorable moments in my life.

But this one tops them all.

Epilogue

Christian

She's spectacular.

It doesn't matter that I've seen her do this sort of thing a hundred times, I'll forever be in awe of her.

My wife.

My teammate.

The girl of my dreams.

We're at one of the biggest comic book conventions in the world, and my wife is a rock star. The crowds are going wild as they see her and listen to her, and all I can do is stand back with pride.

I have it easy. I'm the guy who carries the bags and then stands back until I'm needed. I think back to the years when our roles were reversed. The sacrifices she made. Everything from putting her career on hold for me, moving every six months, watching hundreds of baseball games while listening to me stress over every play, all while embracing my rigid routines and dietary restrictions. And she did it all out of love.

For me.

Now, it's my turn to be here for her.

And there's no place else I'd rather be.

There are two questions I get asked the most while I'm at events with her. First, do I miss playing baseball?

No, I don't. I miss winning games. If every game was like a World Series game, I would still be playing, but I do not miss the grind of being a Major League Baseball player. However, I've found my love for baseball again by helping the next generation of players.

The other question is how it feels to trade carrying equipment bags for carrying Ashla Voss's bags.

The answer? It feels great. I get a front-row seat—or a backstage view, depending on where we are—for the magic.

And trust me, my wife brings love and light and magic everywhere she goes.

I mean, are you kidding me? The way the crowds react to her is like nothing I've ever experienced. Their love and enthusiasm not only for Ashla but also for the entire *Galactic Wars* universe is wild. But seeing Ella Rose's face, the way she smiles at each and every fan, and how much she truly appreciates their support, is a sight to behold.

She's a legend.

I think back on the path we took to get here. It was far from smooth. We had more than our fair share of trials. But the one constant—the one thing that never changed—was how we felt about each other.

And I'll never take that for granted.

The crowd erupts in applause, and I see Ella waving and coming down off the stage with the biggest smile. She spots me and waves before jogging over, and I instantly sweep her up into my arms.

"You did great!" I assure her.

"Be sure to go to booth twenty-two later on today, where Ella Lucas will be signing autographs," the announcer calls out, and we both pull back with wide eyes and grins.

"Twenty-two," she says excitedly.

"It does seem wild how often it comes up for us." I pick up her bags and let her lead the way.

"Because it's lucky," she says with a wink. "Just like us."

And I couldn't agree more.

Acknowledgments from Ashley

I LOVE love! My favorite stories are love stories, and I could not believe my life when my own love story played out like a real-life Hallmark movie. It was always my dream to share our love story with the world one day, but I didn't know how until I met Liz Berry and Jillian Stein from Blue Box Press. Liz and Jillian, two women, two powerhouses in the publishing industry. They are a duo, a FORCE that is unmatched, and I am so very thankful and grateful to have worked with you both to bring this story to life and to call you my friends.

However, I needed someone to help me write this story. I've only really written non-fiction books, and the daunting task of writing a fiction book inspired by my real life in just a few months was too much for me to handle. Enter, Samantha Chase. To be honest, the idea of working with a complete stranger and trusting them with our story was really scary...but after one brunch with Samantha, I knew she was the avocado to my toast. We hit it off immediately, and I was in absolute awe of her throughout this entire process. I truly believe that people are born with their own individual gifts, and Samantha was born to be a writer. Two women who LOVE love, we became our own duo, and now she's stuck with me for life.

Four women working together, two duos...22. I am so lucky that the story of 22 brought us together.

Acknowledgments from Samantha

As a romance author, I write about fictional couples that I create in my head. I control the narrative, create all the sometimes-crazy scenarios, dig deep into the emotions, and find the tension. But my favorite part is always the meet-cute. When I heard about Ashley and David's, I knew exactly why this story needed to be out there.

I thought it would be easy to write this book because…well…they'd done all the hard work for me. The bones were there. I just needed to fictionalize it and turn it into a story inspired by…well…their story.

But it wasn't quite so simple

There were endless emails, phone calls, questions, comments, edits, re-writes, and times when I was pretty sure Ashley dreaded seeing my name pop up anywhere on any electronic device! But the more we spoke and the more I learned, I realized how amazing and incredible and inspirational she is. And this book breathed new life into me as an author in ways I never expected.

So, to Ashley, I say thank you. Thank you for trusting me with your story and for being so willing to put yourself out there to a person you spent maybe a total of six hours with in person!

To Liz Berry and Jillian Stein from Blue Box Press…I have no idea how I got so lucky to be the author you chose to bring this vision to life, but I will forever be thankful. I still kind of pinch myself every day, so…thank you.

About Ashley Eckstein

Ashley Eckstein is an actress, author, entrepreneur, executive producer, fashion designer, inspirational speaker, mental health advocate, podcaster, and a dynamic force in the entertainment and fandom worlds. Best known as the voice of the iconic Ahsoka Tano in *Star Wars*—a character she originated in 2008—she also revolutionized fandom culture in 2010 when she founded Her Universe, a trailblazing fashion and lifestyle brand. Ashley's designs can currently be found at Disney parks and stores around the world.

A leading authority and tastemaker in fandom, Ashley has been featured on *CNN*, *Forbes*, *Fortune*, *Good Morning America*, *Entertainment Weekly*, *The New York Times*, *Los Angeles Times*, *The Washington Post*, and *The Wall Street Journal*, among many others. She was honored by *Good Housekeeping* as one of its "25 Awesome Women," invited to speak at *Fortune* magazine's Next Gen Most Powerful Women Summit, and named one of *CNET*'s "Women Who Inspire." Ashley also serves on the national advisory council for the Kids Mental Health Foundation.

She lives in Orlando, Florida, with her husband, former Major League Baseball player and World Series MVP, David Eckstein. Together, they love traveling the world in search of the best pizza.

About Samantha Chase

Samantha Chase is a *New York Times* and *USA Today* bestseller of contemporary romance that's hotter than sweet, sweeter than hot. She released her debut novel in 2011 and currently has more than 100 titles under her belt – including *THE CHRISTMAS COTTAGE* which was a Hallmark Christmas movie in 2017 and *WEDDING SEASON* which was a Hallmark June Wedding movie in 2023!

A lifelong Disney enthusiast with an unapologetic love for '80s rock, Samantha spends her downtime devouring romance novels, playing far too much online Solitaire, and occasionally donning a tiara while hanging out with her sassy pug, Maylene. She lives in Wake Forest, North Carolina, with her husband of 35 years and their two sons—proof that real-life love stories can have happily-ever-afters, too.

Sign up for my mailing list and get exclusive content and chances to win members-only prizes!

https://www.chasing-romance.com/newsletter

Start a fun new small town romance series:
https://www.chasing-romance.com/the-donovans-series

Where to Find Me:

Website: www.chasing-romance.com
Facebook: www.facebook.com/SamanthaChaseFanClub
Instagram:
https://www.instagram.com/samanthachaseromance/
Reader Group:
https://www.facebook.com/groups/1034673493228089/

Also from Samantha Chase

The Lakeview Harbor Resort Series:
#Resort Romance
#Resort Love
#Resort Fling
#Resort Bliss
#Resort Crush
#Resort Kiss

The Donovans Series (Sweetbriar Ridge):
Loving You
Teasing You
Wanting You
Seeing You
Craving You
Choosing You
Finding You

The Donovans Series (Laurel Bay):
Call Me
Dare Me
Tempt Me
Save Me
Charm Me
Kiss Me

The Wylder Love Series:
Irresistible Love
Indescribable Love
Undeniable Love

The Montgomery Brothers Series:
Wait for Me
Trust in Me

Stay with Me
More of Me
Return to You
Meant for You
I'll Be There
Until There Was Us
Suddenly Mine
A Dash of Christmas
A Merry Montgomery Christmas

The Magnolia Sound Series:
Sunkissed Days
Remind Me
A Girl Like You
In Case You Didn't Know
All the Befores
And Then One Day
Can't Help Falling in Love
Last Beautiful Girl
The Way the Story Goes
Since You've Been Gone
Nobody Does It Better
Wedding Wonderland
Always on my Mind
Kiss the Girl

Meet Me at the Altar
The Engagement Embargo
With this Cake
You May Kiss the Groomsman
The Proposal Playbook
Groomed to Perfection
The I Do Over

The Enchanted Bridal Series:
The Wedding Season
Friday Night Brides
The Bridal Squad

Glam Squad & Groomsmen
Bride & Seek

The Road Tripping Series:
Drive Me Crazy
Wrong Turn
Test Drive
Head Over Wheels

The Shaughnessy Brothers Series:
Made for Us
Love Walks In
Always My Girl
This is Our Song
Sky Full of Stars
Holiday Spice
Tangled Up in You

Band on the Run Series:
One More Kiss
One More Promise
One More Moment
One More Chance

The Christmas Cottage Series:
The Christmas Cottage
Ever After

Silver Bell Falls Series:
Christmas in Silver Bell Falls
Christmas On Pointe
A Very Married Christmas
A Christmas Rescue
Christmas Inn Love
The Christmas Plan

Life, Love & Babies Series:
The Baby Arrangement

Baby, Be Mine
Baby, I'm Yours

Preston's Mill Series:
Roommating
Speed Dating
Complicating

The Protectors Series:
Protecting His Best Friend's Sister
Protecting the Enemy
Protecting the Girl Next Door
Protecting the Movie Star

7 Brides for 7 Soldiers
Ford

7 Brides for 7 Blackthornes
Logan

Standalone Novels
Jordan's Return
Catering to the CEO
In the Eye of the Storm
A Touch of Heaven
Exclusive
Moonlight in Winter Park
Waiting for Midnight
Mistletoe Between Friends
Snowflake Inn
His for the Holidays
Baking it Merry
Karma's a Beach
A Holly Brown Christmas

On Behalf of Blue Box Press,

Liz Berry and Jillian Stein would like to thank ~

Steve Berry
Benjamin Stein
Kim Guidroz
Chelle Olson
Alan Dingman
Chris Graham
Tanaka Kangara
Jessica Saunders
Stacey Tardif
Suzy Baldwin
Grace Wenk
Taryn Fagerness
Ann-Marie Nieves
Dylan Stockton
Peggy Boulos Smith
Richard Blake
and Simon Lipskar